HiddEN

hidden

JERRY B. JENKINS
TIM LaHAYE

with CHRIS FABRY

TYNDALE HOUSE PUBLISHERS, INC.
WHEATON, ILLINOIS

Library of Congress Cataloging-in-Publication Data

Jenkins, Jerry B.
  Hidden / Jerry B. Jenkins, Tim LaHaye.
    p. cm. — (Left behind—the kids) #3 Vol. 9-12
Special ed. compilation of the following four works previously published in 2000: The search; On the run; Into the storm; Earthquake! Summary: Four teens left behind after the rapture battle the forces of evil.
    ISBN 0-8423-8353-0 (hc)
    [1. End of the world—Fiction. 2. Christian life—Fiction.] I. LaHaye, Tim F. II. Title.
PZ7.J4138 Hi 2004
[Fic]—dc22   2003016695

Printed in the United States of America

08 · 07 06 05 04
9   8   7   6   5   4   3   2   1

1

RYAN heard movement in the hospital hallway and scrunched behind Bruce's bed. "I gotta go now," Ryan whispered. Bruce wasn't moving anymore. "You get some rest. I'll tell everybody you said hi."

Ryan squeezed Bruce's hand. Bruce didn't respond.

Ryan tiptoed to the stairwell door without being noticed. He closed it gently and bolted down the stairs. When he came out on the first floor, he ducked into the gift shop and bought licorice and a candy bar. He slipped past the older woman at the desk and calmly walked out the emergency-room doors.

Outside, three women were smoking. For a moment, Ryan couldn't get his bearings. Had he come from the right or left?

"Which way to Kirchoff Road?" Ryan said.

A frail woman tried to speak but coughed violently. She pointed to the right.

"Thanks," Ryan said, and he was off.

It felt good to be on his bike again and heading home. Ryan wanted to tell Judd about his visit with Bruce. He knew Judd would be ticked, but he didn't care. Ryan would just laugh and take Phoenix for a run in the park.

As he rode toward a hill, he heard a plane overhead. It was flying low. Too low. Ryan looked up in time to see the underside of the fighter jet. The roar was deafening. Ryan was sure it was going to crash.

He glanced down just as his front tire hit the curb. Ryan struggled to stay up and swerved into the street. Just as he gained control, an earth-shattering explosion behind him threw him to the pavement. His bike skittered ahead. He saw blood on his elbow and a huge hole in his jeans.

Tires screeched. A van was sliding toward him! He stared, frozen, as it demolished his bike and stopped within inches of his face.

He smelled gasoline. Fire crackled behind him. Screams filled the air. More planes flew overhead. Another explosion. Then another. The van backed up and tried to get around him, but his bike was caught underneath. Ryan grabbed the front bumper and pulled himself up. The driver was looking back. The man on the passenger side was short with a round face and looked like he needed a shave. Ryan saw something move in the back of the van.

The driver turned and yelled. The other man banged on the window and screamed, "Get outta the way, kid!"

Ryan ran to check his bike. The crumpled handlebars

were caught between the back wheel and the bumper. With the explosions and noise around him, his first thought was to run. Find shelter. Get to safety.

But something drew him to the van. He peered through the tinted window. Nothing. He cupped his hand to block the light and was barely able to make out a kid with heavy gray tape over his mouth. Ryan tapped on the window, and the kid turned. *Blindfolded!*

"Get away from there!" the short man yelled as he jumped out and tried to pry the bike loose. "Stupid kid."

Ryan studied the rear license plate, but the short man yelled, "Help me with this!"

Ryan felt the heat from the explosions, and the smoke made it hard to breathe. He yanked the bike loose and watched the short man throw it aside.

"What's wrong with that kid?" Ryan said.

"What kid?"

"The one with the duct tape."

The man looked at him menacingly. "You didn't see nobody, understand?" The man jumped into the van, and it sped off.

Suddenly it stopped and screeched back right at him. He ran to the hill. The van was right behind him as he neared the top. Flames and smoke rose into the air. Before Ryan could see what was on the other side, the van slid to a stop in the grass, and both men jumped out.

"Get him!" the driver yelled. Before Ryan could react, the short man was on him. They threw him into the back of the van. Ryan banged his head on an armrest and lay on the floor. From there he could see only the kid's hands. Riding boots. Long fingernails. *Weird*, Ryan thought.

The men held Ryan down and taped his hands and feet. He kicked and screamed with all his might, but they were too strong. They laid him sideways beneath the seat. "Sorry, kid," the short man said as the van sped away. "Can't take no chances."

"You're king of the double negative," Ryan said, "you know that?"

The man ignored him and wrapped tape around the back of Ryan's head and over his mouth. *Getting this off is really gonna hurt*, Ryan thought. Before the man tied the blindfold, Ryan could see only black smoke out the window. He wondered if he would ever see Bruce or his friends again.

The police, as usual, put Lionel on hold. Finally a cop came on and said, "Your friend will show up, okay?"

"You don't understand," Lionel said.

"No, *you* don't understand," the officer interrupted. "World War III just broke out, in case you didn't notice. We got fires. We got people trapped in rubble, looters, more bombs. Now stop buggin' us. Find him yourself."

Lionel wanted to scream.

"Don't call the police again," Judd said. "All we need is them snooping around here."

"We should at least try to find Ryan," Lionel said. "He'd do that for you."

4

"I wouldn't want him to," Judd said. "That puts everybody in danger."

"Then why'd you go out this morning?" Lionel said. "That put us in danger."

"That was before the bombs started," Judd said.

Vicki and Chaya pleaded with them to calm down. "We need to pull together," Vicki said.

"I don't even want to survive," Chaya said. "Going to heaven has to be better than living without my mother or Bruce or Ryan."

Lionel crossed his arms and shook his head.

Vicki put a hand on Lionel's shoulder. "We all want to find him," she said. "It's just hard to even think straight."

"He probably went to his stash of Bibles," Lionel said. "He could be there hiding—or the place could have been bombed and he's trapped."

"Does anybody know where he hides them?" Judd said.

"I was with him when he started picking them up," Vicki said, "but he never showed me where he put them."

Judd sat on Lionel's bed and rubbed his face with both hands. "Let's go through this one more time," Judd said. "You're sure Ryan wasn't at the hospital?"

"We didn't see him," Vicki said. "And they don't allow kids in intensive care."

"That's what *I* told him," Judd said. "He thought I was trying to shut him out."

"You were!" Lionel said.

"I was trying to take care of him," Judd said. "Let's

back up. Ryan was mad because we didn't let him in on the meeting about Mark."

"So was I," Lionel said.

"He wanted to go see Bruce, and I told him to forget it."

"Yeah, that's when he took off," Lionel said.

"When he came back he brought me a card and asked me to give it to Bruce when I saw him."

"And you said you would, *if you had the chance*," Lionel said. "If you hadn't been so—"

"This is not helping," Judd interrupted.

"What kind of card?" Vicki said.

"Excuse me?" Judd said.

"What kind of a card did Ryan get for Bruce?"

"Why does that matter?" Judd said.

"It was something about heaven," Lionel interrupted, trying to remember. "That's it. He found a card that looked like heaven, and he wanted Bruce to see it."

"What did you do with the card?" Vicki said.

"I left it over there. Hey, it's gone!"

"He *was* there!" Vicki shouted.

"What are you talking about?" Judd said.

"On the nightstand by Bruce's bed there was this card, blue sky with clouds—like heaven. That has to be Ryan's card. He could have gotten someone else to deliver it, but the nurses and the orderly hadn't seen him, so it only makes sense that he gave it to Bruce himself."

"But how?" Judd said.

"You sell him short," Lionel said. "He's a lot smarter than you think."

Judd hung his head. "He may have been inside when the bomb hit."

"You guys don't know him like I do," Lionel said. "If he saw Bruce, he would have come back here fast. He'd have wanted to tell you, Judd. He'd have been juiced about it."

"Then where is he?"

"I don't know," Lionel said. "That's why we have to go back to the hospital."

More explosions rocked the van when they drove away, but then the bombing stopped. The traffic must have been bad. Ryan felt lots of stops and starts. The men didn't say much, and with the tape over his mouth, Ryan couldn't talk to the other kid.

Every time the van stopped, Ryan slid forward and hit his head on the metal posts under the captain's chair. The short man laughed at him. Ryan finally managed to roll onto his side and position himself so he wouldn't get hurt at every stop. The floor of the van felt filthy.

Ryan tried to pick up sounds, but mostly he heard the hum of traffic. Someone kept punching buttons on the radio. Finally a news station interviewed an eyewitness to the bombings. A flurry of reports about the damage followed. There were chaos and terror throughout the world. New York City had been hit.

"Ah, who cares about New York?" the driver said. "Maybe it'll clear up some traffic."

The short man laughed, and someone turned up the radio.

". . . devastating carnage everywhere in the heart of Manhattan," the reporter said. "Bombed-out buildings, emergency vehicles picking their way through debris, Civil Defense workers pleading with people to stay underground."

Ryan thought of Chloe and Buck. Their apartment was in New York. They had been in Chicago the week before, but could they have gone back before the bombing?

Ryan heard the panic in the reporter's voice. "I'm seeking shelter myself now, probably too late to avoid the effects of radiation. No one knows for certain if the warheads were nuclear, but everyone is being urged to take no risks. Damage estimates will be in the billions of dollars. Loss of life is impossible to determine. . . ."

"You think those bombs we came through were *nuc-u-lar?*" the short man said.

"Shh, I'm trying to hear this," the other man said.

"All major transportation centers have been closed or destroyed," the reporter continued. "Huge traffic jams have snarled the Lincoln Tunnel, the Triborough Bridge, and every major artery out of New York City. What has been known as the capital of the world looks like the set of a disaster movie."

The other kid sniffled throughout the ride. They were speeding when a huge blast shook the earth. The short man cursed. "Look at that mushroom cloud!" he shouted.

A few minutes later the Cable News Network/Global Community Network coverage explained the blast. "Our news base in Chicago has been taken out by an incredible explosion. The bomb has flattened O'Hare International Airport. No word yet on whether this was an attack by militia forces or a Global Community retaliatory strike. We have so many reports of warfare, bloodshed, and death in so many major cities around the globe that it will be impossible for us to keep up with all of it."

"What luck," the driver said. "Can you believe this timing? Even if the kid's dad goes to the cops, they'll be so busy, they won't have time to worry about us."

The traffic slowed; then the van took sharp turns. Finally they stopped. Ryan heard a garage door open, and they drove inside. It sounded as if the two men carried the other kid away. Then they came back for Ryan. They cut the tape over his ankles, and he climbed, still blindfolded, three flights of stairs. The place smelled of wood, and boards creaked under his feet. Ryan heard horns, sirens, and a rumbling. *A train*, he thought. He knew from going to Cubs games with his dad that the elevated train snaked through Chicago, and he guessed it was somewhere along the miles of that track that he'd been taken. But he couldn't be sure. He had been in the van an hour and could even be in Wisconsin or Indiana.

Someone pushed him from behind and steered him to a door. He heard a key in a lock and the driver arguing with the other man.

The short man said, "You should have just kept going and left him there."

"Too late now," the other man said.

"I could take him to the river or, well, there's a hundred ways to take care of him."

"Let's keep 'em both for now," the driver said. "Stick him in the utility room."

Someone cut the tape from Ryan's arms and pushed a greasy cheeseburger and some fries into his hands. When the man ripped the tape from Ryan's mouth, it took a patch of hair from his neck, and Ryan yelped.

"There's no easy way to do that," the man said. "Sorry."

He led Ryan into another room and took off his blindfold. The room was dark.

"Keep walking," the man said. "Mattress is on the floor. And you two keep quiet."

Ryan sat, letting his eyes adjust. A thin strip of light sneaked underneath the door. Heavy curtains blocked light from outside. Ryan held his hand in front of his face but could barely see it.

The other kid's voice startled him. He hadn't expected the voice of a girl.

Judd, Lionel, and Vicki hurried back to Northwest Community Hospital through massive traffic jams. Smoke still hung in the air. Emergency crews picked through the rubble looking for survivors. Though there were scores of emergency vehicles and hundreds of people, an eerie silence hung over the search.

Judd explained their situation to a guard.

"Did anyone inside survive?" Vicki said.

"They found a baby," the guard said. "Only others I know of were three women on their smoke break outside. They were taken to Lutheran General."

"Maybe one of them saw Ryan," Lionel said. "Let's go."

RYAN jumped when he heard her.

"Of all the indignities," she said. "It's bad enough being kidnapped by a couple of bumpkins. Now I have to share a room."

He couldn't see her, but her voice was thin and proper. She spoke as if she were drinking a cup of tea with her little finger in the air.

"My name's Ryan," he said.

"Darrion Stahley," she said. "I wish I could say I was pleased to meet you, but under the circumstances, I'm not. Where are we?"

Ryan explained his hunch that they were in Chicago.

"How dreadful. I told my father if he decided to move us to Chicago I wouldn't live anywhere close to the city."

"What's wrong with Chicago?"

"If I have to tell you," she said, "it's not worth the

13

breath. The violence. The dirt. Not to mention the noise." A train passed again, and she paused. "See what I mean?"

"Living in the suburbs didn't protect you from those guys," Ryan said.

"I was riding at the stables. They must have watched me, planned it all along."

That explains the boots, Ryan thought. "Why would they kidnap you?" he said. "Are you rich or something?"

"My father is a powerful man, and yes, he is rich. I'm sure he'll take care of these guys. Until then—" Darrion screamed. "Something's crawling on me! Get it off!"

Ryan banged the mattress. He didn't hit anything, but it seemed to make the girl feel better.

"You stirred up the dust!" She coughed.

"You're welcome," Ryan muttered.

"I can't take this!" Darrion screamed. She kicked at the floor. The short man opened the door a crack, and the light allowed Ryan to see Darrion's face for the first time. She was pretty. She was small with short, brown hair. That's why he had thought she was a boy.

"We need light," Darrion demanded. "The room is filled with little creatures scurrying about. If you have to leave us in such deplorable conditions, the least you could do is give us light so we can stay out of their way."

The short man remained behind the door, out of sight, but Ryan could see his shadow. The man shook his head. "Shut up, kid," he said, and closed the door.

"You don't understand," the girl shouted. "My father won't like this!"

Ryan heard the men laugh. Then the light at the bottom of the door went out.

"Nice try," Ryan said, moving toward the wall.

"You think you can do better?" Darrion said.

"Yeah, I think I can."

"I'd like to see you try," she said.

Ryan felt along the wall, then stood. "Why didn't you tell me you wanted some light?" He switched on a flashlight and pointed the beam to her face.

"Where'd you get it?"

"I saw it when the guy opened the door. They must have put it down when they brought you in and forgot about it."

Ryan handed the flashlight to Darrion. She shone it in his face. "What did you say your name was?"

"Ryan," he said, squinting in the light. "Ryan Daley. What kind of a name is Darrion?"

"What's wrong with it?" she said.

"Nothing. It's just unusual."

"Take that up with my parents," she said. "So, what happened today, with the explosions and everything?"

"Beats me," he said. "A bunch of planes went over, and the bombs started dropping."

"I wonder if they've called my father yet," Darrion said, ignoring Ryan. "He'll be worried, I'm sure. My mother as well."

"Yeah," Ryan said.

Darrion scanned the room with the light. Old

mattresses lined three of the walls almost to the ceiling. Ryan saw bugs scurry into cracks in the corner.

"I hope they come for me before nightfall. There's no way I'll be able to sleep in a place like this."

"How old are you?" Ryan said.

"Almost fourteen," Darrion said.

"Wow, same here."

"Whoop-de-doo," Darrion said. "We're the same age and being held hostage in a padded cell." She rolled her eyes. "I'm hungry. The food they brought was disgusting."

"You don't like cheeseburgers?"

"I'm a vegetarian. The only thing close to edible on the plate was the lettuce, and it was dripping with grease."

"You never eat meat?" Ryan said.

"The thought of eating a cow isn't appetizing to me; is it to you?"

"Well, no, but—"

"That's exactly what you did. Animals and people are the same. We're just a little higher up the food chain. Just because I have the ability to speak doesn't give me the right to eat something that doesn't."

"Yeah, well, I still like cheeseburgers," Ryan said, digging into his pocket. Darrion snatched the licorice from his hands.

"Vegetarians eat licorice?" Ryan said, opening the candy bar.

"Low fat," Darrion said.

16

Lutheran General Hospital was packed with injured people and their families. Vicki and Lionel paced while Judd went to the front desk. He came back dejected.

"They won't tell me anything," Judd said.

Vicki stopped an orderly and asked where the Northwest Community survivors were.

"Are you Dorothy's daughter?" the orderly said. "Your mom's real worried that you'd think she was dead. She's up on the third floor, but you can't go in there."

Vicki thanked her. "I'll go talk with her," she said to Judd and Lionel.

"How you gonna do that?" Judd said.

Vicki grabbed a volunteer's smock from a coatrack and walked toward the elevator. Judd and Lionel gave her a thumbs-up as the doors closed.

Dorothy had fallen as she tried to run from the bombs. She was frail with leathery skin. Her hair was thin, and she coughed violently during the conversation. Even when she wasn't talking, she wheezed through tired lungs.

Vicki fluffed her pillow and tried to make her feel more comfortable. "They said you came over from Northwest Community," Vicki said.

"I'm in the cancer ward," the woman said.

"I have a friend who was over there this morning," Vicki said, "a boy about thirteen or fourteen, riding a bike—"

"A blond kid?" Dorothy interrupted.

"Yes!" Vicki said. "What happened?"

17

"He asked directions. A couple minutes before the explosion."

"Directions where?" Vicki said.

Dorothy rubbed her head. "He was looking for Kirchoff Road. Seemed like he couldn't get his bearings. He took off up the hill. That's the last I saw of him."

Ryan kept the flashlight off to save the battery. He inspected the windows and felt along the wall behind the mattresses.

"What are you doing?" Darrion said.

"Trying to find a way out," Ryan said.

"I already checked."

Ryan scratched at the windows to let some light through.

"It's painted on the outside," Darrion said.

"Wait a minute," Ryan said excitedly. He pulled out his wrist messenger.

"What?" Darrion said, grabbing for the flashlight.

"Our shot at getting out of here," Ryan said. "I can get in touch with my friends using this thing. Douse the light."

Ryan fiddled with the gadget and frowned.

"What's wrong?" Darrion said.

"Smashed. Must have happened when I fell."

"Wait till my father comes," Darrion said. "He'll get us out of here."

"He may get *you* out," Ryan said. "Did you get a look at their faces?"

18

"They wore masks."

"I saw both of them—and their van."

"So?"

"They don't dare release me," Ryan said. "I could identify them."

Judd swung by the house and picked up Phoenix. They took him to the hill above the hospital.

Lionel held one of Ryan's shirts, and Phoenix sniffed it excitedly. Judd and Vicki watched as the dog yanked Lionel toward the yellow police tape surrounding the rescue site.

"Ryan was here," Judd said. "Get Phoenix to turn around."

Lionel tried to drag Phoenix from the tape, but the dog barked and raised up on his hind legs, straining against the leash. Vicki held out Ryan's shirt and got Phoenix back on the trail.

They reached the top and continued down the other side of the hill. Phoenix led them to the middle of a residential street. Bits of broken plastic lay on the ground.

"There are marks on the road back here too," Lionel said. "Like somebody slammed on their brakes."

"That could have happened anytime, couldn't it?" Vicki said.

Phoenix was off before Lionel could respond, zigzagging from the road to the curb and back to the middle of the street. Vicki yelped, and Judd found her on the ground.

"I tripped over that thing," Vicki said.

Judd's heart sank when he saw the twisted piece of metal that had been Ryan's bike. Phoenix barked and strained even more when he caught scent of the bicycle.

"What are you going to do?" Darrion said.

"Pray," Ryan said.

"No, really."

"I'm serious," Ryan said.

"Look, if you're right, you're in real trouble here. You need a plan."

Judd's cell phone rang as they returned to the car. Lionel answered.

"Lionel, it's John. I've been calling hospitals since you guys left. Mark and I finally logged on and accessed admission logs. I think I found him."

"Where?" Lionel said.

"Lutheran General."

"We were just there and talked to a lady who saw him before the bombing."

"The kid on the list is pretty banged up, but he fits the description. Unidentified teenager, blond."

Lionel, Judd, and Vicki sped to the emergency room and said they might be able to identify an injured teen. They were directed to a long corridor filled with anxious family members.

"We have three unidentified kids who are thirteen or

fourteen," an attendant said. "The only boy was unconscious when they brought him in."

"Can we see him?" Judd said.

"Let me check," the woman said.

A few minutes later she returned with a grim face. "I'm sorry," she said. "The boy died. Can you identify him, help us contact his family?"

"We are his family," Lionel said. "His mom and dad are dead."

"Just one of you, please."

"Can you handle it?" Judd said.

Lionel waited in the hallway outside the morgue while they retrieved the body. His stomach was in knots. He thought about Ryan and how they had fought. The little guy wasn't so little anymore. He was annoying at times, got on Lionel's nerves. But Lionel wished he had another chance.

Lionel was led into a cold, sterile room. A sheet covered the body on a metal table.

"Are you okay?" the man said.

"Wait," Lionel said, then took a deep breath. He nodded and closed his eyes as the man lifted the sheet.

Lionel opened his eyes, and a wave of emotion swept over him. The boy on the table had been badly burned, but this wasn't his friend.

"He could have been taken to some other hospital," Lionel told the others. "Don't they sometimes fly 'em by helicopter downtown?"

"It's worth a shot," Judd said. "John can check that out while we follow leads here."

"What leads?" Vicki said.

"We're assuming he was hurt," Judd said. "Let's assume he didn't get hurt."

"Maybe somebody in the neighborhood helped him," Vicki said.

"He would have called us," Lionel said.

Ryan heard a cell phone ring in the other room. He crawled to the door and strained to hear.

"Yeah, boss," the driver said, "she's fine. No, the timing was perfect. We took off with her, and then all those bombs went off. No sir, she didn't see either of us."

Ryan heard the short man whispering to the driver, "Tell him about the other kid."

"No, we didn't see any family members or workers." The man paused. "No, we did just like you said. We haven't made contact with anybody."

The driver was pacing as he talked.

"Tell him about the other kid!" the short man badgered.

"Yes, sir," the driver said. "We understand. She won't be harmed unless you give the word."

The driver hung up, and the short man exploded. "I can't believe you didn't tell him! What's he gonna do when he finds out we got two kids instead of one?"

"He doesn't need to know," the driver said.

"He won't pay us—that's what he'll do!"

"Listen, by the time they're ready to release the girl, we'll have taken care of the other kid."

The two went into another room. Ryan wondered what "taken care of" meant. He went back to the mattress on the floor. Darrion was right. He needed a plan. And fast.

Vicki felt drained. Bruce, the man who had helped change her life, was gone. Her friend Chaya had lost her mother in the bombing. Another Young Tribulation Force member, Mark, had nearly been killed, and where was Ryan? Vicki was hanging by a thread, but there wasn't time to think about that now.

Judd was taking them, along with Phoenix, back to the road where they had found Ryan's crumpled bike. Lionel had been on the cell phone with John.

"John can't find any kids transported by helicopter or anyone fitting Ryan's description."

"It's crazy right now," Vicki said. "The records are probably incomplete. People aren't concerned with keeping record of the dead. They want to help the living."

Lionel looked hard at Vicki. "He's not dead," he said. "Stop talking that way."

Phoenix picked up the trail from the road and took them through tall grass near the hill overlooking Northwest Community Hospital. As they neared the top, Lionel shouted, "Look at these tracks!"

In the grass, Vicki saw two sets of deep tire marks.

Phoenix came back to the tracks and barked. He

sniffed through the area and whined, tipping his head this way and that.

"I'm no bloodhound," Judd said, "but this is where Ryan's trail ends."

"So maybe the bombs caused a car to swerve and knock Ryan off his bike," Vicki said. "Then, whoever was in the car helped him."

"Maybe he didn't get hit at all," Lionel said. "What if he was off his bike? The person in the car gave him a ride because the thing was smashed."

"Then why haven't we seen him or heard from him?" Judd said. "We either find Ryan or we find somebody who saw what happened."

3

RYAN hurdled the toppled trash bin and flew down the alley. He wanted to stop and catch his breath, but he knew he had to keep running. It was his only chance.

He heard the screech of tires. A car flattened a trash bin like a pop can. Ryan kept moving. He passed houses with gang symbols spray painted on the outside.

He jumped the turnstiles of the elevated train. The cashier screamed at him. Ryan shouted back, "Call the police!"

"I'll call them on you!" the cashier said.

His legs were lead as he ran up the stairs. A pay phone. Call Judd, he thought. No money in his pockets. He didn't have time anyway. Two doors slammed, and the men were gaining on him.

People milled about, waiting for the next train. A businessman with his nose in the paper. A woman with a frilly dress and tennis shoes. Ryan ran through the crowd to a chain-link fence at the end of the platform. Trapped! The only way out was to run onto the tracks.

He jumped.

A woman screamed, "No!"

He wasn't trying to kill himself. He wanted to live. So he kept running, staying away from the dangerous third rail. One misstep, and he was dead.

He saw the men jump onto the tracks. Then he heard a noise. Felt it. It started as a low rumbling, like the vibration of speakers on his stereo. He looked up to see the train a hundred yards away and coming fast. He turned, but the men were close now. He ran toward the oncoming train.

Finally, the men retreated. The train blew its horn. Even if the conductor slammed on the brakes, Ryan knew it would be too late. He had to jump the third rail.

The woman screamed again. She was behind the men. It looked like . . . but it couldn't be.

"Mom?" Ryan said, the train bearing down on him. His foot wedged in the track. The sound was deafening.

"Ryan, jump!" the woman screamed.

Ryan sat up in a sweat.

The sound of the elevated train rumbled outside the window. He shuddered and wiped his brow with his shirtsleeve. He was sore from his bike accident. He flipped on the flashlight and saw Darrion sitting on her bed with her legs crossed underneath her.

"Lunch made you a little drowsy, huh?" Darrion said. "What's wrong?"

"Bad dream," Ryan said. "What're you doing?"

"Meditation," she said. "Gets me in touch with myself and my surroundings. So what scared you?"

"I don't want to talk about it."

"Come on," she said, "dreams tell us a lot about ourselves. A window to the soul and all that. My parents let me go to a psychic once. I told her what I'd dreamed, and she said my life was going to be filled with tranquility."

Ryan raised an eyebrow and looked around the room.

"So what's your plan?" she said quickly.

"I have to get out of here," Ryan said, "but first I have to encourage our friends in the next room to let me stay alive."

"I'll demand they not harm you."

"Yeah, that'll work. They wouldn't even give you a lightbulb."

While Lionel and Vicki took the other side of the street, Judd set off alone. He went from house to house asking if anyone had seen Ryan. Chaya called on his cell phone.

"You just got an E-mail from Nina in Israel," Chaya said. "She saw the reports about the war and wanted to make sure you were okay."

"What about over there?" Judd said.

"Didn't say. I gave her your cell phone number. She was anxious to talk to you. Any luck with Ryan?"

Judd explained what they were doing and urged Chaya to pray. "You doing okay?" he said.

"Yeah," she said. "Looking for Ryan is helping me focus on something else. If I stop to think about what happened today, I'm no help to anyone."

A few minutes later Nina called. Judd told her how close the bombings were and the situation with Ryan.

"I'm so sorry," Nina said. "I will be praying for your friend."

"What's it like there?" Judd said.

"We have seen none of the violence the rest of the world is experiencing," Nina said. "But the pressure on my father is intense. I have talked with my mother about plans to come to America, and she is open to it. Does the offer still stand?"

"You bet," Judd said, knowing their money troubles were increasing. He pushed the thought away and said, "We'll work it out. You just get here."

"If my father gives the okay, we could be there as soon as next week."

"Great, keep me posted," Judd said.

Vicki and Lionel approached with puzzled looks.

"Nobody's seen anything," Vicki said, "but there's something strange over there." She pointed to a small white house across the street. "The lady who answered the door wouldn't even talk to us. When we went to the next house, we heard a tapping noise coming from inside. The windows are boarded up. It sounded like somebody trying to get out. Creepy."

"Better go back and check it out," Judd said.

As they neared the house they heard a car start, and the garage door opened. The kids scrunched behind a tree.

"That's her," Vicki said, "the one who wouldn't talk to us."

After the woman drove away, Judd rang the doorbell. There was no answer.

"I know there's somebody in there," Vicki said.

The three kids went to the side of the house. Judd peered through a crack in one of the boards. He saw old furniture covered in dust. Cats were perched on windowsills around the room. Suddenly Judd saw a woman's face.

"Go to the back," the woman said through the glass.

The woman ushered the kids inside and said, "You have to be careful. Anna doesn't like me talking to anyone with all that's going on."

"What's going on?" Judd said.

"There's evil out there," the woman said. "First, all those people disappeared. Then this guy from Romania takes over. Next thing you know, they're droppin' bombs in your backyard."

"We're looking for somebody," Judd said, "a boy on a bike."

"These people hate cats," the woman continued. "There's a shortage, you know. A few months ago the shelves were full. Now there's only a few cans left."

Judd frowned. "What does cat food have to do with—?"

"It has everything to do with it. They want control. First they start with the little animals. Then they come for the children. It's already started."

Judd turned to leave.

"Wait," Lionel said. "What's happening to the children?"

"They're taking the kids away," she said. "Snatching them off the street."

"Did that happen this morning?" Lionel said.

"I can't tell you any more. Anna wouldn't like it."

"Please," Lionel said, "our friend was riding a bike near here. If you saw something, we need your help."

"You know what I think?" the old woman said. "I think the bombs were a diversion. They're taking the kids and brainwashing them so they can have a whole army of little robots."

Vicki picked up one of the cats and stroked it until it purred. "You've been so kind to us," Vicki said, "and you have such beautiful animals. But what we really need to know is if you saw anything."

"When they control the pets—"

"His name is Ryan," Vicki continued, "and he has blond hair. His parents were both killed. We're taking care of him. You can imagine how bad we feel. We thought he was dead, but now we're not sure."

Judd saw a spark in the old woman's eyes. She stared out the window. "My father died when I was ten," she said. "He worked for the electric company. One morning he promised he'd bring me a surprise when he came home. But he didn't make it. . . ."

The old woman wiped her eyes with a paper towel. Vicki put a hand on her shoulder.

"I did see the poor boy," she said. "Anna doesn't like me to go out, but when the bombs went off I stepped onto the porch."

"What did you see?" Vicki said.

"I heard tires squeal and looked down at the curve in the street," she said. "There was a white van. Two men. They'd run over a bicycle and were trying to get it out from under the van. Then they backed up and tried to grab the boy."

"Did they get him?" Judd said.

"Yeah," the old woman said, "they caught him in the grass."

"What happened then?" Vicki said.

"Another bomb went off. I went to the back and saw the smoke and fire. When I looked again, the guys and the kid were gone. I tried to call the police, but Anna said we shouldn't get involved."

"Did you see their license plates?" Judd said.

"Too far away," she said.

Judd opened the back door to leave.

"Thank you for helping us," Vicki said, "and I'm sorry about your father."

The old woman smiled.

Ryan stashed the soda cans under his mattress. "Never know when little things like this might come in handy," he said.

Darrion explained her father's business. "He did a lot of work for the Global Community after the disappearances," she said. "They wanted to promote him, which we thought meant the East Coast. You know, New York, Washington, D.C. But he wound up here in the Midwest."

"So your dad works for Nicolae Carpathia?" Ryan said.

Darrion nodded. "He's met him lots of times," she said. "My dad told me about it. He said when Nicolae shakes your hand, you feel like you're the only person in the room. Like you're really important to him. Nicolae remembers everybody's name, you know."

Ryan felt sick inside. That was exactly what Bruce had said about the Antichrist. He could manipulate people. "Did you lose anybody in the disappearances?" Ryan asked.

"Just an aunt and an uncle," Darrion said. "They were both crazy, though."

"What was wrong with them?" Ryan said.

"Religious wackos," Darrion said. "A few years ago they went over to Europe and got mixed up in some religious group. When they came home, they tried to get my dad to read the Bible and go to church with them."

"And your dad didn't buy it?"

"We've always been religious, open-minded. But they were so narrow. If you didn't believe exactly what they did, you were cooked."

"So if they were wrong, what do *you* think about God?"

"I believe in the unity of all living things. God is in us and in all that exists."

"That's why you're a vegetarian."

"Precisely."

"So, when you eat a carrot, aren't you eating God?" The words were out of Ryan's mouth before he could stop them.

"I'm into Enigma Babylon One World Faith," Darrion said, ignoring the comment. "It takes the best of all the belief systems. It's not trying to hurt people like my aunt and uncle were."

"You didn't tell me they hurt you."

"They tried to scare us. You know, they talked about hell. Made God out to be mean."

The men were moving around in the next room. Ryan put a finger to his lips and silently crept to the door.

"If you'd have just kept going, we wouldn't have to—"

"Don't start!" the man said.

"Why do we have to wait till it gets dark?" the short man said. "Let's do it now."

"And how we gonna do it?"

The two men closed the door and went into another room.

"What did they say?" Darrion said.

"Looks like they're gettin' tired of me quicker than I thought," Ryan said. "I'd better come up with something fast."

Ryan prayed silently for an idea. "Please, God, show me how to get out of here. Unless this is where you want me to be. And if it is, open Darrion's heart and let me talk with her about you."

———

Judd, Vicki, and Lionel regrouped at Judd's house. Judd tried to phone Sergeant Thomas Fogarty of the Chicago Police Department. Sergeant Fogarty had helped the kids before. The line was busy.

"I just talked with Mrs. Fogarty on the other line," Lionel said. "It's almost impossible to reach the police downtown."

"Tell me about it," Judd said.

"She's gonna have him call us when he gets home or if he gets in touch with her," Lionel said.

"What about the local police?" Judd said. "We should call—"

"Already done. They're just as busy. When I got them to listen to the evidence, they said I should come down and fill out a missing person's report. The cop didn't sound too hopeful that it would do any good."

"Probably won't," Judd said.

Judd and Vicki dropped Lionel off at the police station and swung by New Hope Village Church. Judd found Loretta, Bruce's assistant, red-eyed and sniffling. She was nearly seventy and sitting in the outer office in front of a silent television.

"People been callin'," Loretta said. "I don't know what to tell them. Buck and Chloe Williams came in and told me about Bruce. They didn't actually see him, but Rayford Steele did. I wish I could talk with Ray, just to know Bruce didn't suffer."

Judd knelt by Loretta's chair. "I saw him," he said.

Loretta's face was puffy. "How was he?" she said. "I mean, was his body hurt badly?"

Judd was glad he didn't have to dance around the truth. He had seen Bruce under the white sheet. The sight of his face had taken his breath away, it was true. But when he thought about Bruce's face, Judd smiled.

"He looked like he was sleeping," Judd said. "Peaceful. All those sirens and people crying and running everywhere, and there was Bruce—just like he was when he was alive. Calm."

"That young man was like family to me," Loretta said. "He was my only family. You know my story, don't you?"

"I know a lot of your family members were taken in the Rapture," Judd said.

"I lost everybody," Loretta said. "Every living relative. More than a hundred. I came from a church family. I was one of the leading women in this church. I was active in everything, but I never really knew the Lord."

"That's why Bruce meant so much to you," Judd said.

"That young man taught me everythin'," Loretta continued. "I learned more from him in two years than I learned in more than sixty years in Sunday school and church. There's gonna be an awful big hole in my heart now that Bruce is gone. I'm sorry to go on and on. How are your friends?"

Judd explained the situation with Ryan. "The poor thing," Loretta gasped. "I hope he's okay. He learned so much from Bruce in such a short time. He was like a little sponge."

Judd noticed a huge stack of pages on Loretta's desk in the other room.

"It's Bruce's legacy to the church," Loretta said. "It was Buck Williams's idea. I was feelin' all puny, and he said I could still serve the Lord by serving Bruce. He said just from glancing at those pages that Bruce was still with us. His knowledge, his teaching, his love and compassion are all there."

"So what's Mr. Williams going to do?" Judd said.

"He wants me to help print those pages. He says people in the church need access to the material. It's a treasure everyone can use."

"I watched Bruce write some of that while we were in Israel together," Judd said.

"There's powerful stuff there," Loretta said. "Go ahead. I'm sure Bruce would want you to."

Judd leafed through the pages, and tears came to his eyes. *No wonder Buck Williams wants to get this into the hands of people,* he thought.

WHILE Ryan thought of a plan to save his life, Darrion discussed her horse, her private school, her friends in Italy, and more. Ryan thought he was a privileged kid, but his life was nothing compared to hers. Vacations on islands he'd never heard of. A private jet to carry her anywhere in the world. *Her dad must really be loaded,* Ryan thought.

"I don't understand," Darrion said. "My dad should have given them the money by now."

"These guys are working for someone else," Ryan said. "They didn't call your parents."

"So these guys are just waiting for directions?"

"Looks that way," Ryan said. "And they're making a big deal about the pay. That's why I have to be out of the way. They don't want to threaten their paycheck, which is you."

"Why didn't they just ask my dad for the money themselves?" Darrion said.

"I don't know. It's strange."

Darrion sighed and wilted on the bed. "What could those people want?"

Sergeant Fogarty called, and Judd explained the situation. The officer listened with interest. "Why would anyone want to kidnap your friend?" he said.

"That's what we can't figure out," Judd said.

"You can't be positive it was him," Fogarty said. "Some other kid could have—"

"The witness we found described him," Judd said.

"I believe you," Sergeant Fogarty said. "I'm just trying to think of all the angles."

Sergeant Fogarty said he would try to help, but with the mayhem on the streets, the chances of finding Ryan were slim. Even if they did discover some kind of lead, the officers were swamped with just keeping the peace.

Chaya phoned from the church office. "You guys need to get over here right away," she said.

The men wore masks so Darrion wouldn't see their faces. They grabbed Ryan and led him from the room. Darrion barked at the two, saying her father would be upset if anything happened to Ryan.

"Who says we're going to hurt your friend?" the short

man said. "We're just gonna take a little ride down by the lake."

"Shut up," the driver said.

They hustled Ryan into the next room and taped his hands behind him.

"Should we blindfold him?" the short man said.

"What for?" the driver said.

"Good point," the short man said, snorting. "How about his feet?"

"Let him walk down."

The men shoved Ryan at the top of the stairs. He lost his balance and fell. He was groggy as they pulled out of the garage.

On the street Ryan realized his hunch was right. Chicago. The building they were in was surrounded by other apartments. He saw the L tracks and a tiny alley that ran beside them. Cars were parked along the alley with no space between them. A block away Ryan noticed an abandoned factory. Men in old coats stood by a burning trash can outside. A police car was pulling up as they went by. He couldn't make out any street signs until they had gone a few blocks. Then he saw a green sign that said Halsted.

Close to Lake Michigan two huge apartment buildings rose on either side of the road. They were in Lincoln Park, and a few minutes later the men found a marina and parked the van by the pier.

"Too many people around," the driver said. "It'll thin out in a few minutes."

Ryan shook as he prayed.

Judd had never seen Chaya this excited. Loretta was busy on the phone. Vicki had joined Judd and Chaya in Bruce's office.

"You're not going to believe this," Chaya said. "I typed our names into the computer and hit the Search key. You guys show up all the way through here."

"I thought this was just his sermon notes," Vicki said.

"No," Chaya said. "He included lots of personal impressions of his friends. I think we have the answer to a question about Ryan."

Chaya typed in Ryan's name, and Judd read over her shoulder.

"Ryan has finally made his decision," Bruce had written, *"and we are all very thankful. He is the last of the four to see the truth and trust Christ for forgiveness of sins. I pray God will use him mightily in the time we have left."*

"I remember that day," Vicki said.

"The interesting stuff comes a couple hundred pages later," Chaya said as she clicked the keyboard. "Read this."

"Ryan's idea has put me in a difficult situation," Judd read. *"If I trust him with this information, it could jeopardize my relationship with the adult Tribulation Force."*

"What's he talking about?" Vicki said.

"I haven't been able to figure it out," Chaya said. "But it's clear from the other stuff Bruce said that it has something to do with the Bibles Ryan was collecting. Another section of the file mentioned an underground shelter."

"I remember Bruce saying something about how we

need to prepare for the worst," Vicki said, "but where would the shelter be?"

"Remember the excavation they did a few months ago?" Judd said.

"Yeah, sure, but that was just a construction project, wasn't it?" Vicki said.

"Maybe not," Judd said.

The next entry by Bruce read, *"I've decided to go with Ryan's idea and still keep the integrity of the project downstairs. Hopefully, this will provide Ryan with the space and secrecy he needs, without compromising the project."*

"I don't get it," Vicki said. "Is he talking about the downstairs of his house?"

"I don't think so," Judd said. "Follow me."

Ryan mumbled through the tape over his mouth.

"Save your breath," the short man said. "We're not givin' you a chance to scream for help."

Ryan cocked his head and rolled his eyes.

"I think he wants to tell us something," the driver said. He climbed in the back, pulled out a gun, and waved it at Ryan. "If you open your yap and yell, you won't do it twice, understand?"

Ryan nodded, and the man jerked the tape from his mouth.

"I'm trying to figure this out," Ryan gasped through the pain.

"He doesn't need to figure anything out," the short man said. "Put the tape back on."

"I'm not gonna cry for help," Ryan said. "But before you guys whack me, I gotta know why you'd throw away such a golden opportunity."

The driver squinted.

Ryan continued. "I mean, I can understand why you'd grab a girl like Darrion. Her dad's loaded. But what I don't understand is why you'd let me go without even trying to get in touch with my family."

"Are you saying your family can offer us something for your safe return?" the driver said. "As in, money?"

"He's bluffin'," the short man said.

Ryan shook his head. "It just doesn't make good business sense. I mean, I heard you guys talking about how you were going to split the money you got from Darrion." Ryan laughed. "You guys need to start thinking bigger."

The short man grabbed the tape and was about to put it back over Ryan's mouth when the driver grabbed his arm. "Let the kid talk," he said. "What have we got to lose?"

"From what I gather," Ryan said, "you guys aren't working with Darrion's parents. That's your first mistake. You have no control."

"They're payin' us okay for the risk we're takin'," the short man said.

"Are they?" Ryan said. "Compared with what Mr. Stahley is able to pay, I don't think so."

"Our boss isn't in it for the money," the short man said. "He wants the Stahley guy to—"

"Shut up!" the driver said. "Don't tell him everything you know."

"All I'm saying is you've got a bird in your hand that

will pay a limited amount," Ryan said. "But you're throwing away the goose that laid the golden egg."

"And you're the goose?" the driver said.

Ryan nodded.

The short man laughed and slapped the tape back on Ryan's mouth. "Let's get it over with," he said.

"And what if he's telling the truth?" the driver said. "What if we are sellin' ourselves short?"

"I can see it in his eyes," the short man said. "Drive to the end of the pier and we'll open the door."

Judd led Chaya and Vicki to the darkened church basement. They walked through the fellowship hall, down a narrow corridor, past the washrooms and the furnace room. They were now at the end of the hallway with no light.

"They did the excavation on the other side of this wall," Judd said. He felt around the concrete blocks. Nothing. They returned to the furnace room, and Judd flipped on the light switch. A flashlight rested atop the furnace. Judd flicked it on and scanned the back wall closely. He found the furnace and a hot-water heater. Nothing out of the ordinary.

"Wait," Chaya said as Judd turned to leave. "That back wall is weird. There's nothing hanging there or pushed against it. It's wasted space."

The three felt along the back wall. Suddenly, Judd found an indentation about the size of his hand. Judd braced his feet and pushed hard. The three looked in amazement as a section of the wall slid open.

"I'm not goin' in there," Vicki said.

"What if Ryan's down here, hiding?" Judd said. "What if he's hurt?"

"We know that can't be," Vicki said. "Don't we?"

Vicki followed them in, and Judd pushed the wall closed behind them. "Whatever's down here needs to be kept a secret," Judd said.

There was a smell of wet earth and cement. The flashlight illuminated a sign directly in front of them and six steps down: "Danger! High Voltage. Authorized Personnel Only."

They moved down the steps and took a left. Four more steps down was a huge steel door. The sign at the landing of the stairs was duplicated on the door. The knob was locked.

"Dead end," Vicki said.

"Who would have the key?" Chaya said.

"Bruce would," Judd said, "but it doesn't have a keyhole. There must be some other way to get it open." He jiggled the door and banged on it. No luck. Judd led them back up the steps to the entrance.

"Wait," Vicki said. "Shine the light over here."

Judd pointed the light to the wall behind the secret entrance. They ran their hands over it, and this time Chaya squealed in delight.

"It's a handprint, just like the one outside, only a little lower," Chaya said. She leaned into it, and the wall gave way a few inches. Judd put the flashlight down and helped. They moved inside the darkened room and listened. Vicki felt for a light switch but tripped. Judd heard paper rattling. Then Vicki began to laugh.

"Are you okay?" Judd said as he retrieved the flash-light and shone it in her face.

"This is it!" Vicki said excitedly. "We found it!"

Judd found a light switch.

"Incredible," Chaya said.

Around the room, in stacks of fifty each, were the Bibles Ryan had confiscated. Vicki had knocked over a small stack by the door.

"Look at this," Chaya said.

In the corner was a small table with a lamp. Beside it was a picture of Ryan with his mother and father. Next to it was a picture taken only a few weeks earlier of Ryan and Bruce. He also had photos of Lionel, Vicki, and Judd, a photo of Bruce and his family, and one of Phoenix. In the middle of the table was a spiral notebook. Vicki opened it.

"Bruce said I should keep a diary of the things I think about, so I'm going to do it here," Vicki read out loud. *"Bruce said this could be my secret place. If anything ever happens to me, he can tell the others where I'm hiding the Bibles."*

"There must be hundreds in here," Chaya said.

"We've already given a few hundred away," Judd said. "The room must have been packed."

"Listen to this," Vicki said. *"Sometimes I feel really lonely and I want my mom and dad to come back. I wish they could be here so I could tell them what I've learned and what I know about God. But I do have good friends."* Vicki choked up.

"Maybe we'd better not read it," Judd said. "I mean, if he's alive and we find him, he'll be mad."

"Yeah," Vicki said. "I like that attitude."

Lionel returned from the police station and sat by the phone, hating every minute. He wanted to do something to find Ryan. But there was nothing he could do. He had called every possible place Ryan could be. As he sat by the phone, he had an overwhelming urge to pray for Ryan, like he was in danger.

"Give him strength, Father God," Lionel prayed. "Watch over him and protect him."

Ryan felt the crisp lake air on his face as the men drove toward the water. He could hear the sound of cars on nearby Lake Shore Drive, but no people were in sight. Even if he did manage to scream, nobody would hear him.

"Open the door and toss him," the driver said.

Ryan looked at the murky water. If it was shallow, he could get his legs under him. He might be able to bob long enough to stay alive. But if the water was more than six feet deep, there was no hope.

The short man dragged him to the edge of the van. Ryan saw the movement of the water as it lapped against wooden posts. *Too deep*, he thought.

"I'll count to three," the driver said. The short man rocked Ryan back and forth as he counted. "One . . . two . . ."

On the third time, the man stopped and stripped the tape from Ryan's mouth. "You get one more chance. Tell us about your old man."

Ryan trembled, half from fear and half from the cold.

"I-I told you," he stammered, "he puts Darrion's father to shame."

"How much is he worth?" the driver said.

"He owns a lot of cows," Ryan said. "Like, on a thousand hills."

"So he's a rancher?" the short man said.

"Sort of," Ryan said. "My father is rich. He has a mansion, and there's a room he's preparing for me right now."

"What's his name?" the driver said. "We ever heard of him?"

"You've probably seen some of the things he's made," Ryan said, "but I don't know that you know him."

"And you think he'll pay?" the driver said.

"He's already paid a lot for me," Ryan said. "I was adopted into his family. It cost an awful lot."

"Adopted?" the short man said.

"Yeah, I met his Son, and he introduced me to his Father. After that, they made me part of the family."

The two looked at each other. "Sounds hard to believe," the driver said. "Rich guy takes a kid in and makes him an heir?"

The short man shrugged. "How can we reach your dad?" he said.

"I'm not telling until we get back to the house," Ryan said.

"What?!" the driver said.

"If I give you the number, you can throw me in the lake, then call to get the ransom."

"We could just throw you in now and be done with the whole thing," the short man said, tipping Ryan on his side.

"True," Ryan said. "And then you'd probably miss the biggest payday of your life. What my dad can give you could last you forever."

"I got my doubts that anybody would want a kid like this back," the driver said. "But I guess it's worth a try."

Ryan watched the street signs carefully on the way back. If he could somehow get away, he wanted to know where to run. Ryan gave them Judd's number.

"Who do we ask for?" the short man said.

"Ask for Ryan Daley's father," Ryan said.

Ryan prayed someone would be home and would say the right thing to keep him alive. *At least I've been outside and know what I'm up against,* Ryan thought.

Darrion was surprised to see him. It looked like she had been crying. Ryan put his finger to his lips.

"Look," the driver said, "we get in touch with the kid's dad. If it's a hoax, we whack the kid."

"But if he's telling the truth," the short man said, "he knows where we are and what we look like."

"Do I look stupid?" the driver said. "If the dad's rich, we tell him the kid's okay, set up a drop site, and whack him anyway. The kid's outta the picture, and we're a million or two richer."

"What about the boss?" the short man said.

"The boss never knows the difference."

The two were silent a moment. "I'd only change one thing," the short man said. "When you call the guy, make it five million."

5

LIONEL answered the phone on the first ring. The caller ID didn't display the number.

"I'm looking for Ryan Daley's father," a strange voice said.

"Excuse me?" Lionel said. *Ryan's dad is dead,* Lionel thought.

"Ryan Daley's father," the man said. "Do you know where he is?"

Lionel bit his cheek. This could be the break they were looking for. "Yeah, he's not here," Lionel said. "Can I take a message?"

"No," the man said. "When will he be back?"

"I can't say," Lionel said.

The line clicked. Lionel called Judd. "I think we have our first really good clue," Lionel said.

"I thought you were a goner," Darrion said. "I was thinking about all the nice things I'd say at your funeral."

"You don't know how close I came," Ryan said. He explained what had happened and the clues he had learned.

Darrion shook her head. "I haven't told you everything," she said. "You know how I said my aunt and uncle disappeared? Well, they did, but the whole thing was suspicious. My dad started checking it out."

"Wait," Ryan said. "You never really said what your father did for a living."

"He does security stuff. You know, making sure the big guys are safe. He helps out with some of the military jobs, too."

"Military jobs?" Ryan said.

"Disposing of the nuclear weapons," she said. "Planning military assaults, that kind of thing."

Ryan raised his eyebrows. "No wonder your dad's rich," he said. "They have to trust you big time to put you in that position."

"That's just it," she said. "When he started looking into what happened to my aunt and uncle, he got the feeling that somebody didn't like it very much. But he didn't stop."

"Did he find out what happened?"

"He never told me a lot about it directly. I'd pick up things here and there when he talked with my mom. It seemed like the more he looked, the more convinced he became that there was something to the story my aunt and uncle were telling. You know, the Bible and everything. It seemed like what they believed got them killed."

"So they didn't disappear?" Ryan said.

"They were being held in custody in Romania. This was back before there was a Global Community. They had said something against Nicolae Carpathia. I don't know what. My dad found the place where they were held. They weren't released; they just disappeared."

I know what happened to them, Ryan thought.

———————————

Lionel talked again with Mrs. Fogarty. She said she would do what she could. When Judd came in, Lionel told him more about the conversation with the mysterious caller.

"Could it have been somebody from a hospital or the police?" Judd said.

"Don't think so," Lionel said. "Whoever it was sounded like they were outside. Either a cell phone or a pay phone."

Judd called the phone company but was told incoming calls could not be traced. "But this is a serious matter," Judd said. "If the police ask you to trace it, can you?"

"Only in extreme cases," the operator said.

Lionel sat down and scribbled some notes on a pad of paper. "This is what we know. We have Ryan's mangled bike and an old lady who says she saw him being taken from the street."

"In a white van," Judd said.

"We know Ryan would have called us. And he's not in any of the hospitals or morgues in the area."

"At least as far as we can tell," Judd said.

"We know Ryan isn't in his Bible hideout," Lionel said. "And now we can add this strange guy who asks for Ryan's dad."

"If it was from a hospital or the police, the guy would have asked for a parent," Judd said.

"And he would have identified himself as an official," Lionel said.

"Next time he calls, we'll let him speak with Ryan's dad," Judd said.

Ryan told Darrion his story. He began with his friend Raymie and his mom. She was just like Darrion's aunt and uncle. Always going to church. Always talking about God. Raymie lived differently and didn't do some of the stuff Ryan did. Ryan couldn't understand it.

Then, when Raymie and his mom disappeared with the rest, Ryan found a group of kids and a pastor who explained what had happened. Jesus Christ had returned for those who truly believed in him. It was the only explanation that made any sense.

"That sounds so weird," Darrion said.

"It did to me, too, when I first heard it," Ryan said. "But think about it. People vanish. Nothing but their clothes left behind. Babies disappear. Unborn children too. How can you explain that?"

"What about the pastor you met? Why wasn't he taken?"

Ryan explained Bruce Barnes's story in detail. Just

talking about Bruce made Ryan ache to see him again. "It sounds like your dad was thinking a lot about spiritual stuff when he looked into the deaths of your aunt and uncle," Ryan said.

"I think you're right," Darrion said. "In the last few weeks he and Mom have been up late talking. They even started reading the Bible, if you can believe that."

"I can," Ryan said. "I never read the Bible before, but now that I have people who can help me understand it, I—"

The door flew open, and the short man yelled, "Get over here, kid!"

"Did you get in touch with my dad?" Ryan said.

The man jerked Ryan into the next room. "I talked to some kid who said he didn't know when your dad would be back."

"That was probably Lionel," Ryan said. "He's my brother."

"My partner and I have a bad feeling about this. If we don't get a response soon, we're gonna cut you loose."

Ryan didn't want to think about what that phrase meant.

"My father's a busy guy, but I know he really cares for me. Why don't you give him a number to call you back?"

"What do you think, we're stupid?" the short man said. "But if we don't get in touch with him on the next call, that's it."

Vicki met with Chloe at the church. She told Chloe the latest about Ryan. Chloe was visibly upset by the news.

"So much has happened so quickly," she said. "We were on our way to see Bruce when the bombings started. Then, after my dad discovered Bruce's body, Nicolae Carpathia called him. They flew my dad and Amanda away in a chopper."

"Do you know where they went?" Vicki said.

"We believe they're with Carpathia, but we don't know where," Chloe said. "When O'Hare was bombed, I was afraid they might have been caught in the middle, but we're assuming they're safe."

Lionel and Judd came in.

"Who's at the house?" Vicki said.

"We forwarded the calls to Judd's cell phone," Lionel said.

"Any luck on Sergeant Fogarty and the trace?" Vicki said.

"None," Lionel said. "Is Mr. Williams here?"

Chloe led them to Buck, who was waiting for Donny Moore, a computer specialist who attended the church. Buck said he'd be glad to pose as Ryan's father. He and Chloe needed to leave soon, but they would do everything they could.

Chaya rushed into the office with a stack of papers, and Chloe excused herself to talk with Buck.

"I've been going through more of Bruce's manuscript," Chaya said. "Bruce's read on Revelation convinced him that we were at the end of the eighteen-month period of peace, which came right after the treaty Israel made with the Antichrist."

"He's been right about everything so far," Judd said.

54

"Hang on," Chaya said. "Bruce thinks what's next is worse."

Chaya handed them a photocopy of a few pages of Bruce's notes.

If I am right, and we can set the beginning of the Tribulation at the time of the signing of the treaty and what was then known as the United Nations, Bruce had written, *we are perilously close to and must prepare for the next prediction in the Tribulation timeline. The Red Horse of the Apocalypse.*

Lionel smiled. "Remember when Ryan first heard about these verses?" he said. "He told me later he'd started to hate horses."

Vicki put a hand on Lionel's shoulder.

"Look at Revelation, chapter six," Chaya said. Each member grabbed a Bible and read verses three and four: "When the Lamb broke the second seal, I heard the second living being say, 'Come!' And another horse appeared, a red one. Its rider was given a mighty sword and the authority to remove peace from the earth. And there was war and slaughter everywhere."

"This will affect all people," Chaya said. "Bruce believed these verses refer to a prediction of global war."

"Isn't that what we're in now?" Lionel said.

"Let me come back to that," Chaya said. "Bruce thought this would likely be known as World War III. It will be started by the Antichrist, and yet he will rise as the great solver of it, a real peacemaker."

"Carpathia, the great liar," Vicki said.

"He will use this opportunity to gain more power for himself," Chaya said. "After that, Bruce believed the next two horses would be loosed—the black horse of plague and famine and the pale horse of death. I've been doing more study, and I think what we've seen so far is just the start of the war. The strike on the Nike base and the hospital was isolated."

"Tell that to New York City," Judd said.

"But even there," Chaya said, "the bombings seemed targeted. And we don't know how much is coming from the militia and how much from the Global Community."

"I could see Nicolae bombing a place and blaming it on someone else," Vicki said.

Judd's phone rang. He handed the phone to Lionel and quickly went out of the room.

Darrion seemed interested in Ryan's story, but cautious. As they talked, he bent one of his soda cans in half, then worked it until it broke in two. He took the razor-sharp edge and began scratching at one of the small panes of glass in the corner of the window.

"What are you doing?" Darrion said.

"If I'm right," Ryan said, "I may not have that much time before the guys discover the truth about my father."

"You told me your father was dead," Darrion said. "I thought one of the rules you lived by was that you weren't supposed to lie."

"I didn't lie to them," Ryan said. "My father does own a lot of cattle and land, and he is making a place for me."

"I don't get it."

Ryan stopped and turned toward her. "God is my father.

There's a verse in the Bible that says he owns the cattle on a thousand hills. And Jesus said he was going to prepare a place for people who believed in him. All of that's true."

"But you knew those guys would think you were talking about your real dad."

"I didn't plan it that way," Ryan said. "It was the first thing that popped into my head. My family now is everyone who believes in Christ. One day, we'll all be together."

"How can you be so sure about it?" Darrion said. "That's what always got me about my aunt and uncle. They acted like they knew. I'd love to be sure of myself, but I don't want to throw away my brain."

"It's not about being sure of yourself," Ryan said. He dusted the scrapings from the window ledge and put the can down. "That's the difference between what Enigma Babylon One World Faith teaches and what I believe. The new religion says you should trust yourself. Decide for yourself which way you should go. As long as you follow your inner voice, you'll be okay."

"That's not exactly what they teach, but go on."

"The new religion says I should put my faith in faith, in whatever I find that makes me feel like I'm following God."

"You've got a problem with that?" Darrion said.

"Yeah," Ryan said, "it's just plain wrong. You can't let your feelings guide what you believe. You believe what's true."

"And what *is* true? One person's truth might not fit somebody else. See, now *you're* being exclusive."

"You shouldn't believe in belief," Ryan said. "You believe in God. In a person. That's what's true." Ryan could tell he was losing her. "Look, you can't see what's outside now, but if we can get this windowpane out, we can communicate with somebody on the outside."

"So?"

"You're trusting me because I've been outside. For all you know, we might be in some cornfield with nobody around, but you trust me because I've seen it."

"I still don't know what that has to do with—"

"God showed himself to us through Jesus," Ryan said. "He sent his only Son so we could know what God is like. He was God. And he not only showed us the truth, but he also took the punishment for the bad things we've done."

"I believe Jesus was a good person and all," Darrion said, "but I still don't see how you can be so sure."

"I'm not sure because I have great faith. I'm sure because God is great. God showed how great he was by the miracles he performed. The Bible predicts the disappearances and the rise of a one-world government. It's coming true all around us."

"Now you're really talking like my aunt and uncle," Darrion said.

"I don't want to preach to you," Ryan said. "It took me a long time to think it through. But you can't say Jesus was a good man and buy into Enigma Babylon. Jesus said he was the only way to God. And he proved he was God by rising from the dead. That's why I believe in him and can be sure of heaven. It's true not because I want it to be but because I'm trusting somebody who's been there."

Darrion squinted and looked at the window. "Give me the other half of that can," she said.

"Hello?" Lionel said.

"Yeah, I'm looking for your dad."

"Sure, can I ask who's calling?"

"Tell him it's a friend who knows something about his son."

Judd rushed back in with Buck Williams.

Buck took the phone. "What can you tell me about Ryan?" Buck said.

Lionel leaned in close to the phone's earpiece and heard the man say, "First off, if you go to the police, you'll never see your son again. Got that?"

"Is he okay?" Buck said.

"I said, if you go to the po—"

"I got it, all right?" Buck said forcefully. "Now what about Ryan?"

"Second, if you value the kid's life, you'll go to the bank and withdraw five million dollars in cash today."

"I can't get that kind of—"

"Twenties and fifties," the man said.

"I want to talk to him," Buck said. "I want to know he's okay before I do anything."

"Hey, I'm telling you he's okay."

The veins in Buck's neck stood out. "And I'm telling

you, either you let me talk with him, or you never see the money."

Buck punched the cell phone and hung up on the man.

"What are you doing?" Lionel said, horrified.

"It's a hunch," Buck said. "I think it'll work. If we can get control of the situation, we might get a clue from Ryan."

"Control?" Lionel said. "You're playing with Ryan's life!"

"Calm down," Buck said. "For some reason, this guy believes Ryan's father is still living and he's rich. If it's money he really wants, he'll do anything to get it."

"And if you're wrong, the guy gets spooked and never calls again," Lionel said. "And we never find out what happened."

"Unlikely," Buck said. "If Ryan really is alive—"

"He's alive!" Lionel said.

"Right," Buck said, "but it won't work if I'm too anxious. Believe me, I've interviewed enough rich people to know how they act. A guy like that would want to know his son was alive before he shelled out the cash."

Buck took the phone and punched a few numbers on the keypad.

"Hello?" Buck said. "Who is this? Where are you, sir? Okay, good." Buck motioned for a pen and paper. "And what's the closest intersection near you?"

Buck scribbled on the page. "All right. Tell me, did you just see a man at that phone? Okay. Thank you." Buck scribbled some more and hung up.

"I dialed the return call," Buck said. "A guy on the street picked it up. The phone is on Michigan Avenue in Chicago."

JUDD and Lionel stayed with Buck in case the man called again. Donny Moore, a computer whiz, arrived at the church and showed Buck a stack of computer catalogs.

"Whoa," Buck said, "I can see already there are too many choices. Why don't I tell you what I'm looking for, and you tell me if you can deliver?"

"I can tell you right now I can deliver," Donny said. "Last week I sold a guy thirty sub-notebooks with more power than any desktop anywhere. You tell me what you want, I'll get it."

Judd felt a chill go down his spine as Donny said, "When's Bruce gonna be back here?"

"When you said you prayed," Darrion Stahley said, "what did you mean? I know what I do when I meditate, but it sounds like it's something different for you."

Ryan continued working on the window as they talked. "It's like I was saying before, when you pray, you don't follow a bunch of rules or work yourself into a state of mind. You pray to a person."

"I think God's a force in the universe. Why do you say he's a person?"

"A lot of reasons," Ryan said. "The Bible says God created us in his own image. He's communicated with people for thousands of years. And then he showed us exactly what he was like when Jesus—"

The door swung open, and the short man barked for Ryan. Darrion grabbed the soda can from Ryan's hand. "Good luck," she said as he left the room.

Buck asked Donny to sit. "You knew Bruce was sick," Buck said.

"I knew they took him to the hospital, but I just assumed . . ."

Buck touched Donny's arm. "The attack wiped out the hospital," he said. "Bruce didn't make it."

Judd watched as Donny crumpled and fell to his knees. It was painful to go through the feelings again with Donny. "I was able to see him after they recovered his body," Judd said. "Mr. Steele did too, as I understand."

Buck nodded. "I'm really sorry."

Donny looked at him blankly. "Mr. Williams, this has all been hard enough even with Pastor Bruce here. I don't know what we're going to do now."

"Donny," Buck said gravely, "you have an opportunity here to do something for God, and it's the greatest memorial tribute you could ever give to Bruce Barnes."

"Well then, sir, whatever it is, I want to do it."

"First," Buck said, "let me assure you that money is no object."

"I don't want any profit off something that will help the church and God and Bruce's memory."

"Fine. Whatever profit you build in or don't build in is up to you. I just need five of the absolute best, top-of-the-line computers, as small and compact as they can be, but with as much power and memory and speed and communications abilities as you can wire into them."

"You're talking my language, Mr. Williams."

"I hope so, Donny, because I want a computer with virtually no limitations. I want to be able to take it anywhere, keep it reasonably concealed, store everything I want on it, and most of all, be able to connect with anyone anywhere without the transmission being traced. Is that doable?"

"Well, sir, I can put together something for you like those computers that scientists use in the jungle or in the desert when there's no place to plug in or hook up to."

"Yeah," Buck said. "Some of our reporters use those in remote areas. What do they have, built-in satellite dishes?"

"Believe it or not, it *is* something like that. And I can add another feature for you too."

"What's that?"

"Video conferencing."

"You mean I can see the person I'm talking to while I'm talking to him?"

63

"Yes, if he has the same technology on his machine."

"I want all of it, Donny. And I want it fast. And I need you to keep this confidential."

"Mr. Williams, these machines could run you more than twenty thousand dollars apiece."

Lionel's eyes were wide.

Buck whistled through his teeth. "Do it," Buck said.

The short man grabbed Ryan by the collar. "Goin' for another ride," he barked. The driver helped tape Ryan's hands together. On their way to the van, Ryan looked for an escape, but none came. The short man stayed close to him. Ryan knew if he did get free, he would probably endanger Darrion's life. He didn't want to do that.

A few people were on the sidewalk when the van drove by. No one looked at them. The men drove downtown and parked across the street from a bank of pay phones.

"Did you talk with my dad?" Ryan said.

"Shut up and listen," the short man said. "This is how it's goin' down. I'm gonna call your old man again and we're gonna let him know his precious little boy is still alive."

"Fine with me," Ryan said.

"But listen to me," the man said, focusing his steely gaze on Ryan. "You say anything other than 'Hello' or 'Hey, Dad, it's me; give them the money,' and we'll go back to the lake for a little swim."

"A long swim." The driver smirked.

"You got it?"

"I got it."

"And if you try to call out for help to anybody when I roll down the window, I'll hang up, and we forget your old man."

"I understand," Ryan said.

The driver pulled into traffic. He made a U-turn and pulled up to the bank of phones. The short man rolled down his window and dialed the number.

What can I say? Ryan thought. *If I've got only one sentence, or even a few words, what could help Judd and the rest find me?*

———————————

Judd was able to reach Sergeant Fogarty and gave him the location of the pay phone the caller had used. Sergeant Fogarty gave Judd his beeper number and a special code. The officer would dispatch someone to the scene if the man called again.

Judd and Lionel helped Buck box the pages from Bruce's printout. Buck told Judd that Chloe was dropping him off at the Chicago bureau office of *Global Community Weekly*.

As Buck and Chloe made their way out to the Range Rover, Buck lugging the heavy carton, he said to Chloe, "If the guy calls back, give him my private number at the office, and you'd better check with The Drake Hotel and be sure our stuff is still there. We'll want to keep that room until we find a place to live out here."

"I was hoping you'd say that," Chloe said. "Loretta is

devastated. She's going to need a lot of help. I was thinking we could stay with her."

Buck and Chloe talked about Bruce's funeral. Judd
offered the help of the Young Tribulation Force. His cell
phone rang. Lionel answered on the second ring as Judd
raced to a different phone and quickly dialed Sergeant
Fogarty's beeper. If they could keep the man on the phone
long enough, there was a chance they could find Ryan.

"Yeah, I'll get him," Lionel said. "Hang on a minute."

Buck held the phone as long as he dared, then said,
"I'm here. Do you have Ryan with you?"

Buck gave them the thumbs-up signal.

"Before you let me talk with him, I want to
understand your demands," Buck said. "Can any of the
four million be in larger bills, like hundreds?"

Buck pulled the phone away from his ear. Judd could
hear the man cursing through the earpiece.

Ryan heard the man's tirade. "You know I said five
million," he screamed. "Now we're gonna make it six."

The man grabbed Ryan and pulled him to the
window of the van.

"Yeah, I like that attitude a lot better," the man said.
"Six it is. Now would you like to hear the sound of your
kid's voice?"

The man shoved the mouthpiece into Ryan's face.
Ryan froze.

"Talk!" the man yelled.

Ryan opened his mouth, but nothing came out.

"I said talk!" the man said, whacking Ryan in the fore-head with the phone.

Ryan gasped and said as clearly as he could, "Darrion Stahley!"

The short man shoved Ryan to the back of the van and threw the phone out the window. Ryan fell toward the door and struggled to stand. He was close to the door handle when the driver floored the accelerator, and Ryan was thrown hard into the rear seat.

"You've done it now, kid," the short man said. "Those are the last words your dad will ever hear you say."

"What did he say again?" Judd said as they went in the church.

"It happened so fast," Buck said. "I know the first word was *Darien,* but I didn't get the second too well. Sounded like he said *stolley.*"

"What in the world could that be?" Lionel said.

"There's a suburb southwest of Chicago called Darien," Judd said. "Maybe that's where they're holding him."

"Why would they drive all the way downtown to call us?" Lionel said. "And how would they get there so fast?"

"Okay, forget the first word," Judd said. "What's a *stolley?*"

Chaya overheard the conversation and clicked at the church's computer screen. "It sounds more like a name to me," she said, "not a place."

"You think that's the name of the people holding him?" Lionel said.

"I don't know who it is," Chaya said, "but for some reason Ryan chose those words."

Chaya typed in the different possible spellings of the word *stolley*. The Internet search engine provided information about a tennis player, a nineteenth-century geologist, cosmetic surgery centers, and personal pages. On the ninth spelling she slapped the desktop and let out a yell.

"Maxwell Stahley," Chaya said, spelling the name for everyone.

"Who's that?" Lionel said.

"The security magnate," Buck said. "Of course!"

"He's a pretty impressive guy," Chaya said, reading from the screen. "Lives near Chicago. A member of the Global Community special security force. Owns his own international security business. Looks like he's pretty well off."

"How do you know he's the right one?" Lionel said.

Chaya pointed to the screen. "Married seventeen years to Louise Stahley. One child. A girl. Darrion."

"Bingo," Judd said.

"Weird name," Lionel said.

"You think Ryan is being held by an international agent of the Global Community?" Vicki said.

Darrion screamed when the men threw Ryan into the room. Darrion cut the tape with the edge of the pop can. Ryan huddled close to the door and listened as the two men talked.

"The kid said her name," the short man said.

"So what?" the driver said. "If the guy's ready to shell out six million, the kid can say whatever name he wants."

"You know what happens if the boss finds out?" the short man said, an edge in his voice. "You don't know these people like I do. They won't like us sneaking around behind their backs."

"How are they gonna know?" the driver said. "The kid says a name. Maybe his dad didn't hear it right or thinks he said something else."

"But if the boss finds out we're doing freelance on the side when we're supposed to be taking care of the girl, we're in trouble."

"Fine," the driver said. "As soon as it gets dark, we take care of the kid. Then we make one more call to the father. Give him a drop site and see what happens."

"And what if the dad doesn't buy it?" the short man said.

"So we're out the cost of the phone call. But if he does buy it, you and me split six million big ones. The boss doesn't have to know."

Ryan crawled close to Darrion and explained what happened.

"Why did you tell them my name?" Darrion said. "Your friends don't know me from Adam. No offense to your religion."

Ryan smiled. "I couldn't think of anything else. I figured if my friends get in touch with your family, they could work together."

Darrion frowned. "I don't know how they'll get in touch with my mom and dad. Our house is like a fortress, and the number's unlisted."

"I have to get out of here before nightfall," Ryan said. "How far did you get on that window?"

Darrion pulled back the curtain, and a shaft of light hit Ryan in the face. He ducked his head and saw the sun going down over a water tower in the distance.

"I got this one out while you were gone," she said. "It crashed on the fire escape."

Ryan stuck his head through, but the opening was too small for his shoulders.

"I tried that," she said. "Then I yelled, but the alley's deserted. A couple of cars went by, but they couldn't hear me, I guess."

"Good going," Ryan said. "Now if we can get this bigger pane out, I can climb through and go for help."

"We," Darrion said. "You're not leaving me in here alone."

"Okay," Ryan said. "*We* can climb through and get out of here."

Judd and Vicki looked for the access road to the Stahley mansion. They were only a few miles from Northwest Community Hospital. Chaya had called the headquarters of Maxwell Stahley's business, but she was told he had taken a leave of absence from the company.

"I assume that means he's working for the Global Community and I should lay off," Chaya had said. She found an address for the Stahley home, but it took Judd and Vicki a half hour to find the hidden road that led there. Vicki discovered it by poking around behind a riding stable while Judd asked directions at a gas station.

The huge estate was triangular and bordered an exclusive golf course and a forest preserve. Judd parked in a picnic area, and the two hiked into the woods.

Twenty minutes later they came to the twelve-foot iron fence that surrounded the Stahley property. Judd gave a low whistle when he saw the house. The lawn was finely manicured, and several mature trees dotted the backyard. Judd stood on a stump and saw a huge pool with a slide in the patio area.

"See anything?" Vicki said.

"No people," Judd said. "I'm trying to figure out how we can get over this fence. There must be some kind of electronic surveillance system. If this guy is in international security, you'd think—"

Judd stopped and pointed to the sharp spikes at the top of the fence. A tiny sensor emitted a thin strand of red light. Judd scanned the tree line and jogged away, pulling Vicki with him. A hundred yards farther Judd spotted a tall tree whose limbs stretched across the fence.

"If we can climb out onto that branch, we can drop to the ground on the other side," Judd said. "The limb dips. Looks like it's only about a ten- or fifteen-foot drop."

"Looks higher than that to me," Vicki said, "but I'm game."

Vicki was tentative at first. Then she seemed to get the

hang of it. When they were past the sensor, Judd grabbed the branch and swung toward the ground.

"It looks even higher when you get up here," Vicki said.

Judd let go and dropped to the ground, tucking his legs underneath him and rolling into a pile of leaves.

"You okay?" Vicki said.

"Fine," Judd said. "Move out on the limb a little farther. It's closer to the ground. I'll help you."

Vicki inched out onto the limb. The branch bent with her weight.

"Swing your legs down, and I'll see if I can touch your feet," Judd said.

"I don't need help," Vicki said, losing her grip on the limb and grabbing hard. Judd heard a crack behind her and managed to grab Vicki's feet before the branch gave way and Vicki tumbled to the ground.

"I think the branch hit the sensor," Judd said.

"Thanks a lot for the concern," Vicki said.

Judd put his finger to his lips. He expected some type of alarm. He did hear something—a low rumbling of some sort, but he couldn't place it.

The leaves rustled, and Vicki screamed. In the fading light Judd realized the noise was the pounding of paws on the earth. The growling of dogs. And there was no escape.

With the smaller pane out, Ryan and Darrion set to work on the pane in the middle. It was their best chance of escape.

The door opened, and the driver flashed a light around the room. "Where'd you kids go?" the man said.

Darrion stepped out from behind the curtain. "I have to go to the bathroom again!" she said.

"Then come on," the man said. "We have to leave soon."

Ryan's plan, if the men came for him before he and Darrion were through, was to put the tape loosely over his hands and make a run for it as soon as he was in the garage. But he hoped to use the fire escape. That would give Darrion and him more time to put distance between them and the men before they were missed.

———————————

"Don't run," Judd yelled as the dogs neared them. "They'll sense our fear."

"I don't have to run for them to sense my fear," Vicki said.

Judd broke off a stick from the fallen branch and swung it back and forth as the dogs approached. One grabbed the end and hung on as Judd tugged fiercely. The other dogs circled, growling and baring their fangs.

———————————

The window was nearly out. A few more chinks in the putty, and Ryan and Darrion would be free. Ryan heard the men outside the door. Darrion quickly put the tape over his wrists, and the two sat on the floor as if they'd been there all afternoon.

"Time to go," the short man said.

7

VICKI counted five dogs. One would have been enough to paralyze her with fear. Five were terrifying. Ever since she had been a little girl, dogs like these had given her the creeps. Big and black with huge mouths.

One dog lunged at Judd, and he kicked it in the head, only to have another bite at his pant leg. Judd looked like he was losing his balance, so Vicki took off a shoe and threw it as hard as she could. It hit the dog in the neck. The dog let go momentarily and snapped at her.

"I'm gonna try for the fence—maybe they'll follow me," Judd said. "Go to the house and get help."

"You can't!" Vicki said. "They'll tear you to pieces."

"They'll tear us both to pieces if we stay here," Judd said as he took off. "Run!"

Ryan's heart sank. If they only had a few more minutes they'd be free. But the men were at the door, and they meant business.

Ryan wanted to tell Darrion she needed to accept Christ as her Savior before it was too late, but there was no time. He stammered a moment, looked at her, then saw the short man in a mask.

"Wait," Darrion said in a strong voice. "I need to talk with him."

"What's wrong?" he said. "You two lovebirds or something?"

Ryan wanted to tackle the man or hit him with the flashlight.

"I need to ask him a few questions," she said.

"You've had plenty of time to talk," the man said as he grabbed Ryan. "Come on, kid."

"You don't understand," Darrion said. "I need to talk with him about his religion."

Ryan furrowed his brow. *Was she serious or just pretending?*

"Religion?" the man said. "You two are back here talkin' about religion?"

"I have to clear a few things up," Darrion said. "Even condemned criminals get a last meal."

The short man shook his head. "No way," he said.

The phone rang in the other room. The short man stiffened, then turned Ryan loose. "Do your talkin'," he said. "I'll be right back."

Ryan took the tape from his hands, and they stepped behind the curtain.

"Is what you said real or just a ploy?" Ryan said.

"Both," Darrion said. "I thought we could talk while we try to get this window out."

"So what did you want to ask?" Ryan said as they furiously scraped at the putty.

"If this God you talk about can do all those miracles, why can't he get us out of here?" she said angrily.

"He can," Ryan said. "He can do anything he wants. Heal the sick. Raise the dead. Sometimes he lets people go through stuff like this."

"Like being killed for no reason?" she said. "It doesn't make sense. Why would a God who's supposed to be good allow a sweet kid like you . . ." Darrion smashed the can against the window. It gave way a fraction of an inch. "It's not fair!"

Ryan touched her shoulder. "I've been trying to think of a way to explain it since we met," he said. "*I've* been wondering why God would put me here. It makes total sense now."

"What are you talking about?" Darrion said.

"Remember the verse I told you about? The one that says God loved us so much that he sent his only Son into the world?"

"Yeah."

"Well, I think God was preparing you and your family all along. He sent your aunt and uncle. Then me. I think he put me here to tell you the truth."

"But they're gonna kill you!" Darrion said.

Ryan smiled. He had the feeling he'd finally solved the riddle. "I promise you, I'm not going without a fight."

"How can you say that?" Darrion said. "Why aren't you scared?"

"I am scared," Ryan said. "But it's clear to me now. God loves you. He cared enough for you that he put me here. Pretty cool, huh?"

"I still don't understand."

"You will," Ryan said. "There's something you need to do, and I don't want to leave before you do it."

Ryan dropped his can.

"We're not gonna get this window out of here, are we?" Darrion said.

"Not before the guy gets back," Ryan said. "But I don't think God let us come all this way for nothing." Ryan grabbed the flashlight.

"You're not going to hit him with that, are you?"

"I'd like to," Ryan whispered, "but I'm thinking of something else."

Ryan bunched the curtain up at the bottom and placed it against the window. "Hold this," he said. "I'm gonna give it a kick. Hopefully the whole pane will come out. When it does, you go through and get down the fire escape as fast as you can. I'll be right behind you."

Ryan gently pushed the door closed and propped two mattresses behind the doorknob. Then he shone the flashlight toward the window. He ran a few steps and jumped into the air feetfirst.

———

Vicki's heart raced as four of the dogs sprinted toward the fence after Judd. The fifth dog, poised like a loaded gun, stood between her and the house.

Judd was climbing the fence now. When he was a few

feet from the top, the dogs lunged and bit his pant leg, dragging him back to the ground.

Vicki knew she had to get help, but the growling dog before her was inching closer. She looked into its eyes. Hollow.

"Nice doggie," she said nervously.

The dog lunged at her. Vicki jerked backwards. She took off her other shoe and waved it in front of the dog's face. "Come and get it," she said, waving it high over her head.

Vicki threw the shoe as far as she could and yelled, "Fetch!" Without blinking, the dog turned and ran.

Vicki was gone, running with bare feet over the cold ground. She heard Judd struggling and the dogs at the fence barking. She couldn't help looking over her shoulder, and there was the dog, a few yards behind, shaking its head as it tore the shoe to bits.

Vicki hit a sudden slope in the yard, lost her balance, and fell. When she looked up the dog was beside her, growling. He dropped the shoe and inched closer. His teeth were bared.

"No!" Judd yelled from the fence. "Vicki, get up!"

But it was too late. There was nothing Vicki could do but cover her face with her arms and scream.

When Ryan's feet hit the glass, he heard a crunch. The window didn't pop out like he had hoped. He grabbed the curtain and kept his balance. Only half the glass had broken.

"Hey, what's goin' on in there?" the short man said.

Ryan took the flashlight and beat furiously against the

window. Shards flew everywhere as the glass shattered and fell through the fire escape.

The short man was at the door now, but he couldn't get in. "Carl, they're breakin' something in there!" he yelled. "And the door's stuck."

The sharp pieces of glass around the window looked like the jagged mouth of a jack-o'-lantern. Ryan ran the flashlight around the window and tried to get it as smooth as possible so they could get through.

Both men lunged at the door. "Why didn't you bring him out in the first place?" the one called Carl shouted.

Ryan helped Darrion through just as the men broke the door open.

"Hurry!" Darrion said.

"Go!" Ryan said, "I'm right behind you."

Ryan went through the opening headfirst, then suddenly stopped. The man had him by his shoe. Ryan kicked with his other foot, but the man wouldn't let go. Someone grabbed his hands and pulled. Darrion.

"Ow!" the man yelped. "I'm cut!"

Ryan landed on Darrion in a heap. They were down the first flight of stairs before the men discovered they couldn't fit through the window. Then Ryan and Darrion were on the ground and running.

"It's not much of a head start," Ryan panted as he caught up with her, "but at least we're free."

The dog was over Vicki, inches from her face, when it perked up its ears. He straightened, whimpered, and ran toward the house. The other four dogs near Judd did the same. They ran past Vicki in a flash, barking and whimpering.

Judd caught up to her. "You okay?" he said.

"Better than your pants," Vicki said. "Why'd the dogs run off like that?"

Judd pointed toward the house. Vicki saw a man standing by a shrub with his arms folded. He had a goatee and was nicely dressed. As they neared, they saw an electronic monitor in his hand.

He spoke precisely. "This is private property," the man said. "You are fortunate the animals didn't hurt you. They are trained to kill."

"Are you Mr. Stahley?" Vicki said.

The man ignored her question. "You came onto my property for a reason. What is it?"

Vicki saw Judd square his jaw. "We're looking for Ryan," he said. "We want him back."

"Ryan who?" the man said. "I know no Ryan."

"Ryan Daley," Judd said. "We talked with him this afternoon. He gave us your daughter's name."

The man looked startled. "Come with me," he said.

Vicki had never seen a home so spotless and so empty. Mr. Stahley led them through a huge, sparkling kitchen. The living room was decorated totally in white. A slender woman with brown hair looked lost on the huge couch.

"Was it them, Max?" the woman said.

Vicki noticed the woman's eyes were red and puffy.

"No, just a couple of kids," Mr. Stahley said.

Vicki and Judd got right to the point.

"We're here because we believe you know where our friend Ryan is," Judd said. "Tell us where he is and we'll leave, no questions asked."

"But we don't even—," Mrs. Stahley said.

Mr. Stahley gave her a look. "Tell me what your friend said," he said to Judd. "You talked with him by phone?"

"To be honest," Judd said, "I don't know if we can trust you. We know you work for the Global Community."

Mr. Stahley raised a hand. "Let me tell you our circumstances. Our daughter, Darrion, was taken from us this morning. She was at the riding stables where she goes every day. We received a call from her captors that she is well. That is all we know."

"I'm sorry for you," Vicki said.

"Now tell us about your friend," Mr. Stahley said.

Judd told them. When he was finished, Mr. Stahley scratched his chin.

"Is Ryan your brother?" Mrs. Stahley said.

"In a sense," Vicki said. She quickly explained that they had found each other after the disappearances. When she mentioned that a pastor had actually helped unite them, Judd flinched. Vicki noticed a change in the Stahleys as well.

"How much are they asking?" Judd said.

"Darrion's captors do not want money. They have taken her because of my position with the Global Community."

"You mean they're with the militia?" Judd said.

"No. It comes from within the Global Community. Let us say I have been somewhat at odds with the leadership regarding the current engagement."

"I don't understand," Vicki said. "Why would people from the Global Community want to kidnap your daughter?"

Mr. Stahley explained the situation with his brother and sister-in-law. "After I took this position with the Global Community, I began to look into the circumstances more fully. The further I looked, the more I was told I should not look."

"They were being held by the Global Community for being Christians?" Vicki said.

"They were being held by Nicolae Carpathia," Mr. Stahley said, "before the world knew him. My brother and his wife were working with the church in Romania. They were outspoken Christians."

"I still don't understand why Darrion was kidnapped," Vicki said.

"A few days ago I objected to the targets the potentate himself suggested," Mr. Stahley said. "After that they cut me off."

"Targets?" Judd said.

"The bombings here and around the world have been planned," Mr. Stahley said gravely. "The loss of innocent lives disturbs me greatly. I threatened to go to the media. That is when Darrion was taken from us."

"And you think if you keep quiet, she'll be returned," Judd said.

"We have to think that!" Mrs. Stahley said. "We have

no indication of where she is. I have tapped every source I know. Have you any idea where Ryan is?"

"Chicago," Judd said. "The ransom calls came from the North Side."

"Why would Ryan be mixed up in all this?" Vicki said.

"Perhaps your friend somehow got in the way of Darrion's captors."

Vicki felt frustrated. All the talk of the inner workings of the Global Community made her even madder at Nicolae Carpathia. She wanted to find Ryan and bring him home. She wanted everything to be okay again, but it wasn't. And it didn't look like things would ever be okay again as long as Nicolae was in control.

"What do we do now?" Vicki said. "Sit and wait?"

"There is nothing I can do," Mr. Stahley said. "I am under constant observation. No doubt you were detected when you came over the fence."

The phone rang. Mr. Stahley spoke in hushed tones. When he returned he was ashen faced. "Darrion remains unharmed," he said. "Within the hour cities around the world will be annihilated."

"What does *annihilated* mean?" Vicki asked.

Mr. Stahley's voice was grave. "*Annihilated* means just what it sounds like it means—totally destroyed."

"What cities?" Judd said.

"Nicolae Carpathia said that he intends to make North America an object lesson to those who oppose the Global Community. Attacks will hit Montreal, Toronto, Dallas, Mexico City, Washington, D.C., New York, Los Angeles, San Francisco . . ." Mr. Stahley's voice trailed off.

"What?" Mrs. Stahley said.

"And Chicago . . ."

Though she was smaller, Darrion was able to keep up with Ryan well. They came to a cross street. Ryan tried to stop a passing car, but the driver honked his horn and drove past. They both screamed as they ran, but the noise of the nearby L track drowned them out.

Ryan ran to an apartment building. He made it through the outer door, but the inner one was controlled by a buzzer. He gave up and ran back outside. He heard a garage door opening and doors slamming.

"This way!" Darrion said, as she ran for the abandoned building.

Ryan could only make out the word *candy* on the rickety sign in front. Windows were broken from the second floor to the top. The rest of the building was boarded with plywood. Darrion raced ahead of Ryan to the back. Burned-out trash cans lined the wall. The men Ryan had seen earlier were gone.

"Stop here," Ryan said. He peeked around the corner and saw the van. When it passed, they both jumped behind a trash can. The van slowed, then sped up and zoomed to the end of the street. Trash littered the parking lot, and weeds grew through the broken asphalt.

"Not many places to hide," Darrion said, looking at the emptiness behind them. They could see the Chicago skyline to the south. "Who would have thought you could be in a city this big and feel so alone."

"If we can make it to a phone, we'll be in good shape," Ryan said. "A gas station or a restaurant or something."

Gravel spun behind them. Ryan turned as the van raced across the empty lot toward them.

"We have to get inside," Ryan said. "They'll catch us for sure out in the open."

They sprinted to the front and pulled at the boards until one gave way. They climbed through the small opening just as the van rounded the corner. Ryan turned on the flashlight, and the carpet seemed to move. Then he realized it wasn't carpeting. Rats.

"I want to get outta here!" Darrion said.

"Keep moving," Ryan said.

They climbed over the rats and out the door of the musty office. Around the corner was the factory area. A heavy layer of dust covered the machinery. The place smelled like the inside of an old refrigerator. They found a stairwell and ran up a few floors. More offices. A lunchroom. More rats.

"What are we gonna do now?" Darrion whispered.

"We have to hide," Ryan said. "If those guys catch me, I'm finished."

"How about if I let them catch me, and I tell them you ran for help," Darrion said.

"I couldn't ask you to do that," Ryan said. "Besides, they'd probably move you, and there'd be no way to find you."

Ryan chose the fourth floor. They ran to the other end and found a phone on an old desk. Ryan picked it up, but there was no dial tone.

"Look at this," Darrion said. She pointed to a hole in the wall and an empty space inside. "It looks like a safe was in here. If we could get inside and move something in front of the opening, they'd never find us."

They heard the men ripping boards from the side of the building.

"Hurry!" Ryan said.

Darrion swept their tracks from the dust. Then they ran around the fourth floor, into and out of rooms.

When they heard the sound of the men on the stairs, they retreated to their hiding place and pulled the desk tight against the wall. The safe hadn't been huge, but the space was big enough for Ryan and Darrion to sit cross-legged and listen.

"They've definitely been up here," the short man said when the two men walked near them. The man's cell phone rang. The one named Carl answered. "Yes, sir," he said, "everything's fine."

Ryan punched Darrion in the shoulder. "Right," he whispered.

"We'll move her first thing in the morning, boss," Carl said. "What time you want us there? Okay. No problem. We'll call you from there."

"What'd he say?" the short man said.

"He said he'd meet us at sector four tomorrow morning," Carl said.

"Great," the short man said. "Now all we gotta do is find the little vermin."

JUDD and Vicki jumped into Mr. Stahley's silver Mercedes and watched the man maneuver the car swiftly through the security gauntlet. Mrs. Stahley had supplied Vicki with new socks and a pair of shoes.

"I don't care who's watching," the man said, "I'm going to save my daughter."

They sped toward the expressway that led to Chicago. Mr. Stahley zigzagged through slower traffic, rode on the shoulder, and screeched around construction cones.

Judd gave Mr. Stahley the location of the pay phone. Mr. Stahley punched up the cross streets on his in-dash computer, and the screen flashed the correct route.

"I think we have company back here," Vicki said.

Judd turned to see a late-model car following the Mercedes.

"I see them," Mr. Stahley said. "They've been with us since we left the house."

"If they were any closer," Vicki said, "they'd be in front of us."

"Global Community," Mr. Stahley said. "They know I'm out of my safety zone. But if they dispose of me, Darrion might be safe."

"You can't bank on that," Judd said. "We have to find her before the bombing starts."

"Hang on," Mr. Stahley said as he pushed the accelerator to the floor.

The men came close to the desk, then clomped down the hall.

"They were so warm, and now they're getting colder and colder," Darrion said.

"When they move to the next floor," Ryan said, "we have to do something. The way I see it, we can hunker down here and hope they leave, or we can kick our offense into gear."

"I have a feeling you think we should do the latter."

"Exactly," Ryan said. He explained his plan. Darrion was skeptical at first, bringing up objection after objection. Then she said, "If it weren't for you, I'd still be in that dingy apartment. I'll do whatever you say."

They quietly moved the desk and stole into the hallway. The men were above them now. Darrion and Ryan timed their actions to the movements of the men. When they heard noise, they moved. When they didn't, they stopped.

Ryan led the way to the lunch area and put his plan in motion.

Judd watched as the car behind them followed closely. Once, Mr. Stahley cut from the extreme left lane to an exit on the right. The car behind them nearly crashed into a truck. The truck swerved, narrowly missing the car, and careened into a wall. Then the Global Community guards were again behind them.

"How important is it for us to lose these guys?" Judd said.

"If we want to find Darrion and your friend," Mr. Stahley said, "we have to lose them. It's their job to keep us away, but—"

"If that's true," Vicki interrupted, "why don't we let those guys lead us to Darrion and Ryan?"

"What do you mean?" Judd said.

"If they're trying to keep us away, they must know where the kids are being held. If we can somehow lose them and make them think we know where we're going, they'd go right to the hideout, wouldn't they?"

"Brilliant," Mr. Stahley said.

"Yeah," Judd said, "but how are we gonna lose them and follow them at the same time?"

"Brace yourself," Mr. Stahley said as he pulled onto the shoulder and slammed on his brakes. Judd heard the squeal of tires and then a sickening crunch as the car behind them smashed into them.

Mr. Stahley opened the glove box and handed Judd two small items. "Stick this one on their front tire, and put this somewhere under the car, out of sight," he said. "It's magnetized."

Mr. Stahley got out of the car and calmly walked back. Judd slipped his cell phone to Vicki and slithered out of the car. He crawled on the ground, praying he wouldn't be seen.

"Do it now," Ryan whispered.

Darrion was inside the entrance to the fourth-floor lunchroom facing the stairs. "Here goes," she said softly, then with a loud voice shouted, "Hey, Carl, get yourself down here!"

Ryan crouched behind the door to the stairwell and watched as Carl came running. The short man was farther away. When Carl got to the bottom of the stairs, Darrion was in clear view.

"I got you now!" the man said gleefully.

I think not, Ryan thought.

Carl's feet flew out from under him as he hit the slick mixture of leftover candy goo that Ryan had put together. The man slid from the door to Darrion's feet.

"I'll be needing this," she said politely, and before the man could protest, she grabbed his cell phone and ran toward the back of the room.

"Got it!" she yelled triumphantly.

Carl tried to get up, but his hands and feet were so slick he flopped like a walrus. When the short man rushed into the room, Carl called out, but it was too late. The short man went down in a heap and slid into Carl, who was on all fours. When he hit, they both went face first into the slime.

Ryan turned and hit the stairwell two and three steps at

a time. He raced to the front of the building. Darrion had taken the back stairs and was there a few seconds later.

Ryan grabbed the cell phone and punched the familiar numbers as he ran.

"What's happening?" Vicki said as the Mercedes sped away.

"Not to worry," Mr. Stahley said. The car was right behind them again. Mr. Stahley gave a nod, and Judd pushed a button on a small black box. Immediately the car behind them skidded to the right and stopped. Vicki saw the two men exit the car and shake their fists in the air.

"I don't understand," Vicki said.

"Judd placed a transmitter on their car. I'll be able to follow it here on the screen."

"But how are we supposed to follow them if they're on the side of the road?"

"Judd also placed a small explosive device on the front right tire," Mr. Stahley said. "By the time they change the tire and get back on the road, we'll be a safe distance away and can follow them."

Vicki was amazed. "You have those things just lying around?" she said.

"I keep a few odds and ends for emergencies," Mr. Stahley said as he looked in the rearview mirror. It was the first time Vicki had seen him smile.

"They could have killed you," Vicki said.

"I think I surprised them. I walked to the back of their car to give Judd enough time. It was a calculated risk, but it worked."

Judd's cell phone rang. Vicki answered, and it was Lionel.

"You have to tell me what's going on," Lionel said.

The home phone was busy. Ryan called the church but got the answering machine. Mr. Williams's voice was on it. He didn't listen to the message.

Ryan and Darrion ran through the garbage-strewn lot behind the factory and up over a mound of dirt. The elevated train tracks snaked through the neighborhood. Ryan could make out a stop about three blocks away. If nothing else, they could get lost in the crowd. As they ran, Ryan dialed Judd's cell phone number. Busy.

Great, he thought, *I finally get to a phone and I can't talk to anybody!* He punched the numbers for Bruce's house, but before he could push the Send button, the cell phone rang.

Ryan stopped. Darrion looked over her shoulder. "Answer it," she said.

"Hello?"

"Who is this?" a man said.

"I've got the same question," Ryan said. "Who are you?"

"Where's Carl?"

"That's a lot of questions. How about an answer from you?" Ryan said.

"Put Carl on the line now!" the man said.

"Well, he's in kind of a sticky situation. I don't think he'd want me to use up his cell minutes. Better go."

Ryan hung up and immediately dialed Judd's number again. Still busy.

"This way," Darrion yelled, and she led Ryan underneath the L tracks. A train approached above them with a deafening clatter. In the dimming light, sparks flew from the rail overhead. Abandoned cars and shopping carts littered their path. They hit a cross street. A police car rounded the corner, its lights flashing. Darrion and Ryan waved their arms wildly, but the car sped on, ignoring their cries for help.

"Dial 9-1-1!" Darrion shouted.

"Duh," Ryan said. "Why didn't *I* think of that?"

The line rang and rang. Then Ryan heard a recording.

"Due to the heavy number of calls—," the voice said.

Ryan punched the phone off and tried Judd's phone again. Still busy.

They were close now. People stood in line up ahead. The two sprinted into the street and headed for the entrance to the L stop. From their left the white van shot in front of them. The short man jumped out.

"Thought you could get away, huh?" the man said.

"Lionel's going crazy at home," Vicki said.

"I hope we have something good to report next time we talk," Judd said. "Let me have the phone."

The short man grabbed Darrion. He was still covered with goo. She bit the man's arm and kicked his legs. Carl jumped out of the van and ran to help. But Ryan was there.

"Hey, Candyman," Ryan yelled. "There's some guy on

the phone for you. Wants to know where Darrion is. Wanna talk to him?"

Ryan threw the phone in the air, and the short man watched as it smacked against the underside of the train tracks. In that split second Darrion kicked him hard and slipped free. The short man doubled over in pain. Carl tried to grab her, but she darted behind the van and into the street. A car screeched to a halt. Someone screamed.

Ryan grabbed the phone, dodged both men, and rushed around the van. A man was standing in the middle of the street with his car door open.

"She ran right out in front of me!" the man said.

Ryan prepared for the worst. He looked at the pavement in front of the car. No body.

"Where is she?" Carl yelled.

The man in the car held his hand over his chest like he was in pain. "She ran right out," he said again. Then Ryan saw Darrion's boots as she bolted up the stairs. The cashier was yelling at her. The next second the cashier yelled at Ryan as he vaulted over the turnstile.

"Call the police!" Ryan shouted to the lady behind the glass.

Judd's cell phone rang.

"Judd," a familiar voice said, "it's Ryan."

Judd nearly broke down from relief. "Ryan!" he shouted.

"Look, I can't explain right now, but I need help."

"Tell me where you are," Judd said.

The train pulled into the station as Ryan and Darrion
rushed onto the platform. The men were coming up the
steps. The train doors opened and people streamed out.
As Ryan and Darrion ran for the front car, Ryan heard a
droning sound above him. He glanced up in time to see
a plane streak by. It looked like the same type of plane he
had seen earlier in the day in Mt. Prospect.

"We're at the L," Ryan said to Judd. "I don't know
which stop. The train just got here."

"Is Darrion with you?" Judd said.

"You figured it out?" Ryan said. "She's right here.
We just made it onto the L, but the guys are getting
close."

"Ryan, we're in Chicago. Tell us where to go. Which
L line are you on?"

"I don't know," Ryan said.

"Ask somebody!" Judd screamed.

Ryan and Darrion hunkered down behind a seat and
watched the men push their way onto the platform. The
cascade of people had slowed them. Ryan looked up to
see the train doors closing.

The conductor spoke over the scratchy speakers. "This
is Ravenswood, the Brown Line. Next stop, Diversey. Next
stop, Diversey. Stand clear of the doors."

When Ryan glanced back, he couldn't see the men.

"Did they get on?" Darrion said.

Ryan shrugged and told Judd their next stop as the
train pulled out. A few moments later someone in the
front screamed, "Look out!"

A plane swept low above the buildings, and Ryan saw the explosion. The train rocked, and the cell phone went dead. In the mayhem Ryan turned and saw the two men looking through the window of the next car. Ryan looked to the front and saw a fireball in front of the train. The tracks had been blown to bits, and they were heading right for the chasm.

Ryan and Darrion grabbed a metal pole and braced themselves. The train stopped before the gaping hole. Everyone breathed a sigh of relief. Some clapped.

"That was close," Darrion said.

"Yeah, but it looks like we have company," Ryan said, pointing toward the door.

People around them were crying. Some were banging on the doors to get outside.

"I need to tell you something," Darrion said. "I've made my decision."

Ryan sat up straight. "What do you mean?"

"You know," she said, "about God and everything. What you said makes a lot of sense. I think he did send you to tell me the truth. I'm ready."

Ryan's eyes widened and he smiled.

Before he could say another word, another explosion pummeled the tracks. It felt like an earthquake. The train tipped and Ryan saw the ground. If the train fell that way, the impact would surely kill them. But the train righted itself and tipped the other way, crashing onto the tracks. Darrion and Ryan still clung to the metal pole in midair as glass smashed and people screamed.

Judd told Mr. Stahley to find Diversey. They kept the
L tracks in sight as they flew through the city.

"This is what I was afraid of," Mr. Stahley said.
"They've triggered the second attack on Chicago just as
the potentate planned."

Judd noticed the attack seemed concentrated to his
left toward the lakeshore. It looked like Michigan Avenue,
known as the Magnificent Mile, was under heavy bombing.

Mr. Stahley stopped only at intersections where emergency vehicles were passing. Otherwise he honked his
horn and ran through stop signs and red lights. A bicycle
messenger darted out in front of the car, and Mr. Stahley
swerved to avoid a head-on collision.

"The world's at war and you still have to dodge those
guys," Mr. Stahley said.

Cars were abandoned in the middle of the road while
people sought some kind of shelter. But where the bombs
landed, there was no shelter. Smoke and flames rose into
the air as they drove.

They passed an L stop, and Vicki screamed. "A white
van! We must be close."

Mr. Stahley floored the accelerator and sped down
a street parallel to the tracks. He jumped the curb and
barreled through an alley, winding through a maze of
trash cans and parked cars.

Mr. Stahley slammed on his brakes and cursed. Judd
looked up and saw a horrifying sight. Before them was the
L track with a huge hole in one section. At the edge of the

flames, a train sat on its side, as if some giant had pushed it over. People were scrambling to get out of windows.

"Do you think that's the one?" Vicki said.

"It has to be," Judd said.

———————————————

Darrion pulled herself up on the pole and grabbed Ryan's hand. "All that work on the uneven parallel bars finally paid off," Darrion said. "Now what do we do?"

Ryan reached for the door, but he was short a few inches.

"Here, son," a man below him said. "Use this."

The man handed him an umbrella. Ryan stuck it into the soft rubber between the doors and jabbed at it. Nothing happened. Darrion pointed to an emergency button beside the door. When he hit it with the umbrella, the door popped open.

The two stood on top of the train and tried to get their balance. They could see into apartment buildings and the burning city around them. People were trying to crawl on top of the train. Some made it and spilled onto the tracks. Smoke and debris spread through the area, making it difficult to see.

"Please remain inside the train car," the conductor said through the scratchy speakers. "Do not walk on the tracks. The rail is electrified. You are in danger."

"As soon as we get on the ground and away from those goons," Ryan said, "I want to pray with you."

"Sounds like a plan," Darrion said.

When they came to the end of the first car, Darrion

and Ryan jumped and landed safely on top of the second car. When they reached the caboose, Ryan took Darrion's hand and dropped her gently to the tracks.

"Wait for me," Ryan called down to her. "I don't want you to get close to the third rail."

Another bomb fell close to the tracks, and Ryan braced himself. The tracks swayed but didn't buckle. He regained his balance and was surprised to see Darrion running away through a cloud of smoke.

Ryan jumped to the tracks. Darrion was headed back to the station. He was about to scream at her to stop when two men passed him. Carl and the short man.

We're too close to let them catch us now, he thought. As Ryan took off, he noticed something strange underneath the tracks. A silver car drove wildly, honking its horn and racing toward the station.

"Judd!" Ryan said.

VICKI felt vibration in the backseat as the Mercedes clattered underneath the tracks. The muffler had come loose and was banging the ground.

"There she is!" Judd shouted, pointing overhead. "She's going back the other way."

Mr. Stahley whipped the steering wheel to the left and slammed on his brakes. The car spun perfectly, kicking dust into the air, then was pointed in the right direction.

Something on the instrument panel of the car beeped, but neither Mr. Stahley nor Judd paid it any attention. Vicki craned her neck and saw Darrion sprinting down the tracks. She was small but very fast.

The Mercedes was a block away from the train stop when Vicki saw a flash of headlights to her left. She braced herself for impact and screamed a warning as a car blindsided them, sending the Mercedes into a chain-link fence.

Vicki was stunned. Judd and Mr. Stahley struggled to release their seat belts.

"Everybody okay?" Mr. Stahley said.

Vicki and Judd nodded. The driver's side door was smashed, so the three climbed out Judd's side. When they were finally out, a voice behind them said, "Hold it right there."

Vicki glanced at the other car and recognized it from the expressway.

So that's why the light was beeping, Vicki thought.

Ryan ran behind the men a few paces. He was careful to stay in the middle of the track and keep his balance. Darrion was almost to the platform now.

He heard a crash of metal underneath the tracks. The silver car was against a fence. One of the men in the other car jumped out. He had a gun.

Ryan looked up and saw Darrion struggling to climb onto the wooden platform. The men following Ryan were closing in when someone in a trench coat reached out and helped her up.

"All right!" Ryan shouted.

But the man didn't let go. He held Darrion by her elbow and roughly dragged her to the stairs. The men in front of him stopped and turned.

"No!" Ryan screamed.

"Get him," Carl said.

Vicki saw the gun and put up her hands. The man motioned for the three of them to move beside a concrete slab underneath the tracks.

"Where's your boss?" Mr. Stahley said.

"That's none of your concern," the man said. He had short hair and wore a long, black coat. "You should have stayed home."

"And leave my daughter to the likes of you—"

"Your daughter would have been returned," the man said.

"And how long would it have taken to send a guided missile into my living room?"

The man with the gun smiled and put his finger to his lips. "Time for talking's over," he said. "I have my orders."

"Your orders didn't say anything about them," Mr. Stahley said, nodding toward Judd and Vicki. "They're innocent."

The man looked at the two teenagers. "Sorry," he said. "They know too much."

Ryan was better at running the tracks than the men. The short man was red in the face and puffing behind Carl. A hundred yards ahead the train lay on its side, and beyond that the burning tracks. Ryan knew he had to act fast. As he went past the silver car below and saw the man with the gun, he caught sight of a metal ladder built onto the track. He would have to cross the electrified rail to get to it, but if he could reach it before his captors, he could make it to the ground.

105

It killed him not to go after Darrion. But what good would he be if he were caught? He looked back to the platform once, but Darrion was gone. Then he spotted the man with the trench coat below the tracks. He still had Darrion by the arm.

Judd saw a man holding a young girl by the arm.

"Darrion!" Mr. Stahley cried.

The man in the trench coat threw the girl into the other car. He looked at Mr. Stahley. "Take care of him," the man snapped.

"Yes, sir," the man in the black coat said.

The car sped away. Judd held Mr. Stahley's arm. They had only one chance now.

Ryan met a group slowly making its way from the train. He dodged them, then quickly jumped the third rail and grabbed the rungs of the ladder. A woman in the group screamed. The short man had a gun. He leveled it at Ryan.

Suddenly, a huge explosion sent the entire group to the tracks. Ryan held on to the ladder with all his might. When the vibrations stopped, Ryan saw that the two men had fallen on the electrified third rail.

Judd fell to the ground at the explosion. Mr. Stahley rushed the man with the gun. Before he could reach him, the man had regained his balance and pulled himself up by the concrete support.

Judd noticed movement overhead. Someone was climbing down the side of the tracks.

Ryan!

Judd looked away and coughed. He caught Vicki's eye.

"We don't really know what this is about," Judd said, walking a few paces.

"Stay where you are," the man with the gun said, turning slightly as Ryan climbed down the ladder behind him.

"It's not fair," Vicki said, putting a hand over her eyes. "We're just kids. We didn't know!" She wept bitterly. Only Judd knew it was an act.

Ryan slowed until the man with the gun moved slightly. Vicki was crying. That would cover the noise of his descent.

Ryan stepped onto a ledge about ten feet above the ground. He knew he wasn't big enough to wrestle the gun from the man, but if he jumped him, Ryan guessed the surprise and the weight of his fall would give Judd, Vicki, and the other man the chance they needed.

Ryan's feet landed squarely on the man's shoulders, and they both tumbled to the ground. Judd put his foot on the man's wrist, and the gun fired. Mr. Stahley wrestled the gun from him.

"Ryan Daley, meet Maxwell Stahley," Judd said as they subdued the gunman.

107

"Darrion's dad?" Ryan said.

"I am," Mr. Stahley said. He held the gun on the man while Judd looked for something to bind him.

"Sure is good to see you," Vicki said. "Lionel wouldn't let us give up."

"Can't wait to see him," Ryan said. "Bruce too."

Judd and Mr. Stahley tied the man with some rope Judd found in the Mercedes. They opened the damaged trunk, shoved the man in, and shut the lid.

The car was sluggish when they pulled away. A huge pool of antifreeze was on the ground. As they drove, Ryan quickly explained what he had heard the two men say about moving Darrion. "They said something about taking her to sector four, whatever that means," he said.

"Sector four is the northern quadrant of Chicago," Mr. Stahley said. "The Global Community has different security offices in each quadrant."

"So you know where the place is?" Ryan said.

"It could be any one of a dozen I can think of," Mr. Stahley said calmly.

A cell phone rang. It took Ryan a few seconds to realize it was in his back pocket. "This could be the boss guy," Ryan said.

"Don't answer it," Mr. Stahley said.

"But how are we going to know how to find Darrion?" Ryan said.

Mr. Stahley pointed to the screen in the dashboard.

"The tracking device!" Vicki said.

"Cool," Ryan said as he watched Mr. Stahley weave in

and out of traffic. Cars coming into the city were at a standstill. Emergency vehicles tried to get near the injured.

"We have to find her," Ryan said. "We talked a lot about God, and she said she was ready."

Mr. Stahley was quiet as Judd and Vicki asked Ryan questions about what he and Darrion had discussed. When they were on the expressway, Mr. Stahley turned on the radio.

"It's not clear whether this attack on Chicago was nuclear," the reporter said.

"If it had been nuclear," Mr. Stahley said, "the radiation would've gotten us by now."

". . . and in just a moment we understand we will go live to the potentate," the reporter continued. "Recapping our top story, a massive attack on Chicago has leveled much of Michigan Avenue. Thousands are feared dead. . . ."

Ryan gave a low whistle. "That could have been us," he said.

"Ladies and gentlemen," the reporter said, "from an unknown location, we bring you live, Global Community Potentate Nicolae Carpathia."

There was a slight pause.

"He's probably in a plane somewhere," Mr. Stahley said. "He'll use his most emotional voice."

"Brothers and sisters of the Global Community," Carpathia said. "I am speaking to you with the greatest heaviness of heart I have ever known. I am a man of peace who has been forced to retaliate with arms against international terrorists. You may rest assured that I grieve with you over the loss of loved ones, of friends, of acquaintances. The horrible toll of civilian lives should haunt these enemies of peace for the rest of their days.

"As you know, most of the ten world regions that comprise the Global Community destroyed 90 percent of their weapon hardware. We have spent nearly the last two years breaking down, packaging, shipping, receiving, and reassembling this hardware in New Babylon. My humble prayer was that we would never have had to use it.

"However, wise counselors persuaded me to stockpile these weapons in strategic locations around the globe. I confess I did this against my will. Now it appears that decision was a good one.

"In my wildest dreams, I never would have imagined that I would have to turn this power against enemies on a broad scale."

Carpathia talked about two members of his inner circle who had conspired against him, and another who had carelessly allowed militia forces in his region to do the same. "The forces were led by the now late president of the United States of North America, Gerald Fitzhugh," Carpathia said.

"Did he say the 'late' Gerald Fitzhugh?" Vicki said.

"They wouldn't allow that man to live any more than they want to let me live," Mr. Stahley said.

"I thought you said you were just raising concerns about the air strikes," Judd said. "Couldn't you go back and say you'd made a mistake?"

"I could try," Mr. Stahley said, "but I don't think it would do any good. Now that the attack has been successful, my fate is sealed. There is no reason for them to allow me to live. I only hope I can get my wife and daughter to safety before they accomplish their goal."

Carpathia was still going. "While I should never have to defend my reputation as an antiwar activist, I am pleased to inform you that we have retaliated severely and with dispatch. Anywhere that Global Community weaponry was used, it was aimed specifically at rebel military locations. I assure you that all casualties were the work of the rebellion."

"Is that true?" Ryan said. "Those were militia planes today?"

"Of course not," Mr. Stahley said, "but everyone will buy it because they want to believe in Carpathia."

"There are no more plans for counterattacks by Global Community forces," Carpathia continued. "We will respond only as necessary and pray that our enemies understand that they have no future. They cannot succeed. They will be destroyed.

"I know that in a time of global war such as this, most of us live in fear and grief. I can assure you that I am with you in your grief but that my fear has been overcome by confidence that the majority of the global community is together, heart and soul, against the enemies of peace.

"As soon as I am convinced of security and safety, I will address you via satellite television and the Internet. I will communicate frequently so you know exactly what is going on and will see that we are making enormous strides toward rebuilding our world. You may rest assured that as we reconstruct and reorganize, we will enjoy the greatest prosperity and the most wonderful home this earth can afford. May we all work together for the common goal."

Judd thought of Rabbi Ben-Judah, his wife and children. They might be on their way to America at that very moment. Their situation paralleled the Stahleys, but for different reasons. The Stahleys were a risk to Nicolae for political and security reasons. The Ben-Judahs were at risk because of their faith.

Judd was exhausted. He helped Mr. Stahley follow the transmitter until they drove up beside what looked like a ritzy office complex. The building was made of granite. The top of the building was smaller than the base, and the polished sides sloped down.

"There it is!" Vicki said as they rounded the corner. A car with a smashed front fender was parked askew at the back entrance to the building.

"What's the plan?" Judd said.

"I'll get into the building alone with my security card," Mr. Stahley said.

"No way," Ryan said. "I'm going too."

"We'll need someone who can drive to keep the car running," Mr. Stahley said. "Judd, that means you. We also need someone at the front in case Darrion gets free."

"I can do that," Vicki said.

"And in case something happens to me, Ryan, you stand inside the back door. I'll call if I need help. It's the best plan."

"It could be a trap," Ryan said. "If that guy can't reach his friend in the trunk, they'll suspect you're coming, right?"

"I'll take that chance," Mr. Stahley said. "My one goal is to get Darrion out of there alive. Outside of that, I don't care."

Mr. Stahley took the gun he had taken from the man in the trunk. Vicki ran to the front of the building. Judd stayed behind the wheel.

"Stay here and listen," Mr. Stahley said to Ryan. "And I need something else. It's very important."

"Whatever you say," Ryan said as they entered the building.

"Pray," Mr. Stahley said.

Vicki stole to the front of the building and tried to look in the windows. The glass was so clean she could see her reflection in the dim moonlight. In the distance she could see the city of Chicago in flames.

She moved away from the building a few paces and noticed a light on the fifth floor. It was the only light on in the building.

Judd fidgeted and turned on the radio. He heard more news of global devastation. World War III was raging. He hadn't heard the man in the trunk for a while. The man had thumped and kicked throughout the ride. Now he wondered if the guy had been overcome by fumes.

He took the key from the ignition and went to the back of the car. He knocked on the trunk. "You okay in there?" Judd said.

No answer.

Judd put the key in and turned it till it clicked. Suddenly the trunk burst open, and the man who had been bound was on Judd. Judd struggled, but the man was bigger and stronger.

"Where's Stahley?" the man yelled as he held Judd down.

"Ryan, help!" Judd yelled. The man was after the car key. Judd kept struggling, but the man had Judd's hand and was prying it open.

A shot rang out inside the building, and the man leaped to his feet. Then another shot, and another. Judd jumped in the car and locked the doors. The man ran toward the building. Judd honked the horn, hoping Ryan would lock the back door.

Vicki backed up on the lawn to get a better look at the building. Suddenly the curtain pulled back. It was Darrion. Mr. Stahley stood behind her. He raised his gun and shot at the glass. The window didn't break. He shot again and again. Then he threw himself against the window. It cracked slightly but didn't give way.

Then she heard a horn honk. She ran to the back and

was nearly knocked over by the man in the black coat, who sprinted toward the roadway. The last time she saw him, he was flagging down a car on the access road to the building.

As soon as Ryan heard the gunfire, he bolted up the stairs. The door closed behind him. Ryan stopped at each landing to listen. When he got to the fifth floor he heard a voice. He gingerly opened the stairwell door and stepped inside the hallway.

Ryan stayed a safe distance away and kept quiet. The man in the trench coat was down the hall talking to someone through a closed door.

"It's no use," the man said. "The glass is unbreakable. I have you both."

"You've failed," Mr. Stahley said from inside the room. His voice was muffled, but Ryan could make out his words.

"And how have I failed?" the man said.

"My laptop," Mr. Stahley said. "If I don't disable it in the next five minutes, an E-mail is sent to every news organization in North America. I'm sure the information is something Mr. Carpathia would not want disseminated."

"Where is the computer?" the man said flatly.

"Release my daughter and I'll take you to it," Mr. Stahley said.

Ryan heard a huge crash of glass downstairs. The man quickly turned the key to unlock the room. Now there were footsteps on the stairs behind him. He stepped inside a doorway and watched Judd bolt through the stairwell door, with Vicki right behind. The man in the trench coat turned and fired. Judd hit the floor and rolled toward Ryan. Vicki stopped just inside the stairwell.

The door to the room flew open, and Mr. Stahley faced his enemy. The men were only two feet apart when they both fired and fell to the ground. Judd, Vicki, and Ryan ran to Mr. Stahley's side.

"Take the gun out of his hand," Mr. Stahley gasped.

Ryan pulled the gun from the other man's hand, but he could tell there was no reason to fear. The other man was dead.

Darrion knelt over her father. "Dad, are you gonna be okay?"

"I don't know, honey. I'm just glad you're safe."

There was blood on Mr. Stahley's shirt. "We need to get you to the hospital," Darrion said.

"Wait," Mr. Stahley said, grabbing his daughter's arm. "Ryan told us what you talked about. He said you've made a decision. About God."

"Yeah," Darrion said. "I'm sorry, Daddy, but I think Aunt Linda and Uncle Ken were right. I think—"

Mr. Stahley interrupted her. "I believe they were, too, honey. I was blind to the truth."

Darrion looked at Ryan. "How do we do it?" she said. "What do we say?"

Ryan took a breath.

"The Bible says if you confess with your mouth that

Jesus is Lord and believe in your heart that God raised him from the dead, you will be saved. Just pray something like this. God, I know I've sinned. I'm sorry."

As Ryan prayed, Darrion prayed out loud. Ryan watched Mr. Stahley's lips move as well.

"Right now I confess I believe you died for me on the cross. I accept your forgiveness for my sin and I put all my hope and trust in you. Come into my heart right now, in Jesus' name. Amen."

Vicki and Judd both said, "Amen."

Darrion opened her eyes and smiled at Ryan. Mr. Stahley was silent.

"Daddy?" Darrion cried. "Daddy!"

RYAN knew they had to leave Mr. Stahley and get to safety. When Judd crashed the car through the back door, an alarm would go off somewhere. If they hung around, no telling who might show up. Plus, knowing Mr. Stahley was dead might satisfy others in the Global Community who wanted the rest of the family dead.

Darrion was overcome with grief. Ryan held her arm as she walked down the stairs.

"What about the laptop?" Ryan said to Judd, explaining what Mr. Stahley had said.

"It had to be a ruse," Judd said. "Mr. Stahley didn't have a laptop with him."

"This car won't make it much farther," Vicki said when they made it to the Mercedes.

"We only need to get to the forest preserve," Judd said. "We'll pick up my car and—"

"My mother!" Darrion cried as they pulled out. "We have to get my mother. They'll come for her."

Vicki dialed the number Darrion gave. Twenty minutes later they met Mrs. Stahley at the stable where Darrion had been abducted. The two embraced and wept bitterly. Judd and Ryan drove to the forest preserve. They scoured the car to remove any clues of their identity. Judd drove them all to Mt. Prospect.

It was dark when they pulled into Judd's driveway. Lionel rushed out to greet Ryan. The kids helped Mrs. Stahley and Darrion inside. When Darrion was able to speak, she talked about the decision she and her father had made.

"You should have seen his face, Mom," Darrion said. "He seemed at peace. All those things we said, the way we ridiculed Aunt Linda and Uncle Ken for what they believed. They were right. We missed the truth."

"I want to thank you for saving my daughter's life," Mrs. Stahley said to Ryan. "I don't know what to say."

Darrion turned to Ryan. "Where is he now?" she said. "Does my dad's soul go to heaven, or does that happen some other time?"

"I asked Bruce that same question," Ryan said. "The Bible is clear. When a Christian dies, he or she goes to be with God. That means there's a big reunion going on right now with your father and your other family members who were Christians."

"That's comforting," Darrion said. Then she turned to her mother. "Mom, are you ready to listen?"

"Not just yet," Mrs. Stahley said.

"He would want you to," Darrion said.

Mrs. Stahley wiped her eyes and turned to Ryan. "Then tell me what you told my daughter and my husband." she said.

Ryan opened a Bible and let Mrs. Stahley read the verses he had quoted to Darrion earlier. Mrs. Stahley wept more when Ryan explained the depth of God's love. "Even though we're sinful," Ryan said, "Christ died so that we might live with him."

Mrs. Stahley asked questions and stared at the Bible. Finally she took Darrion's hand. "I knew in my heart there was something to what Ken and Linda were saying," she said. "But I didn't want to believe it. Now I know it's true. Whatever time I have left on this earth, I want God to have control. I want him to use me in some way."

Judd and Vicki prayed with Darrion and Mrs. Stahley, then took them downstairs to Vicki's old room. They would spend the night at Judd's, then move to a safer location.

Judd walked to Ryan's room and asked if they could talk about something important.

"Sure," Ryan said. "Hey, I told you I'd get to see Bruce. Didn't think I could even get in, but I did."

"I'm glad you did," Judd said. "It must have been something, getting through all those people at the hospital without being seen."

"Wasn't that hard," Ryan said humbly. "What did you want to tell me?"

Judd wished he didn't have to tell Ryan the bad news, but he knew he couldn't keep it from him any longer. If they did survive the next few years before the return of Christ, there would be more bad news.

"Ryan," Judd said, "you took a bunch of chances today, and it seems God used you. Part of me wants to scold you for taking off and not telling us. But I have to say I'm really proud of the way you trusted God."

"I'd be lying if I said I wasn't scared," Ryan said. "Especially when those guys kept talking about dropping me in the water."

"You didn't let your fears keep you from doing what was right. You put your life on the line for somebody else. I know that kind of sacrifice pleases God."

"Yeah, Bruce always said God can do big things through you when you feel the weakest. That way he gets the glory."

Judd thought hard. *How can you tell someone their best friend is gone?*

"So, when can I call Bruce?" Ryan said. "You guys didn't tell him anything about me being gone, did you? I wouldn't want him to have a relapse or whatever you call it."

Judd bit his lip. "Ryan, God has one more thing he wants you to trust him with."

"Hey, you don't have to be dramatic," Ryan said. "Just tell me."

"Do you remember this morning when you left the hospital? You heard all the explosions, right?"

"You bet. Smoke was everywhere. I didn't think I'd make it out alive."

"The target was the Nike base. It was a militia outpost. A lot of people were killed in there—"

"Is it Mark?" Ryan said gravely. "Was he at that Nike base thing?"

"He was there," Judd said, "but they sent him out before it was bombed. He's okay, but still a little shaky."

"Then what's the deal? Tell me. I can take it."

"Ryan, one of the first bombs fell on the hospital. The only survivors of the blast were outside when the bombs hit."

Ryan's eyes looked vacant. "It's about Bruce, isn't it?" he said.

"Yeah."

Ryan shook Judd's arm loose and stood. "Are you sure? I mean, couldn't he be under the rubble some-where? I've heard of people in buildings like that who live for a week."

"Ryan—"

"Come on," Ryan said as he pulled Judd's arm, "we have to go back and make sure."

Judd stood and grabbed Ryan's shoulders. He looked Ryan square in the face, knowing what he was about to say would crush the boy. "We're not going back," Judd said. "There's no point. Bruce is dead."

Ryan narrowed his eyes. "How do you know if you don't even try!" he said through clenched teeth. "How can you just give up on him like that, after all he's done for you?"

"I saw him," Judd said. He was emotional but controlled. "I pulled the sheet back from his face."

123

Ryan turned away and looked out the window. He ran for the bedroom door, but Judd grabbed him.

"I don't want to hurt you," Judd said tenderly. "I'd do anything if I could bring him back, but I can't. It tore my heart out to see him like that, and to have to tell you is just as hard. But we have to face the truth."

Ryan fell onto the bed and put his arm over his face.

"It's gonna be hard," Judd said, "but we'll get through this together."

"Leave me alone," Ryan said.

"Come into the other room with us," Judd said.

"I want to be alone," Ryan repeated. He didn't seem angry. "It's okay. I just want to think a little."

A thousand thoughts flashed through Ryan's head. In the terror and excitement of the day, with his goal of staying alive and telling Darrion about the love of God, he hadn't thought much about Bruce possibly being hurt. Now Bruce was dead.

Dead. *What does it mean?*

Ryan had been able to talk with Bruce like with no one else. He hadn't even talked with his mom or dad like that. Bruce listened. He cared. When Lionel got on his nerves or Judd bossed him around, Ryan could go to Bruce. Even when Bruce was on a trip, he took time to e-mail and always brought back some kind of souvenir.

Then Ryan thought of Israel, and the tears came. Bruce had promised to take him. Ryan had tried to make Bruce feel bad about passing him by, and now he felt empty. He'd heard Judd and Bruce talk about the things they'd seen on their trips. He'd looked the different sites up on the Internet and had even done reports for religion class. Now he'd never get to go.

What about the Bible room? the church?

There were thousands of people around the world who depended on Bruce and his teaching. Why would God take a man so totally committed, so sold out to the cause of Christ? Who could God provide to take his place?

Ryan brought back the last moments he had spent with Bruce in the hospital. He had opened the card that looked like heaven and held it in front of Bruce's closed eyes. And then a wonderful thing had happened. Bruce had raised his hand and placed it on Ryan's shoulder. A tear ran down Bruce's cheek as they said good-bye. *Somehow, Bruce must have known,* Ryan thought.

Through the sadness and the feeling of loss, Ryan thought of something that made him smile. Bruce taught him that no matter how bad things seem, if God was in control, there was always something good to think about. The thought came when Ryan remembered the pictures in his Bible room. Bruce had given Ryan a treasured photo of his family. Ryan closed his eyes and saw it. Bruce and his wife. His two older children beside him and the little baby on his wife's lap. Ryan knew Bruce didn't have to grieve for his family any longer. Bruce was with his wife. He could see his children and talk with them.

Ryan had brought up the subject of heaven numerous times in their studies. He knew heaven was a real place. He knew people would recognize each other there. He knew he would have a different type of body, one that wouldn't get sick or die. People who were blind or couldn't walk wouldn't have those problems anymore. He tried to picture the moment when Bruce saw his family again.

Then a thought overwhelmed Ryan. He sat up on the bed. Bruce was now in the presence of the person he loved most and who loved him. Jesus. For some reason God had allowed Bruce to die, and even though Ryan couldn't understand it, the thought of Bruce face-to-face with Jesus made the tears pour. But they weren't tears of grief.

"God," Ryan prayed, "I do trust you. I believe you can help me get through this. Thanks for bringing me home. Thanks for answering my prayers about Darrion. Thanks for my friends. Help me get over Bruce's death. And tell him I said I'll miss him. Amen."

Before Ryan stood, he heard a scratching at the door. When he opened it, Phoenix bounded in and bowled him over, licking his face and smothering him with affection.

Judd wanted to check on Ryan, but Vicki shook her head. "He needs the time," she said. "You did a good job in there."

"How do you know I did a good job?" Judd said.

Vicki squirmed. "I kind of listened at the door."

Judd took Vicki in the kitchen to talk alone. "We can't keep Darrion and Mrs. Stahley here," he said. "In fact, I don't think any of us can stay. The Global Community guys have our number. They could follow the trail right here."

"We could take them to Bruce's house," Vicki said. "There's plenty of room with Bruce gone. . . ." Vicki's voice trailed. She looked up with teary eyes. "What are we going to do, Judd? Bruce was like a parent to all of us."

"I've been thinking a lot about that," Judd said. "The Young Tribulation Force is going to grow. Our money's gone. We can't stay here and don't have the time to sell the place. And we've got company coming." Judd explained that the Ben-Judah family was coming to live with them.

"I wish we could solve all this like they do on TV," Vicki said. "Just hire a nanny or something. Everything works out in thirty minutes."

Judd lifted her chin with his hand. "Can I tell you something?" he said. "The way you acted today," Judd said, "the way you faced danger and didn't give up. I really admire how strong you are. How resourceful you've become."

"Thank you," Vicki said, blushing. "I've always thought we made a pretty good team."

The doorbell rang. Judd checked before he opened the door and was surprised to see Chaya.

"Thank God you're all right," Chaya said. Darrion and Mrs. Stahley came back upstairs. Chaya explained how she had been able to help decipher Ryan's clue on the phone.

Mrs. Stahley raised a hand. "My daughter and I face an uncertain future without my husband," she said. "I'm not sure how this is supposed to work, but I suddenly feel as if I'm needed."

Judd didn't understand what the woman was trying to

say. "We're here for *you*, ma'am," Judd said. "We're going to take care of you."

"And I thank you," she said. "But I feel as if I should offer something. Not as a reward, but as a fellow family member."

"What are you saying?" Vicki said.

"As you and Judd know, our family has no lack of resources. It could very well be that the Global Community will freeze our bank assets. But I want you to know the money, the cars, the land, all we have I want to share. I will withdraw our money as quickly as possible so it can be used for a good purpose. I know Maxwell would agree with me."

Judd was stunned. "We have huge financial needs," he said. "But you can't—"

"It's already been decided," Mrs. Stahley said. "I said I wanted God to use me, and this is just a small way to do that." Mrs. Stahley asked to use a computer to transfer funds from her account. "If I wait, it may be too late."

Judd showed her the computer in his father's office. Within a few minutes she had successfully transferred funds to Judd's account and to another secret account in another country.

"Now we must rest," Mrs. Stahley said, taking Darrion downstairs.

Vicki looked at Judd. "Can you believe it?" she said.

"I'm still trying to take it in," Judd said.

"I don't mean to be the bearer of more bad news," Chaya said, "but I'm afraid some things are getting worse. Have you heard anything from Buck Williams?"

"No," Judd said, "the last time I saw him he was headed to *Global Community Weekly*."

"That's where he went," Chaya said. "I just got off the phone with Loretta, who filled me in. Chloe dropped Buck off at the office, then went downtown to get their stuff out of The Drake Hotel. They were planning to stay with Loretta tonight. But when Chloe got to the hotel, she took a message from her dad. He said they should get out of Chicago as fast as they could."

"Captain Steele must have found out about the bombing," Judd said. "Did she get out?"

"Buck was on the cell phone with her when the first bombs hit," Chaya said. "She was on Lake Shore Drive."

"Oh no," Vicki said. "Lake Shore is really close to Michigan Avenue, where most of the damage was done."

"Where's Buck now?" Judd said.

"He borrowed a car from somebody he works with, and now he's headed downtown to see if he can find Chloe," Chaya said.

"When we came from there it looked pretty hopeless," Judd said. "Traffic was a mess. I can't imagine what it's like now."

Judd grabbed his jacket and asked Vicki and Chaya to spend the night at his house. "I'll call you as soon as I find out anything," he said.

Judd flipped on the radio as he drove toward Loretta's. The reporters confirmed Mr. Stahley's fears. Chicago wasn't the only target.

"We've just received confirmation of the attack on San Francisco," the announcer said. "It's impossible to estimate the number of dead at this point, but airports and other transportation centers have been destroyed."

Judd shuddered. He recalled the news of the devastating attack on Heathrow Airport in London. The main centers of transportation were being bombed. Communication centers. Trade centers. This would allow Carpathia to have a stranglehold on the world's economy, transportation, and communication.

A coworker of Buck's, Verna Zee, met Judd at Loretta's door and let him in. Loretta was on the phone with Buck. Verna looked distraught.

"Here, Verna," Loretta said, "Buck wants to talk to you."

Verna took the phone. "Oh no, Cameron," she said, "what happened?"

Loretta told Judd that Buck was somewhere near Lake Shore Drive in Chicago but hadn't found Chloe. "Buck showed up with Verna a while ago, and I opened my home to her," she said. "She seems like a nice person, but confused. I've just been tellin' her my story."

Verna got off the phone. "He wrecked my car," she said. "Said he'd replace it with a better one. Can't argue with that. He's close to Michigan Avenue. I'm not sure he's going to find anything tonight."

Verna dialed the newsroom and talked with a staff member. She thanked the man and told him to call if there were any more messages.

"Buck got three calls," Verna told Judd, "but none from his wife."

The phone rang. It was Buck.

"No," Verna told Buck, "but you did get a call from a Dr. Rosenzweig in Israel, and another was from a man claiming to be your father-in-law."

Judd blocked out the rest of the conversation. Loretta offered him something to drink, but he couldn't concentrate. The name of Chaim Rosenzweig made him think of Dr. Tsion Ben-Judah. Dr. Rosenzweig was a mentor to the rabbi. Judd thought about Ben-Judah's children, Nina and Dan, and their mother. He prayed they would be safe and able to make it to Chicago.

From the living room, Judd heard the phone ring again. This time Verna let out a whoop. She hung up and dialed another number.

"No, Cameron, it's Verna," Judd heard her say, "but the office just called. Chloe just tried to reach you. She didn't say where she was or how she was, but at least you know she's alive."

Judd put his head down on the couch for a moment. Since the night of the disappearances, it had been the most tumultuous day of his life. He had lost a dear friend. He had seen Darrion, her mother, and her father accept the gift of salvation. He had witnessed Mr. Stahley's death and the deaths of others. He had seen destruction near his home and in downtown Chicago. In the midst of it all, he had seen the power of God's love at work in the lives of his friends.

Judd closed his eyes only for a moment. When he opened them, light streamed through the window, and he heard familiar voices of the people he loved.

11

"JUDD, help!"

The girl sounded desperate. He tried to place her voice, but he couldn't. Judd called back, but she didn't seem to hear.

"Judd, we need you! Hurry!"

"Nina!" Judd said as he awoke. He tried to shake the dream but couldn't. Judd had met Nina in Israel while traveling with Bruce. Because her father was such an outspoken Jewish believer, Nina, her brother, Dan, and Mrs. Ben-Judah were in constant danger.

Nina's helpless cry haunted Judd as he collected himself. There was a pain deep in his chest. Could the previous day have been a dream? Could Bruce really be dead? Judd sat up and listened to voices in the other room. Judd had come to Loretta's—Bruce's secretary at New Hope Village Church—house when he heard Chloe Williams was in trouble. The search for Ryan had been exhausting. Judd had fallen asleep before he found out what happened to Chloe, and now he listened as Loretta and Buck Williams talked in hushed tones in the kitchen.

Loretta wept about Bruce. Buck assured her she wouldn't have to handle the arrangements for Bruce's body.

"But I don't think I can handle the memorial service either," Loretta said. "There's so much to prepare."

Buck said he would take care of both.

"It feels so good to have people in this place again," Loretta said. "Y'all stay as long as you need to or want to."

"We're grateful," Buck said. "Amanda may sleep till noon, but then she'll get right on those arrangements with the coroner's office. Chloe didn't sleep much with the ankle cast, but she's sleeping hard now."

When Loretta left for the church, Judd went to the kitchen to talk with Buck.

"I heard you had quite an experience with Ryan," Buck said. "How is he?"

Judd told him. He asked Buck's advice about Mrs. Stahley and Darrion.

"That's a tough one," Buck said. "You want to get them into hiding as fast as you can," Buck said. "If the Global Community wanted Mr. Stahley that bad, they'll come looking for the rest of his family. Sounds like they know too much."

"What happened with Chloe?" Judd said.

Buck quickly explained that Chloe had received a message from her father to get out of downtown Chicago. She was talking with Buck on a cell phone with a cop right behind her. Chloe didn't want to stop. Then the

bombing began. Chloe's Range Rover was thrown off
Lake Shore Drive and landed in a tree. That's where she
stayed until Buck found her.

Buck was interested in Ryan's story. Judd explained
how they found him and how Ryan helped save their
lives. "Mr. Stahley gave his life for his daughter," Judd
said.

"We may all be asked to do that," Buck said. "I'm not
sure how much Nicolae Carpathia knows about my faith,
but he's sure to find out at some point. We have to be
ready for whatever comes."

"Is Verna Zee a Christian too?" Judd said, referring
to Buck's coworker, also staying at Loretta's house.

"No," Buck said. "I may have put myself in real
danger when I brought her here. My hope is that she'll
hear the message and respond. If not, I'm in trouble.
Carpathia hasn't given any indication he suspects
anything, but if Verna tells my superiors, it's only a
matter of time."

"Do you talk with Carpathia?" Judd said.

"Last night in fact," Buck said. "He wanted to know
about the coverage of the war here. His voice got real
emotional when I told him. He said it was a tragedy."

"Makes me sick," Judd said. "Is that all he said?"

"No, he wanted me to come over there and cover
meetings in Baghdad and New Babylon."

"You're not going?" Judd said.

"I told him I was working another story," Buck said.
"He's getting another guy."

As they talked, Buck turned his attention to the papers

scattered across the dining-room table. "Bruce's notes," he said. "Chloe had them with her in the Rover. I have to put them back together."

Judd helped get the transcripts in order. Buck had a huge job ahead of him. He not only had to read the massive pile of pages but also edit it for the church.

"Can I ask about the other story you're working on?" Judd said.

Buck reached for the phone. "Hang on," he said.

Buck called Ken Ritz, a pilot who had flown him to New York just after the disappearances. "I know you're busy and probably don't need my business," Buck said, "but you also know I'm on a big, fat expense account and can pay more than anyone else."

Judd wondered where Buck needed to go so soon after his wife's accident.

"Israel," Buck said to Ken Ritz. "And I have to be back here by Saturday night at the latest."

Vicki awoke and heard someone crying. For a moment she couldn't figure out where she was. *Judd's house*, she thought. He had asked them to stay at his house while he went to Loretta's. Vicki had crashed in Judd's parents' room. Chaya sat on the edge of the bed, her shoulders shaking.

"Are you OK?" Vicki said.

Chaya shook her head. "I couldn't sleep," she said. "I called my father about my mother's funeral. He said I shouldn't bother. He doesn't want me there."

"That's all he said?" Vicki said.

"He asked about Bruce; then he told me this would be our last conversation."

"He can't keep you away from your own mother's funeral," Vicki said.

"He said he would turn his back if I came. I have betrayed the Jewish faith by becoming a Christian. I have betrayed him and the memory of my mother."

Vicki put an arm around Chaya as the older girl sobbed. "I prayed that her death would soften him," Chaya said. She was clutching the note she had found in her mother's hand.

"At least you know where your mom is now," Vicki said.

"I know she's in a better place," Chaya said, "but my father . . ."

Lionel and Ryan were in the kitchen fixing breakfast. Ryan held out a plate to Vicki when she sat down.

"You're our guests so we're pulling out all the special food," Ryan said.

"If I can keep him from eating it all," Lionel said.

Ryan and Lionel seemed to be working together. Their rivalry the past year had been fierce at times, bickering and fighting almost daily. Vicki wondered how long the truce would last.

As they ate, although they were sad, they kept remembering funny stories.

"When I moved into Bruce's house, I forgot my toothbrush," Vicki said. "I asked Bruce if he'd take me to buy some toiletries, and he got all serious. He told me he'd never had a teenager in his house and knew there were things I'd need. He was about to launch into this big speech about growing into womanhood when I stopped him and said, 'Bruce, I just need a toothbrush.' "

Everyone laughed.

"What do you think Bruce would say about Darrion and Mrs. Stahley?" Ryan said.

"He'd be proud of what you did," Lionel said. "If you hadn't been there, they might not have made it. They sure wouldn't have heard about God the way you told them."

"None of it would have happened if I hadn't gone to see Bruce," Ryan said. "He started the whole thing."

Chaya had talked with Loretta late the previous night and brought everyone up to date on Chloe and Buck. Though Amanda was safe, Rayford Steele remained with Nicolae Carpathia. Amanda said Rayford was flying to New Babylon.

"Carpathia gives me the creeps big time," Ryan said. "I think he's Satan himself."

"That's not what Bruce told us," Lionel said.

Chaya nodded. "Bruce taught that the Antichrist would not be indwelt by Satan himself until halfway into the Tribulation. The guy's evil, no doubt. But even with the war and all the death, things will get worse."

Darrion rushed up the stairs. "Turn on the television!" she said.

———————————

"Why Israel?" Judd asked Buck. "I've heard that's the one place the war hasn't touched."

"I'm not covering the war," Buck said.

"Then why go?" Judd said.

"I'm not sure how much I should tell you," Buck said, "for your own safety."

"With what we've been through," Judd said, "I don't think you could tell me anything that would endanger my life more than us hiding family members of a Global Community traitor."

"In the middle of trying to find Chloe yesterday, I got a call from Dr. Chaim Rosenzweig," Buck said. "He's friends with Rabbi Tsion Ben-Judah."

Judd reminded Buck he had met the rabbi's wife and two adopted children on his trips to Israel. Buck looked away.

"We watched the rabbi's televised speech too," Judd said. "And Bruce kept us up to date. It was exciting to watch the rabbi speak to all the new believers in Teddy Kollek Stadium. What's happened?"

"They can't find him," Buck said, "Dr. Rosenzweig said he was going to Nicolae for help, and I begged him to leave Carpathia out of it. I haven't heard anything more, but I assume the prophecy from the two witnesses at the Wailing Wall is correct. Dr. Ben-Judah will be protected in spite of the murders. So I feel I have to—"

"Wait," Judd said. "What murders?"

Buck stared at him. "You'd better sit down."

Lionel flicked on the television in the kitchen. The Stahley girl looked upset. Mrs. Stahley was there a moment later and watched with her arms folded.

The news anchorwoman was nicely dressed, but the worry showed on her face.

"This report out of Chicago has pushed aside war news," she said. "An international business leader and a high-level member of the Global Community is dead this morning. Maxwell Stahley, who made his fortune in international security, was found dead of a gunshot wound in an office building in a suburb of Chicago."

Video footage showed men carrying Mr. Stahley's body from the Global Community building.

"Mr. Stahley was found alone in a pool of blood in a first-floor entryway," the woman said.

Mrs. Stahley covered her mouth and turned her head.

"He wasn't on the first floor," Ryan said. "He was on the fourth floor with the other guy."

"Also missing are Stahley's wife and daughter," the anchor said. A picture of the Stahley family flashed on the screen.

"I hate that picture," Darrion said.

"The motive is not clear," the woman continued, "but a source close to the Global Community confirmed that a large amount of money had been taken from one of Stahley's bank accounts in the U.S."

"They found it already," Mrs. Stahley said. "I transferred the funds last night."

"Will they be able to trace it to Judd?" Vicki said.

"I put the money into several different accounts to be safe," Mrs. Stahley said. She looked at Vicki. "One of them was Judd's."

A spokesman for the Global Community appeared on

a satellite hookup. He vaguely answered questions about the war, then turned to the Stahley report.

"We must let the investigation run its course," the man said. "This is a great personal loss of a devoted colleague. I do believe it will be important to focus on the mother and daughter at this point. They may be in danger, or perhaps they know something about the murder."

"You wanna find them because they know what's really going on," Ryan said to the TV.

"Are you suggesting his wife and daughter might be responsible for the murder?" the woman said.

"We're not ruling anything out at this point," the spokesman said, "but we would like anyone who has any information on the whereabouts of these two to get in touch with the Global Community immediately."

A phone number flashed on the screen.

"That guy looks nervous," Vicki said.

"My husband left important documents behind," Mrs. Stahley said. "Documents that might save our lives."

"Where are they?" Vicki said.

"That's the problem. They're at our house in a secret place."

The phone rang. Chaya answered. She looked startled, then covered the receiver with her hand.

"It's Loretta," Chaya said. "The police just called the church."

Who was murdered?" Judd said, sitting warily.

"I found this out from Dr. Rosenzweig," Buck said.

"He respects Dr. Ben-Judah but couldn't understand why such an educated man would throw away his reputation by proclaiming Jesus as the Messiah. He was afraid religious zealots would kill Ben-Judah."

"And they did?" Judd said, holding his breath.

Buck shook his head. "Chaim called to tell me about the rabbi's wife and children."

"No!" Judd gasped.

Buck's voice grew tense. "All killed," he said. "I'm very sorry."

The words felt like a sledgehammer. The air went out of the room and Judd couldn't speak. Couldn't think. Buck kept talking, but Judd couldn't concentrate.

"Chaim said Ben-Judah's house was burned to the ground," Buck was saying.

"You sure it was them?" Judd managed.

"Chaim says it was a public spectacle. I assume the rabbi is in hiding. At least I hope so."

"That's why you're going to Israel?" Judd said.

"It's not what Carpathia thinks, but yes. I need to find the rabbi."

Judd put his face in his hands. "The dream," he said. "I had a dream about Nina last night." Judd explained his relationship with Nina, Dan, and their mother. They had taken Judd in. They had driven him to historic sights in Israel and explained their social customs. They had eaten together and talked about their faith. Judd had invited them to America. Now they were dead.

Or were they? He could hope. Judd thought a moment. "Maybe they're just trying to lure the rabbi out of hiding. If he thought his family had been killed, he'd come out for sure."

"What could he do if they're dead?"

Judd slammed his fist onto the table. "I don't get it," he said. "The two witnesses promised protection, right?"

"Moishe said anyone who threatened the rabbi would answer to him," Buck said. "I thought the rabbi's family would be protected, too."

"I don't think they're dead," Judd said.

"Dr. Rosenzweig wouldn't have told me that unless it was true," Buck said.

"You said yourself Carpathia has the power to make people believe a lie," Judd said.

"But there's no reason," Buck said. "You've just gone through a gut-wrenching experience with Ryan. You've lost Bruce. Now this. I don't blame you for being upset. But you have to face the facts."

Judd wanted to keep arguing, but he knew he shouldn't. "I need a favor," he said.

12

"**DON'T** panic," Lionel said, though mention of the police startled him. "We don't know what they want."

Chaya looked upset. "The officer told Loretta someone used the church phone to call Mr. Stahley's office yesterday," she said. "Loretta told them it might have been Judd. She hung up and realized he might be in danger."

"Great," Lionel said. "The church was our best hiding place for the Stahleys. Now that's out."

"I was the one who made the call," Chaya said. "They're looking for me, not Judd."

"Doesn't matter," Lionel said. "We're in this together."

The phone rang again. Lionel waved the rest off and looked at the caller ID. It was blank. "Yeah, he's not here right now. Can I take a message?" Lionel said.

"This is the police," the man said. "We're investigating a murder. Do you know where Judd Thompson is right now?"

"I'm not sure," Lionel said. "He was gone all night. What precinct are you with? I'll have him call when he gets back."

The phone line clicked.

"Funny," Lionel said. "Since when do the police not want anyone to know who they are?" He looked at Mrs. Stahley and Darrion. "We need to get you out of here fast."

Before anyone could move there was a knock at the door.

"I don't like it," Buck said.

"Don't treat me like a kid," Judd said. "I've been to Israel before."

Buck folded his arms. "That's not the point."

"It can't cost much more to let me fly with you," Judd said. "As soon as we touch down, I'll be gone."

"I'm not against you going to Israel," Buck said. "I'm just not in a position to let you go with me."

"Where else am I going to find a way over there when there's a war on?" Judd said.

Buck sighed. "I don't know. I just can't handle the responsibility of—"

"You don't have any responsibility," Judd said. "All I need is a way to get over there so I can check on Nina and Dan. That's all I'm asking."

"I know this news hurts," Buck said, "but I'm doing something that could get me killed. I just can't take you. I'm sorry."

146

"If you don't help me out, I'll find my own way," Judd said.

Judd dropped the subject. If God really wanted him to go to Israel, God could work it out without Buck's help.

Judd helped Buck finish organizing Bruce's transcripts. Buck said he was going to pack and then try to reach Dr. Rosenzweig. "The old man knows he's being watched," Buck said. "But I think he's trying to tell me, in a cryptic way, that Dr. Ben-Judah is alive and safe somewhere."

Chaya slipped to the garage with Darrion and Mrs. Stahley. The girl and her mother climbed into the trunk. Chaya waited for Lionel's signal and opened the garage door.

"I hope this works," Chaya said to herself.

Vicki opened the door. A tall, thin woman with glasses greeted her. Vicki remembered the woman from the hearing she had been given at Nicolae Carpathia High School.

"Candace Goodwin," the woman said. Vicki showed her into the living room. As she did, a huge crash of pots and pans clattered behind Vicki. Lionel stood in the kitchen in the midst of the furor. The noise lasted a good twenty seconds as the boy clumsily picked up, dropped, and kicked several pans. Vicki could tell that the social worker was ready to get down to business. Her face was tight, and she looked like she had aged since the last time Vicki had seen her.

"If you recall," Mrs. Goodwin said, "I'm with Global Community Social Services." She pulled out a yellow legal pad and scribbled some notes.

"I remember," Vicki said. "I told my story to you and got sent to the Northside Detention Center."

Mrs. Goodwin grimaced. "I didn't want to do that, but you wouldn't cooperate."

"What are you doing here?" Vicki said.

"It's my job to know these types of things," Mrs. Goodwin said grimly. "The real concern before us is what you're going to do now."

"What do you mean?" Vicki said.

"We received a report about your guardian's death," Mrs. Goodwin said.

"How could you possibly—"

"Do you deny it?" Mrs. Goodwin said.

Vicki bit her lip. "No," she said. "But he wasn't my guardian. He was my adoptive father."

"We have some important matters to discuss," Mrs. Goodwin said. "You're a ward of the state now."

"Does that mean what I think it means?" Vicki said.

"Unless we find a suitable alternative," Mrs. Goodwin said, "you could return to NDC."

Vicki gasped. With the war and mayhem around the world, she had thought she might be able to slide through the cracks in the system. *How could they have discovered Bruce's death so fast?* she thought.

"I have a place to stay and friends—"

Mrs. Goodwin's beeper sounded. She handed Vicki

her card. "I need to talk with you about something later," she said. "I'll be in touch."

Judd came through the door as Mrs. Goodwin was leaving. Vicki explained the situation and told Judd about the police call.

"Chaya drove the Stahleys somewhere," Vicki said. "I don't know where. We just wanted to get them out of here."

"If it was the Global Community on the phone rather than the police," Lionel said, "we might have company soon."

"Better they find us than Chaya," Judd said.

"I'd rather they didn't find any of us," Vicki said.

———————————

Judd called Ryan into the meeting and told them about the Ben-Judah family. The kids were crushed. Ryan said he had been looking forward to meeting Nina and Dan and helping them adjust to American society. Vicki stared off into space.

"I wonder if that's what we'll have to go through," Lionel said. "The persecution of people who believe in Jesus is increasing."

"This is going to hit Chaya hard," Vicki said. "She thought the Ben-Judahs might talk to her father."

Judd told them of his desire to go to Israel. "I want to make sure," he said. "I think God is drawing me back there, and it may be because the family isn't really dead."

"You don't trust Dr. Rosenzweig?" Vicki said.

"I don't trust anyone who says Nicolae Carpathia is a good man," Judd said.

"It's not fair," Ryan said. "You've been to Israel twice, and Bruce promised. You ought to take me."

"Hang on," Lionel said. "You're going to Israel because you have some kind of feeling?"

"I can't explain it," Judd said.

"What if it's a bad piece of pizza?" Lionel said. "Come on, Judd, we can't just go running off whenever we feel like it."

The phone rang. Lionel looked at the caller ID. "No number," he said.

"Let's get out of here," Judd said.

Chaya drove Mrs. Stahley and Darrion to Bruce's house and put them in a secluded room downstairs. When they were settled, Mrs. Stahley became emotional. "What will they do with my husband's body?" she said.

"I assume they'll keep it until the investigation is complete," Chaya said.

"I want to see him," Mrs. Stahley said. "It doesn't seem real to me."

"Mother—," Darrion said.

"It's not that I don't believe your report," Mrs. Stahley said. "I need to see my husband's face."

"You have to resist that," Chaya said. "The Global Community wants you to come forward. If they find you, they'll twist things and make you look like the murderer."

"She's right, Mother," Darrion said. "We must hide."

Judd and the others joined Chaya at Bruce's house. Mrs.
Stahley and Darrion excused themselves while the group
met. When Judd told them the news about the Ben-Judah
family, Chaya shook her head. "When will the insanity
end?" she said.

Judd asked Chaya's advice on the trip to Israel.

"Travel anywhere is risky right now," Chaya said.

"I still don't get it," Lionel said. "Why does God want
you in Israel?"

"I woke up thinking about the Ben-Judah family this
morning," Judd said. "Maybe they're still alive. And who
knows, if Buck can't find Dr. Ben-Judah, maybe God will
let me help."

"I don't see how it's possible," Vicki said. "Mr.
Williams won't take you, and you sure can't get a flight
anywhere with the war going on."

"Maybe you're right," Judd said. "Maybe this was all
in my head."

"I'm sorry for interrupting," Mrs. Stahley said, slipping into the room. "I know how you can get there."

"You do?" Judd said.

"The only person who worked with my husband
that I trust is Taylor Graham," Mrs. Stahley said. "I
wanted to call him when Darrion was taken, but
Maxwell wouldn't allow it. He knew Taylor can be pretty
high-strung."

"Sounds like my kind of guy," Ryan said. "How can
he help us?"

Judd glanced warily at Ryan. "Us?" he said.

"He's been our family pilot for years," Mrs. Stahley said. "He's flown us around the world several times."

"Cool guy," Darrion said. "He's let me fly before."

"Right," Ryan said.

"No, really." Darrion rolled her eyes and smiled. "Okay, it was on autopilot, but it still felt like I was flying the plane."

"Wouldn't they have taken possession of your plane by now?" Judd said.

"We keep it in an underground hangar near the house," Mrs. Stahley said. "Maxwell used the Global Community–supplied aircraft for business, but no one knows where our private jet is. The trick will be getting onto the property. I'm sure the Global Community is watching it."

"Can you get in touch with this guy?" Judd said.

"I can try."

Mrs. Stahley reached the pilot's answering machine, then dialed his pager.

"What do you hope to accomplish with the trip?" Mrs. Stahley said.

"To find out about the Ben-Judah family," Judd said.

"Which brings us back to me," Ryan said. "What happens if you're over there and you get into some real trouble?" Ryan flexed his muscles and Darrion smiled.

Judd explained Ryan's wish.

"Judd won't admit I can take care of myself," Ryan said.

"After what you accomplished yesterday," Vicki said, "I would think Judd would jump at the chance."

"I agree Ryan proved himself," Judd said. He held up his passport. "But it's not practical. He doesn't even have one of these."

Chaya's eyes widened. "I'll be right back," she said, running from the room. Soon she returned, holding a white envelope.

"What you said about Ryan going with you?" Chaya said. "It *is* practical."

She handed Judd the envelope. Judd opened it slowly, then let out a low whistle.

"What?" Ryan said, grabbing the envelope.

"It was going to be a surprise," Chaya said. "Bruce told me that on his next trip to the Holy Land he was taking Ryan with him. He filled out the paperwork and sent in Ryan's—"

"That little picture!" Ryan said, his mouth open wide. "Bruce wouldn't tell me what he was going to do with it."

Ryan pulled out the crisp, blue passport and opened the cover to see his picture inside. He touched it gingerly, as if it were a treasure. A yellow Post-it note was stuck to the back. In Bruce's familiar handwriting Ryan read out loud, *"For Ryan. It's your turn finally."*

Vicki gave Judd a look.

"Don't take sides on this," Judd said. "You know it's too dangerous—"

"Judd," Vicki said, "we watched Ryan dodge bombs and bullets yesterday and save Darrion's life. I'd say he's earned a chance, don't you think?"

"If God wants you to go," Lionel said, "it looks like he wants you to have some company."

Chaya handed Ryan a page from Bruce's manuscript. "I copied this for you," she said.

Over Ryan's shoulder, Judd read the page.

Bruce had written: *I'm so excited the process is complete. The next time I set foot on Israeli soil, I'll get to take Ryan. He talks constantly about going. I've had to say no twice. This is going to be such a surprise. I can't wait to see his face when I show him the passport and tell him he's going with me.*

Ryan looked at Judd with tears in his eyes.

Judd shook his head. "We don't even know if this Graham guy will fly us," Judd said.

"Us?" Ryan said.

"Yeah." Judd smiled. "Us."

Judd and Ryan arranged a meeting with Taylor Graham at a donut shop in Prospect Heights. "I don't want to tell him everything," Judd said. "I know Mrs. Stahley trusts him with her life, but we have to be careful."

Graham looked like a swimmer—tall, tanned, and muscular. They bought coffee and donuts and sat in Judd's car.

"I have to tell you," Graham said, "I didn't know I'd be dealing with a couple of kids."

Judd glanced at Ryan, who rolled his eyes.

"I wouldn't even be talking to you unless the Mrs. had asked."

"I understand your concern," Judd said. "You're safe with us. I assume the Global Community is looking for you, too."

"They found me already," Graham said. "Since my

boss was grounded for a few days, which I still don't understand, the GC had me do a VIP run to Dallas yesterday. Didn't get in until early this morning."

"The GC told you Mr. Stahley was going to be grounded?" Judd said.

"Said he was out for at least a few days and might not be back," Graham said. "I do what I'm told, but first thing on the list when I got back was to check with him and find out what's going on."

"So you don't know anything about why Mr. Stahley was out?" Judd said.

"If you know something, tell me," Graham said.

"You sure you can trust us little kids?" Ryan said.

Graham ignored him and listened intently as Judd explained the events of the previous day. Ryan told the pilot how he had gotten entangled in the kidnapping and about some of the kidnappers' conversations on the phone.

"What did the guy in the trench coat look like?" Graham asked.

Judd told him.

Graham shook his head. "Corny bit it, huh?"

"What?" Ryan said.

"Cornelius Van Waylin," Graham said. "Supposed to be Max's friend. They were together a few years ago before this whole Global Community deal. Had a falling out. Corny had it in for Max from the get-go."

Ryan described the other man who had gotten away. "Doesn't ring a bell," Graham said, "but Corny had lots of people working for him, inside and outside the GC."

"So will you take us?" Ryan said.

"It's probably about the safest airspace in the world right now," Graham said, "but you have to pass through some hot spots. Why Israel?"

"It's a personal trip," Judd said. "I promised Ryan we'd—"

"OK, you can cut that stuff," Graham said. "I'm not gonna risk my neck on a joyride to Jerusalem because somebody has an itch. I'll ask you one more time. Why are you going?"

Judd was in a corner. If Graham was working with the GC, Judd and Mrs. Stahley were in trouble. But if he offended Graham, he might lose his best chance for a trip to Israel.

Before he could answer, Graham turned to Ryan. "What's your name again?" he said.

Ryan told him.

"I want you to buckle your strap tight around you," Graham said. "Now." He turned to Judd. "As fast as you can, flip the front seat back and climb next to your friend."

"What's going on?" Judd said.

"Two GC guys walked into the donut place after we ordered," Graham said. "I didn't think much of it. When the second car pulled up I got a little antsy. Then I saw someone who looks a lot like the guy you said ran away from sector four last night. I figure we ought to do something."

Judd was in the backseat and barely buckled in when Taylor Graham pulled away from the curb. Judd had no idea his car could move that quickly or that it could look so easy.

"Yeeehigh!" Ryan said.

"While we're in the process here," Graham said, "tell me why you need to go to Israel."

"Some friends of ours were killed," Judd said. "I don't believe it. We want to find out what happened."

"You think they're still alive?" Graham said, taking a curve hard.

"Maybe it's blind hope," Judd said, "but I have to know. They'd do the same for me."

Judd couldn't see either of the other cars now. Graham turned onto a frontage road that paralleled an expressway and sped toward an intersection.

"I'll take you on one condition," Graham said.

"We're not telling where Mrs. Stahley is," Ryan said.

"I don't want you to," Graham said.

"Then what's the condition?" Judd said.

13

VICKI met with Chloe later in the day. Chloe hobbled around on a cane, needing crutches but unable to manage them with her sprained wrist. Chloe brought Vicki up to date on the adult Tribulation Force. Buck's coworker, Verna Zee, was back at the Global Community office and would return later that night.

"We need your advice about Darrion and Mrs. Stahley," Vicki said. "Where do you think they should stay?"

"Here," Chloe said. She told Vicki where to find a key in the kitchen. "Bring them over while we take Buck to Palwaukee Airport. Verna's staying downstairs. You can put Mrs. Stahley and Darrion in the garage apartment. It's not fancy, but no one will find them."

"What about Loretta?" Vicki said. "She'll need to know."

"I'll tell Loretta," Chloe said. "You stay with them and bring whatever they need. I'll have Loretta say you're trying to get over Bruce's death and you need a little privacy."

"That wouldn't be far from the truth," Vicki said.

Chloe put a hand on her shoulder. "Hang in there until the memorial service," she said. "I'm sure that will bring healing to us all."

The phone rang and Chloe handed it to Vicki.

"You'll never believe it," Judd said. The car phone was noisy, and Judd sounded out of breath. "We're on our way to Israel!"

"Great," Vicki said. "When do you leave?"

"The pilot will take us on one condition," Judd said. "He wants to go right now—no packing, no good-byes. Ryan hasn't let go of his passport, and I have mine."

"Why does it have to be all of a sudden?" Vicki said.

"Can't explain," Judd said. "Just be careful. And make sure you get Mrs. Stahley and Darrion to a safe place."

"It's already taken care of," Vicki said.

Vicki told Judd the group would pray for him and Ryan, even though she didn't know exactly what to pray. When she hung up, Buck came in with his luggage. Rayford Steele's wife, Amanda, was there to drive him to the airport.

"I want to ride along," Chloe said.

"Are you sure you're up to it, hon?" Buck said.

Chloe's voice was quavery. "Buck, I hate to say it, but in this day and age we never know when we might or might not ever see each other again."

"You're being a little dramatic, aren't you?" he said.

"Buck!" Amanda said in a scolding tone. "You cater to her feelings now. I had to kiss my husband good-bye in front of the Antichrist. You think that gives me confidence about whether I'll ever see him again?"

Vicki smiled. Buck had been properly chastised. Vicki got in touch with Chaya. "We have a couple people to move," Vicki said.

Judd was impressed with Taylor Graham's abilities behind the wheel. He also had keen insight. Graham whipped the car under a drive-through canopy and let the car idle.

"What's wrong?" Judd said.

"Helicopter," Graham said. When the pilot was sure they weren't being followed, he headed for the Stahley mansion. "The place'll be watched closely, so we'll have to go the long way around," he said. "I hope you guys are in good shape."

On their way, Nicolae Carpathia's voice interrupted the news reports on the radio. He talked in his usual overly humble manner.

"Make no mistake, my brothers and sisters," Carpathia said, "there will be many dark days ahead. It will take a huge supply of resources to begin the rebuilding process, but because of the generosity of the seven loyal global regions, the world will see the largest relief fund in the history of mankind. This will be given to needy nations directly from New Babylon. The relief effort, under my direct orders, will be handled in a swift and generous way.

"Continue to resist those who speak out against us. Continue to support the Global Community. And remember that though I did not seek this position, I accept it with resolve to pour out my life in service to the brotherhood and sisterhood of mankind. I appreciate your support as we set about to stand by each other and pull ourselves out of these troubled days to a higher plane."

Ryan shook his head. "He's saying that because people want to hear it."

Judd waited to see any reaction from Taylor Graham. The pilot concentrated on the road ahead. Judd explained how he and Vicki had gotten onto the Stahley property.

"You're lucky the dogs didn't tear you apart," Graham said.

Graham drove into a different entrance to the forest preserve, farther from the Stahley estate. Instead of staying in the parking lot, he stopped at a hidden gate in a wooded area. Graham unlocked the gate and drove deeper into the woods. A few hundred yards farther they found a gravel path with warning signs posted every few yards.

"I didn't know this was here," Judd said.

"No one's supposed to," Graham said. "I usually have my four-wheel drive. It can get nasty out here when it's wet."

The car snaked through the underbrush, and the terrain gradually inclined. Finally they went straight uphill until the ground leveled and they came to a clearing. Graham parked the car under a huge willow tree, and the three hiked along the edge of the woods.

"See anything out there?" Graham said.

Judd saw the edge of the Stahley estate in the distance and the iron fence he and Vicki had climbed. Between them and the fence were acres of rolling, green land.

"I see some pine trees and a lot of grass," Judd said, "but nothing that looks like a plane or a landing strip."

"Good," the pilot said.

Graham showed them to a small grove of trees and knelt in front of a brick-sized stone. Underneath, Judd saw what looked like a fishing-tackle box. Graham opened the lid. Inside was an airtight instrument panel covered with buttons and knobs.

"I'll need you to stay here and work the runway," Graham said to Judd. "Ryan, you come with me, but you have to stay low. When we're in the clearing, we'll be easy to spot."

Ryan smiled at Judd and raised his eyebrows.

"We have an underground tunnel that connects the mansion with the plane hangar," Graham said. "It's hard to find, so I'm assuming the Global Community people haven't located it yet."

Graham pointed to the panel. "This is our backup entrance," he said. "When Ryan and I make it to the entrance, I'll give you a thumbs-up. You press the black button and hold it until we get inside."

"How long will you be in there?" Judd said.

"It'll take a few minutes' prep, maybe fifteen or so," the pilot said. "When you hear the plane start, flip the green switch to the "on" position. Pull the top down and replace the stone, then run like mad straight toward that tree."

Graham caught Judd's eye. "This is important," Graham said. "If something goes wrong, you'll need to find the road and get back to Mrs. Stahley. If we're clear in there, the sound of the plane is bound to alert them. If you're slow and don't make it, I'll leave you in a New York minute."

"I'm not slow," Judd said. "I'll make it."

"Good," Graham said. "There's an old stump about ten yards in front of the tree. The door to the plane will be open. Got it?"

Judd nodded. Ryan held up both thumbs and the two took off, running close to the ground.

Vicki and Chaya helped Darrion and Mrs. Stahley get settled in the garage apartment. Mrs. Stahley had found some clothes in Bruce's wife's closet that fit, but the two had little else.

"The apartment doesn't have a phone," Vicki said, "so we'll get you a cell phone to use in case of an emergency. It does have a complete kitchen, so you won't need to go out."

"This is very kind of you," Mrs. Stahley said, "but where will the hiding end? At some point they'll track us down. And when they do, you'll be caught in the middle."

"God put us together for a reason," Vicki said. "He wants us to help. We'll take this a day at a time and pray God leads us."

Darrion flipped on the television. The reporter stated that Nicolae Carpathia would speak from New Babylon within the hour. "I can't wait," she said sarcastically.

Ryan watched Taylor Graham give Judd the signal. Before them, a grassy door in the side of the mountain opened. Ryan and the pilot scurried in. Graham hit a button that closed the door.

While the pilot readied the Learjet, Ryan walked around the hangar. The place was massive. Tools hung from one wall. In another area Ryan found fuel pumps. Ryan couldn't believe the interior of the plane. Leather seats complete with video monitors were neatly positioned about the cabin. In the rear of the plane Ryan found electronic equipment.

"We can hook up with satellites," Graham said. "We can hear and see just about anything we want up here."

"Cool," Ryan said.

Graham showed Ryan how to close the rear door once Judd was aboard. "You do what I say," Graham said, "whether your friend makes it or not. Understood?"

Ryan nodded, but he knew he wasn't going anywhere without Judd.

Outside, Judd waited for any sign of the plane. He had seen the hill open, but now, as he looked closely, he couldn't tell where the door had been. If Graham hadn't given him the tree as a reference, he would never have found the correct spot. He still couldn't see the landing strip.

A line of geese flew overhead in a perfect *V*. A squirrel skittered about searching for nuts in the dry leaves. Winter was coming. Instinct told the animals to prepare. Judd felt the same way about his life. He had survived nearly two years of the Tribulation. What lay ahead was more frightening than anything they had been through.

Judd heard an engine and at first thought it was the plane. To his left he saw a four-wheel-drive vehicle

bounce up the hill and around the tree line. A man with
binoculars surveyed the landscape. Judd hit the ground
and stayed there. Moments later he heard the engine rev.
He lifted his head and saw the car near the willow tree.
Two men disappeared beneath its branches.

Come on, Graham. Hurry! Judd said under his breath.

———————————————

Ryan watched the pilot leave the plane and grab a nozzle. "If we didn't have this," Graham yelled, "we'd have
to refuel somewhere along the East Coast. Once we're
airborne, I'm not stopping until we hit the Holy Land."

Ryan heard something beep behind him.

"Hey, Mr. Taylor, sir," Ryan said, "there's something
going on with your computer back here. The one with all
the lines on the screen."

The pilot shut off the fuel and replaced the nozzle. He
jumped into the cabin and quickly closed the door. He
had a worried look on his face as he ran to the cockpit.

"What's wrong?" Ryan said.

"We've got company," Graham said. "Better get
strapped into your seat."

"But I thought you wanted me to close the door once
Judd—"

"There's no time to pick him up," Graham said. "I just
hope Judd has the sense to throw the switch and stay
where he is."

"But you can't leave him!" Ryan said.

Ryan's words were drowned by the roar of the jet
engine as it came to life.

Loretta was glad to see Vicki. "You can use that apartment as long as you need it," she said.

"I don't want to impose," Vicki said.

"That's the last time I want to hear a thing about it," Loretta said. Vicki smiled, and the two hugged.

Verna Zee joined them at the kitchen table. Vicki could tell by the way Loretta served food and coffee that hospitality came naturally to her. She could also tell that Verna wasn't a people person. When Loretta talked, Verna fidgeted with her napkin. Verna was probably perfect at barking orders in the newsroom, but she was out of her element here over coffee and cookies.

The conversation turned to Bruce. Loretta politely asked if Verna had ever been involved in a church.

"That's a laugh," Verna said. "I've probably been to church about a dozen times my whole life. And that includes weddings and funerals.

"My dad was an atheist," Verna continued. "My mom grew up in a strict home. Her parents said it was evil to watch TV. Couldn't go to dances or drink anything stronger than Kool-Aid, and that may have been too strong, I don't know. When she got old enough, she turned her back on religion and said yes to my father. Then I came along."

"So you never went to church as a child or as an adult?" Loretta said.

"The idea of attending church was never discussed," Verna said. "Wasn't an option."

"And what do you think about God now?" Loretta said.

"I don't think about it," Verna said. "I figure if there is a God out there, a force or a being of some sort, he'll weigh my good and bad points."

"But haven't you ever been curious?" Loretta said. "Most people look for some kind of deeper meaning in life than what they see from day to day."

"I don't have time for deeper meaning," Verna said. "I do what I do and leave it at that."

"That seems kind of sad to me," Vicki said. "Mr. Williams talks about journalism as a noble profession. Seeking truth and all that. But you're saying—"

"Buck Williams and I are different people," Verna said. "If he wants to be motivated by the truth, fine. But I don't do it because a God is standing over me wagging his finger."

Vicki backed off and let Loretta take over.

"I think what Vicki is saying is that without some kind of deeper purpose, life is empty. To do what you do, you have to be motivated by more than your paycheck, right?"

"Look, I'll admit I don't live the happiest life on the planet," Verna said. "I'm skeptical. I see the glass as half empty. But I like being this way."

"What did you make of the disappearances?" Loretta said.

Verna shook her head.

Loretta took a long sip of coffee and leaned back in her chair. "Verna," she said, "I'd like to tell a skeptical journalist the true story of what happened to me. That is, if you want to hear it."

Verna looked about nervously and sighed. "I guess I don't have anything better to do," she said. "I'm listening."

Judd heard the plane engine come to life. He flipped the green switch to the "on" position as Graham had said. He shut the box, replaced the stone, and kept his head down.

The door in the side of the hill opened, and Judd spotted the plane. Then his jaw dropped. The grass in the middle of the clearing moved. As it did, a black line of asphalt appeared as far as he could see.

Judd looked left and saw the two men hop in their vehicle and speed toward the clearing. *Should I run or stay?* Judd thought. *If I hunker down here, they won't find me. But what about Ryan? I can't leave him alone.*

Judd waited until the men were a safe distance past him; then he stood and ran.

"How'd you get the runway to do that?" Ryan said.

"If you look closely at the field," Graham said, "you'll notice that part of the grass is greener than the rest. We put in artificial turf and motorized the strip so it would stay hidden. When I trip the wire at the end of the runway, it triggers the turf to return."

Ryan saw something move in the distance and let out a whoop. Judd was running like the wind.

The pilot cursed. "He should have stayed put," he said.

"He's going to make it," Ryan said.

"Not if those guys see him," Graham said, pointing to a car in the middle of the runway.

Judd ran as fast as he could up the hill, then picked up speed as he reached the clearing. He could see the stump of the tree. To his right, Mr. Stahley's Learjet whistled and picked up speed. To his left were the men in the car. He heard them honking their horn and yelling, but he focused on the tree stump.

He crossed the runway and jumped onto the stump as the jet roared toward him.

"Slow down!" Ryan yelled.

"There isn't time," the pilot screamed.

"He's right where you told him to be!" Ryan said. "It's not fair. Those other guys will get him for sure if we don't pick him up."

"Those guys will get all of us if we don't get out of here right now," Graham said.

The car sped toward Judd. He saw one man pull a gun and hold it out the window. The plane was going too fast. Suddenly it slowed and nearly came to a stop as he timed his jump and fell perfectly onto the cabin floor at Ryan's feet.

"The pilot was going to leave you," Ryan said. "I convinced him to stop."

"Stay low," Graham said from the cockpit. "These guys are armed to the teeth."

"I've never seen you run that fast before," Ryan said, as he buckled his seat belt and leaned toward the floor.

"I've never had to run that fast before," Judd said.

"Hang on," Graham said from the cockpit. He swerved off the runway and barely missed the four-wheel drive. Judd heard a bullet ping off the glass in the cockpit.

Graham smiled. "Bulletproof," he said. "But I hope he doesn't try for the fuel tank."

The car turned around and followed them. Graham had trouble getting back on the runway, but when he did, the plane shot forward.

"They're gaining on us!" Ryan shouted.

"I'm not worried about them," Graham said. "I'm worried about those guys up ahead."

Through the front of the plane Judd could see another car parked across the runway near the end.

"How are you gonna get around that?" Judd said.

"Hang on," Graham said. "We either get this rig in the air now or we're finished."

The plane accelerated and lifted its nose. Judd heard a thud beneath them, and then they were airborne.

"Yahoo!" Ryan shouted. "We're on our way to Israel."

"What was that noise?" Judd said.

"Landing gear," Graham said. "One of the tires clipped the car. We're on our way, but we might have trouble landing."

14

LORETTA began with her childhood. She had been raised in the South, where church was part of her routine.

"It was our meeting place," Loretta said. "Social and spiritual at the same time. My father taught Sunday school. My mother led Bible studies in our home. But something was missing, and I didn't realize what it was until the disappearances."

Verna rolled her eyes. "You mean that it was God," she said.

"You said a little bit ago that if there was a God, he could weigh your good and your bad," Loretta said. "I've been a member of this church for more years than I care to admit. I've served on just about every committee and group they have. If somebody had made a list of people most likely to go to heaven, I'd have been at the top, right up there with the pastor."

"And you don't think you measured up?" Verna said.

"I know I didn't measure up," Loretta said.

Verna shifted in her seat and put her hand on her chin.

"The night people vanished, I went to the church and found Bruce Barnes, one of our pastors. We knew what had happened. We watched a video the senior pastor made. That's when I understood my life was a fake. I wasn't a true Christian."

"This is all fascinating," Verna said, "but—"

"Bruce Barnes taught me everything," Loretta continued. "I learned more from him in the last two years than in the sixty before it combined. I'm not blamin' anybody but myself. My daddy had gone on before, but I lost Mama, all six of my brothers and sisters, all of their kids, their kids' husbands and wives. I lost my own children and grandchildren. Everybody.

"A couple of weeks before it happened, one of my daughters was over here with her children. I was reading one of those picture Bibles for little kids to my grandbaby. The child was no more than three years old, and she looked up at me with these huge, brown eyes and said, 'Grandma, do you have Jesus living in your heart?' I was so pleased. I was glad my grandkids were growing up in a good home. And if I'd have listened closer to what that little child was saying, I wouldn't be here today."

"If that were true, then I wouldn't have a place to stay and you wouldn't have a new sermon," Verna said.

Loretta leaned closer. "I had the sermons memorized," she said. "I didn't have a relationship with God."

When the plane made it past the East Coast, Judd and Ryan relaxed a little. Judd told Ryan he was lucky he didn't have to endure the scrunched legroom of a commercial flight. In the Stahley jet, they could both get up and walk around.

"There are soft drinks and snacks in the kitchen area," Graham said. Judd made the pilot some coffee and sat near the cockpit.

"I knew the Global Community boys underestimated how tight Max and I were when they asked me to run the Dallas flight for them," the pilot said. "I didn't know what was up, but it was clear they trusted me and not him."

"Did you find out stuff about Carpathia?" Judd said.

"Enough to make me think there was something wrong with the guy," Graham said. "Max felt that way when he was checking out his brother's death."

Ryan looked at Judd. Judd knew what he was thinking. Maxwell Stahley's brother and his wife hadn't died. They had been raptured. Judd nodded at Ryan. "What else do you know about Carpathia?" he said.

"From Max and some of the security taps we had, I know he's not too happy with that rabbi."

"What do you think Carpathia's next move will be?" Ryan said.

"The war has put him in a perfect position," Graham said. "This is what he wanted. With people vulnerable, they'll look for help. The Global Community will give it. With the one-world currency almost in place, he's moving toward a cashless society."

"Everything will be electronic?" Ryan said.

"Exactly," Graham said. "And if he taxes every transaction, you can imagine the billions he'll rake in for his New Babylon then."

"How can people let him get away with all that?" Judd said. "You know he's a fake, right?"

"I know Max had strong suspicions," Graham said. "Carpathia wants to own the major media so he can control the press. He'll replace the three ambassadors who revolted with leaders who agree with him. That'll bring the Global Community back to ten regions."

"Ten leaders!" Ryan said. "Can you believe it?"

"What?" Graham said. "Did I miss something?"

Judd wondered again if Graham could be trusted fully. A man who would risk his life for them surely needed to know *why* Nicolae Carpathia was doing these things. *But should he hear it from me?* Judd thought. *Could giving him that information prove costly in the future?*

Vicki was content to listen to Loretta's story. Chloe and Amanda arrived and joined the others at the table. When Loretta was finished, Chloe told Verna how she and Buck had met because of the Rapture, and how she, Buck, and her father had become believers in Jesus Christ.

Loretta refilled Verna's cup with coffee. Verna warmed her hands over the steam and sighed. "You guys like to gang up on people, don't you?"

Everyone laughed. Verna shook her head. "Those are interesting stories, but it seems a little wacky."

"What's so strange?" Loretta said.

"The whole thing," Verna said. "My dad warned me there'd be people like you. And not only you, but Buck is mixed up in it too. Nicolae Carpathia trusts him!"

"Verna," Chloe said, "Loretta didn't have to welcome you in here. We didn't have to offer this information. We're telling you this because we care."

Amanda defended Buck. "If there's one person on the planet you should trust, it's Buck Williams," she said.

"You and Buck have been at each other's throat for a long time," Chloe said. "He's told me about your fights."

"I think the war made our skirmishes look petty," Verna said.

"Your skirmishes *were* petty," Chloe said.

Verna stood and leaned against the wall. "I'll tell you the truth," she said. "I've been a little bit jealous of Buck's assignments. Buck is everything I wanted to be, and the more I look at his copy, the more it steams me. Compared to him, I feel like a college kid trying to put sentences together."

Amanda wandered out of the kitchen, then called for Chloe to come into the living room. Vicki followed and saw a news bulletin on television. People were crowding around an airplane tarmac.

"There comes Rayford," Amanda said. "Thank God he's OK."

The flight crew, followed by seven ambassadors, gathered around the microphones. Finally the camera pulled back to show Nicolae Carpathia descending the plane's steps. Vicki was amazed at the man's ability to strike just the right pose and expression. He appeared concerned, grave, and yet somehow purposeful and confident.

As lights flashed and cameras whirred, Carpathia resolutely approached the bank of microphones. Every network insignia on each microphone had been redesigned to include the letters GCN, the Global Community Network.

A woman broke from the crowd and ran directly for him. Security guards who stepped in her way quickly realized who she was and let her through.

"Is that Hattie?" Chloe said suddenly.

"Who's Hattie?" Verna said.

"Carpathia's fiancée," Chloe said. "It *is* her."

Vicki thought Carpathia looked embarrassed and awkward for once. He welcomed the woman to his side, but it was clear he was upset. Hattie leaned in to kiss him, and Carpathia pulled her ear to his mouth and whispered something. Hattie looked stricken.

"Poor girl," Chloe said.

Hattie tried to pull away from Carpathia, but he grabbed her wrist and kept her standing next to him at the microphones.

"It is so good to be back where I belong," Carpathia said. "It is wonderful to reunite with loved ones. My fiancée is overcome with grief, as I am, at the horrible events that began a few hours ago. This is a difficult time in which we live, and yet our horizons have never been wider, our challenges so great, our future so bright.

"Even though we have all suffered a great tragedy, I

believe we are destined for prosperity if we commit to standing together. We will stand against any enemy of peace and embrace any friend of the Global Community."

The crowd, including the press, applauded with just the right solemnity. It made Vicki sick. Besides, she was eager to see how Darrion and Mrs. Stahley were.

Ryan sensed Judd's uneasiness. The pilot needed to hear the truth, and Ryan wanted to give it. If Graham was interested, Judd could join in. If not, Ryan could play the mouthy kid. Judd flinched when Ryan first began; then he saw where Ryan was going and backed off.

Ryan told his whole story. When he got to the end and described his last meeting with Bruce, Graham was quiet.

"Must have hurt a lot to lose a friend like that," Graham said.

"More than you can know," Ryan said. "Bruce taught us a lot about the Bible and about what's going to happen in the future."

"OK, I'll bite," the pilot said. "What *is* going to happen in the future?"

"If I'm right," Ryan said, "everyone's going to go through some scary stuff. But people who don't believe are going to be in worse trouble than they could ever imagine."

"Max's brother talked to me once about this stuff," Graham said. "I didn't listen all that closely because I thought he was a kook. But if what you say is right, the end isn't that far off."

"Exactly," Ryan said.

Judd took over. Graham spent the hours throwing questions to both boys. Ryan was amazed at how much they both remembered from Bruce's teaching.

After the press conference, Vicki listened as Chloe pulled Verna aside.

"Verna, the information you know about Buck could ruin his career."

"It could ruin a lot more than that," Verna said.

"Will you keep quiet about what you know?" Chloe said.

"It depends. What do you think Buck would be willing to offer in exchange?"

"You know as well as I do Buck would never work that way," Chloe said.

"I figured that."

"As far as we're concerned, the most important thing is what you decide to do about Christ," Chloe said. "But you know our very lives depend on you protecting Buck from your bosses."

"Cameron's only boss is Carpathia," Verna said. She shook her head. "As much as I admire Carpathia and what he's been able to do for America and the world, I hate the way he controls the news. We journalists are supposed to be fair. Unbiased."

"So you'll help us then?" Chloe said.

"When will Cameron be back?" Verna said.

"Sometime over the weekend," Chloe said. "And one

more thing. Promise me you'll come to the memorial service for our pastor."

Verna bit her lip. "I don't know why I'm saying this, but OK. I'll wait till I talk with Buck, and I'll be at that meeting Sunday."

Chloe smiled, then laughed when Verna said, "I just hope the floor doesn't fall through when I walk in."

Taylor Graham landed the Learjet on a private airstrip near Tel Aviv. Judd and Ryan prepared for a rough landing. Graham masterfully landed the plane, then got out to inspect the damage.

"Doesn't look too bad," Graham said. "I know a guy who can fix it and keep quiet. We won't have to go through customs, but we'll probably run into some Global Community checkpoints on the way."

"We?" Judd said.

"If you don't mind the company," Graham said, "I'd like to go along. I might be able to help you find the people you're looking for."

Judd stammered. "We . . . wanted to do this on our own."

"Hey, I'll back off," Graham said, putting up both hands. "A little rest by the seashore sounds good to me. I'll wait to hear from you."

Judd conferred with Ryan.

"What about the checkpoints?" Judd said to Graham. "Won't the GC be looking for you?"

"I have a fake ID," Graham said. "My GC connections could come in handy, but—"

"If you're willing to follow our lead," Judd said, "we want you to come with us."

"Hey, I've followed so far," Graham said. "I'll give my mechanic a call and get a car."

Vicki checked on Darrion and Mrs. Stahley. Chaya was with them. She had brought dinner and the cell phone.

"We saw Carpathia," Mrs. Stahley said.

"Made me sick," Darrion said. "That man is the reason my father is dead."

Chaya motioned for Vicki to step outside. "I didn't want them to know this, but there's a strange car across the street all afternoon."

"You think it's GC?" Vicki said.

"I'm not sure," Chaya said. "I had Lionel create a diversion so I could come over here. The social worker, Mrs. Goodwin, called. She wants to meet with you."

"At the house?"

"I told her you were out and she seemed nervous," Chaya said. "She said she'd meet you at nine o'clock at that coffee place on Rand Road."

"I don't like leaving Mrs. Stahley and Darrion," Vicki said. "Did she say what she wants?"

"She wouldn't tell me," Chaya said. "Just to meet her there tonight."

Vicki told the Stahleys she had to go out and that they should not answer the door if anyone came. Chaya drove Vicki to the coffee shop, and they looked for Mrs. Goodwin. They parked across the street and waited until they saw the woman walk in.

Chaya stayed in the car while Vicki went inside.

"I'm glad you're here," Mrs. Goodwin said when she saw Vicki. "Let's go to my car." The woman looked upset.

Vicki didn't know if she should get in. It could be a trap. Vicki looked inside. The car was empty.

"Is there a problem?" Mrs. Goodwin said.

Vicki shook her head and climbed in.

"What did you want to talk about?" Vicki said.

The woman shook her head. "I know I shouldn't be here," she said. "Your house is being watched by the Global Community. They say you may be hiding a murder suspect."

Judd and Ryan located the garage near the hangar and found three vehicles stashed by Mr. Stahley.

"He was prepared for everything," Ryan said.

Judd chose a late-model sedan that looked like it could move fast. Graham got behind the wheel, and Judd did a double take. The man had sunglasses, a mustache, and a goatee.

"You grow hair that fast?" Ryan said.

"Another precaution," Graham said, with a hint of British accent. "From here on out, I'm Geoffrey Croton. Jolly old chap from just outside London, you know."

"I always wanted to meet somebody who talked like that," Ryan said.

"Sit back and relax," the pilot said, as he revved the engine. "We've got a long drive ahead and who knows what in between."

"Murder suspect?" Vicki said, stunned. Was this woman giving information for Vicki's own good, or was she a pawn in the hands of the Global Community? "Who am I supposed to be hiding?" Vicki said.

"I don't know exactly," Mrs. Goodwin said, "but it must be someone pretty important. I got wind of it earlier this afternoon."

"Why are you telling me this?" Vicki said.

Mrs. Goodwin looked about nervously. "Ever since that day at the school, I've thought of you. The way you handled yourself under the pressure of our questions and the way you talked about what you believe."

"That's why you're here?" Vicki said.

"Partly," Mrs. Goodwin said. "You deserve every chance I can give. First, you need to know about the call that came in about you. All calls are monitored. It was from Barrington, from a Mr. Stein."

"Chaya's dad!" Vicki gasped.

"He told us about your father's death and gave us information about your religious views, things I already knew from your answers at the hearing."

"Did he say anything about me hiding someone?" Vicki said.

"No, that was another source," Mrs. Goodwin said. "All I know is that you're in great danger." Mrs. Goodwin started the car. "I can't stay here. We need to keep moving."

―――――――――――――――――――

Vicki looked behind her to see if Chaya was following them. She thought she saw her once, but lost sight of the car in traffic.

MRS. GOODWIN drove through town and parked on a residential street. "This should be OK," the woman said.

"What are you afraid of?" Vicki said.

"The Global Community," Mrs. Goodwin said. "You have to find another place to stay tonight."

"I have one," Vicki said, "but I still don't know why you're helping me."

Mrs. Goodwin had avoided eye contact with Vicki. Now she turned in her seat and pursed her lips. "I work with troubled kids every day," Mrs. Goodwin said. "There are thousands who have been left homeless because of the disappearances. I'm sure a lot of them have fallen through the cracks."

"I wish I had," Vicki said.

"I'm glad you didn't," Mrs. Goodwin said. "I talk with some pretty tough kids. You're the first one who seemed to have more direction than the people trying to help her."

"Ma'am?" Vicki said.

"Your principal, Mrs. Jenness, and the other teacher, Mrs. Waltonen," Mrs. Goodwin said. "They put up a front that they had it together. I could tell they were scared."

"Do you know anything about Mrs. Waltonen?" Vicki said. "I saw her at Judd's graduation, but I haven't heard anything more."

Mrs. Goodwin said that Mrs. Waltonen and Coach Handlesman were both at a reeducation facility. Mrs. Goodwin said, "From the moment I heard you, I knew at some point I needed to talk with you."

Vicki held her hands open as if to say, "I'm all ears."

"I've tried to be a good person all my life," Mrs. Goodwin said. "When I was a kid, they called me Goody Two-Shoes. I was at the top of my class academically. I volunteered for social organizations. I was popular."

"You look like you could have been a cheerleader," Vicki said.

Mrs. Goodwin smiled. "Varsity squad. When I went to college, I studied to teach disabled children. I worked with Social Services and saw how much help they needed, so I took this position."

"How does that fit with me?" Vicki said.

"When you spoke of your faith," Mrs. Goodwin said, "you didn't talk about living up to rules and regulations. That's what I've always thought about religion. You do your best and hope."

"That's what most people think," Vicki said.

"I've cornered the market on helping people," Mrs. Goodwin said. "I've gone overseas to feed the starving;

I've worked at soup kitchens in the city. I've even taken
people into my home to give them a place to stay. But
I've never felt accepted by God. I've never really been sure
like you. Over the last few months, I couldn't get what
you said out of my mind. I knew I had to talk with you.
When the call came about your father, and I got wind of
what the Global Community was saying, I had to come."

"I'm glad you did," Vicki said.

"So tell me," Mrs. Goodwin said, "how can you be
sure God accepts you?"

The sun was coming up when Ryan, Judd, and Taylor
Graham neared Jerusalem. Ryan pointed each time he
saw a familiar biblical landmark. He couldn't believe they
were so close to the Sea of Galilee. Then came Nazareth.

Judd pointed out other spots he and Bruce had seen
from their earlier trips. Ryan asked questions as they
passed roads leading to Jericho, the Dead Sea, and the
Jordan River. A few miles from Jerusalem, Ryan spotted
a sign for Bethlehem.

"Don't get too excited," Graham said. "Look up ahead."

Ryan saw a line of cars and what looked like toll-
booths.

"It's a GC checkpoint," Graham said. "Let me do the
talking."

They waited in line a few minutes, then pulled
forward to a uniformed Global Community officer, who
asked the nature of their visit.

"My good man," Graham said in his cockney accent,

"we're on holiday. Seeing the sights. Enjoying the safety, if you know what I mean."

Graham laughed and handed the man the passports. "Don't suppose you'd know how we could get in to see those shouting chaps down at the Wailing Wall, would you?" he continued. "We've seen them on—"

"This is not a tourist center," the guard said, looking closely at the passports. "Why do you have the two Americans with you?"

"They're in my charge for a few days," Graham said innocently. "As I said, we're on holiday."

The guard bent down to look at Ryan and Judd. He handed the passports back. "You may go," he said.

"We passed our first test," Graham said. "Now where?"

Judd handed him an address. "We're going to the Ben-Judah house," he said. "I want to see it myself."

Vicki remembered praying that God would use what she had said in the meeting at the school. She hadn't planned on it affecting Mrs. Goodwin.

"You know about my parents and how the rest of my family disappeared," Vicki said.

"And I know about Pastor Barnes and how he helped you," Mrs. Goodwin said. "I want to *know* that God accepts my efforts. And I want to be sure about what's to come."

"God always keeps his word," Vicki said. "The prophecies in the Bible are coming true all around us. So you can be sure that what God says will happen."

"I believe that," Mrs. Goodwin said.

"The Bible says that if you confess with your mouth that Jesus is Lord and believe in your heart that God raised him from the dead, you will be saved."

"That's it?" Mrs. Goodwin said.

"That's the beginning," Vicki said.

"So all the good I've done is worthless?" Mrs. Goodwin said. "All I needed to do was believe something?"

"Somebody explained it this way," Vicki said. "Suppose everybody in the world is required to jump to the moon. That's the goal. Some people jump really high. Some people can't jump at all. Some don't even try. But no matter who they are, no one can jump to the moon."

"What's the point?"

"God is holy. He's perfect in every way. So those who want to follow him have to be perfect. But we're not. We sin. And sin separates us from God. The good things you've done are like those jumps. They were a good try, but you're never going to make it unless someone takes you there."

"And that's where Jesus comes in. . . ."

"Exactly," Vicki said. "Jesus was God in the flesh. He lived a perfect life and paid the penalty so you could be accepted by God. That's why I know you can be sure about heaven. Jesus said whoever believes in him will not die but will have eternal life."

Mrs. Goodwin looked toward the street, deep in

thought. "So if you don't do good things to get to God," she said, "why do them at all?"

"When somebody has given his life for you," Vicki said, "you want to love and serve him with everything you have."

Judd gasped when he saw the Ben-Judahs' house. It was nothing but a charred pile. Smoke still filled the air. The area was cordoned off by police tape.

"The reports about the fire were right," Ryan said.

Judd asked Graham and Ryan to stay put while he looked around.

"Be careful what you say," Graham said.

Judd walked the street, asking for anyone who spoke English. He came to the house next door where he, Nina, and Dan had slipped through a secret passage. A boy who looked about fifteen sat in a small garden with a water fountain.

"I speak English, yes," the boy said.

Judd let himself inside the gate and sat down.

The boy was average in size, but a little heavy. "You have seen the news," the boy said. "My house is famous because it's the one next to that mess."

"I'm Judd Thompson," Judd said, as he stretched out his hand.

"My name is Samuel," the boy said.

"Nina and Dan were friends of mine," Judd said.

Immediately, Samuel closed his eyes and let his head fall to his chest. "You could get in trouble mentioning their names in this neighborhood," he said. "I can't talk about them. My father does not permit it."

"I remember your house," Judd said. "Nina, Dan, and I went through the tunnel—"

Samuel put up his hand. "I must go," he said.

"Please," Judd said. "I don't believe they're dead."

Samuel shook his head. "You are wrong," he said softly.

"I've come a long way," Judd said. "Tell me what you know."

Samuel raised his voice. "I am glad they are dead! We are better off without those who would blaspheme the name of God."

Judd saw two men pass near the garden and walk on. Samuel lowered his voice. "Why should I believe you?" he said. "You could be working with the attackers. You could be one of them."

Judd knew he had to be careful, but he felt he should trust this boy. "I am a believer in Christ, as were Nina and Dan," Judd said. "For some reason, God sent me here. If you know anything that would help, I want to hear it."

Samuel looked toward the street again and leaned close, barely moving his lips. "I will do better than that," he said. "I will say good-bye to you and go inside the house. Wait a few moments, then go to the side entrance. The door will be unlocked."

Samuel stood, shook hands with Judd, and left. A few moments later Judd went inside. Judd heard a noise and found a stairwell leading to a basement.

"Welcome to my hideaway," Samuel said. "My

mother no longer lives with us, and my father has left for work. He let me stay home today."

"I'm glad," Judd said. "Now maybe I can get to the bottom of this."

Samuel led Judd to a small room with a computer and some electronic gear. Judd waited while the boy retrieved a video camera.

"You must understand that what I am about to show you must not be revealed to anyone," Samuel said.

"I understand," Judd said.

Samuel hooked up the connections. "You were right about the passageway," he said. "We allowed Nina and Dan to go through our home. But my father said the risk was getting too great. When the rabbi went on television and proclaimed Jesus as the Messiah, our whole community was under suspicion.

"I have known Nina and Dan for years," Samuel said. "I knew them before their father died and Mrs. Ben-Judah married the rabbi. It was a shock that their stepfather had betrayed the faith, but I never held them personally responsible."

"Do you know anything about what they believed?" Judd said.

"We had many talks in this very room," Samuel said. "After my father sealed up the entrance, I still met with them. They were very frightened."

"And for good reason, it sounds like," Judd said.

"I will tell you about the day it happened," Samuel said. "But I must warn you. You may not wish to hear or see what is on this videotape."

Judd nodded. "I want to see all of it," he said.

Vicki led Mrs. Goodwin in a simple prayer. "God, I know I'm a sinner and I need your forgiveness. I believe Jesus died for me, and I ask you to come into my life now. Forgive me of my sins. I don't trust in myself or my own goodness anymore but in your Son, Jesus. Amen."

Mrs. Goodwin said, "Amen."

Samuel prepared the equipment and sat in front of the video monitor. "Before I show you this, I will tell you about that day," he said.

"I'm ready," Judd said, taking a deep breath.

"I was sick that day. My father let me stay home but told me not to go outside. I couldn't sit in the garden or go onto the patio. I had nothing to do but watch television and read. In the afternoon, I sat near the window and watched traffic, waiting for my father.

"That's when I saw the van. It pulled into a parking space down the street. No one got out. The glass was tinted, so I couldn't see who it was. It just sat there. Mrs. Ben-Judah came outside for something, and I saw movement inside the van, just shadows.

"I had no idea how it would turn out," Samuel continued, "and you should not think I am able to tell the future, but I pulled out my video camera and used the zoom lens to get a better look. As I turned it on, Dr. Ben-Judah's driver pulled up. Nina and Dan got out."

Samuel paused. Judd nodded, and the boy pushed the Play button on the camera.

———————

Mrs. Goodwin drove Vicki back to the coffee shop. Headlights flashed brightly in the rearview mirror.

"Someone's getting out of that car," Mrs. Goodwin said. "Do you want me to keep going?"

"No!" Vicki said, recognizing Chaya. Chaya tapped on the driver's window. She looked angrily at Mrs. Goodwin, then at Vicki.

"Are you all right?" Chaya said.

"It's OK," Vicki said. "Mrs. Goodwin and I were just talking about some really important stuff."

Chaya looked relieved. "Good," she said, "but I need you to come with me, if you're through."

"We're finished." Mrs. Goodwin smiled. She took Vicki's hand and squeezed it. "Find a safe place and stay there." She handed her card to Vicki. "Call me at this number when you get settled. I'm sure I'll have more questions."

"How did you find us?" Vicki said when she was in the car with Chaya.

"I lost you when you turned off the main road," Chaya said. "I thought she might take you to the detention center, so I went there. I waited a while and then went to Loretta's to see if you were there. That's when I found this."

Chaya handed Vicki a piece of paper. Vicki unfolded it and saw Mrs. Stahley's elegant handwriting.

"They're gone, Vick," Chaya said. "Darrion and Mrs. Stahley are gone."

Samuel's camera work was shaky. Judd could see the unmarked van in the background. Nina and Dan got out of the car and went into their house. They passed the two guards at the front door, posted by Dr. Ben-Judah for his family's safety.

Judd felt queasy watching the video, like there should be an eerie soundtrack to go along with the pictures.

"I turned off the camera, and then it started," Samuel said. "I turned the camera back on as quickly as I could."

The tape jumped to a horrifying scene. Several hooded thugs shot automatic weapons at the house. Judd couldn't see the guards of Dr. Ben-Judah, but there was little return fire.

The camera pulled away from the window, and Judd heard the heavy breathing of Samuel saying something in Hebrew. There were shouts on the street and confusion.

"I did not know what to do," Samuel said, as Judd watched. "I froze. Then I placed the camera on the windowsill and went into the other room."

With the camera's zoom pulled back, Judd could see the entire scene. One thug stood by the van and waited. Shots rang out inside the house. More shouting. Then Mrs. Ben-Judah was dragged outside. Judd heard Nina cry out. He couldn't watch.

"What did Nina say?"

"She cried for her mother," Samuel said. "I will translate for you."

Next, Nina was brought into the street. *They're making an example of them,* Judd thought.

"Where is he?" the thug said. "Where is the rabbi?"

"I will not betray my father!" Nina screamed.

"Tell us now!" the man screamed back.

Such courage, Judd thought. In the face of death, Nina would not give them any information. Dan was dragged out last. A man ran to the van and then carried a container inside the house.

"Spare your life," the thug sneered at Dan. "Tell us where your father is."

Dan stammered and looked into the face of his hooded captor.

"Now! Before it is too late!" the man screamed.

"Let me see your face," Dan finally said.

The man was standing over Dan and facing the camera. He lifted his mask and bent low. Judd could see the man had a heavy, black beard and a mustache. "Now, tell me! Where is Tsion Ben-Judah?"

Dan spat in the man's face.

"You insolent—"

"I would rather die than betray my father!" Dan said.

Those were Dan's last words.

A crackling sound grew in the background. One of the thugs yelled, "The rabbi is not inside. What now?"

"To the university," another said.

As the van pulled away, Judd heard a siren in the distance. Neighbors waited a few moments, then rushed to look at the three lifeless bodies. Then the screen went blank.

Judd could not speak. The horror of what he had seen was too much.

"No matter what one thinks of their beliefs," Samuel finally said, "they died honorably."

"They were treated like animals," Judd choked.

"I do not know where the rabbi is," Samuel said. "Maybe his driver saw what happened and found him before the others. No one knows where he took him. On the news, the driver claims he knows nothing."

"The report I heard was true," Judd said. "My friends are dead. We came here for nothing."

"I have not been able to show this to anyone," Samuel said. "Not even my own father. I do not know what to do with it."

Judd heard the front door open, and a man called for Samuel.

"Here he is now," the boy said.

Judd went to the side door. Samuel ran after him. "Take this with you," Samuel whispered, shoving the small videotape into Judd's jacket pocket.

16

WHAT'S *taking Judd so long?* Ryan thought, as Taylor Graham snored. When Judd finally returned to the car he looked worried. Ryan woke the pilot, who suggested they find a hotel. They checked into the King David and found their room.

"I'm gonna crash for a couple hours," Graham said. "Wake me when you need me."

Ryan sat with Judd. He had never seen his friend so depressed. Judd flicked on CNN, but Ryan turned it off with the remote.

"Talk to me," Ryan said.

"Why did we come here?" Judd said flatly. "And with a guy we've just met. It was crazy."

"You know we had to check on the Ben-Judahs," Ryan said. "God wanted us here."

"Maybe he did; maybe he didn't," Judd said. "Looks like a wasted trip to me."

"What did you see in that house?" Ryan said.

Judd told him about the video. Ryan cringed when he heard the details. Judd pulled out the cassette.

"No one sees this, and no one gets access to it," Judd said. "I'm putting it in the safe downstairs."

"Then what?" Ryan said.

Judd shrugged. "As long as we're here, you might as well see the sights," he said. "And the most impressive one is at the Wailing Wall."

"What do you mean they're gone?" Vicki shouted. "I told them to stay put."

"Read the note," Chaya said.

Vicki couldn't believe what she saw. Mrs. Stahley's beautiful handwriting cut Vicki to the heart.

Dear Friends, the note read, *Darrion and I have appreciated your concern and sacrifice. You have risked your lives for our safety and we thank you. However, our very presence puts you in danger. We cannot do that any longer. We believe God will protect us and you. Thank you for your kindness. Sincerely, Louise Stahley.*

"They must have overheard me when I told you the house was being watched," Chaya said.

Vicki shook her head. "I hope she knows what she's doing," she said.

"Where do you think they went?" Chaya said.

"I don't know," Vicki said. "I just hope we can find them before the Global Community does."

Judd secured the videotape at the front desk. He placed the key in his wallet. Near the elevator Ryan tapped Judd on the shoulder and nodded toward the front of the hotel. Judd saw Buck Williams.

"He's traveling as light as we are," Ryan said.

Buck was shocked to see Judd and Ryan. "You're taking a big chance," Buck said.

Judd explained what they had learned about the Ben-Judah family. "Have you heard anything from Dr. Ben-Judah?" Judd said.

"Nothing firsthand," Buck said. "I just came from the airport and met one of the rabbi's friends. He said Rabbi Ben-Judah called him once and said that I would know where to start looking."

"Where's that?" Ryan said.

"No way," Buck said, shaking his head. "You two are out of this. The authorities are even trying to pin the murders of his family on the rabbi."

"That's loony!" Ryan said.

"I agree," Buck said, "but the people out to get Tsion will stop at nothing. His driver was killed in a car bombing. That's why I'm saying you two should get back to the States."

"If that's so," Judd said, "they're following you right now."

"I've taken precautions," Buck said. "I'm registered

here under the name of Herb Katz. I'm going to my room to make a few calls and get some sleep. I'll see you when I get back home."

Vicki and Chaya went back to Bruce's house. Lionel was still there, and the two brought him up to speed.

"If Mr. Stahley had a secret hangar for his plane," Lionel said, "you can bet he had another secret house or cabin somewhere."

"Still," Vicki said, "you have to believe Mrs. Stahley will try to get back to her place for the documents she talked about."

"There's no chance," Lionel said. "The Global Community goons will be crawling all over the place. Plus, we've got problems of our own."

"What?"

"School is back in session starting tomorrow," Lionel said.

Vicki thought a minute. "That might not be a problem," she said.

Judd and Ryan took turns napping in the lobby of the hotel so they wouldn't miss Buck. Near sundown, Buck briskly walked to a cabstand. Judd and Ryan followed.

Judd paid the cabbie when they reached the Wailing Wall. They saw Buck walk toward a wrought-iron fence, where the two witnesses prophesied.

The two men called themselves Moishe and Eli, and

truly they seemed to have come from another time and another place. They wore ragged, burlap-like robes. They were barefoot with leathery, dark skin. Both had long, dark gray hair and unkempt beards. They looked strong and had bony joints and long-muscled arms and legs. Anyone who dared get close to them smelled smoke. Those who dared attack them had been killed. Several had rushed them with automatic weapons, only to seem to hit an invisible wall and drop dead on the spot. Others had been overcome by fire that had come from the witnesses' mouths.

They preached almost constantly in the language of the Bible, and what they said angered the devout Jews. They preached about Jesus Christ, proclaiming him the Messiah, the Son of God.

Judd had seen the witnesses with Bruce. Hearing their voices again made a chill go down his spine. Ryan was excited at the sight and drank it in. As usual, a huge crowd had gathered, though people kept their distance.

This evening the witnesses were doing as they had done every day since the signing of the treaty between Israel and Nicolae Carpathia. They were proclaiming the terrible Day of the Lord. They acknowledged Jesus Christ as "the Mighty God, the Everlasting Father, and the Prince of Peace. Let no other man anywhere call himself the ruler of this world! Any man who makes such a claim is not the Christ but the Antichrist, and he shall surely die! Woe unto anyone who preaches another gospel! Jesus is the only true God, maker of heaven and earth!"

Judd pointed out all the different people of various

races and cultures in the crowd. "They're understanding the message in their own language," he said.

"Unbelievable," Ryan said.

Judd saw Buck edge farther into the crowd of about three hundred. Suddenly, both preachers stopped and moved forward toward the fence. The crowd seemed to step back in fear.

"I think they see him," Ryan said. "They're both staring straight at Buck."

Without gesturing or moving, Eli began to preach. "He who has ears to hear, let him hear! Do not be afraid, for I know that you seek Jesus, who was crucified. He is not here, for He is risen, as He said."

Judd was riveted. Moishe stepped forward and looked directly toward Buck. "Do not be afraid, for I know whom you seek. He is not here."

Eli again: "Go quickly and tell His disciples that Christ is risen from the dead!"

Moishe, still staring at Buck: "Indeed, He is going before you into Galilee. There you will see Him. Behold, I have told you."

The witnesses stood and stared silently for so long, unmoving, it was as if they had turned to stone. The crowd grew nervous, and some left. Some waited to hear the witnesses speak again, but they remained still. Judd and Ryan moved farther to the back so Buck wouldn't see them. Soon, Buck was left standing alone, with the two witnesses still staring at him. The witnesses seemed not even to breathe. No blink, no twitch. Their faces almost glowed with the final rays of sunlight. Neither opened his mouth, and yet Judd heard, plain as day in English, "He who has ears to hear, let him hear."

"What's Buck saying to them?" Ryan said.

"I can't hear," Judd said. "Let's move closer."

Buck asked the witnesses, "If I came back here later tonight, might I learn more?"

Moishe backed away from the fence and sat on the pavement, leaning against a wall. Eli gestured and spoke aloud, "Birds of the air have nests," he said, "but the Son of Man has nowhere to lay his head."

"I don't understand," Buck said. "Tell me more."

"He who has ears to hear—"

Judd thought Buck looked frustrated. "I'll come back at midnight," Buck said, interrupting Eli. "I'm pleading for your help."

Eli backed away. "Lo, I am with you always, even to the end of the age."

Judd and Ryan hid as Buck left.

"Was that something, or what?" Ryan said. "Those were the words Jesus spoke to his followers. You think they'll actually help him find Rabbi Ben-Judah?"

"If anyone can help him," Judd said, "those two can."

"You're not thinking about reviving the *Underground*, are you?" Lionel said.

Vicki smiled. "It's a perfect chance to invite those who haven't heard the message yet."

"Wait," Chaya said, "I'm not following either of you."

Vicki told Chaya about the *Underground* and what

they had been through with the secret newspaper. Vicki and Judd had paid a great price for their involvement. Since the graduation ceremony in the spring, the *Underground* hadn't made an appearance.

"And you want to invite people to do what?" Chaya said.

"Come to Bruce's funeral," Vicki said. "If we get started on the copy now, we can get it into their hands by Friday. The service is on Sunday, and you know it's going to be evangelistic."

"But if they catch you—," Lionel said.

"I'm past worrying about that," Vicki said. "We're in a war for people's souls now. We can't afford to be careful."

Judd and Ryan didn't want to go back to the hotel. They would let Graham sleep and wait until Buck returned. They wandered the old city, visiting the sights of the ancient world. The newly rebuilt temple was lit up to look like something in a three-dimensional picture show. It seemed to hover on the horizon.

"You know what Bruce said about that place," Ryan said. "One day Nicolae Carpathia will sit in that new temple and proclaim himself God."

Judd shivered. "I wouldn't want to be near that guy for a million bucks," he said.

Judd showed Ryan the Garden of Gethsemane, the Garden Tomb, and the Mount of Olives, where Jesus would return in triumph.

"It won't be too long," Ryan said. "One day we're

going to be able to sit down with Bruce and get answers
to all the questions we've ever had."

Judd and Ryan ate dinner, then returned to the
Wailing Wall before midnight. They came upon a small
group of sailors strolling past the fence.

"Where are the two weirdos?" one sailor said.

"Over that way," another said.

Buck drove up in a cab and hurried toward them.
Ryan and Judd stepped out of sight. Buck was carrying his
overnight bag.

"Looks like he's on the move," Ryan said.

Buck hung back and waited for the sailors to leave.
When he moved forward, Eli and Moishe raised their
heads and looked directly at him. Buck walked to the
fence. He whispered something to the witnesses, and Eli
said, "He who has ears to hear—"

Judd inched closer and listened as Buck said, "I know
that, but I—"

"You would dare interrupt the servants of the Most
High God?" Eli said.

"Forgive me," Buck said.

Moishe spoke. "You must first communicate with the
one who loves you."

Judd gave Ryan a puzzled look.

"What does he mean?" Ryan said.

Before Judd could answer, Buck's cell phone rang.
Judd heard Buck say "Chloe," and understood. These
witnesses knew so much.

Buck got off the phone. Moishe and Eli huddled and
seemed to be whispering. They approached the fence.

Suddenly the two began shouting at the top of their lungs. Judd and Ryan stepped back, startled, then listened as Eli and Moishe traded off quoting verses.

"And it shall come to pass in the last days, says God," they shouted, "that I will pour out My Spirit on all flesh; your sons and your daughters shall prophesy, your young men shall see visions, your old men shall dream dreams."

The men looked at Buck.

"What's that all about?" Ryan whispered.

"Shh, listen," Judd said.

The witnesses continued: "And on My menservants and on My maidservants I will pour out My Spirit in those days; and they shall prophesy. I will show wonders in heaven above and signs in the earth beneath: blood and fire and vapor of smoke. The sun shall be turned into darkness, and the moon into blood, before the coming of the great and awesome day of the Lord. And it shall come to pass that whoever calls on the name of the Lord shall be saved."

Buck picked up his bag and moved closer. Judd heard others in the crowd warn him. "Better not do that. You'll regret it!" someone said.

Buck whispered something, and Eli spoke softly. Buck retreated to the crowd. "Did they hurt you, son?" a man said. Buck shook his head.

Moishe began to preach in a loud voice: "Now after John was put in prison, Jesus came to Galilee, preaching the gospel of the kingdom of God, and saying 'The time is fulfilled, and the kingdom of God is at hand. Repent, and believe in the gospel.'

210

"And as He walked by the Sea of Galilee, He saw Simon and Andrew his brother casting a net into the sea; for they were fishermen. Then Jesus said to them, 'Follow Me, and I will make you become fishers of men.'

"They immediately left their nets and followed Him."

Ryan tugged on Judd's arm. "It's like they're speaking in a biblical code," he said. "They're telling Buck where to look for the rabbi, but nobody knows it but Buck."

Buck drifted from the crowd, lugged his bag to a short taxi line, and climbed into the back of a small cab. "Can a fella get a boat ride up the Jordan River into Lake Tiberius at this time of night?" Judd heard Buck ask the driver.

"Well, sir, to tell you the truth," the cabbie said, "it's a lot easier coming the other way. But, yes, there are motorized boats heading north. And some do run in the night."

Judd and Ryan watched as the driver sped off. "Looks like we're not gonna follow this time," Judd said.

"Why not?"

"I'm almost out of cash," Judd said. "Besides, I think Buck's right. We need to get back home."

Judd headed for a cab and noticed Ryan wasn't budging. "It'd be different if Bruce were here," Ryan said.

"How?" Judd said.

"He wouldn't give up this easy," Ryan said. "God brought us here for a reason. I don't know what it is, but if those two guys can help Buck find somebody, they might be able to help us figure it out."

Judd looked at the witnesses. His first reaction was to tell Ryan to cut the guilt trip. But he knew being in Israel was a dream come true for Ryan.

"All right," Judd said. "Let's see what they say."

Ryan was glad Judd had changed his mind. The crowd was much smaller as they approached. The witnesses were silent. Ryan boldly made his way to the front, and Judd followed.

"This is the chance of a lifetime," Ryan whispered. "I never thought I'd see them this close."

"Be careful, boys," an older man said. "They can breathe fire."

Ryan turned and looked at the man. He had graying hair and wore the clothing of a religious man. "Thank you, sir," Ryan said, "but we don't have anything to fear from these men. They're preaching the truth about Jesus. I believe what they say. He died, was buried, and rose again on the third day. He's alive right now. Those who believe in him don't have to worry about these witnesses. . . ."

A murmur went up in the crowd. People around Ryan stepped back as if they had seen a ghost. When Ryan turned, he saw both witnesses at the fence, looking straight at him.

17

RYAN didn't know what to say. The two witnesses stared at him. Judd stood at Ryan's side.

Eli was the first to speak. "Blessed are those who mourn," he said.

Ryan's eyes widened. "You're talking about my friend, Bruce, right?" he said.

A single tear fell onto the leathery face of the man at the fence. "Blessed are those who mourn," he said again, "for they shall be comforted."

Moishe spoke. "The kingdom of heaven is like a mustard seed, which a man took and sowed in his field, which indeed is the least of all the seeds. . . ." When Moishe said the word *least*, he paused, looked at Ryan, then continued. "But when it is grown it is greater than the herbs and becomes a tree, so that the birds of the air come and nest in its branches."

Eli again: "Assuredly, I say to you, unless you are converted and become as little children, you will by no means enter the kingdom of heaven."

Ryan was awestruck. Judd stood with his mouth open. The crowd had retreated, and the boys were alone with the witnesses.

Eli and Moishe looked at Judd with their piercing eyes. Their lips did not move, but Judd heard them distinctly.

"The Lord is slow to anger and great in power, and will not at all acquit the wicked."

Will not acquit the wicked, Judd thought. God was telling them that he would never let guilty people go unpunished.

Judd and Ryan were quiet on the trip back to the hotel. Their experience had left them speechless. A note from Taylor Graham lay on Judd's pillow.

You two obviously don't need me hanging around. I found an airstrip close to Jerusalem. Call me on my cell phone when you're ready to leave.

"Should we have told him where we went?" Ryan said.

"I'd rather have it this way," Judd said. "I just hope he doesn't take off and leave us."

Judd and Ryan both slept hard through the morning and into the afternoon. When Judd awoke, he found Ryan watching the news. Ryan turned it off and asked to talk.

"The first thing the witnesses said to me was clear," Ryan said. "They knew I was mourning Bruce. It's the part about the mustard seed I don't understand."

"I don't think they were trying to tell you something

214

as much as report it," Judd said. "You've got a lot of faith for a young person. God can use you or anybody who puts their trust in him."

"That makes sense," Ryan said. "What about that stuff about God being slow to get angry?"

"At first I was scared that I'd done something bad," Judd said. "But I can't help but think it has something to do with the tape."

"I don't get it."

"Maybe God is going to judge the people who killed the rabbi's family."

"And he's going to use us to help do it?" Ryan said.

"Exactly," Judd said.

"You're not thinking of going to the authorities with the tape?" Ryan said.

"I know it sounds dumb, but—"

"It's worse than dumb," Ryan said. "It's suicide. If the murderers are just religious zealots, you're fine. But if they're connected with the Global Community, they'll want that tape. And then they'll want to do away with anyone who's seen it."

"The Ben-Judahs were my friends," Judd said. "They didn't deserve to be killed."

"You want revenge," Ryan said.

"I don't!" Judd said. "I want to do what God wants me to."

Judd called Vicki to check in. He was aghast that Mrs. Stahley and Darrion were gone. He promised to get in touch with Taylor Graham to see if he had any ideas where they might have gone.

"I wanted to call you earlier," Vicki said. "Something really strange happened to Loretta."

"Fill me in," Judd said.

"I was at Loretta's house with Chloe and Amanda. Loretta called and said she was working alone at the church, and she had an urge to pray for Buck. She said she was so overcome with emotion that she stood up, then got dizzy and fell to her knees. Once she was kneeling, she realized she wasn't dizzy but was just praying for Buck."

"Weird," Judd said. "Have you heard anything from him?"

"Just that he's still looking for the rabbi," Vicki said.

Judd told Vicki about seeing Buck the previous night. "Some strange things are happening over here," he said. "It might just be me, but God seems to be working in more direct and dramatic ways all the time."

"He's about to work in more dramatic ways here," Vicki said. She explained their plan with the *Underground.*

"Don't take any unnecessary risks," Judd said.

Vicki laughed. "I could say the same to you."

Ryan fought with Judd about the tape, while Judd tried to call Taylor Graham.

"I don't see how God could be saying two totally different things to two people," Ryan said. "I've got a feeling that we should head over to the rabbi's office and have a look around. Maybe Buck hasn't found him yet and we can help."

"This is what I've decided," Judd said. "If you don't want to help, you don't have to."

Ryan rolled his eyes. "Pulling seniority again," he said.

"It's late," Judd said. "First thing in the morning we'll head to the police station."

Vicki looked over the *Underground* and smiled. It had been a long time since she had been involved in writing and producing the paper.

The front page dealt with the bombings and what was predicted in the Bible. The story continued inside with specific prophecies that had already been fulfilled. On the back was an invitation to Bruce's funeral Sunday morning. The kids scanned in a picture of Bruce.

Vicki wrote: *He was the only pastor on the church staff to be left behind. But the disappearances of most of his congregation changed his life. The prophecies that appear in this edition were taught by Bruce Barnes, but he left many more. Hear his story and what he believes is coming after World War III Sunday morning at New Hope Village Church.*

"You think they'll come?" Lionel said.

"Wouldn't you want to know what's coming next from somebody who had nailed the future so accurately?" Vicki said.

Lionel nodded. "How are we going to get the paper inside the school? You know how tight security is."

"We have one day to figure it out," Vicki said.

Ryan didn't want to hold Judd's passport or wait outside the police station, but Judd was set on the idea. Ryan was glad Judd had compromised with him and left the tape in the vault at the hotel.

"You wait here and if anything happens, call Taylor Graham right away," Judd said.

"As if that's going to help," Ryan said.

"He was probably out of range when I called," Judd said.

"On a satellite phone?" Ryan scoffed. "He didn't answer last night or this morning. He's probably on his way back home without us."

Ryan stood by the door and watched as Judd strode through the door to the police headquarters.

Judd got nowhere being polite. He was an American in a foreign country. He stood in one line, then was told to wait in another. Finally he grabbed the arm of an officer going by. The man looked at him sternly.

"I have information about the murders of the rabbi's family," Judd said.

The man immediately took Judd into a corner office. Judd waited until a police captain arrived.

"Why did you come to our country?" the man said.

"Friends," Judd said. "The Ben-Judah family. I wanted to be sure the reports were right."

"Their bodies are in the morgue now," the man said. "Would you like to see them?"

"No," Judd said. "I know they're dead. But I saw something. The face of one of the murderers."

"And how could you have seen that?"

"First, I need to know that you're serious about finding the murderers," Judd said.

The man stood and picked up a phone. "We are serious," he said. He spoke softly into the phone, then put it down. "I am so serious about this matter that I want you to talk to the people heading up the investigation."

"Who's that?" Judd said.

"The Global Community," the man said. "They have asked us to give them any leads we might find."

Outside, Ryan saw a Global Community van pull up to the police station. *If I don't try now, I might never see Judd again,* Ryan thought. He walked confidently into the station and spotted Judd sitting in a holding area. Ryan finally got Judd's attention but didn't dare go close to him.

Judd's eyes darted to the GC officials, then back to Ryan. Judd pointed to his chair.

"What?" Ryan said.

Judd didn't have time to explain. Two men led him outside. He was careful not to look at Ryan.

Ryan waited a moment, then rushed to the chair. It was empty. He moved the cushion. Underneath was the key to the lockbox at the hotel. He grabbed it and ran outside. The van had already pulled away and was lost in traffic.

Please, God, Ryan prayed, *show me what to do.*

Vicki and Lionel packed the *Underground* the night before and were ready the next morning. Vicki called her friend

Shelly, and the two had stayed up late sewing a special pouch into the lining of Lionel's and Vicki's jackets. They hoped that the GC monitors who checked every backpack and duffel bag wouldn't notice.

At school, Vicki and Lionel walked through different entrances. When she reached her locker, Vicki took off her jacket and unzipped the pouch. She took the stack of pages and quickly placed it in the bin where school newspapers were distributed.

At lunch she met with Lionel. "I had a close call at the door," Lionel said. "The metal detector went off when I went through, and they made me take off my backpack and jacket and walk through again."

"They didn't find anything?" Vicki said.

"I thought for sure they'd feel how heavy the jacket was, but they gave it back and didn't say a thing. A bunch of kids in my third-period class had copies."

"Same here," Vicki said. "I wonder what the principal will do this time?"

In Vicki's next class, Mrs. Jenness, the principal, made an announcement condemning the illegal paper. The school secretary then interrupted Vicki's class.

"Would you please send Vicki Byrne to Mrs. Jenness's office?" the secretary said.

Ryan made his way back to the King David Hotel and gave the key to the man at the front desk.

"One moment," the man said.

He returned with the tape. As Ryan walked out,

another man called after him. The man had a phone to his ear. "Yes, we just gave him something," the man said into the phone.

Ryan briskly walked toward the revolving door.

"All right, we'll keep him here until you arrive," the man said.

Ryan ran.

"Stop him!" the man yelled. Then Ryan heard on the loudspeaker, "Security to the front lobby!"

A doorman stepped in front of him. Ryan faked left, then ran through the automatic handicapped exit. The doorman gave chase, but Ryan was too fast.

He kept running, not knowing where he was or where he was going. He knew Judd's life was at stake if the tape wound up in the hands of the Global Community.

Ryan ran through crowded streets. Once he thought he saw a security patrol nearby, but he ducked inside a building and hid in the bathroom. When he came out he realized he was in the university where Tsion Ben-Judah taught.

He looked in the directory and found the rabbi's office number. He ran to the third floor and saw the door covered with police investigation tape. A guard sat in an adjacent office.

"May I help you?" the guard said.

"Just looking around," Ryan said. "Whoever had this office must have done something really bad."

"He murdered his family," the guard said. "We're keeping watch in case he tries to come back."

Ryan wandered down the hall, feeling something

strange. Maybe it wasn't an accident that he had stumbled into the university. Maybe there was something in here he needed. He found an empty classroom and camped in the corner. He would wait until nightfall. He had to get inside the rabbi's office.

Judd was placed in a holding cell. He knew the Global Community officials wanted to scare him. When they finally brought Judd upstairs, he gave them his name and where he was from.

"Where is your passport?" the GC officer said.

"It's probably back at the hotel," Judd said.

"And where is the item you had locked in the hotel safe?"

"What item?" Judd said.

The man tilted his head and looked over his glasses. "Mr. Thompson, we can make this as easy or as difficult as you wish."

"I don't know where it is," Judd said. "That's the truth."

"Who is in possession of it?"

"A friend."

"Would this be your young friend?" The man described Ryan.

"I don't understand," Judd said. "I come here to tell you about a murder you're investigating, and now I'm the bad guy. What's up with that?"

The man nodded to the guard, and Judd was taken back to his cell. Another guard came with some dinner a few hours later. Judd wondered about Ryan. Maybe Buck had been right. Maybe he had endangered both of them needlessly.

After midnight the guards brought a bearded man into the next cell and threw him on the cot. The man was bleeding and had dark bruises on his face.

Ryan waited until it was dark, then slipped into the wing where the rabbi's office was located. He heard the guard snoring at the end of the hall. He placed a stack of books on the railing of the stairwell and attached a spool of thread he had found in a utility closet. He backed into the bathroom and pulled hard on the thread. The books clattered down the stairs, echoing through the massive building. A moment later he heard the guard's keys jangling.

"Who's there?" the guard shouted.

Ryan slipped past the secretary's desk and into the rabbi's office. Ryan gasped. Books lay on the floor. Maps and artifacts had been shredded. Old parchment with funny writing had been stomped on.

The drawers of the rabbi's desk had been ripped out, the contents strewn on the floor. The lock on the middle drawer had been shot through. Framed awards and citations lay broken on top of the desk.

"It would kill Dr. Ben-Judah to see this," Ryan muttered.

He spotted something in the rubble. A small, round picture frame had escaped the thugs. In the picture were the rabbi's wife and their two children. Ryan smiled and put the picture in his pocket.

Ryan heard the jangling of keys outside. He hid under what was left of the rabbi's desk.

Mrs. Jenness looked sternly at Vicki. "I had hoped this foolishness would stop with what happened to your friend last year."

"I saw the newspaper in the bin," Vicki said. "Why do you think I had anything to do with it?"

Mrs. Jenness shook her head. "Don't play innocent this time," she said. "We know about your father, or at least your adoptive father."

Vicki fumed.

"We received a call from an anonymous parent who told us about his death," Mrs. Jenness continued. "I'm sorry for your loss. But no matter what emotions you're going through, you must abide by the rules."

Vicki remained silent.

"I don't think you want us to go further up the ladder with this," Mrs. Jenness said. "You know what happened last year. If you'll confess, we'll figure out something, taking into account your . . . state of mind."

Vicki knew if she confessed, Mrs. Jenness would have grounds to send her back to Northside Detention Center.

"I won't confess," Vicki said. "You'll have to call whoever you need to call."

The next morning Judd was again interrogated.

"I suppose you've had time to think about your situation," the man said.

"I'm an American citizen," Judd said. "I came here to

find out about my friends. I wanted to give information to the authorities, but I don't think I can trust you."

"You are a citizen of the Global Community," the man corrected. "You only have the rights granted by such. We know who killed the woman and the children. We do not need your help to solve this crime. As a matter of fact, there is the man now."

The officer pointed a remote-control device to a television in the corner. A picture of Rabbi Tsion Ben-Judah flashed on the screen. The Global Community Network News reported that a Michael Shorosh had been arrested in connection with the harboring of a fugitive from justice. "Global Community spokesmen say that Ben-Judah, formerly a respected scholar and clergyman, apparently became a radical fundamentalist. They point to this sermon he delivered just a week ago as evidence that he overreacted to a New Testament passage and was later seen by several neighbors slaughtering his own family."

Judd watched in horror as the news ran a tape of Tsion speaking at a huge rally in a filled stadium in Larnaca, on the island of Cyprus. "You'll note," the newsman said, as the tape was stopped, "the man on the platform behind Dr. Ben-Judah has been identified as Michael Shorosh. In a raid on his Jericho home shortly after midnight, peacekeeping forces found personal photos of Ben-Judah's family and identification papers from both Ben-Judah and an American journalist, Cameron Williams. Williams's connection to the case has not been determined."

Judd recognized the man named Michael as the

person in the cell next to him. In the photo on television he had no cuts or bruises.

The tape showed Dr. Ben-Judah reading from Matthew. The verses, of course, had been taken out of context. "Whoever denies Me before men, him I will also deny before My Father who is in heaven.

"Do not think that I came to bring peace on earth. I did not come to bring peace but a sword. For I have come to 'set a man against his father, a daughter against her mother, and a daughter-in-law against her mother-in-law'; and 'a man's enemies will be those of his own household.' He who loves father or mother more than Me is not worthy of Me. And he who loves son or daughter more than Me is not worthy of Me."

The news reporter said solemnly, "This was recorded just a few days before the rabbi murdered his own wife and children in broad daylight."

MRS. JENNESS set up an appointment to meet with
Vicki and a social worker that evening. "I may need to
have someone from the Global Community present as
well," Mrs. Jenness said.

"I'll be there," Vicki said.

Vicki was unable to reach Mrs. Goodwin before the
meeting. She wasn't surprised to see her walk in with a
representative of Global Community Social Services later
that evening.

"Mrs. Jenness," Mrs. Goodwin said, "as I told you on
the phone, we've been working on Vicki's case for a few
days. The evidence you've submitted doesn't implicate
her, except that Bruce Barnes was her adoptive father."

"Well, I—"

The social worker spoke up. "Have you made a list of
students who attend that particular church?" the man
said.

227

"Well, no, but—"

"I don't mean to tell you how to do your job," the man continued, "but I think I speak for the office on this. We can't waste our time on frivolous accusations such as this."

Mrs. Jenness looked stunned. Vicki thought Mrs. Goodwin would stick up for her, but she didn't count on this much support.

Mrs. Goodwin and the man stood to leave. Mrs. Jenness apologized, then glared at Vicki. "This is the last time you'll embarrass me like that," she seethed.

When Judd wouldn't talk, he was taken to his cell. The man named Michael was gone, but was roughly returned a few minutes later. Judd pulled close to the bars and whispered. The man looked at Judd, then lay back again.

Michael looked awful. One eye was swollen shut. "I'm a friend of Buck Williams," Judd said.

Michael's voice was low and gravelly. "The Global Community can do better than this. I told you already, I do not know where the rabbi is."

"I'm not one of them," Judd said. He tried to explain who he was and why he was in Israel, but Michael wouldn't listen. "I was there when the witnesses talked with Buck," Judd said in desperation.

Michael sat up. "What did the witnesses say?"

"They quoted verses about going into Egypt," Judd said. "Buck got in a cab and was looking for someone who had a boat who could take him up the Jordan River."

Michael slid close to the bars and looked at Judd with his good eye. "You are not a plant by the Global Community?" he said.

"I'm a friend of Buck's from America," Judd said.

"And you are looking for the rabbi as well?" Michael said.

"I came here to find out about his family," Judd said. Judd briefly told Michael about his trip and discovering the truth about the Ben-Judah family.

"You must be very careful what you say," Michael said. "You are a believer?"

"I am," Judd said.

Michael sat back against the bars. Judd saw a trace of a smile. "We are like Paul and Silas now, except I do not sing very well," Michael said. "Moishe and Eli are my mentors. I became a believer under their preaching and that of Tsion."

"Are you an evangelist?" Judd said.

"In the manner of Paul the apostle, according to Dr. Ben-Judah. He says there are 144,000 of us around the world, all with the same assignment that Moishe and Eli have: to preach Christ as the only everlasting Son of the Father."

"Tell me about Dr. Ben-Judah," Judd said.

"An escape plan has been in place for some time. For months we thought the guarding of his family was unnecessary. The zealots wanted him. At the first sign of a threat or an attack, we sent to Tsion's office a car so small it appeared only the driver could fit in it. Tsion lay on the floor of the backseat, curled into a ball, and covered himself with a blanket. He was raced to my boat, and I took him upriver."

"He knows about his family, right?"

"Yes, and you can imagine how awful that is for him. On the boat I could hear his loud sobbing over the sound of the engine throughout the entire voyage. I can still hear it in this prison cell."

"What about Buck?" Judd said. "Are they together?"

"They are," Michael said. Michael described his meeting with Buck. "I had killed two enemies of God who were searching for the rabbi. I was prepared to kill your friend. He was more than a little surprised when I pointed a high-powered weapon at his head. After he answered my questions, I showed him where we had hidden Tsion."

"How did you know he was for real and not just a journalist looking for a great story?" Judd said.

"I had my doubts," Michael said, "but when I asked him to describe the fulfilled prophecies of the Messiah, I knew it was more than just a story for him. He was the deliverer."

"Buck?" Judd said.

"God spoke through the two witnesses and assured us a deliverer would come. He would know the rabbi. He would know the witnesses. He would know the messianic prophecies. And most of all, he would know the Lord's Christ. Buck fit the description perfectly."

"What's Buck gonna do with the rabbi?" Judd said.

"He has to get him out of the country," Michael said.

"But the rabbi has to be one of the most recognizable

people in Israel," Judd said. "How in the world will Buck get him through customs?"

Michael smiled. "How else? Supernaturally."

Ryan picked up the phone that was still on the floor and dialed the secretary's desk. He heard the guard jump when it rang, then the deep, "Hello?"

Ryan spoke in a whisper. "There's somebody in the stairwell," he said. "A guy with a gun!"

"Who is this?" the guard said.

Ryan hung up. The guard's chair scraped the floor. The man unsnapped his holster. Ryan crept to the hall and saw the guard peeking over the railing. Ryan went down the other stairwell.

"Stop!" the guard called after him, but Ryan was already into the street.

Judd and Michael talked like old friends. They were fellow prisoners, united in their belief in Christ.

"I do not want to tell you too much," Michael said. "If the Global Community thinks you know something about Tsion, they will get you to talk."

"Are Buck and Tsion safe?"

"When you are in the will of God, there is no weapon formed against you that can prosper," Michael said. "God rides with Tsion and Buck. I believe they will be saved."

Judd sat back against the cell bars. Just talking with

Michael was worth the trip. But how did God want to use him? Why did he have him here?

"I have been thinking about the verses Tsion said were comforting to him," Michael said. "The joy of the Lord is my strength." Michael repeated the phrase again and again. Judd thought about joy. Behind bars it took on a different meaning. It wasn't just being happy and smiling all the time. It was deeper. Joy came from believing God is in control and knows what he is doing.

"Our God is working his will through Tsion and Buck," Michael said. "Buck told me of a dream. That he would leave through Egypt rather than through Israel. And as we were praying together, God made his will clear to us."

Michael bent forward, inches from Judd's face, and said, "I believe my life is destined to be short. My assignment is to preach in Israel, where the real Messiah is hated. But if God is for us, who can be against us?"

Judd shivered. He was face-to-face with one of the most courageous Christians on the planet. It made him want to exhibit courage as well.

"My only concern now is for my loved ones," Michael said. "I have a wife and family. A small child. I pray they do not suffer the same fate as Dr. Ben-Judah's family."

Ryan found a pay phone and called Taylor Graham. This time the pilot answered.

"They probably took Judd to the main headquarters in Jerusalem," Graham said. "Where are you?"

Ryan told him, and the pilot gave him directions.

"You'll go past the Wailing Wall on the way," Graham said. "Stay as far away from there as you can. I'll meet you in a half hour right across the street from GC headquarters."

Ryan walked briskly through the moonlit streets. He heard dogs barking. He stayed as close to the buildings as he could, clutching the picture and the tape in his pocket.

When he passed the Wailing Wall he saw a small crowd gathered near the fence where the preachers sat. He wanted to go closer but knew he should get to Judd as quickly as possible.

Then he heard it. Was it inside his head? A whisper? A voice? A thought? Whatever it was, it stopped Ryan in his tracks. He turned and faced the witnesses.

The tape, Ryan thought. *They'll be after the tape. Where can I keep it safe?*

Then the plan was clear to him. He could see it. God's justice. The purpose of their trip. He took the tape from his pocket and ran toward the crowd.

Vicki, Chaya, and Lionel met at Bruce's house late that evening. Vicki described her ordeal with Mrs. Jenness.

"Mrs. Goodwin called before you got home and suggested you stay with an adult in the area," Chaya said. "I told her about Loretta's house, and she said that would be fine."

"I was thinking of going over there anyway," Vicki said, "in case Mrs. Stahley and Darrion show up again."

The phone rang. Lionel answered and put Ryan on the speaker.

"What's happening?" Lionel said.

"I need you guys to pray, and pray hard," Ryan said. "I can't go into it all, but Judd's in big trouble. I have to go into the Global Community headquarters and see if I can—"

"Global Community?!" Lionel shouted.

"He was arrested," Ryan said. "Look, just pray that I'll be able to get him out of there and back to the plane. If I can do that, we'll be back for the memorial service."

"And if you don't get him out?" Vicki said.

"We may have a memorial service of our own over here," Ryan said.

The guard came for Judd, led him upstairs to another office, and told Judd to wait. The same interrogator stepped in the room and left the door ajar. He told Judd to go through his story again, and Judd reluctantly did. Another man stepped inside and closed the door. He looked familiar, but Judd couldn't place him.

"We understand you paid a visit to a neighbor of the Ben-Judah family," the officer said.

Judd studied the face of the other man.

"A concerned father called and said his son had talked with an American who knew the rabbi's children," the officer continued. "Would that have been you?"

"I went to the Ben-Judah house to see for myself," Judd said. "There was a kid next door in a garden."

"You took something with you when you left," the officer said. "What was it?"

The video! Judd thought. *That's the man in the mask!*

"What did you take with you?" the officer said sternly.

The man by the door was looking directly at Judd now. His eyes were dark and piercing.

There was a knock at the door. An officer handed the interrogator a note. The man held it out to read it, then glanced at Judd.

"You were expecting a visitor?" he said.

"No, I don't think so," Judd said.

"Stay where you are," the man said.

He left and to Judd's surprise came back with Ryan. Ryan smiled as he sat. The other men left the room. Judd held his finger to his lips.

"You know they can hear us," Judd whispered.

"It's OK," Ryan said. "I had to see you about the tape."

Judd's eyes widened. "Don't do this!"

"I went exactly where you told me to go, but the tape wasn't there," Ryan said. "You have to get out and help me find it."

"I told you it was—"

"I won't listen," Ryan said, sticking his fingers in his ears. "You said the tape would be where we were the other night. With our two friends. Remember?"

Judd stared at Ryan. Finally he understood. "Where should I meet you if I can get out of here?" he said.

Ryan smiled. "I'll be waiting where we last saw the journalist," Ryan whispered. "Meet me there."

"They'll follow you when you leave," Judd whispered.

"I have that figured out, too," Ryan said. He leaned closer. "Vicki, Chaya, and Lionel are praying up a storm. I'll see you outside."

Ryan left and Judd was returned to his cell. Judd told Michael the news.

"I am praying for you," Michael said. "I believe you will see Tsion. I may not see him until we are in heaven together. Tell him I am praying for him. I have told him I would risk everything to protect him. He is my spiritual father. Now may God give you the same. Do not lean on your own strength. Go with God."

Ryan walked out of the Global Community building and hopped straight into a cab parked outside.

"Hit it," Ryan said.

"Yes, sir," Taylor Graham said.

Ryan glanced back to see two Global Community guards rush outside. The cab was around the first corner by the time the men made it to their vehicle.

"Where'd you get it?" Ryan said.

"Friend of mine owns a cab company," Graham said. "This is the fastest one they have."

Ryan slid from one side of the backseat to the other as the pilot drove the car through the narrow streets of Jerusalem. With the speed of the cab and the ability of the driver, Ryan knew those following them didn't stand a chance. Now if Judd could convince them to let him go, his plan could work.

"I want to speak with the other man alone," Judd said when the officer came into the interrogation room. The officer looked startled, turned, and said something in another language to the man with the beard.

"It's out of the question," the officer said.

"I have some information I only want to give to *him*," Judd said. "I believe it will clear up the questions you have."

The man nodded, and the officer reluctantly left the room. The man who had taken the life of Judd's friends now sat before Judd. Judd's palms were sweaty.

"What do you have to tell me?" the man said with a thick accent.

"How does it feel to know you've killed innocent people?" Judd said.

"I do not know what you're talking about," the man said.

"I know it was you," Judd said.

"We are trying to apprehend the real murderer right now—"

Judd interrupted. "I saw you take off your mask before you killed Dan, Dr. Ben-Judah's son."

The man kept his steely gaze on Judd. "Then you are a liar," he said. "You told the officer you arrived from America after the killings."

"I saw a videotape," Judd said.

The man was silent. He scratched his chin. Finally he spoke. "Where would you come upon such a tape?"

"Where I found it isn't the point," Judd said. "It proves the rabbi is innocent. And if the media gets it, you're in big trouble."

"There are channels the media must go through—"

"And you know it would embarrass you and your superiors," Judd said. He couldn't believe how he was standing up to this cold-blooded killer, but he was.

"What do you want?" the man said. "I am not admitting anything, you understand. But you must want something."

"I want you to let me out of here with the promise that I'll have safe passage back to the U.S."

The man scoffed. "If I am the man you say I am, why wouldn't I kill you right now?" he said. "What would prevent that?"

"Because you don't have the tape," Judd said. "And that little kid who just walked out of here knows exactly where it is. And if I don't show up within a half hour, he'll hand it to those headline-hungry journalists."

"We are following the young man as we speak." The man smiled.

"And I'd be willing to bet a few minutes of video that your guys have lost him," Judd said. "Go ahead and check. I'll wait."

The man picked up a phone and dialed a number. He spoke softly, then raised his voice. He finally put the phone down gently and turned to Judd.

"Was I right?" Judd said.

"We have failed to locate him for the moment," the man said. "It is only a matter of time."

"Yes, it is, isn't it?" Judd said knowingly.

The man leaned forward. "You will take us to the tape," he said. "You will hand it over and be safely on your way."

238

19

JUDD waited nervously while the men finished the paperwork for his release. As far as Judd could tell, the man who had killed the Ben-Judah family wasn't an official Global Community officer, but he was working closely with them.

Judd questioned the man again before they led him to the car. "When this is over I'm free, right?" he said.

"You have my word," the man said.

Judd sat alone in the backseat of the car. Judd glanced behind them as they pulled out. A van followed that looked like the same one used in the Ben-Judah murders.

So the whole crew is here, Judd thought.

___

Taylor Graham drove Ryan through the exact streets he and Judd would need to take to get to the airstrip. "It's pretty secluded outside of town," Graham said. "I'll have the plane running and ready to go. You just keep the directions straight."

They drove back to town and parked in a line of cabs near the Wailing Wall. It was the wee hours of the morning, and there were only a handful of people looking at the witnesses.

"Are you sure Judd'll be here?" Taylor Graham said.

"As sure as I can be of anything right now," Ryan said.

"For what it's worth," the pilot said as he got out of the car, "you two don't act like any kids I've ever known. See you at the plane."

Judd didn't tell them they were going to the Wailing Wall. Instead, he gave them directions as they came to each intersection. Finally, Judd told them to stop.

"What is this?" the man said.

"You wanted the tape, right?" Judd said. "This is where it is."

The driver pulled his gun. "This is a trick," he said. "He has no tape."

Judd tried to remain calm. He didn't know exactly where Ryan had put the tape, but he had an idea. He opened the door and slowly got out. The driver jumped out and held his gun on Judd.

"Put that away," the other man said.

"I've kept my end of the bargain," Judd said.

"You haven't given us anything," the man said.

Judd pointed toward the witnesses. "The tape's over there. I told you it was in a safe place."

The van pulled up, and several men exited. They didn't have black hoods, but Judd placed each of them as the masked gunmen.

The driver started forward, but the leader stopped him. "If he wants to be released," the man said, "he'll have to bring the tape to us himself. Everyone wait here."

Judd scanned the cabs and noticed one at the end with no driver. Then Ryan popped his head up and winked.

Judd made his way to the front of the small crowd, then inched farther. "Don't let their stillness fool you," someone said. "They'll kill you if you get too close."

Judd spied the tape lying near the fence. Moishe and Eli appeared to be sleeping, their leathery skin rising and falling with each breath. Judd got close enough to bend down and grab the tape when he heard a voice.

"God shows his anger from heaven against all sinful, wicked people who push the truth away from them-selves," Eli said. "Stand back."

Judd stood and left the tape. The small crowd had retreated when they heard Eli's voice.

"What are you doing?" the leader called behind Judd. "Bring it here."

"I can't," Judd said, moving away from the fence. "If you want it, you'll have to get it yourself."

The driver reached for his weapon, and the other man

held his arm. He stepped forward and slowly pushed his way through the crowd.

Ryan started the car when he saw Judd move away from the fence. "Just like I thought it would be," Ryan said to himself.

Vicki joined a nervous Chloe and Amanda at Loretta's house. She asked that they pray for Judd and Ryan. Then Chloe filled them in on Buck's situation.

"I talked with him briefly, but I have no idea where or how he is," Chloe said. "My dad said I shouldn't worry, but I think something's wrong."

Chloe punched the number of Buck's cell phone.

"Do you know if he found the rabbi?" Vicki said.

Amanda shook her head.

"Buck! It's Chloe!"

Chloe listened, frowned, then tried to talk. "But,Buck—," she sighed. "You call me when you're safe," she said.

"What did he say?" Vicki said.

Chloe was busy dialing more numbers. "He said to not ask questions. He's safe for now, but everybody needs to pray. And he wanted me to get on the Internet and find the phone number for an airport in the Sinai desert. There's a pilot there—"

Amanda grabbed Chloe's hand and squeezed hard. Chloe's father, Rayford, answered, and Chloe told him the story. Chloe asked Rayford to get the phone number and call the pilot. Rayford agreed.

"Hurry, Dad," Chloe said.

Judd stepped a safe distance from the fence. The leader of the group was seething. "You will regret this," the man said.

"What do you mean?" Judd said. "You told me—"

"You didn't actually think I would let you out of the country, did you?" the man said. "You and your little friend in the cab will be dealt with most severely."

The man strode toward the fence and picked up the videotape. He turned to leave but stopped when Moishe's voice thundered behind him.

"We proclaim the power of God Almighty," Moishe said, "whose majesty is over Israel, whose power is in the skies."

"Woe to you, evildoers," Eli said. "Woe to those who shed the blood of the innocent."

Judd watched the man's face turn white with terror. He clutched the tape to his chest and turned. People behind Judd fell to the ground.

"The blood of the righteous cries out," Moishe thundered.

The man stiffened. "What do you want with me?" he cried. "I have done nothing to you!"

Eli and Moishe looked with piercing eyes at the man.

The man gasped at their faces and turned to run.

"Behold, the Lord says vengeance is mine," Eli and Moishe said in one loud voice. "I will repay, says the Lord."

With that, the two witnesses opened their mouths, and fire gushed forth, engulfing the man. Judd was so close, his clothes were singed. The tape in the man's hands melted instantly. Judd stumbled backward. People behind him fled.

Judd heard a gun blast. A bullet whizzed past him. Eli and Moishe turned their gaze on the men at the van. With lightning accuracy the two opened their mouths and consumed the entire company of murderers. One man fled to the van, only to have it catch fire and explode. The driver of the car had barely pulled his handgun from its holster when the fire fell. The gun melted in the man's hand.

Judd ran toward the last cab. He dodged several burning figures. As he got in, he looked toward the witnesses. Eli and Moishe looked straight at Judd and nodded. Without moving their lips Judd heard them say, "May the glory of the Lord be your rearguard."

Ryan's hands were shaking when Judd got in. Nothing could have prepared him for that horrifying scene. Judd got behind the wheel, and Ryan pointed the way. He heard sirens behind them.

Judd tried to drive like Taylor Graham, but the streets were unfamiliar and the car felt stiff. As they rounded a corner, Ryan yelled. A Global Community patrol car careened out of an alley and pulled behind Judd.

"We can't stop now," Ryan said. "We're almost at the airport."

"But we can't lead them to the plane," Judd said. "We'll have to lose them."

"How?" Ryan said.

Judd saw a man with a gun leaning out the window. Just as he fired, Judd swerved. The patrol car followed, nearly sending the man out the window.

"They're shooting at our tires," Judd said.

"Can't you go any faster?" Ryan said.

Judd took an alley, then another, but the patrol car stayed right behind them.

"Don't take too many of those or I won't be able to remember the way to the airport," Ryan said.

"Call Taylor and tell him we've got company," Judd said.

Ryan dialed the number. "He says there's an access road around the back that might help," Ryan said. "We can drive right onto the runway from there."

Judd floored it and pulled slightly away from the car. When they neared the airport, another GC vehicle with its lights flashing joined the chase. Judd saw the plane taxiing to the end of the runway.

"When I get close," Judd said, "we're both making a run for it."

Judd barrelled through a sandy area and onto the runway. He screeched to a halt beside the plane. Ryan jumped out and ran up the stairs. Judd put the car in reverse and jumped out. The plane was moving as he entered the cabin. While he and Ryan pulled the stairs up, Judd saw the two GC cars swerve and narrowly miss the taxi.

"Take a seat fast," Taylor Graham shouted as the plane picked up speed. The cars pulled to within fifty yards of them, then faded in the distance as the plane took off.

Judd and Ryan explained what happened at the Wailing Wall. The pilot seemed impressed.

"How did you know to take the tape there?" Graham asked Ryan.

"I can't explain it," Ryan said. "I knew God would take care of us."

When they reached cruising altitude, the pilot suggested Judd and Ryan check the GC frequencies in the rear of the plane. They played with the knob, hearing static and foreign languages. Finally, Judd found a transmission from an Egyptian border guard.

"He just slammed on his brakes and sent me off the side of the road," an officer said.

"We have backup coming, as you requested," another man said. "The roadblock is in place at the airport. How many are on the bus?"

"Did he say bus?" Judd said. "Michael said Buck and Tsion are on a bus."

The radio squawked. "I'm not sure," the first man said. "I am now in front of him and—"

There was a crash, and the transmission ended.

"What happened?" the other man on the radio said.

"He rammed me! I have lost my hood, but I'm giving chase."

"You should be able to see your backup soon," the other man said.

"What's going on?" Taylor Graham said from the cockpit.

"The Global Community guards are chasing Buck," Judd said. "I'm assuming he has Tsion Ben-Judah with him. They're headed for an airport in Egypt."

"Probably Al Arish," Graham said. "It's south of the Gaza Strip on the Mediterranean."

"Unable to stop him, sir," a different voice said on the radio. "We'll turn around and give chase."

"How far to the airport?" a man said.

"We can see it now," a guard said. "Less than a kilometer."

Judd and Ryan held their breath.

"The blockade is in place, sir," another man said. "There is no way he can get into the airport from here. We can see him now."

The radio went silent. Ryan looked at Judd. "They're caught," he said.

"Unit one, report," a man said.

There was static on the man's transmission. Judd could make out the words *bus* and *fire*, but little else. The leader was frantic, calling for information. Finally a man in a squad car broke through.

"The bus ran into the roadblock and scattered the officers," the man said. "It nearly tipped over, then burst into flames. Several officers are down."

"What about the occupants?" the first man said.

"We opened fire into the bus immediately," the second man said.

"Have you found their bodies?"

Silence. Then, "I'm sorry, sir, officers are firing again!"

"Go to a secure frequency," the base said.

Judd and Ryan scanned the frequencies but couldn't find more information.

"I hope they made it," Ryan said. "I can't imagine losing Bruce *and* Buck in one week."

Vicki answered the phone when the pilot of Buck's plane, Ken Ritz, called a short while later. She handed the phone to Chloe, who was relieved to hear that Buck and Tsion were on their way home.

Later, Buck called Chloe and assured her that when she heard the whole story she would understand. Chloe told Vicki and Amanda that no one outside the Tribulation Force but Loretta could know about Tsion.

"Buck didn't know Verna had moved out," Chloe said. "He's really uptight about her knowing about his faith."

"He'll be even more surprised if he sees Verna at Bruce's memorial service," Amanda said.

Ryan heard Taylor Graham's satellite phone ring. "I'm so glad to hear from you, Mrs. Stahley," he said. "We heard you moved."

The pilot listened intently and briefly told the story of their trip to Israel. Finally, he handed the phone to Ryan.

"Ryan, it's me, Darrion!"

"Are you guys OK?" Ryan said.

"We are for now," Darrion said. "We've had some pretty close calls."

"Where are you?" Ryan said.

"I can't say," Darrion said. "My mom told Taylor we were in Wisconsin, but that's not true. Don't tell him, though."

"Why not?" Ryan said.

"My mom was worried about you guys," Darrion said. "She thinks she might have set you up."

"How?" Ryan said.

"It's a long story," Darrion said. "Just make sure he doesn't land at the strip near our home. If my mom is right, Taylor is working with the Global Community."

"But that's not possible," Ryan said.

"I can't tell you any more," Darrion said. "But when you land, we think Taylor will suggest he be taken into custody. Then he'll try to help you two escape somehow. If that's what he does, it's a trap. They'll follow you to try and find us. Be very careful, OK?"

"We will," Ryan said. "Thanks."

Ryan hung up. "What was that all about?" Taylor Graham said.

"She said she was sorry she left our friends," Ryan said. "She wanted to thank me for what I did when she was kidnapped."

"Is that all?" the pilot said.

"Yeah, that and something about a reunion she wants to have in Wisconsin or someplace," Ryan said. "I don't know how we're gonna pull that one off."

Ryan jotted a note to Judd: *Darrion says the pilot is dirty.* He placed it on a tray and handed it to Judd.

"Care for a cookie?" Ryan said.

It was as if Tsion Ben-Judah was in some international witness protection program. Vicki was at Loretta's home when he was smuggled in under the cover of night. Amanda and Chloe greeted him warmly and compassionately. Vicki had talked with Judd briefly from their plane and knew the truth about his family. She stayed in the background and watched.

Loretta had a light snack waiting for all of them. "I'm old and not too up on things," she said, "but I'm quickly getting the picture here. The less I know about your friend, the better, am I right?"

Before anyone could answer, Tsion said, "I am deeply grateful for your hospitality."

Loretta soon trundled off to bed, expressing her delight in offering her home in service to the Lord.

Buck and Tsion had been injured. Chloe hobbled with them into the living room, followed by a chuckling Amanda. "I wish Rayford were here," she said. "I feel like the only one who can walk without a limp. I'm going to have to do every chore that requires two good legs around here."

Chloe leaned forward and reached for Tsion's hand with both of hers. "Dr. Ben-Judah, we have heard so much about you. We feel blessed of God to have you with us. We can't imagine your pain."

The rabbi took a deep breath and exhaled slowly, his lips quivering. "I cannot tell you how deeply grateful I am that God has brought me here. I confess my heart is broken. I cannot deny God's presence, yet there are times I wonder how I will go on. I must pray for relief from bitterness and hatred. Most of all, I feel terrible guilt that I brought this upon my wife and children. I don't know what else I could have done, short of trying to make them more secure. I could not have avoided serving God in the way he has called me."

Amanda and Buck each put a hand on Tsion's shoulders. They all wept and prayed. They talked well into the night, Buck explaining that Tsion would be the object of an international manhunt, which would no doubt be approved by Nicolae Carpathia himself.

20

RYAN was dying to tell Judd more of what Darrion said, but he couldn't risk it. If Taylor Graham saw them whispering or passing notes, he'd know something was up. Ryan went to the front and asked if he could watch. "I just put it on auto," Graham said. "The thing will fly itself."

Ryan climbed into the tiny cockpit and put on the headset. The pilot showed him what not to touch. The sun was sneaking up behind them, and it put a purplish glow on the horizon ahead. *I have to tell Judd*, Ryan thought. *But how?*

Vicki went back to Loretta's apartment to get some sleep. She couldn't believe she had just met the rabbi. She had trouble sleeping and turned on the television. The reports of the war around the world continued. Already, Nicolae Carpathia was putting his spin on it.

"World health care experts predict the death toll will rise to more than 20 percent internationally," the reporter said. "Global Community Potentate Nicolae Carpathia has announced a new health care plan. He and his ten global ambassadors have outlined the new regulations. Here is renowned heart surgeon Samuel Kline of Norway."

"The current agencies cannot handle disease and death on this scale," Dr. Kline said. "Potentate Carpathia's plan is not only our only hope for survival, but also a blueprint for the best health care agenda ever."

Vicki was distressed over the reports of the war, but for some reason, this doctor scared her.

"Should the death toll reach as high as 25 percent," the doctor continued, "we will need these new directives to govern life from the womb to the tomb. Our planet can be brought from the brink of death to a shining new state never before imagined."

Right, Vicki thought. *Carpathia kills 25 percent of the world's population and we're all healthier for it.*

Ryan stayed at the controls, loving the feeling. The pilot tapped him on the shoulder. "I'm gonna catch a little nap," Graham said. "Wake me in twenty minutes, OK?"

Ryan said he would. When he could hear the pilot snoring, he motioned for Judd to join him. Ryan whispered what Darrion had told him, making sure the pilot was really asleep.

"Why would he rescue us in Israel if he's with the GC?" Judd said.

"They must think we know where the Stahleys are," Ryan said. "Darrion and her mom are priority one."

"If Graham is working with the GC," Judd said, "he knows almost everything about us."

"And he also knows about Buck getting Dr. Ben-Judah."

"It just doesn't seem right," Judd said. "He seemed genuine, like he was really trying to help."

"How about when he took off from the hotel?" Ryan said. "You think he was really mad at us, or was he using that chance to communicate with the Global Community?"

Judd grimaced. "How did you know where to find me after the GC took me from the police station?"

"I tried to follow you, but they went too fast," Ryan said. "I called Graham and he told me."

"That's what I thought," Judd said. "We could use a couple parachutes right now."

"What can they do to us when we get back?" Ryan whispered.

"I can cover for you," Judd said, "but they're gonna have my record on file. They could slap me on the wrist and say I can never go outside the country again. . . ."

"Or what else?"

"Remember what happened to Coach Handlesman?" Judd said. "They could send me to one of their reeducation camps. And I'd probably be there a long time."

"So what are we gonna do if he wants to land at the Stahley place?" Ryan said.

"How good are you at acting?" Judd said.

A few minutes later Judd woke Graham. "It hasn't been twenty minutes, but I need your help," Judd said frantically. "Something's wrong with Ryan."

Graham shook himself awake and followed Judd to the bathroom. Ryan was leaning against the sink, beads of sweat on his forehead.

"I didn't feel well when I got on," Ryan said, "but I thought it was just all the excitement."

Graham felt his head. "You're burning up," he said. Graham retrieved a first-aid kit with a thermometer. Ryan passed out on the floor.

Judd and the pilot moved Ryan to a seat and made it recline. Judd asked what Graham thought it could be.

"It might be food poisoning," the pilot said. "I've also seen guys with a bad appendix act this way. Could be a hundred things."

"We'd better get him to a hospital right away, don't you think?" Judd said.

"I wanted to make it back to Chicago so we'd be safe," Graham said. "I'd like to touch down at the Stahleys' landing strip."

Ryan writhed in pain and moaned loudly.

"Let me check where we are," Graham said.

Vicki saw Buck embrace Rayford Steele at the house later that day. Amanda had picked Rayford up in Milwaukee after his exhausting flight from New Babylon. "I'm really fighting the jet lag," Rayford said. "I'm going to try and stay up until tonight so I can go over what you've put together for Bruce's funeral."

Rayford looked awestruck when Buck took him to Tsion Ben-Judah.

"It's truly an honor to meet you," Rayford said.

"I have heard much about you as well," the rabbi said.

Rayford, Buck, and Tsion moved downstairs while Vicki talked with Amanda.

"We might need to use the apartment for another visitor," Amanda said. "I don't want to kick you out or anything—"

"That's fine," Vicki said. "Who's coming?"

"We hope a woman named Hattie Durham will be here in a few days," Amanda said. Amanda explained that Hattie had been Rayford's senior flight attendant on the night of the Rapture. Since then she had taken a job with the Global Community.

"She's romantically involved with Carpathia," Amanda said gravely. "And from what Rayford tells me about their talks on the plane coming over here, she's struggling with a lot of decisions she has to make."

Judd was relieved to see Ryan's pains pick up as they entered North American airspace. They seemed to become unbearable the closer they got to Chicago.

"I'll divert to Indianapolis," the pilot said. "I thought we might make it to Chicago, but he's in too much pain. Did you get a read on his temperature?"

"It's really high," Judd said.

Graham declared an emergency, and an ambulance met them at the gate of the airport. "They'll take you straight to the hospital," the pilot said. "I'll need to stay with the plane."

"You've been a lot of help," Judd said. "We'll call you when we get back."

"No, I feel I should stay until I make sure he's OK," the pilot said. "Mrs. Stahley would want it that way."

"OK," Judd said. "We'll meet you over at the hospital."

"I'll be there as fast as I can," Graham said.

The paramedics put an oxygen mask on Ryan and checked his vital signs as they sped to the hospital. Judd stayed in the back with Ryan.

"Your heart rate and blood pressure look normal," the man said. "Are you feeling better?"

"A little," Ryan managed to say.

"I'm going to start an IV," the man said.

"No, don't," Ryan said. "I'm feeling a lot better."

"It'll help—"

"No, I don't want you to stick me if you don't have to," Ryan said.

Judd was watching the roadway for car rental dealerships. "Stop!" Judd shouted to the driver. "You have to stop!"

The startled driver pulled over, his lights still going, and Judd quickly had Ryan off the gurney and out of the ambulance.

"We're really sorry about this," Judd said as he shut the door. Judd glanced back as they ran through the parking lot and saw the paramedics watching them with opened mouths. One was talking on the radio.

Judd and Ryan darted into the car rental office. "We're in a really big hurry," Judd said. He quickly filled out the forms, paid for the car, and left.

Three hours later they were nearing Chicago and trying to make sense of their trip. "That was a pretty convincing job of acting," Judd said.

"I always wanted to be a movie star," Ryan said.

"I noticed your acting ability ended when that paramedic was going to stick a needle in your arm."

"What are we gonna do?" Ryan said.

Judd shook his head. "We have to take it a step at a time," he said. "We'll check in at Loretta's house first. I have to know about Buck."

"The memorial service is tomorrow," Ryan said. "Will it be too risky, since Graham heard us talking about it?"

"I don't know," Judd said. "We'll have to get everybody together and go over our options."

Back home, Judd went to Loretta's house and found Vicki and Amanda in the front living room. Judd and Ryan were relieved to know Buck was alive and were thrilled to hear that he, Rayford, and Tsion Ben-Judah were downstairs preparing for Bruce's memorial service.

"Let me take you to return the car," Amanda said. "You can meet him a little later."

After returning the car, Amanda dropped the three kids off at Bruce's house. Lionel and Chaya were overjoyed to see Judd and Ryan and listened to their story.

"I hope Buck has time to tell us what happened to him," Ryan said. "We heard about his chase from the border guards."

Judd and Ryan listened as Vicki explained what had happened to them while the two were gone. Judd paced as she talked.

"We're under suspicion of hiding Mrs. Stahley and Darrion," he said, "which is true."

"But they didn't do anything," Vicki said.

"Which is also true," Judd said, "but the truth doesn't make any difference to the Global Community. Also, the pilot who took us to Israel knows a lot more than we want him to. It's pretty clear he's mixed up with the GC, and he might have had something to do with Darrion's kidnapping and Mr. Stahley's death."

"Which makes Mrs. Stahley look pretty smart for getting away from us," Vicki said. "After she made those calls to her pilot, somebody started following us."

Judd sighed. "We might have to do something drastic," he said. "Relocate. Maybe all of us move back together."

"I don't care how much trouble we're in," Lionel said, "I'm not missing the service tomorrow for Bruce."

Judd agreed. "We need to be there," he said. "But now I want to hear Buck's story and meet Dr. Ben-Judah."

Ryan wanted to hear Buck's story too, but he was more excited about meeting the rabbi.

When they arrived at Loretta's house, Rayford Steele met them. "We need to go over a few things," he said. "Tsion is an international fugitive. I can't tell you everything I know, or how I know it, but the Global Community wants Tsion dead. One slip could cost him his life."

The kids said they understood.

"Buck can't speak in public," Rayford continued. "And with all the suspicion surrounding you kids with the Stahley situation, I'm wondering if it would be smart to have you guys go underground."

"You mean like, disappear?" Lionel said.

"Not forever," Rayford said, "but until things cool down, it's best to be safe."

Judd glanced around the room. "I don't mean to be disrespectful," he said, "but are you going underground?"

"I know what you're thinking," Rayford said, "but the fact is—"

"We had this same conversation with Bruce," Judd said. "He finally understood that God can use us just like he can use grown-ups."

"I'm not saying God can't use you," Rayford said.

"We want to live for Christ," Judd said. "We don't want to be foolish or careless, but we want to be bold and believe in God with all our hearts."

Rayford nodded. "I know you do. But you have to be careful not to think everything you feel is straight from God. The trip to Israel turned out OK for the moment, but the final results aren't in."

"I understand," Judd said. "Knowing God is more than a feeling."

Rayford nodded. "I believe in you guys. God will show you what's best. I've heard you all know something about the shelter Bruce built."

The kids nodded. "We understand we won't be able to go there or know how to get in," Judd said. "We'll never tell anyone about it."

"Good," Rayford said. "I'm tired and need to prepare for tomorrow. I know you want to see Tsion, but he's very emotional right now."

"We won't stay long," Ryan said.

Rayford led the kids downstairs, where Buck and Tsion sat at a table. Buck greeted the kids warmly and smiled at Judd and Ryan.

"Good to see you two," Buck said. "We'll trade stories later."

"It's a deal," Judd said.

Buck introduced Tsion to Lionel and Chaya. Chaya said something in Hebrew, and Tsion embraced her. He spoke with a thick Israeli accent.

"Praise God!" Tsion said. "I am so happy to know God is calling the Jewish people all over the world to himself through Jesus."

Vicki shook the rabbi's hand, then he shook Judd's.

"You knew my daughter," Tsion said.

"I did," Judd said. "I'm very sorry for your loss."

Tsion wept. "Forgive me," he said. "Looking at you reminds me of what I have lost. But I know that today my wife and children see God. Part of me very much wants to die so I can be with them. Only God's grace keeps me going. Only God can take away my thoughts of revenge."

Judd looked at Ryan.

"I feel called to serve God, even in my grief," Tsion continued. "I do not know why he has allowed this. God

must have something new for me to do with the time I
have left. I am grateful for your friendship and for your
prayers."

"What will you do now, sir?" Vicki said.

"I know my life is worthless in Israel. My message has
angered all those except the believers, and with the silly
murder charges against me, I had to leave. If Nicolae
Carpathia wants me dead, I will be a fugitive everywhere.
But if God wants to use me to help others know him better,
I will go anywhere and do whatever he calls me to do."

Tsion craned his neck. Ryan had been standing
slightly behind Judd as he listened.

"And who is this young man?" Tsion said.

"My name is Ryan, sir." Ryan put out his hand, and
the rabbi clasped it in his own.

"I have something for you," Ryan said. He pulled out
a crudely wrapped package and handed it to the man.

"A gift for me?" Tsion said.

"I didn't do a very good job with the paper," Ryan
said, "but I think you'll like it."

Ryan hadn't told Judd about the picture. Judd
frowned and elbowed him.

"I think we need to get back to our meeting," Rayford
said.

"No, let me open the gift," the rabbi said, as he
gingerly tore at the package. When he could see its
contents, he gasped and reached for a chair. The rabbi
put his face in his hands and wept.

"What did you do now?" Judd said.

"I think that's enough," Rayford said.

The rabbi put up his hand. "Please," he said after a few moments. "What he has given me is priceless."

Tsion held up the picture frame and showed the others his wife and children. "I kept this on my desk in my office at the university," Tsion said. "I do not know how you were able to find it, or who you bought it from, and I will not ask you. But I thank you."

Tsion hugged Ryan hard. Then he turned the picture over and opened the back of the frame.

"I was overcome because I remembered the occasion my wife used to give me this picture," he said. "I was well into my research about the Messiah. The disappearances had taken place. I knew I had been left behind. And I knew my decision to follow Jesus would cost me greatly.

"My wife also knew the reality of such a decision. I explained my studies to her and the children. I also explained the dangers. If they followed me in faith, they could become outcasts.

"One by one, I prayed with them. My wife, then my son, and then Nina placed her trust in Jesus."

Tsion stopped and bowed his head, his whole body shaking with emotion. Ryan looked at Vicki. Her eyes filled with tears. Finally, the rabbi continued.

"The next day, my wife went to the photographer's studio and had this portrait taken of the three of them. And on the back," Tsion choked, "she wrote a note to me. I had thought it was lost forever."

Ryan and the others listened as Tsion read the note in Hebrew, then translated.

"*To my beloved Tsion,*" the rabbi read, "*you have shown*

*us the way of life, the path of peace. May God grant you
wisdom and courage in the days ahead. May he be, to you,
Jehovah Jireh."*

"What does that mean?" Ryan said.

With tears in his eyes Tsion said, *"Jehovah Jireh* is a
name that means 'the God who provides.' In the Old
Testament God provided for his people again and again.
And God will provide the strength I need at this time of
despair." Tsion looked at Ryan. "This means so much to
me. I have artifacts in my office, texts of ancient manu-
scripts that are priceless. But you have given me back
what is most valuable."

Tsion hugged Ryan so hard he picked him up off the
floor.

Judd led the others to Loretta's living room. He knew
trouble might be ahead. How long would it take Taylor
Graham to find them? And after him, the Global
Community? Would the people from Nicolae High show
up at the service tomorrow? Would Buck's coworker,
Verna Zee, be there? And what had happened to Darrion
and Mrs. Stahley?

Tomorrow, Judd thought. *We have to make it through
tomorrow.*

JUDD THOMPSON JR. held his breath. The head of the Tribulation Force was about to ask the rabbi to become their new spiritual leader. The other kids joined Judd to listen outside the door. The Trib Force was meeting with a man Nicolae Carpathia hated. Judd couldn't help thinking about the danger.

Rayford Steele, Nicolae Carpathia's pilot, led the rabbi into the room. Rayford looked at Judd and smiled, then left the door slightly ajar. The other kids crowded around.

"Tsion, my brother," Rayford said, "we would like to ask you to join our little core group of believers. We're not asking for an immediate decision, but we need a leader, someone to replace Bruce."

As Judd watched, Tsion rose and placed his hands atop the table. The man was only in his forties, but to Judd he looked much older. The rabbi spoke with a shaky voice.

"My dear brothers and sisters in Christ," Tsion said,

"I am honored and grateful to God for saving my life. We must pray for those who helped me escape.

"I am sad, but I see the hand of God Almighty guiding me. I am right where he wants me. I need no time to think it over. I have prayed already. I will accept your offer to become a member of the Tribulation Force."

Judd saw tears in the eyes of the other group members as Tsion said, "I cannot promise to replace Bruce Barnes, but I will dedicate the rest of my life to sharing the gospel of Jesus Christ, my Messiah."

With that, the man seemed to collapse in his chair, and the others in the room knelt.

"Come on," Judd whispered.

"I knew he'd accept," Ryan said when the kids returned to the living room, "but how do you pronounce his name?"

"Just say 'Zion,' " Chaya said. "That's pretty close in English."

"Do you think he'll teach us like Bruce did?" Lionel said.

"I don't think we'll have much contact with him," Judd said. "After the memorial service tomorrow, they'll probably keep him hidden."

———————————

Lionel awoke Sunday morning knowing it might be the toughest day of his life. The excitement and tension of the past week had kept him from thinking much about Bruce. But now, on the day they would say good-bye, he felt a pain deep in his chest.

There had been no funeral for Lionel's family. On the morning of the disappearances, he had discovered only the clothes of his parents and siblings. His older sister, Clarice, had been reading her Bible. His mother had been kneeling in prayer. Lionel still wondered if she had been praying for him at the moment she vanished. He felt so guilty for being left behind. He had known the truth but had not acted on it.

But today was different. Unlike his family, the body of Pastor Bruce Barnes would be there. He could see it. Touch it.

Lionel thought back to his first meeting with Bruce. He had felt so alone that day. The man let them watch a video that explained what had happened. Then Bruce told his own story. God had Lionel's attention. He finally understood that being a Christian wasn't following a set of rules or doing certain things. It had to do with his heart.

And his heart ached. It was hard to lose every member of his family. He had taken them for granted, his mom and dad especially. But losing Bruce was different. When Bruce spoke of spiritual things, Lionel really listened. Now Bruce was gone. Lionel wondered if he would ever have another teacher like him.

Vicki and Chaya stayed at Loretta's house overnight. The next morning they kept to themselves as the adults got ready for the morning service.

"I need a favor," Chaya said. "My mother's funeral is

this afternoon as well. You know my dad doesn't want me there, but I have to go."

Vicki placed her hand on Chaya's shoulder. "You don't have to say anything more," Vicki said. "I'll go with you."

Two hours before Bruce Barnes's service began, the Young Trib Force met at New Hope Village Church. Judd prayed, "Give us wisdom and help us do what's right."

Judd welcomed John and Mark. The two cousins quickly updated the group. John was off to college in a few days. Mark had rebounded from his scrape with death in the militia. "I'm not going back to school," he said. "I'd like to help you guys any way I can."

"We can use it," Judd said. He looked at the kids gravely. "This is not how Bruce planned it," he said. "I'm sure he wanted to live until the Glorious Appearing of Christ. But that won't happen now. Nobody elected me leader, so I'm open to a vote—"

"We don't need that," Lionel interrupted. "You go ahead."

The others agreed.

"I haven't done things perfectly," Judd said. "When Ryan and I went to Israel with that pilot, Taylor Graham, we may have led the Global Community straight to us. And I've done other stupid things. More than once, I was mad at Bruce because I thought he was treating us like kids. Now I know he just cared."

Judd saw Vicki wipe her eyes, and he looked away. He had to hold it together until the service.

"For some reason, God let this happen to Bruce," he continued. "And one of the things Bruce told us was that when bad things happen, they will either turn you away from God or draw you closer to him. You'll run away or become more committed."

"I want to be more committed," Ryan said.

"Me too," Lionel said.

"Then we have to face the facts," Judd said. "First, Bruce is gone and we need to grieve for him. It's OK to cry. In fact, it's good. Second, we're hopefully going to see a lot of people from school here. The *Underground* got the word out. But a few might not be here to mourn."

"You mean spies?" Lionel said.

"Or worse," Judd said. "I wouldn't be surprised if there were some people from the administration here to see if they can catch somebody."

"I hope they do come," Vicki said. "They need to hear it like everybody else."

"But we still have to be careful," Judd said. "You know the school will clamp down hard if they can figure out who put the last issue of the *Underground* together."

"I think we ought to spread out during the service," Lionel said.

"Good idea," Vicki said. "That way they won't see us together."

Judd brought the group up to date on Buck and Tsion. "Buck told me about their drive across the desert," he said. "They were in an old bus. Once a Global Community officer searched the bus while Buck was stopped.

271

Buck thought Tsion was sleeping in the back, but the officer didn't find him."

"Where was he?" Ryan said.

"Buck found him after the officer left," Judd said. "Tsion said he had to go to the bathroom, so when the bus stopped he found some bushes by the road."

"God works in mysterious ways," Lionel said. Everyone laughed.

"He does," Judd said. "At one checkpoint a guard actually found the rabbi hiding."

"Did they arrest him?" Lionel said.

"No," Judd said. "Tsion was praying God would blind the guard or make him careless, but the man shined a flashlight in Tsion's face and grabbed him by the shirt. The guard said, 'You had better be who I think you are, or you are a dead man.'"

The kids stared at Judd.

"Finally, the rabbi told him his name. The guard said, 'Pray as you have never prayed before that my report will be believed.' Then he said a blessing and walked off the bus."

"Incredible," Lionel said.

"If that's not God, I don't know what is," Ryan said. "But what happened when they got to the airport? That's where we lost the transmission."

Judd explained that he and Ryan had picked up a radio report of the chase on their way back from Israel.

"There were so many squad cars at the roadblock," Judd said, "that Buck and Tsion set the bus on fire and ran. Buck got shot in the foot, but they were able to take off and get back home safely."

As the service grew near, Judd suggested they meet afterward in the same room. Everyone agreed. Judd then asked Chaya to lead the group in a brief Bible study. She took them to several passages in Luke and John that spoke of the cost of following Jesus.

"The Scriptures are clear," Chaya said. "A life of following God is not easy, but when we give our lives to him, he gives us the power to live and the promise of eternal life. What more could we need?"

Vicki couldn't believe her eyes when she looked outside. The service was still a half hour away, but the parking lot was full and cars lined the street as far as she could see. Inside, the crowd sat in silence, staring at the casket or looking at their programs. Many cried, but no one sobbed. Vicki hoped she wouldn't either.

She sat at the end of a pew toward the front. She stared at the closed casket. She had been to only a couple of funerals, and she hadn't paid much attention.

She opened the program and read the contents. A verse on the back read *"I know that my Redeemer lives."*

She had known Bruce since the day of the disappearances. She had lived under his roof and had even been adopted by him. And yet, she felt there were many things she didn't know. The program listed his date of birth, and she realized she had never thought to ask how old he was. Vicki did the math in her head. *Bruce was preceded by his wife, a daughter, and two sons, who were raptured with the church,* the program read. Their names were listed.

Several times Vicki looked up from the page to keep from crying. She spotted Buck and Chloe Williams behind her near Rayford Steele's wife, Amanda. Rayford would be on the platform soon, talking about Bruce. If there was anyone who could give a tribute to Bruce and speak the message Bruce would want these people to hear, it was Rayford.

Loretta entered and sat near the back. It took Vicki a second look to realize she was with Rabbi Ben-Judah.

The other members of the Young Trib Force were scattered throughout the crowd. She thought she would make it without crying until she spotted Ryan. He was in the front row of the balcony, his eyes red. He waved and tried to smile, then buried his face in his hands.

At ten o'clock Ryan saw Rayford Steele walk through a door at the side of the platform. Another elder stepped to the pulpit and asked everyone to stand. He led them in singing two hymns. Ryan couldn't get the words out.

Vicki smiled when she remembered Bruce's singing. Bruce had admitted he couldn't sing well, but that didn't stop him from belting out what he called a "joyful noise" during congregational songs. At the end of one service he had leaned over to Vicki and said, "What I lack in tone, I make up for in volume."

She smiled again as the songs ended. The elder told the congregation there would be no offering or announcements, just the tribute to Bruce. "Our speaker this morning is Elder Rayford Steele. He knew Bruce as well as any of us."

Judd sat in the back. Bruce had died more than a week earlier, but it still didn't feel real. Hearing Rayford's voice, calm and in control, eased the pain a bit.

Rayford opened his notes and welcomed everyone. "I need to tell you I'm not a preacher," he began. "I am here because I loved Bruce. And since he left his notes behind, I will, in a small way, speak for him today."

Judd imagined himself at the pulpit, wondering what he would say, when an old woman and a young boy walked in. The woman wore dark sunglasses. Judd stood and offered them his seat.

"I want to tell you how I first met Bruce," Rayford was saying, "because I know that many of you met him in much the same way. We were in the greatest crisis of our lives, and Bruce was there to help."

Judd moved to the back of the sanctuary, but people were standing shoulder to shoulder from the last pew to the back wall. He looked into the balcony and saw a space near the sound booth.

Ryan had heard Rayford's story before. He had been best friends with Rayford's son, Raymie. Ryan had even been at their house once when Mrs. Steele had talked about the rapture of the church with her husband.

Rayford explained that he had called the church when

he discovered his wife and son were missing. Then he met Bruce and saw the video the former pastor had left behind.

"If you had asked people five minutes before the Rapture what Christians taught about God and heaven," Rayford said, "nine in ten would have said to live a good life, do the best you can, be kind, and hope for the best. It sounded good, but it was wrong! The Bible says our good deeds are worthless. We have all sinned. All of us are worthy of the punishment of death."

Ryan looked around the room and saw a lot of new faces. The *Underground* had done a good job of bringing people in. Now it was Rayford's turn to give them the message.

"I would fail Bruce if I didn't say this," Rayford said. "Jesus has paid the penalty. The work has been done. We can't earn our salvation; it's a gift from God."

Judd exited through the back doors and swiftly made his way to the balcony stairs. The overhead speakers carried Rayford's voice throughout the building.

Judd stopped and listened as Rayford said, "If I can get through this, I would like to speak directly to Bruce. You all know that the body is dead. But Bruce, we thank you. We envy you. We know you are with Christ. And we confess we don't like it that you're gone. We miss you. But we pledge to carry on. We will study, and this church will be a lighthouse for the glory of God."

Tears in his eyes, Judd put his hand on the railing. As

he did, someone grabbed his arm roughly and turned him around. The man clamped his hand over Judd's mouth and leaned close.

"Don't make a sound," Taylor Graham whispered. "You're coming with me."

22

VICKI hung on every word. Rayford was about to preach the very sermon Bruce would have given. "But before I do that, I want to give you a chance to say something in memory of our brother."

Vicki looked around. No one moved. Finally, she heard a voice from the back. Loretta stood and described how she had worked with Bruce since the disappearances. She challenged people to give their lives to Christ as Bruce did, then she broke down. The man next to her gently put his arm around her.

People around Vicki wept. Loretta was crying. Vicki wanted to stand and say something, but she felt nervous. Would anyone care what she thought about Bruce? Finally, she knew if she didn't say something, her heart would break. She stood.

Taylor Graham hustled Judd through the front door and around the side of the church. Judd tried to pull away, but the pilot was strong. Judd looked for Global Community officers or a squad car. Two blocks from the church, Graham found his car, unlocked the passenger side, and pulled Judd in after him.

Vicki shook, but she knew what she was doing was right.

"I've done some bad things in my life," Vicki said. "When my family disappeared, I thought I hadn't been good enough. Then I met Bruce, and I heard the message.

"He was always kind, and it never bothered him that I asked a lot of questions. When I got sent to a detention center, he visited me. When I heard someone wanted to adopt me and make me his daughter, I couldn't imagine who. But I should have known."

Vicki's voice trembled. She pushed her hair behind an ear and bit her lip.

"I can't tell you how much Bruce helped me understand God's love," Vicki continued. "Mr. Steele is right. God loved us enough to want to adopt us into his family, even when we didn't deserve it. That's what Bruce did for me, and I'll always love him for it."

Vicki scanned the crowd. Some wiped their eyes. Others nodded. Everyone looked at her.

"Don't let this day go to waste," Vicki said. "If you don't know God, ask him to forgive you today and become his child. You'll never regret it."

Vicki sat and bowed her head. From all over the sanctuary people stood and told what Bruce meant to them. After more than an hour, Rayford said they could take one more person before a brief break.

Vicki heard a voice with a thick accent behind her. "You do not know me," Tsion Ben-Judah said. "Many Christian leaders around the globe knew your pastor, learned from him, and were brought closer to Christ because of him. My prayer for you is that you would continue his ministry and his memory, that you would, as the Scriptures say, 'not grow weary in doing good.' "

At Rayford's request, Vicki and the congregation stood and stretched. "We're long past our normal closing time," he said, "so I'd like to excuse any who need to leave."

As Rayford backed away from the pulpit, everyone sat down and looked at him. Someone giggled, then another, and a few more. Rayford smiled, shrugged, and returned to the pulpit.

"I guess there are things more important in this life than personal comfort, aren't there?" he said. Vicki heard a few amens. Rayford opened his Bible and Bruce's notes.

A thousand thoughts flashed through Judd's mind as Taylor Graham drove in silence. Was Graham turning him over to the hands of the North American Global Community? Was he out for revenge for Judd's and Ryan's escape? Judd had always been able to think quickly. Now he didn't know what to say or do.

Graham turned into the forest preserve that led to the Stahley property.

They wound along the access road and to the edge of the woods. Graham stopped the car, flipped on a gadget on his dashboard, then sped into a clearing. The pilot activated a remote control device, and the side of the hill opened. Graham drove into the secret plane hangar and punched the door closed.

"Why didn't you do that the first time we came here?" Judd said.

"Ground was wet," Graham said. "The tracks would have led them right to us." The pilot got out of the car. "Follow me," he said.

———————————

Ryan listened carefully as Rayford outlined his message. The words were Bruce's, written on an airplane while returning from a trip. Some of the things Bruce wrote sounded spooky.

Rayford said, "Bruce writes, *'I was ill all night last night and feel not much better today. I was warned about viruses, despite all my shots. I can't complain. I have traveled to many countries without problem. God has been with me. If I'm not better upon my return, I'll get checked out.'*

"This message is particularly urgent, because he was convinced we are at the end of the time of peace. Bruce writes, *'If I am right, we must prepare for the next prediction: The Red Horse of the Apocalypse.'*"

I don't like the sound of this, Ryan thought.

Rayford continued reading from Bruce's writing.

" 'Revelation 6:3-4 predicts what I believe is a global war. It will likely become known as World War III. This will immediately usher in the next two horses of the apocalypse, the black horse of plague and famine, and the pale horse of death.' "

Ryan watched Rayford look up from his notes. "Do any of you find this as astounding as I do?" Rayford asked.

Ryan nodded. *It's happening right now!* he thought.

"This was written just before or just after the first bomb was dropped in our global war. I don't know about you, but I want to listen to a man like this."

Ryan quickly thumbed through his Bible as Rayford read from Revelation 6.

" 'And I looked up and saw a horse whose color was pale green like a corpse. And Death was the name of its rider, who was followed around by the Grave. They were given authority over one-fourth of the earth, to kill with the sword and famine and disease and wild animals.'

"Bruce says, *'I'll admit I don't know what the wild animals refer to,'*" Rayford continued. *"'They could be real animals or perhaps the weapons used by the Antichrist and his enemies. Whatever it means, one-fourth of the world's population will be wiped out. Of the quarter of the earth's population that will perish, surely many, many of these will be tribulation saints.'* "

Ryan shuddered. *A fourth of all the people on earth. Will I be one of them?*

Judd sat and Taylor Graham pulled a chair near him. The pilot shook his head and frowned. "You guys gave me the slip in Indy," he said. "Got me in big trouble."

Judd gritted his teeth. "You sold us out," he said.

"Why do you say that?"

"Never mind why," Judd said. "Do you admit it?"

Graham looked at the floor. "There's a lot you don't know," he said. "A lot I still can't tell you. I guess you deserve to hear my side."

Vicki felt lost. The meeting was a tornado of emotion. And now she was listening to Mr. Steele talk about the first four of seven Seal Judgments. She tried to focus.

Thankfully, Mr. Steele asked for a five-minute break. "We'll meet back here at one o'clock. Then I'll make us all aware of what we have to look forward to within the next few weeks."

Vicki looked for Judd in the front hallway but couldn't find him. Lionel slipped in beside her.

"Pretty intense, huh?" Lionel said.

"Imagine sitting in there and not knowing any of those predictions from the Bible," Vicki said. "You'd have to believe this is true."

"It might be too scary," Lionel said. "People can shut out what they don't want to hear."

"Mr. Steele is telling us stuff I haven't heard yet," Vicki said. "And I don't get the four horses and the seven seals."

Lionel leaned against the wall as some people crowded by, eager to get back into the service before Rayford began again.

"I talked with Chaya yesterday," Lionel said. "She's got it down. The four horsemen are the first four judgments from God. The red horse is the start of the war. Then the rest of them—famine, plague, and death— happen right after. Bruce thought we're right in line for numbers five, six, and seven."

"And then Jesus comes back?" Vicki said.

"No," Lionel said. "There are two more seven-part judgments after this one." Lionel frowned. "I guess that's why they call it the Tribulation. There's a lot of trouble ahead."

Vicki held up a hand. "Speaking of trouble," she said. "What is it?"

Vicki nodded toward the stairs. Coming toward them was the principal of Nicolae High, Mrs. Jenness.

Before Taylor Graham could speak again, Judd took over. "You sold us out," Judd said. "You were going to give us over to the Global Community."

"Is that why you took off?" Graham said. "Darrion tipped you off on the phone?"

Judd didn't answer.

"I thought I could trust you guys," Graham said. "That whole thing with Ryan being sick was a big act."

"You thought you could trust *us?!*" Judd yelled. "If we'd stayed with you, the GC would have been all over us."

"You don't understand. If you'd stayed with me, I could have pointed them *away* from you. It's too late for that now."

"I thought you were working with the GC," Judd said. "They're after us."

"No, they're after *you*," Graham said. "They're interested in Ryan, but only because he can lead them to you."

"We shouldn't be seen together," Lionel said.

Vicki was thinking the same thing, but it was too late now. Mrs. Jenness spotted Vicki and Lionel and came directly toward them. She pursed her lips and looked down.

"I know we've had our differences," Mrs. Jenness said, "but I'm genuinely sorry for your loss."

"Thank you," Vicki said.

"My guess was that the people who wrote the *Underground* newspaper would be here today," Mrs. Jenness said, looking suspiciously at Vicki.

"Could be," Vicki said. "But there are an awful lot of people from the school here."

Mrs. Jenness frowned. "I have to go," she said. "The memorial service was very . . . enlightening." She fixed her stare on Lionel. "You're Lionel Washington, aren't you?"

Vicki didn't know Mrs. Jenness even knew Lionel's name, and it startled her.

"Yes, ma'am," Lionel said.

"I need to see you in my office, first thing in the morning," she said.

"What is it?" Vicki said.

"That's between Lionel and me," Mrs. Jenness said, "and his family."

Mrs. Jenness walked out the front door.

"You think she knows I'm involved with the *Underground*?" Lionel said.

"I can't think what else it would be," Vicki said, "but what does your family have to do with it?"

"I don't have any family," Lionel said, "except you guys."

Vicki saw Rayford Steele head toward the podium. She and Lionel hurried back into the service.

———————————

Judd watched Taylor Graham closely. The pilot ran a hand through his hair and sighed. "I don't know what else to do other than tell you," he said.

"Tell me what?" Judd said.

"First of all, you kids really showed me something in Israel."

"We're not kids," Judd said.

"I didn't mean it like that," Graham said. "Gimme a break."

"I'm listening," Judd said.

"I'm not with the GC like you think," Graham said. "They gave me an order, and the best thing I could do—"

"If you're not with the GC, why are you taking orders from them?" Judd said.

"I worked for the GC just like Mr. Stahley did," Graham said. "But you don't always agree with your bosses. Mr. Stahley uncovered a lot of shady information about them. I helped him. When he died, I got even more suspicious. He had some kind of evidence that could blow the lid off Carpathia and the whole GC machine."

"And that's why you were going to deliver Ryan and me to them?" Judd said.

287

"Just listen," Graham said. "I can't know what the GC are doing unless I stay close. They took me in for questioning after I got back to Chicago. Now I know the time's right."

"For what?" Judd said.

"To get those secret documents out into the open," Graham said. "And to do that, I'm going to need your help."

Vicki slipped into her pew. Buck talked with Chloe and Amanda a row behind her.

"Rayford has to be exhausted up there," Buck said.

"I took him some orange juice," Amanda said. "That ought to help."

"Did you talk with Dad?" Chloe said.

"Yes," Buck said. "He really wants people to know what's about to happen so they can be ready."

"I just hope they can handle it," Chloe said. "I've seen the pages Dad's about to read. It's terrible."

"After you tricked Ryan and me, you want my help?" Judd said.

"I have to find Mrs. Stahley," Graham said.

"This is really good," Judd said. "You pretend you're our friend, you cut it real close when you took off, put on the beard and the accent to get us past those GC checkpoints, and you even rescued us and flew us out of Israel. That was all fake."

"How do you know it was fake?"

"Because you flew back here to give us up! I'm not trusting you at all."

"I promise you, I didn't fake anything," Graham said.

"So those GC guys at the donut shop were for real?"

"I had no idea who they were following," Graham said. "Could've been either one of us."

"The close calls on the runway here and in Israel, those were real?" Judd said.

"Yes," Graham said. "Let me explain. When Mrs. Stahley called and asked me to help, I did it because she's family. Her friends are my friends. I wasn't happy about taking two teenagers, but you grew on me.

"When we arrived at the hotel, I got a call from GC Command. They figured out where I was and wanted me to bring you in. I went back to Haifa to get the plane and get out of there."

"You were going home without us?" Judd said.

"I figured I had to bolt and hoped you two could find a way back on a commercial flight," Graham said. "It was the safest thing to do. But they found me in Haifa, and I was forced to fly to Jerusalem. By then, you were in custody."

"This makes no sense at all," Judd said. "If you're supposed to be my friend, let me go right now!"

"I can't do that," Graham said. "You don't know what kind of danger you're in. Do you know what a double agent is?"

"Yeah, somebody who works for one government but really works for somebody else."

"That's what I am," Graham said. "I work for

Carpathia and the Global Community, but I'm really working for someone else."

Judd thought a moment. He was pretty sure Graham wasn't a believer. At least he hadn't let on that he was. But if he was working for someone else, who could it be? The militia? Or was this whole conversation being taped? Maybe Graham was saying this so Judd would tell all he knew about Mrs. Stahley.

"If you're not working for the GC," Judd said, "who are you working for?"

23

LIONEL returned to his seat. It looked like no one had left. They all wanted to hear the next segment of Bruce's teaching, which was life-and-death stuff. Rayford Steele was reading again from Revelation 6 about those believers in Christ who would give their lives during the Tribulation. The Bible called these people martyrs.

"The Scripture says, 'I saw under the altar the souls of those who had been slain for the word of God and for the testimony which they held. And they cried with a loud voice, saying, "How long, O Lord, holy and true, until You judge and avenge our blood on those who dwell on the earth?" Then a white robe was given to each of them; and it was said to them that they should rest a little while longer, until both the number of their fellow servants and their brethren, who would be killed as they were, was completed.'

"I put Bruce in this category of one who has died for

his faith," Rayford continued. "While he may not have died specifically for preaching the gospel, clearly it was his life's work and it resulted in his death."

Lionel closed his eyes. What Rayford said next gave him chills.

"I envision Bruce under the altar with the souls of those who have been killed because they believed in Jesus. He will be given a white robe and told to rest a while longer until even more martyrs are added to the total."

Lionel pictured Bruce's face, remembering the first time he had met him. Bruce was there when Lionel needed him most. Now he was waiting patiently for his white robe. Maybe he was there with Mrs. Ben-Judah and her children. *I wonder who will be the next to join them?* Lionel thought.

Rayford paused and scanned the congregation. "I must ask you today," he said, "are you prepared? Are you willing? Would you give your life for the sake of the gospel?"

As Rayford took a breath, Lionel heard a young voice cry out, "I will."

Across the balcony, Lionel spotted Ryan standing, tears streaming down his face. It was clear Rayford hadn't expected anyone to say anything out loud, but there was Ryan.

"So will I!" Lionel said as he stood. Ryan looked at him across the balcony and smiled. Three or four others in the congregation said the same. Quickly Rayford thanked those who had spoken. "I fear we may all be called upon to express our willingness to die," Rayford said. "Praise God you are willing."

Judd waited for Taylor Graham to answer. The pilot rubbed the back of his neck. Judd still didn't know if he could trust the man.

"I guess I don't know who I'm working for now," Graham said. "I was working for Mr. Stahley, but he's dead. I'm committed to keeping his wife and daughter safe. And I'm working to expose the people who killed him."

"I'm supposed to buy that?" Judd said.

"Whether you buy it or not," Graham said, "it's the truth."

Judd studied the man. Flying to Israel without knowing his loyalties had probably been a mistake. But now what?

"If all the secrets of the Global Community are down here somewhere, why aren't the GC crawling around?" Judd said. "You brought me in here like you knew they weren't going to stop you."

"They still don't know about the hangar," Graham said. "The entrance from the house is hidden. I know it's in this room, but that's all. I knew we'd be safe talking here."

"What if you're still working for the GC," Judd said, "and all this stuff about protecting Mrs. Stahley is a lie?"

Taylor Graham shook his head.

"What about the things we told you on the plane?" Judd said.

"What things?"

"The stuff about the Bible and God," Judd said. "You seemed interested."

"I am," Graham said, "but I can't say I believe it yet."

If he were really lying to me, Judd thought, *he would have told me he believed the whole thing. Maybe he's for real.*

Vicki paid close attention to the judgments and found she was finally understanding. Rayford said the scene in heaven with the martyrs could be happening that very moment.

"And if it is," Rayford said, "we need to know what the sixth seal is. Bruce felt so strongly about this judgment that he cut and pasted different translations of Revelation 6:12-17. Just remember that the Lamb in these verses refers to Jesus Christ."

As Rayford read the passage, Vicki looked at the verses in her own Bible.

" 'I looked when He opened the sixth seal, and behold, there was a great earthquake; and the sun became black as sackcloth of hair, and the moon became like blood. And the stars of heaven fell to the earth, as a fig tree drops its late figs when it is shaken by a mighty wind. Then the sky receded as a scroll when it is rolled up, and every mountain and island was moved out of its place. And the kings of the earth, the great men, the rich men, the commanders, the mighty men, every slave and every free man, hid themselves in the caves and in the rocks of the mountains, and said to the mountains and rocks, "Fall on us and hide us from the face of Him who sits on the throne and from the wrath of the Lamb! For the great day of His wrath has come, and who is able to stand?" ' "

Vicki looked up, her face white with fear. She knew

that some words in Bible prophecy stood for other things, but these words seemed clear.

"I'm not a Bible teacher or a scholar," Rayford said, "but I ask you, is there anything difficult to understand about a passage that begins, 'Behold, there was a great earthquake'? Bruce has carefully charted these events. I believe the Four Horsemen of the Apocalypse are at full gallop. And I also think the fifth seal, the tribulation martyrs whose souls are under the altar, has begun."

It all fits, Vicki thought.

"Bruce's notes say more and more people will be killed because of Jesus. Antichrist will come against tribulation saints and the 144,000 witnesses springing up all over the world from the tribes of Israel.

"If Bruce is right—and he has been so far—we are close to the end of the first twenty-one months."

Vicki saw Rayford grip the podium with both hands.

"I believe in God. I believe in Christ. I believe the Bible is the Word of God. And I believe Bruce taught us well. Therefore, I am preparing to endure what this passage calls 'the wrath of the Lamb.' An earthquake is coming, and it is not symbolic."

Vicki was proud of Rayford. He had delivered the message with passion, just like Bruce. She agreed with everything he had said, but she couldn't help fear the earthquake and what might happen when it came.

Judd mulled over his next move. He could refuse to talk with Taylor Graham and see what the man did, or go ahead and trust him.

"OK," Judd finally said. "Tell me why the GC are so hot on my trail."

"There's the torching of those guys in Israel," Graham said. "But in one sense having those guys out of the way was a favor. What they really want is Mrs. Stahley."

"I don't know where she is," Judd said.

"You know more than they do," Graham said. "There was some money transferred to your bank account. They traced it back to Mrs. Stahley."

"Maybe *you* told them we were hooked up," Judd said.

"I wouldn't do that. I told you, the safety of Mrs. Stahley and Darrion are my—"

"Yeah, yeah, they're your biggest concern," Judd said.

"There's something else," Graham said. "When I got back from Indy I caught wind of something new. The top GC guys love the idea."

"What is it?" Judd said.

"Carpathia thinks he can build a world of peace and brotherhood," Graham said. "That's why he blew up just about everything when the militia attacked."

"He wants people to get along with each other and live in peace, so he blows people up?"

"I know it sounds screwy, but it's true," Graham said. "He says the people who agree with him are going to be happy. Those who oppose him are toast."

"That means he'll wage war against people who believe what I believe," Judd said.

"And he's taking a new step toward that," Graham said. "He wants to form an organization of healthy, strong young people who are devoted to the Global Community. So devoted that they would want to make sure everybody is in line with the GC objectives."

"People ripe for brainwashing," Judd said.

"I wouldn't put it past him," Graham said.

"Would they wear uniforms, insignias, the whole thing?"

"No," Graham said. "Carpathia wants them to blend in with everyone else, but they would be trained in psychology. They would secretly inform the GC about people who oppose their views. I assume anyone who doesn't line up with the Enigma Babylon Faith would be in big trouble."

"So there goes free speech," Judd said. "What's he calling them?"

"I'm not sure," Graham said. "But he doesn't want to use the words *police* or *secret*, though that's exactly what they'll be."

"What kind of power would they have?"

"They'll carry guns," Graham said. "If they have reason to stop someone or question him or even search him, they can do it."

"Their own judge and jury," Judd said.

"Exactly. Whoever is perceived as an enemy, whoever says something negative about the Global Community, can be eliminated right there."

"Where's he going to get these people?" Judd said.

"All over the world," Graham said. "That's why I've been going along with them."

"What do you mean?"

"When they called and threatened me in Israel," Graham said, "they had no power. I could've refused and walked away. But they brought up Conrad, my brother."

"What does he have to do with it?" Judd said.

"He had nothing to do with it until they got him," Graham said. "He's in one of the camps for these new GC monitors down South somewhere. They said if I didn't help them find Mrs. Stahley, they'd put an end to his education."

"So you are cooperating with them," Judd said.

"Only to buy time," Graham said.

"How old is he?"

"About your age," Graham said. "Maybe a little younger. If I can find Mrs. Stahley and get those documents, I might be able to use them as barter. If not, I'll take them to the media and hope I can find my brother before it's too late."

Ryan could tell Rayford Steele was near the end of his message. The pilot wiped his forehead and closed his Bible.

"The seventh Seal Judgment is mysterious because Scripture is not clear what form it will take. All the Bible says is that it is apparently so dramatic that there will be silence in heaven for half an hour. We will study those judgments and talk about them as we move into that period. However, for now, I believe Bruce has left us with much to think and pray about."

Rayford stepped to the side of the pulpit, just behind Bruce's casket. He looked down and said, "We have loved this man. We have learned from this man. And now we must say good-bye. Though we know he is finally with Christ, do not hesitate to grieve and mourn. The Bible says we are not to mourn as those who have no hope, but it does not say we should not mourn at all. Grieve with all your might. But don't let it keep you from the task. What Bruce would have wanted above all else is that we stay about the business of bringing every person we can into the kingdom before it is too late."

Rayford closed in prayer. As Ryan looked up, he saw the pilot sit and lower his head. Most stayed seated, while a few quietly stood and made their way out. Ryan stayed for a few moments, then went downstairs to the meeting place.

"Why didn't they open the casket?" Ryan said.

"I think they want people to come back for a viewing later," Vicki said. "I'll be with Chaya at her mom's funeral."

Ryan looked around and saw a boy helping an old woman down the steps. As they moved toward him Ryan said, "Has anybody seen Judd?"

"I saw him, young man," the frail old woman said. "He gave up his seat for me and my . . . my daughter."

The woman took off her dark glasses and raised her silver wig.

"Mrs. Stahley!" Ryan said.

The woman put a finger to her lips and closed the door to the meeting room.

———————————————

"If what you say is really true," Judd said, "I need to get back and warn my friends."

Taylor Graham looked away. "I don't think that's a good idea," he said. "With the level of risk, I'm not sure you should ever see them again."

24

RYAN hugged Darrion. She had cut her hair even shorter to look like a boy.

"Where did you guys go?" Ryan said.

"Wisconsin," Darrion said. "We have a—"

Mrs. Stahley interrupted her daughter. "We can't tell you exactly where our cottage is. It's not safe for you to know. But we had to find out if you and Judd made it back OK."

"You came all that way for us?" Ryan said.

"Taylor Graham is not our friend," Mrs. Stahley said. "He's been with us so long, I can't imagine him being disloyal to us, but now I think he's working solely for the Global Community."

"What tipped you off?" Ryan said.

"My husband's E-mail is still on the Global Community list," she said. "He received a coded message that says

Taylor is cooperating. He's trying to find Judd, and in turn, trying to find me."

Vicki put her hand on Mrs. Stahley's shoulder. "Judd should be hearing this," Mrs. Stahley said. "Where is he?"

"Maybe he's back talking with Rayford or Buck," Ryan said. "I'll go get him."

"No, you stay here," Vicki said. "I'll look."

"I don't have much time," Mrs. Stahley said. "I know the GC are looking for me. I wouldn't be surprised if they were somewhere in that crowd this morning."

"But I have to get back to them," Judd said.

"If you let the others know where you are, you'll put them in as much danger as you're in," Taylor Graham said. "You can't do that. I'll get a message to them for you."

Something felt wrong. If Graham *was* working for the GC, it would make sense that he would want to find the other kids. They might lead him to Mrs. Stahley. But Graham could be telling the truth. What he said next sent a shiver down Judd's spine.

"There's also a report that your friend Buck Williams has Tsion Ben-Judah with him," Graham said. "Is that true?"

Rayford Steele told Vicki he hadn't seen Judd all morning. Vicki ran to the parking lot and spotted Buck and Chloe getting into their car. Before she could reach them, Buck's coworker Verna Zee arrived.

Vicki knew from her talks with Verna at Loretta's house

that the woman did not believe in Christ. Vicki also knew that Buck was nervous about Verna and her knowledge of what he believed. She stood a few feet away and listened as Verna said, "I recognized Tsion Ben-Judah!"

"I'm sorry?" Buck said.

"He's going to be in deep trouble when the Global Community peacekeeping forces find out where he is. Don't you know he's wanted all over the world? Buck, you're in as much trouble as he is, and I'm tired of pretending I have no idea what you're up to."

"Verna, we have to go somewhere and talk about this," Buck said.

"I can't keep your secret forever, Buck," Verna said. "Do all these people believe Nicolae Carpathia is the Antichrist?"

"I can't speak for everyone," Buck said. "Verna, I took a huge risk in helping you out the other night and letting you stay at Loretta's home."

"You sure did. And you may regret it for the rest of your life."

Vicki turned and slowly walked back to the church. She heard Verna threaten Buck. If Verna told her superiors about Buck's beliefs, he could lose his job or even his life. She would talk with Chloe after the funeral and find out what happened.

If Judd was reluctant to give information about his friends, he was even more hesitant to talk about Tsion Ben-Judah. Judd knew the Global Community would stop at nothing to silence this man who had caused such a stir around the world.

"Why are you asking about him?" Judd said.

"I have to know what I'm up against," Graham said. "I don't think the GC have put you and this Williams guy together yet, but if they do, it could be bad news for everybody."

Judd silently prayed. He had acted so quickly in talking with this stranger. Now if he said the wrong thing, not only could Judd endanger his friends but the adult Trib Force as well.

"I'm not giving you any information," Judd finally said. "Maybe you're who you say you are, and maybe you're not. I'm not taking the chance."

Taylor Graham stood and walked to the other side of the room.

"Let me go, and I'll be careful," Judd said. "Or you can lock me up here; I don't care. You can kill me if—"

"I'm not going to kill you," Graham said, slamming his fist against the wall. "I'm helping you, can't you see that?" The man moved closer. "What can I tell you that'll prove I'm telling the truth?"

Judd shook his head.

"Then I'll go back and get your friends," Graham said. "And I'll bring them here one by one if that's what it takes."

Ryan noticed that Mrs. Stahley looked tired. Even though she wore heavy makeup and the wig, he could see there were big circles under her eyes.

"What are you going to do?" Ryan said.

"They'll find us sooner or later," Mrs. Stahley said. "I could try to hide, but I'm tired. And I don't like the thought of cooping Darrion up for the next few years. I have a plan."

Mrs. Stahley said she wanted Darrion to stay with the kids. "She could live with Vicki and you, couldn't she?"

Chaya nodded. "We'd be glad to take her in," she said.

"Mother, why didn't you tell me this?" Darrion said. "What are you going to do?"

"I'm going to give myself up," Mrs. Stahley said.

"No!" Darrion shouted.

Mrs. Stahley put her hand on Darrion's shoulder. "It's the best for all of us. If I come forward peacefully, maybe I can convince them I was just concerned for you when I went into hiding."

"But you know what they'll do," Darrion said.

"Your safety means more to me than my own life," Mrs. Stahley said.

"Why do you have to choose?" Darrion said. "We can both be safe."

Mrs. Stahley shook her head. "I have to go now," she said.

"At least tell us where the secret documents are," Ryan said. "We might be able to use them to free you."

Mrs. Stahley shook her head. "I have never seen them," she said. "I only know what my husband said about them."

"And you told us they could be used to help fight the GC," Ryan said.

"I also told you they were in a secret place," Mrs. Stahley said. "I know the combination is in a file in Maxwell's upstairs office. I never asked, and he never told me where the safe was located."

"Mother, I won't let you go!"

Mrs. Stahley hugged her daughter. "Do not risk yourself for me," she said to Ryan. "Take care of my daughter."

When Vicki returned, the group brought her up to date on what had happened. Mrs. Stahley and Darrion were hugging and saying good-bye. Vicki was concerned that Judd still hadn't shown up.

Vicki made sure Darrion would be OK at Loretta's house until they returned from Chaya's mother's funeral.

"What can I expect?" Vicki said as she and Chaya drove toward South Barrington.

"I expect my father to be cold," Chaya said. "He won't look at me. He'll be upset the burial has taken so long."

"Why?" Vicki said.

"Jewish custom is to bury the dead quickly," Chaya said. "Because of the bombing, he no doubt had difficulty getting her body released."

"What about the service?" Vicki said.

"You won't see anything fancy," Chaya said. "Jewish law forbids it. We are taught we are all equal in death, so the coffin is plain wood. My mother will be dressed in a simple linen shroud."

"You told me something about prayers for people who have died," Vicki said. "Will they do that?"

"You mean *shivah*," Chaya said. "Another form of that Hebrew word means 'seven.' For seven days we mourn the person who has died. People will come and sit with the family and pay their respects. There are morning and evening prayer services at the home."

By the time they arrived at the service, Chaya had explained more about Jewish beliefs. Vicki left the flowers she had brought in the car, since Jews believe a funeral is not a time for decoration.

"I can tell this is going to be different from Bruce's funeral," Vicki said.

As Vicki and Chaya walked toward the group, a man met them. Chaya seemed to recognize him.

"I am sorry for your loss," the man said. "I have been asked to do a difficult thing."

"My father . . . ," Chaya said.

"Yes. He requested if I saw you, that I tell you it would be best for you not to be here."

Chaya looked sternly at the man. "This is my mother," she said.

"Your father says you have left the faith," the man said. "Out of respect for him and your mother, I beg you. Please go."

"Out of respect for my mother," Chaya said, "I will stay."

Instead of going to the front, Chaya and Vicki sat in the back. The rabbi recited a psalm and read a passage from the Scriptures, and the group chanted a memorial prayer.

The coffin was carried to the grave site and lowered. Chaya's father, weeping uncontrollably, took a shovel and placed some dirt on the coffin. Then people formed two lines, and the mourners passed through.

"They're saying something to your father," Vicki said.

A tear fell down Chaya's cheek. She recited the greeting, then translated it. "May God comfort you together with all the mourners of Zion and Jerusalem," she said.

Vicki noticed Chaya's father did not look at them during the entire service. When the group had left for their cars, Chaya slowly went forward to the edge of the grave. She picked up the shovel and let some dirt fall on her mother's casket. Then she pulled a small Bible from her pocket and opened it to the New Testament.

"Your mother isn't in that box," Vicki said.

"I know," Chaya said. "I believe she is with God."

She held the Bible up and read with a trembling voice, "'When this happens—when our perishable earthly bodies have been transformed into heavenly bodies that will never die—then at last the Scriptures will come true:

"'Death is swallowed up in victory.
O death, where is your victory?
O death, where is your sting?'"

Chaya wept, and Vicki stayed with her until she was ready to return home.

Ryan inched through the line with Lionel in front of him. Hundreds of people filed past Bruce's body. The casket was open now, and on both sides of the casket were beautiful flowers.

Lionel stopped at the head of the casket, then patted Bruce's folded hands. Ryan came next. Bruce looked like he was asleep. Ryan touched Bruce's hands. They were cold and rigid.

"Good-bye, friend," Ryan managed to say. Then he broke down.

Rayford Steele, who was shaking hands with people as they filed past, helped Ryan to the front pew.

"You OK?" Rayford said.

"I'm sorry," Ryan said.

"Don't ever apologize for feeling bad about things like this," Rayford said. "This is a really sad thing. Would you like a glass of water?"

Ryan wiped his eyes. "Why do people always give you water when there's something wrong?" Ryan said.

Rayford smiled. "I don't know," he said. "The other thing they do is try to make you feel better. They say things like, 'Bruce is in a better place now' or 'Bruce is with his family.' That's true, but it's still hard to know he's gone."

"I just thought of something," Ryan said. "He's with Raymie and Mrs. Steele, too."

Rayford looked away.

"There's something I never told you, Mr. Steele," Ryan said. "Can I tell you now?"

"Go ahead," Rayford said.

"On the day of the disappearances, I came over to your house. My mom and dad weren't home, and I didn't know what to do. I came to see Mrs. Steele or Raymie. The door was open a little, so I walked in."

Rayford listened carefully and paid no attention to the mourners who were passing by.

"I went up to Raymie's room and saw his nightclothes in a neat pile on the bed," Ryan said.

"When I found them on his bed, I folded them," Rayford said.

"Then I heard a noise down the hall," Ryan said. "You were on the floor of your bedroom, your shoulders shaking. I didn't want to disturb you, so I ran home. That's when I found out that both my mom and dad had died."

"You should've said something," Rayford said. "I could've helped."

"It still makes me sad to think about it," Ryan said. "But even though it was bad, it made me go to Raymie's church. And that's where I met Bruce."

Rayford put his hand on Ryan's neck and squeezed it. "I'm really proud of you," he said. "I wasn't around much when you and Raymie played, but I know he liked you. I can see why."

"I miss him a lot," Ryan said.

Rayford stood.

"Can I ask what you're going to do next?" Ryan said. "Are you still going to work for the Global Community, or can you stay around here?"

"I wish I could stay," Rayford said. "But I'm still flying for the GC. I've decided I want to be obedient to God, even if that means I'm giving service to Carpathia. He wants me to be back in New Babylon next week."

25

WHEN Vicki hadn't heard from Judd by Sunday evening, she grew more concerned. Lionel and Ryan had no idea where he might be. Chaya wanted to be alone, so she dropped Vicki off at Loretta's house.

Chloe Williams and Amanda Steele asked about Chaya.

"I guess she's doing OK, considering what she's been through today," Vicki said.

"She's facing two big losses at one time," Amanda said. "It's important for her to grieve and not shove it under the rug."

"She'll be doing fine and then, all of a sudden, she loses it," Vicki said.

"That's common," Amanda said. "It's a process. You don't grieve once and move on. Most people feel waves of bad feelings wash over them. There could be regrets or other memories that come back again and again. You realize the person is gone and is never coming back.

That's really tough. Then, over time, the waves slow down, and you have longer periods where you think normally. You get back into your routine."

"But it's sad that you do that," Vicki said. "For me, I lost a father. He's never coming back. But the world just goes on."

"And that's what Bruce would want you to do," Amanda said. "Think about his own story. When his wife and children were raptured, he grieved and grieved. But God used that grief. Bruce went into action and helped others come to know God."

"Is there anything I can do to help Chaya?" Vicki said.

"When I lost my mom," Chloe said, "it really helped when I chose a keepsake of hers. I gave her a necklace before I went to school, and that's one thing I still cherish."

"Maybe she can go back to her house," Amanda said, "not tonight, or even this week, but in a couple of weeks, and find something that reminds her of her mother."

"As sad as it is, I don't think her dad would allow it," Vicki said.

The talk turned to the memorial service and what had happened afterward with Verna Zee. Vicki was interested.

"Buck and I met her at the magazine office later," Chloe said. "Basically she said she knew it was Tsion Ben-Judah in that service, and I planted a little doubt in her mind."

"Did she buy it?" Vicki said.

"Not at first," Chloe said, "but then she called here, and Loretta didn't give her any information. She backed off a little, and Buck challenged her. I think she'll leave it alone for now."

"At least she came to the service like she promised," Amanda said.

"Did she mention anything about what Mr. Steele preached?" Vicki said.

"She said it was strange, all those predictions coming true," Chloe said. "When I asked her what it would take to convince her about God, she said an earthquake would be pretty hard to argue with."

Taylor Graham had been gone a long time. Judd wondered if he really would get each of the kids and bring them to the hideout, or if that was a bluff to get him to talk.

Judd sorted the facts in his mind. He wanted to believe the pilot. To have someone inside the Global Community who could give information and help him escape seemed too good to be true. Maybe it was.

Judd thought of escaping. He knew the woods nearby well enough. He could make it to the road in ten or fifteen minutes of hard running. But something told him to stay.

Then he thought about Bruce. It was evening, and the viewing of Bruce's body was long over. Judd had missed his chance of saying good-bye to his friend.

Ryan was reading in bed when he saw Phoenix sit up. The hair on the dog's back stiffened, and he growled.

"What is it, boy?" Ryan said.

Phoenix jumped off the bed and whined. He put both paws up and scratched at the door.

"OK, show me what's out there."

Ryan followed Phoenix up the stairs. There was a light on in the kitchen, but the hallway and the living room were dark. Ryan noticed a thin strip of light under Lionel's door. Judd's door was open, and the room was dark.

Phoenix went to the front door and sniffed. He turned and barked loudly.

"What is it?" Ryan said.

As his eyes adjusted to the room, he saw the figure of a man sitting quietly in an easy chair. Ryan saw a red glow and smelled smoke in the room.

"Remember me?" the man said in a low voice.

Ryan shivered. Whoever it was had broken into the house and was waiting. Ryan did remember the voice, but he couldn't place it.

"I can't even see you, let alone remember you," Ryan said.

Phoenix was barking wildly and moved toward the man.

"Grab your dog and put him away before I do," the man said.

Ryan moved closer and grabbed Phoenix's collar.

"Put him in the closet and shut the door," the man ordered.

"I'll put him back downstairs in—"

"I said, put him in the closet," the man said, gritting his teeth.

Ryan obeyed. He felt bad putting the dog in such a small place, but he didn't have a choice.

A door opened down the hall. Lionel entered the room.

314

"What's all the noise?" Lionel said. "And why is
Phoenix—"

"Shut up and sit down," the man said.

"We have company," Ryan said.

"How did you get in here?" Lionel said.

Ryan heard the click of a gun.

"Doesn't matter how I got in. What matters is that
I'm here. Now sit down."

Lionel and Ryan sat.

"Where's your friend?" the man said.

"We have more than one," Ryan said.

"Don't get cute. The tall kid. Judd."

"We haven't seen him since this morning," Lionel
said. "Why?"

"'Cause I need to talk to him," the man said.

Phoenix's muffled barks came from the closet. He
scratched harder at the door, frantically trying to escape.

"You really don't remember me, do you?" the man
said. He fiddled with a lamp shade and clicked on a light.

The flash nearly blinded Ryan. The man had turned
the lamp away from himself and onto the boys. Ryan
shielded his face with his hand, and the shadowy sight of
the man sparked his memory. The long black coat. Short
hair. Under the L tracks. The man with the gun.

"Remember me now?" The man laughed.

"He's with the Global Community," Ryan said to
Lionel. "He was going to kill Judd and Vicki and Mr.
Stahley."

"Until this little runt jumped me," the man said.

"What do you want with Judd?" Ryan said.

"It's personal," the man said. "We're looking for a few missing people. That Stahley woman and her kid. A pilot named Graham. You know where any of them are?"

"For a professional bad guy, you have a hard time keeping track of people," Ryan said.

Lionel flinched. "Cool it," he whispered to Ryan. "I think I know how we can get out—"

"Knock it off," the man yelled.

Lionel sat up.

"Maybe I need to show you I mean business." The man raised his gun at Lionel, then pointed it a few inches to the right. "This will quiet the little pooch," the man said.

"No!" Ryan screamed.

Ryan heard a quick spurt from the silencer and a thwack behind him as the bullet went through the hollow door and into the closet. Phoenix stopped barking. Ryan turned to see the huge bullet hole. The hole was at the same height as the doorknob.

"Stay where you are," the man said, "unless you'd like one of these for yourself."

"You better not have hurt my dog!" Ryan said.

Phoenix whimpered inside the closet and barked again.

"Listen to him," the man said. "Your dog's fine. But I'll aim a little lower next time unless you tell me where your friend is."

"We don't know," Lionel said. "He was supposed to meet us after a funeral today, but he didn't show up."

"Not good enough," the man said, raising his gun again.

"It's the truth!" Ryan screamed, standing to block the closet door.

316

"Sit down!"

"No!" Ryan said.

"I told you, get out of the way—"

Ryan heard a loud bang and closed his eyes. Then he heard another spurt from the gun. Glass shattered. Ryan opened his eyes and saw the man running for the front door. He opened it, held his gun in front of his face, then pivoted into a shooting stance. When he didn't see his target, he shouted at the boys to stay where they were. Then he was gone.

"What happened?" Ryan said.

"Get Phoenix and let's get outta here," Lionel said. "I'll explain on our way to Vicki's place."

Lionel collapsed on the couch when they arrived at Vicki's house. Ryan fell to his knees, gasping for air, as Phoenix bounded through the door. Vicki got Phoenix a bowl of water and waited for Lionel and Ryan to catch their breath.

"What happened?" Vicki said when they could finally talk.

"First," Lionel said, "I don't think they followed us, but in case they did, who's here?"

"Darrion, Chaya, and me," Vicki said. "What's going on? Did you find Judd?"

"No," Lionel said, "but we did find out we're not the only ones looking for him."

Ryan explained who the man with the gun was and what had happened. "I still don't know why the guy took off like that," he said.

"You didn't see him?" Lionel said.

"Who?" Ryan said.

"Just before I whispered for you to cool it," Lionel said, "I saw a guy look in the window."

"Another GC guy?" Vicki said.

"I don't know who he was," Lionel said, "but he got a good look at Ryan and me. He moved around to the front to get a look at the other guy. I figured they weren't together. That's when you stood up."

"I wasn't about to let him blow Phoenix away," Ryan said.

"He shot at the window, and the other guy took off," Lionel said. "That's when we bolted."

"What did the guy at the window look like?" Vicki said.

"It was pretty dark, but I could tell he was tall," Lionel said. "Looked like a swimmer."

Ryan asked a few more questions and then shouted, "It was Taylor Graham!"

"What would he be doing at the house?" Vicki said.

"Looking for Judd," Ryan said, "or me. Whatever the reason, I'm glad he showed up."

"I feel like the walls are closing in," Lionel said. "Let's get Darrion and Chaya and get outta here."

"Wait," Vicki said. "First, I'm not going anywhere until we find Judd. Second, if we run, they'll think we're guilty of something, and we're not! If you miss the meeting with Mrs. Jenness tomorrow, people from the school could be looking for you as well."

"If they find us here, they'll find Darrion," Lionel said. "That'll connect us with Mrs. Stahley, who's wanted for murder!"

"And we all know it was the GC who killed Mr. Stahley," Vicki said. "We have to keep our lives as normal as possible until we find Judd and figure out what to do."

———————————————

Judd looked for a way to escape from his underground prison, but he found none. Taylor Graham had locked him in a room deep inside the hangar. The heavy metal door was impossible to open, so Judd spent his time looking through the desk and the bookshelves that lined one wall of the room.

In the center drawer of the desk Judd found paper clips and stationery. In the back he discovered a shoe box filled with old baseball cards. *These have to be worth a fortune,* Judd thought. Mixed in was what looked like a key card to a garage. Judd tossed the box back into the desk and kept looking.

In the bottom drawer Judd found huge pages rolled into a scroll. He cleared the desk and unrolled it, looking at the precise drawings.

A blueprint, Judd thought. As he studied it closer, he realized it was a drawing of the Stahley home and underground hangar.

There has to be a passage from the house to here, Judd thought.

He found drawings for the upstairs, the kitchen and patio area, the basement, and then he found an arrow with the word *entrance* scrawled underneath.

Judd flipped the page over and saw a drawing of the underground hangar. He found another arrow drawn in

319

a small room in the back of the hangar. When he studied it further, he realized he was in that very room.

Now we're getting somewhere, Judd thought. *If I can get into the house, I'm free. But how?*

The arrow on the drawing pointed to what looked like the bookshelf. Judd pulled books away, hoping a panel would move. He took each book off the shelf and put it back, but nothing happened.

Next he tried moving the actual shelves, but they were somehow anchored to the wall. Mr. Stahley had placed decorative plates and mugs along the shelves. Behind one was a square, silver plate with a slot in the middle. A red light flashed above the slot. He studied it for a moment, then quickly went back to the desk and retrieved the weird card in the shoe box.

It fit perfectly, but when he inserted it, nothing happened. When Judd pulled the card out, however, a green light flashed below the slot. Something was moving behind Judd. A door? A vault?

Judd turned and was amazed to see a section of the tile floor rising. Underneath, a safe with an electronic combination came into view.

26

THE NEXT morning Lionel retrieved some clothes from Judd's house and headed for school. Vicki said she would be praying for him and stood across the hall from the principal's office while Lionel went in.

The school secretary was just getting in and asked him to wait. Finally, she buzzed Mrs. Jenness.

The principal opened the door and ushered Lionel in. Inside, a burly, black man about the size of Lionel's father stood and embraced him.

"I don't mean to scare you," the man said. "I've just heard so much about you, I feel like I know you."

"Who are you?" Lionel said.

"This is Mr. Sebring," Mrs. Jenness said. "He called me last Friday about meeting you."

"Nathan Sebring," the man said, "but my friends call me Nate. Your mother called me that when we were kids."

"My mother?" Lionel said.

"Lucinda was one of my dearest friends," Nathan said. "I called her Cindy. I knew your father as well. Fine man."

Mrs. Jenness asked them to sit. "We had trouble locating you with your current address, Lionel," she said. "The house was empty. Boarded up, actually."

Lionel didn't speak. He didn't want to talk about where he was staying until he was asked.

"I knew your mama when we were little kids," Nathan said. "Some of your family's still down South, and when I asked about you, they said—"

"I didn't think I had any family left down South," Lionel said. "Didn't they get taken in the disappearances?"

"Sure, some of 'em did," Nathan said, "but a couple were left. I think they heard through your Uncle André that you were still alive. I'm sorry to hear about his passin'."

The two stared at Lionel as if he was supposed to know what to say. Lionel stood. "Well, it was really nice meeting you," he said. "I'd better get to class."

"Now hold on a minute," Nathan said, taking Lionel's arm. Lionel looked at the man's hand, and he took it away. "Your family asked me to come for you," Nathan continued. "They gave me papers."

"They're in order," Mrs. Jenness said.

"I told them I'd come and get you. They made me promise not to come back unless I brought you back."

Lionel forced a smile. "That's very kind of you," he said, "but I don't know the family back there anymore. I wouldn't feel comfortable."

Nathan looked at Mrs. Jenness. "He'll get used to it in time," Nathan said. "He'll be like a bird let out of a cage down there."

"Lionel," Mrs. Jenness said, "if it's true that you have no family here and there are relatives who want you to live with them, I don't see that you have any real choice in the matter."

"Now you've got that right, ma'am," Nathan said. "The boy just doesn't understand how much love those people have for him." Nathan looked at Lionel. "If you knew how much they cared, you wouldn't put up a fuss."

"I don't want to go," Lionel said. "I'm happy where I am."

Nathan cocked his head. "Now if that don't beat all," he said. "I'm sorry. I guess I just don't understand the culture up here. A man rides hundreds of miles on a train to find somebody he's never met, and when he finds him . . . *mm mm mm.*"

"You could have phoned," Lionel said.

"I did phone the only place that has contact with you," Nathan said. "And Mrs. Jenness, who has been a wonderful help, offered her complete assistance."

"Lionel," Mrs. Jenness said, "you have a right not to go, but Mr. Sebring and the family also have the right to petition the Global Community Social Services."

"And I'll do it, too," Nathan said. "Out of respect for your relations down South, of course."

"Can he really do that?" Lionel said.

"I can and I will," Nathan said.

Lionel felt alone. Bruce was dead. Judd had disappeared. He was glad Vicki was outside waiting for him.

"Can you give me some time to think it over?" Lionel said.

"You can have the whole day," Nathan said. "I scheduled train tickets leaving tomorrow for the two of us. Where can I come talk to you?"

"Why don't you leave me your hotel number?" Lionel said. "I'll call you this evening."

Judd had slept fitfully on a cot Taylor Graham left outside the door. Judd dragged it inside and heard the door lock.

"Hey, don't I get something to eat?" Judd had yelled, but Graham didn't respond.

Judd awoke the next morning and heard moaning in the next room. He banged on the door and yelled. In a few minutes, Graham returned with orange juice and sweet rolls, but the man winced when he put the food on the desk.

"What's wrong?" Judd said. Then he noticed the bloodstain on the back of Graham's shirt.

"Had a little trouble at your house last night," Graham said.

"*My* house?" Judd said.

"I told you I was going to bring your friends here one by one," Graham said. "But I was a little late. The GC had a guy talking with Ryan and another kid."

"Right." Judd smirked. "You're just saying that to—"

"I'm telling the truth," Graham said sternly. "The guy

saw me and fired. It only grazed my shoulder, but it hurts like crazy."

"I've gotta get outta here," Judd said. "Do you know what happened to my friends?"

"Don't have a clue," Graham said. "But I'm not letting you go."

Judd stood and ran past the pilot. Graham stuck out his foot and held it tightly against the door. Judd turned and lunged at Graham, who easily stepped aside. Judd went sprawling on the floor.

"Whether you believe it or not," Graham said, "I'm doing this for your own good."

Vicki called an emergency meeting of the Young Trib Force that afternoon. The kids ordered pizza, but everyone was so upset, no one felt like eating.

"I can't believe it," Ryan said. "Why do they come for Lionel now, after all this time?"

"Don't ask me," Lionel said. "Seems like I'd have some kind of say in it. I don't even know these people."

"What about your friend at the GC Social Services," Chaya said to Vicki. "Couldn't she help?"

"I called Candace from the school this morning," Vicki said. "She told me she'd do everything she could, but it doesn't look good. If the guy really is empowered by the family, Lionel could fight it, but he'd eventually have to go."

"And if that's true, I'd only be making them mad if I draw this thing out," Lionel said. He put his head on the table. "I don't know what to do."

"Maybe you should go with Judd," Ryan said, "wher-ever he is."

"Don't joke about it, OK?" Lionel shouted.

"What'd I do?" Ryan said.

"This is my life we're talking about," Lionel said. "They're taking me away. Do you understand that?"

Ryan got up and slammed his chair into the table.

"I hope you do go," Ryan said. "The sooner the better." Ryan ran out of the room.

Chaya stood, but Vicki motioned for her to stay. "Let him go," Vicki said.

The kids sat in awkward silence. Finally, Lionel said, "I wish Judd were here."

Vicki did too, but she didn't say it. Judd had been their anchor. Whether he made the right decision or not, he took charge. The kids could lean on him. Even though she wasn't the oldest, she felt a responsibility to take his place.

"Judd's not here," Vicki said, "and neither is Bruce. We've been saying all along we want to make our own decisions and that God can lead us just as well as he can lead older people."

Lionel looked at Chaya. "Please tell me there's some-thing in the Bible that'll let me stay," he said.

"The closest thing I can come up with is the verse about obeying authorities," Chaya said. "I know it's not what you want to hear."

The group threw around ideas and options. Lionel could go into hiding. He could stay and fight the system. Or he could go with Nathan. After a few minutes Chaya took the floor.

"No matter what you decide," Chaya said, "there are some things in Bruce's notes we need to talk about. He made it no secret that we would one day become the mortal enemies of the Antichrist. We've done a lot of worrying about money, but one day, even to buy a loaf of bread, you'll have to take a mark on your forehead or your hand."

"Wait a minute," Lionel said. "What do you mean? Like a stamp or something?"

"It's not clear what form it'll take," Chaya said, "but if you don't have it, you'll be in trouble. We won't be able to fake it. And once you take the mark, you've chosen sides with the devil. You're lost forever."

"What if you don't take it?" Vicki said. "Is there any hope for those people?"

"The people who don't have the mark will have to live in hiding," Chaya continued. "Their lives won't be worth anything to the Global Community, so they'll have to take care of themselves."

"I don't like the sound of that," Lionel said.

"Bruce wrote about this, and I think Dr. Ben-Judah agrees," Chaya said. "Cash is going to be meaningless soon. We need to take what money we have left and convert it to gold."

"What I have left wouldn't buy an ounce," Lionel said.

"Why gold?" Vicki said.

"Cash might be phased out pretty soon," Chaya said. "Gold can still be used for food and supplies. That is, until the day comes when we're forced to choose whether to take the mark of the Beast."

"Then we have to put that in an edition of the *Underground*," Vicki said. "Especially this thing about taking the mark."

"I agree," Lionel said. "Buck Williams is coming out with a *Global Community Weekly* article that spells out the great earthquake that's coming. You could use some of his material, too."

"What do you mean *I* should?" Vicki said. "You're not going to be part of it?"

"I've made up my mind," Lionel said. "It tears me up to say this, but I'm going to call the guy and tell him I'll go."

Judd was angry. He didn't know why he was being held. If the Global Community wanted to question him, they could have done it at any time. But here he was, alone, separated from his friends.

"Let's say I believe you," Judd said. "Let's say you are keeping me here for my own good. What happens then?"

"We work together," Taylor said. "We find Mrs. Stahley and Darrion and figure out where those documents are."

"Can you get a message to my friends?" Judd said.

"I can send an E-mail right now," Graham said.

Graham plugged in an incredibly lightweight computer and turned it on. A window opened with a video display of news. Graham was about to open his E-mail program when Judd stopped him.

"Look at that," Judd said.

On the screen was a news anchorwoman with a

graphic of Maxwell Stahley behind her. Graham turned up the audio as the anchor introduced a reporter.

"We're live at police headquarters," the reporter said, "where only moments ago a dramatic arrest was made in the Maxwell Stahley murder case."

Judd was horrified to see video footage of Mrs. Stahley being led away from a hotel parking lot.

"She was dressed as an old woman," the reporter continued, "but someone at the hotel recognized her from news reports, and police took Louise Stahley into custody."

The video footage ended, and the reporter was shown outside police headquarters. "Authorities tell us the woman will remain here overnight. Then she'll be handed over to the Global Community early tomorrow morning."

Taylor Graham cursed and slammed his hand against the desk. "There goes our chance to find those documents," he said.

Judd stood and took the key card from his pocket. He knew Graham was telling the truth now. He slid the key card into the slot, and the safe rose from beneath the floor.

"I know where the documents are," Judd said. "Now all we have to do is figure out the combination."

Lionel put his suitcase down in the foyer of Bruce's house. It was late. No one seemed to want to look at him. Lionel shook hands with some and hugged others. Vicki was in tears.

"Do you know where he is?" Lionel said.

"Bruce's room," Vicki managed.

Lionel found Ryan staring out Bruce's window.

"I'm sorry for snapping at you," Lionel said.

"Yeah, it's OK," Ryan said flatly. "I didn't mean what I said either."

"I don't hold it against you," Lionel said. "We're all pretty raw right now."

"So you're giving up?" Ryan said.

Lionel frowned. He didn't want to get into it with Ryan again. If things had to end, he wanted them to end well.

"I don't think you're rid of me yet," Lionel said. "A couple of years and I'll be on my own."

"A couple of years is a long time when there's only five left altogether," Ryan said.

"I don't know why this has happened," Lionel said. "I keep thinking maybe there's somebody down South who needs to hear the truth. My going might be the only way they'll hear it."

Ryan turned. "I'm sorry . . . about everything," he said.

"We had some good fights," Lionel said.

Ryan smiled.

Lionel saw a van pull into the driveway. Nathan Sebring got out.

Lionel shook hands with Ryan.

"Call me," Ryan said.

"You bet," Lionel said.

As Lionel grabbed his suitcase, Darrion came out of

her room, crying. "They've arrested my mother," she said. The others came to comfort her.

As he got in the car, Lionel looked back at the house. The kids were standing outside. He had been through so much with these friends. He allowed a thought to cross his mind: *This might be the last time I see any of them in this life.*

27

JUDD looked at his E-mail early the next morning, but there were no answers from Vicki, Lionel, or Ryan. Taylor Graham had showed Judd how to send and receive mail without tipping the GC. "It's unsafe to use the satellite phone," Graham had said.

Judd tried to think of who else he could reach to get to the kids. He sent a message to Buck, Chloe, and even Dr. Ben-Judah. While he was on-line, the computer blipped.

"Incoming message," a voice said.

The screen switched, and Judd saw words being typed by Dr. Tsion Ben-Judah. *Judd, I have had no contact with your friends, but I must ask you a question.*

Go ahead, Judd typed back to him.

I am receiving hundreds of responses already to postings on the Internet, Dr. Ben-Judah wrote. *As you can imagine, I am unable to respond to them all. A few are from younger readers. I would like to send a note of thanks and tell them a colleague will respond to their questions or concerns. Would you assist me with this important task?*

A colleague with Tsion Ben-Judah? Judd thought. Judd certainly had the time now that he was also in hiding.

I would be honored, Judd wrote. *Send the messages immediately.*

Vicki was glad Ryan didn't argue about staying at Judd's house. When a neighbor approached them and asked about a strange man snooping about, Vicki told Ryan to get back in the car. Ryan slept on the couch at Vicki's place and was ready for school early the next morning.

Vicki checked her E-mail before she left and let out a yelp when she opened the message from Judd. Ryan read over her shoulder.

Vicki, Judd wrote, *I'm safe and staying with a friend. Ryan knows him, too. He's convinced I'm in real danger. Ryan knows this place—it's behind a "green hillside that opens up." I've made a discovery but need more information to help D's mother. Let me know when you get this.* The note was signed JT.

"What does he mean?" Vicki said. "Is he in Israel?"

"The only green hillside I can think of is the one that leads to the underground hangar at the Stahleys," Ryan said.

"You think his discovery is the secret documents?" Vicki said.

"That's something that could help Darrion's mother," Ryan said. "Write him back and tell him the combination is in Mr. Stahley's office upstairs."

Judd read Vicki's message carefully. Vicki told him Lionel was gone. Judd was stunned.

When Taylor Graham returned later that morning, Judd asked if they should bring Ryan into hiding with him.

"Not yet," Graham said. "I went to your house last night but couldn't find him. From the reports I get, he's safe. Which is more than I can say for myself."

"What are you hearing?" Judd said.

"I picked up a radio transmission a few minutes ago," Graham said. "They have GC posted in Stahleys' house. They've found out about the documents, but they don't know where they are. We have to get that combination."

Judd showed him Vicki's message. "The combination is inside the house," Judd said. "Do you know how to get inside?"

"Max never told me how he came and went from the house," Graham said. "I always used the outside entrance."

"Can't we just use some kind of explosive on it?" Judd said.

"Material's too strong," Graham said. "Plus we'd draw attention to ourselves with a blast that big."

"What are you going to do?" Judd said.

"I'll have to try and sneak in from the outside," Graham said.

A knock on the hotel room door awakened Lionel. He stretched and felt something crawling on his arm. Nathan Sebring had chosen a shabby hotel near downtown

Chicago. During the drive Lionel could tell the man didn't want to talk. He wouldn't explain where they were headed or what time their train left the next day.

Nathan answered the door and welcomed an overweight man he called Tom.

"Good work, Chuck," Tom said to Nathan. "They bought the accent?"

"I told you not to worry," Nathan said.

The two exchanged papers, and Tom handed Nathan a wad of cash.

"This is your next assignment," Tom said.

Nathan looked at Lionel. "Change of plans, big boy," Nathan said. "You're getting a ride from my friend."

"I thought we were going on a train," Lionel said. "And why is he calling you Chuck?"

Nathan grabbed his overnight bag and laughed. "Nice meetin' ya," he said. Then he was out the door.

"What about my family?" Lionel said.

Tom told Lionel to get dressed.

"I need to take a shower, bugs are crawling all ov—"

"I said, get your clothes on and get in the van!" Tom yelled.

———————————

Vicki was in a daze at school. The loss of Lionel made her feel more alone. Mrs. Jenness called an all-school assembly, and Vicki found her friend Shelly sitting near the back.

"You're not gonna believe this," Shelly said. "I was working in the office yesterday when the Global Community called. This is mandatory."

"They made the school call this assembly?" Vicki said.

"It's a grief awareness seminar," Shelly said.

Mrs. Jenness introduced the speaker as a therapist. She also attended an Enigma Babyon One World Faith congregation and had personally met Nicolae Carpathia.

"Two good reasons to get up and walk out," Shelly whispered.

The speaker began by asking how many people had lost family members and friends in the last two years. Almost every hand went up.

"You have the power within yourself to overcome anything," the woman said. "No matter how bad your situation, if you learn to trust yourself and your feelings, you can become the person the Global Community needs."

Judd had free rein of the hangar. For exercise, he jogged. Graham showed him a stash of food that could last months if they needed it. Judd and Graham tried in vain to find the passageway from the hangar to the house.

"I'm headed topside," Graham said. "I'm gonna chance it. Wish me luck or whatever you do."

Judd turned to the computer. He spent most of his time there, communicating with his friends and those who e-mailed Tsion. Some of the kids who wrote the rabbi wanted more evidence, but most of them had come to Christ and were asking what they should do with their faith.

One message stood out. The screen name was Pavel. The boy wrote Tsion and said he wanted to understand the truth about the man named Jesus. Tsion suggested that Judd send him a copy of the Scriptures and excerpt some of Bruce's teachings. Judd did that, but he also struck up a conversation. Judd asked where Pavel lived and what his family had been through during the war.

We have not experienced any harm during the war, Pavel wrote. *My father works for the Global Community here in New Babylon. One day he mentioned the potentate was upset by the message of the rabbi in Israel and of the men who preach at the Wailing Wall. I became curious. I read the rabbi's messages and listened to the men at the Wailing Wall.*

Judd couldn't believe it. The son of someone at Global Community headquarters was interested in the gospel!

Judd explained the life of Christ as clearly as he could. *Jesus was born of a virgin and remained sinless his entire life. He was not just a good man; he was perfect. He was God in the flesh. Sin separates a person from God forever, and every person on earth has sinned. But Jesus' death paid the penalty for anyone who believes in him. If a person asks for God's forgiveness, God answers and freely gives salvation.*

Judd included Scripture references and a personal message at the end. *If you have video capabilities and other questions,* he wrote, *tell me when it would be safe and we'll talk.*

As he wrote the message, Judd wondered if this boy was actually who he said he was. For all Judd knew, Pavel could be Nicolae Carpathia himself.

Judd said a prayer and pushed the Send button. *I don't care who it is or what his motives are,* he thought. *Everybody needs to hear this before it's too late.*

Vicki couldn't wait until it was time for questions. Two microphones were positioned in the front and back of the auditorium. At each end, students lined up and waited their turn. Vicki was second in line at the microphone in the back.

Kids who had lost family members in the bombings were in tears. Most of the kids were energized by what the therapist said. They were into the positive message. Vicki's heart went out to them. What the speaker had said made her angry.

"I can tell you loved your brother very much," the woman said to a freshman at the front of the room. "And I can tell you where he is right now. You have him right in your heart. You have to keep your brother alive. And you have to trust yourself to do that."

Vicki rolled her eyes. She was up next.

Judd's video hookup with Pavel was successful. The kid looked small and wore thick glasses. He had blond hair and sat low in his chair, so he stayed in the bottom of the picture while he spoke. Pavel could understand six languages, but he could speak only four. He apologized for his English.

"I cannot tell you who my father is," Pavel said, "but it is true. I am in the apartment building in Nicolae Carpathia's compound."

"You know that Dr. Ben-Judah's message is not very popular with the potentate," Judd said.

"I understand," Pavel said. "But since the disappearances and the war, I have been searching for answers. The ones the Global Community gives do not satisfy."

Judd's computer blipped. "Hang on, Pavel, I need to check something," Judd said.

The message looked weird. He could tell from the message window that it wasn't from any of his friends. He gasped when he saw it was from the Global Community. It read: *Global Community Priority Directive: The pilot is in custody. Continue the search for the daughter and the two boys. Search their homes and schools first.*

The speaker pointed to Vicki and smiled. "You have a question?" she said.

"Yes," Vicki said. "If you knew for sure where a person was after they had died, wouldn't that be the best hope of all?"

The woman looked bewildered. "I don't understand the question," she said.

Mrs. Jenness stood and moved toward the woman.

Vicki continued. "Let's say your father dies on the day of the bombings and you're really bummed," she said. "But you know without any doubt that your dad went to heaven. Wouldn't that help in your grief?"

Mrs. Jenness whispered something to the woman, and she nodded. "Heaven is a state of mind, not a real place," the woman said. "I think we should leave matters of faith to our religious leaders. Next?"

"No, answer the question!" Vicki said.

"You, in front?" the woman said.

The girl at the next microphone looked back at Vicki. It was Shelly!

"I'd like to hear you answer her question," Shelly said.

Someone in the crowd yelled, "Answer it!" Vicki heard a few boos and some applause. Things were quickly getting out of hand.

"All right," the woman said, trying to regain control. "If a person knew what happened after a loved one had died, in a psychological sense that would give him or her hope. But we have to deal with reality here. And the reality is, we can't know what's beyond this life until we've gone there."

"That's where you're wrong," Vicki said. "We *can* know."

"So you're saying you can judge whether a person is good enough to go to heaven?" the woman said.

"Yeah, who made you God?" someone said.

"I can tell you that *nobody* is good enough to go to heaven," Vicki said. "Every one of us has sinned. But God made a way for us—"

"That's enough," Mrs. Jenness said. Global Community guards moved toward Vicki. "Byrne," the principal shouted, "sit down or you'll be escorted out of here."

Vicki stepped away from the microphone. Everyone turned to look at her. She didn't want to betray her faith, but she also didn't want to give Mrs. Jenness any more ammunition against her.

She sat. During the rest of the meeting, three girls passed notes to her asking to talk with her when the assembly was over.

Judd gave Pavel some new materials and asked if he could get in touch with him later in the day. Pavel said he could safely talk at midnight Judd's time.

As soon as the line was free, Judd contacted Tsion Ben-Judah. He had to find some way of protecting Ryan and Darrion.

Lionel was hustled into the van by another man. Several other boys were already inside. They all looked scared. A cage separated the driver and the backseats. Lionel felt like he was going to prison.

"Where are they taking us?" Lionel asked an older boy in the seat in front of him. The boy didn't respond.

Lionel watched the traffic from inside the tinted windows of the van. They went south on the expressway until the road forked. One sign said Memphis; another said Indianapolis. The driver stayed to the right and drove toward Memphis.

Ryan was playing dodgeball in gym class. He was one of three remaining players when the teacher blew his whistle. "Daley!" he yelled. "Get over here."

"I wasn't hit, Coach, really," Ryan said.

"Get over here."

The coach was a long-faced, thin man who acted tough. But Ryan knew he was fair.

"Somebody wants to see you in the office," the man said.

"Can I finish the game?" Ryan said.

The coach smiled. "You go on. It looks pretty important."

Ryan ran out of the gym and up the stairs to the long hallway that led to the office. He felt weird wearing his gym uniform in this part of the school. He looked out the big window by the office and stopped. Pulling into the parking lot was a white car that said "Global Community Security." Two men got out and walked toward the school. Ryan didn't know the one on the left. The one on the right wore a long, black coat and had short hair.

"This doesn't look good," Ryan muttered. He turned to head back to the gym for his clothes. Before he took a step, someone grabbed his arm.

28

VICKI met with the three girls at lunch after the assembly.

"You really showed that Global Community lady," one girl said.

"I only stood up because I don't think she was telling us the truth," Vicki said. Vicki briefly told her story. The other girls listened while they ate. When she was almost finished, Shelly tapped Vicki's shoulder and nodded toward the entrance.

Mrs. Jenness scanned the room with a scowl.

The three girls picked up their lunch trays and moved away.

Ryan felt the viselike grip on his arm and heard a man whisper, "Move down the hall and don't look back."

When they were nearly to the gymnasium, Ryan glanced up. "Buck!" he said.

Buck Williams hustled Ryan out the back entrance. "My car is still around front," Buck said.

"I just saw GC Security pull in," Ryan said.

"They're after you," Buck said. "Dr. Ben-Judah reached me at the office. Judd heard they were coming to get you."

"How would he know that?" Ryan said.

"We can find out later," Buck said. "Right now I need to get the car and get you somewhere safe."

Ryan hid in the parking lot and watched the school carefully. He could see the gym entrance through a window. The vice-principal and two GC goons were talking to his teacher.

Ryan hopped in the backseat when Buck arrived. Someone was hunkered down on the floor.

"I guess this is Buck's witness protection program," Darrion said.

"What did you say in the office?" Ryan asked Buck.

"I told them I was with the Global Community, flashed my credentials, and asked to see you," Buck said. "They took one look at my clearance card and didn't ask questions."

"Where are we going?" Ryan said.

"We have to get you to safety," Buck said. "The GC have both Mrs. Stahley and Taylor Graham in custody."

Ryan gave a low whistle. "We must have been wrong about Graham," he said.

As they drove, Ryan asked Buck questions about the adult Tribulation Force. Rayford Steele was preparing to return to New Babylon. Amanda, his wife, was staying to help Chloe with the materials Bruce left behind. Tsion Ben-Judah was in hiding, though Buck didn't say where, and Buck was working on a *Global Community Weekly* article.

"What's it about?" Ryan said.

"I'm taking Bruce's message and turning it into a cover story," Buck said. "I've assigned reporters from offices in several countries to interview different religious leaders. I'll include their answers in my article."

"What are the questions?" Darrion said.

"Just one," Buck said. "Will we suffer the 'wrath of the Lamb'?"

"Wow," Ryan said. "Has anybody been assigned to talk with that Enigma Babylon guy?"

"Peter Mathews?" Buck said. "I did that myself. He thinks the book of Revelation is just literature. He says the earthquake is symbolic and that if God exists at all, he or she is a spirit or an idea."

"Sounds like what I used to believe," Darrion said.

Buck pulled up to a stoplight in Mount Prospect. "The only question is, where do I take you?" Buck said.

Ryan smiled. He knew a place where no one would find them.

Vicki sat through the geology lecture, wondering if she would get another chance to talk with the girls she met in the assembly. She was thinking of the *Underground* and what the next issue would contain when she heard her teacher say something about an earthquake.

"I have a friend who attended a funeral the other day," the teacher said, "where someone brought up the idea of a worldwide earthquake." The teacher laughed, and several students snickered as well.

"People who buy into religion put their minds on the shelf," the teacher continued. "There has never been nor will there ever be a global earthquake."

The teacher drew a diagram on the chalkboard. "We've talked about this before. Earthquakes are caused by faults. These underground plates rub against each other. But tell me, if this one smacks against this one, do you think there will be an earthquake over here?"

"No," the class responded.

"Of course not," the teacher said. "It's not logical. If you believe there's going to be a worldwide earthquake, you probably believe in a global flood and that a man and his three sons saved all the animals in a boat."

While the others laughed, Vicki took notes.

Lionel sat in the dark van, his stomach growling. He hadn't eaten since the night before. When the driver stopped for gas, he yelled, "Nobody talks!" Both the driver and the other man got out.

Lionel knocked on the window and asked, "When are we gonna get something to eat?"

The driver stuck his head in the door and cursed. "I said nobody talks!" he screamed.

"Better keep your mouth shut," a boy behind Lionel

whispered when the man was gone. "He'll probably give us something before too long."

Lionel introduced himself.

"I'm Jake," the other boy said.

"Where are you from?" Lionel asked.

"Detroit. They got me yesterday."

"Where's he taking us?" Lionel said.

"Someplace down South," Jake said. "We don't know for sure, but somebody heard the guy mention Alabama."

Lionel shook his head. "They told me there were family members looking for me," he said. "I thought the man who took me was a friend of my mom's."

"That happened to a couple others in here," Jake said. "They grabbed me right off the street."

"Your family will come for you, won't they?" Lionel said.

"Don't have family," Jake said.

Lionel felt sorry for him but didn't know what to say. "What could they possibly want with us?" Lionel said.

The large boy in front of Lionel turned. "They'll have to give us a bathroom break before long," he said. "We're jumping them when they do. Got it?"

Lionel nodded as the driver and Tom got back in the van. The driver pulled over to the side of the road, opened a cooler, and passed bottles of water to the boys. Lionel thought it was the best thing he had ever tasted.

Ryan asked Buck to drive to the church. Buck's eyes widened when Ryan opened the secret entrance to the

Bible hideout. "Bruce had this built at the same time . . . as the other construction."

"I got you," Buck said.

Ryan knew Dr. Tsion Ben-Judah was probably only a few yards away in his underground shelter, but he didn't dare bring up the subject. He didn't want to endanger the rabbi or Darrion by revealing it. Still, he wished he could sit and talk with the man. It seemed clear to Ryan that the rabbi was destined to preach the gospel to thousands in the next few years.

Buck ran out for fast food and brought it back. Ryan and Darrion ate hungrily as they planned their next move.

"I think I should stay here," Ryan said. "Can you find a place for Darrion that's safe?"

"We can use Loretta's apartment," Buck said.

"I don't want to hide," Darrion said. "I want to help my mother."

"Hang tight," Ryan said. "We'll do our best."

Judd was on-line at midnight. Through the video link, Pavel said he did not go to a conventional school but had teachers come to him.

"I am alone for another hour," Pavel said. "But I need to tell you something."

"What is it?" Judd said.

"Here," Pavel said. He reached toward the camera and positioned it lower. Judd saw a wheelchair.

"You may not want to talk to me any longer," Pavel said, "but I feel you should know the truth."

"You're in a wheelchair," Judd said. "Big whoop."

"What did you say?" Pavel said.

"I said it's not a big deal," Judd said. "It doesn't make a difference to me."

"It makes a big difference to most people I know," Pavel said. "I cannot do what others do. When some find out, they no longer want to be my friend."

"Their loss," Judd said. "You're smart, you ask questions, you think things through. You may never win the one-hundred-yard dash, but there are more important things in life."

Pavel beamed. "You sound like my mother," he said.

"Your mother's a sharp lady," Judd said.

"Was," Pavel said. "She vanished."

Judd felt a chill go down his spine. "Pavel, do you know why she disappeared?"

"I do not know," Pavel said. "She never complained, but I thought it might be because taking care of me was so difficult."

"I'm sure that wasn't it," Judd said. "Did your mother ever read the Bible?"

"My father would not allow it," Pavel said. "He says religion is for those who are weak, and I do not want to be weaker than I already am."

The boy paused and reached beneath his desk. "I found this on my mother's bed the morning of the disappearances," Pavel said. He held up a small black book.

Judd told Pavel why his mother had disappeared. Jesus Christ had come back for true believers. His mother had to be one of them.

"She tried to talk with me about God, but I wouldn't allow her to," Pavel said. "My father can be a very stern man."

"Don't wait any longer," Judd said. "You can be sure right now that you're a true follower of Jesus."

"How?"

"You've read the material I sent," Judd said. "Do you believe what those verses said?"

"Yes," Pavel said.

"You know you can't work your way to God or do enough good things to get you into heaven, right?"

"Before now I didn't even believe in heaven," Pavel said, "but yes, I do believe."

"If you know you've sinned, you can pray right now and ask for forgiveness." Judd outlined a prayer and then watched as Pavel bowed his head.

"God, I am sorry for what I have done," the boy said quietly, "and I have done so many bad things. I believe you sent your Son, Jesus, to die for me. And I believe he did rise from the dead. Please forgive me. Amen."

Pavel looked up. "Was that all right?" he said.

"That was great," Judd said.

"Does that mean when I die I will see my mother again?" he said.

"It sure does," Judd said.

Lionel awoke, his head bobbing up and down with the bouncing of the van. He saw the exit for Tupelo, Mississippi. Then the van pulled into a rest area.

"You boys have two minutes each," the driver said. "We'll take you in groups of three." The man held up a gun and shoved in a cartridge. "In case you get any ideas, we both have one of these."

As the men exited, the boy in front of Lionel turned. "This is it," he said. "Whoever is with me helps me jump these guys, all right?"

The kids around Lionel nodded. Lionel stiffened. He didn't mind giving his life for a good cause, but this one seemed stupid.

"Why don't we just see where they're taking us first," Lionel said.

The bigger boy turned and held up a fist. "I hope you're not in my group," the boy said, "but if you are and you don't help, I'll get you."

"I'm just saying we might be making a mistake—"

"You'll make a mistake if you don't help," the boy said.

The first group went into the rest area with the driver and quickly returned. The man named Tom herded the next three—Lionel, Jake, and the bigger boy. He sneered at Lionel. "Better do what you're told," the boy said.

The driver was a wiry-looking man with a stubbly beard and bad teeth. He mumbled for them to go to their right, sticking the end of the gun deep into his coat pocket and waving it.

The lobby was empty. There were slots with maps and brochures of vacation destinations. Pictures of Elvis Presley dotted the walls. Lionel went into the bathroom first, followed by Jake. The last boy stumbled, dropped something on the floor, then knelt in the open doorway.

"Giddup," the man with the gun said.

"Can't without some help," the boy said.

"Wait!" Lionel shouted from inside the bathroom.

But it was too late. As the man looked up, the boy on the floor punched him hard in the stomach. The man wheezed and fell backward. The boy jumped to his feet, pulled the bathroom door closed, and locked it.

"Couldn't get his gun," the boy shouted. "Open that window!"

Jake was on it. "It's stuck," he said.

Lionel heard coughing and sputtering outside, then a shout from the man at the van.

"Don't do this," Lionel said.

"Too late now," the boy said. "You're in this as much as me."

The boy yanked at the window. The second time, the window broke from its hinges, leaving a small opening. "You first," the big kid said to Lionel.

"No way," Lionel said.

"Suit yourself," the boy said.

Jake went out, then the bigger boy. Lionel heard footsteps, then gunfire. If he stayed, he might get hit.

Lionel hopped up to the opening and fell to the ground in some bushes. He easily caught up with the other two as they crossed a creek.

In the distance Lionel heard the door break and more shots. He was glad to be alive, but he had no idea what trouble he was in.

29

JUDD was anxious to leave the hangar and be with his friends, but he couldn't leave without the secret documents. They were the only hope for Mrs. Stahley and Taylor Graham. As the hours passed, his hope faded.

He spent most of the day on the computer, answering questions and sending material. Every chance he got, he moved around the room looking for the entrance to the house.

He was at the computer when he heard a noise. Voices. People moving around. Knocks on the wall.

Judd sat still. He could hear himself breathe.

"It sounds hollow here," a man said on the other side of the wall.

"It sounds hollow in a lot of places," another said. "Keep looking."

When the men moved on, Judd let out a sigh of relief. He had to have a plan of escape in case the GC discovered the entrance to the hangar.

Lionel and the other two boys ran through the night. When they came to a swampy area, Lionel warned them of snakes. "They have water moccasins down here," he said.

"They're not out this time of year," Jake said. "Are they?"

The boys went around the swamp and came upon an abandoned farmhouse. Lionel couldn't see inside and didn't want to chance going in. With no flashlight or matches, they huddled on the porch and waited for light.

Something moved inside.

"Probably a raccoon," the big boy whispered. "Maybe a possum."

A bat flew through the window, and the boys heard an earsplitting screech. "I'll take my chances with the snakes," Jake said, as all three fled the house.

Lionel said very little as he and Jake followed the bigger boy. By morning they were tired and hungry. Lionel was covered with burrs from head to foot.

"You think they'll get the police on us?" Jake asked the big boy.

I hope they do, Lionel thought. *Then I can tell them what really happened.*

"They won't chance using the cops," the big boy said. "What they're doing is illegal." The boy looked at the sunrise. "I have a good feeling. If we've made it till now, we're probably all right."

The boys followed a dirt road that eventually led them to a small general store. Lionel had enough change for one bottle of soda. They were sharing the drink when Lionel saw the van. Jake and the other boy ran. Lionel just stood by the store and waited.

Vicki assigned the articles for the *Underground* and worked late into the night on each one. Judd had done an excellent job providing material from Dr. Ben-Judah. Chaya was editing Bruce's sermon notes from the memorial service. Mark had written about the "wrath of the Lamb" prophecy and what damage a worldwide quake would do.

She hoped to add these to Buck Williams's material and an article about taking the mark. If it all came through, it would be the most convincing newspaper the kids had ever published.

Vicki talked with Buck after reading an advance copy of his *Global Community Weekly* article. "As you can see," Buck said, "I've tried to take an objective viewpoint."

"But there's enough truth in here for people to figure it out," Vicki said. "How does this kind of reporting compare with the other things you've done?"

"I've done Man of the Year stories, covered famous personalities, breaking news events," Buck said, "but I've enjoyed this more than all the others combined."

"You have everybody in here," Vicki said. "Nicolae Carpathia, faith guides from around the world . . ."

"But the scoop of the year is getting Tsion Ben-Judah," Buck said.

"How are you going to explain getting an interview with him to your bosses?" Vicki said.

"Simple." Buck smiled. "Dr. Ben-Judah learned about the story over the Internet and submitted his view from a secret location."

Vicki could see the excitement in Buck's eyes. Within a week, millions of people would read what she held in her hands.

"My hope is that people will get far enough into the article to see what a converted Jew from Norway says about the earthquake," Buck said.

Vicki flipped to the next-to-last page.

"No one should assume there will be shelter," the man was quoted as saying. "If you believe, as I do, that Jesus Christ is the only hope for salvation, you should repent of your sins and receive him before the threat of death visits you."

As much as he liked the Bible room, Ryan hated being cooped up. Buck was able to find an old laptop computer for him, but since there was no telephone in the room, Ryan had no connection for E-mail. He knew he shouldn't bother the rabbi.

Bruce had equipped the room with a cable hookup, so Ryan kept up with the news. News stations ran footage of the arrest of Mrs. Stahley and Taylor Graham, but nothing more was said. They were being held in connection with the murder of Mr. Stahley.

Each day Ryan was supplied with food by Chloe or

Amanda. Ryan loved his visits with Amanda because she reminded him of his mother. Chief in his mind was Darrion's safety.

"You don't need to worry about her," Amanda said. "We have a visitor coming next week, so we asked Sandy Moore if she could stay with her."

"Is that the computer guy's wife?" Ryan asked.

"Right," Amanda said. "At first, Sandy said she didn't know if it would work. Then she talked with Donny, and he said he had the perfect place."

"Good," Ryan said. "The GC would have no reason to look there."

Amanda asked how Ryan felt about being alone.

"I'm OK," Ryan said. "I just want to get out of here as fast as I can."

"I'm counting the days until I see Rayford again, too," Amanda said. "He's in New Babylon. I enjoy the work Chloe and I are doing, but I'd give anything for us to be together."

"Must be tough," Ryan said.

Amanda Steele pulled a chair close to Ryan. "I'm not sure anything can be as tough as what you're going through," she said. "You've lost everything you've ever known. Your parents. Your best friend, Raymie."

"But I've gained a lot, too," Ryan said. "That's what Bruce said when I talked about his family. He said it was worth losing everything just to make sure he was right with God."

"Bruce was right," Amanda said. "If he were here, he'd tell you how proud he is of you."

———————————

Lionel had been placed in the locked van while the two men caught Jake and the other boy. The men had given up the search the night before and delivered the other kids. Then they returned.

"We knew we'd catch you kids someplace where there was food," the guard with the bad teeth said.

"You're gonna pay for gettin' away," the other said.

They crossed the Mississippi state line into Alabama and finally reached the compound. Several older teens roughly led the three into a small, dingy building. Lionel was locked in a single room with no light.

He awoke to the sound of birds. It was morning. Lionel imagined the nest of little ones breaking through their eggs, waiting for their mother to bring food. *What freedom*, he thought.

It had been two days since he had eaten a full meal. Lionel could tell he was getting weaker. He had always said he was "starving to death" when he was the least bit hungry. Now he felt like he really was.

———————————

Ryan finally got up the nerve to knock on Tsion Ben-Judah's door. He was sure the rabbi was being hidden there. He just didn't know if the man could hear his knock.

"Dr. Rabbi, sir," Ryan called, "it's me. Ryan. I don't want to disturb you. I know you're doing important stuff and all."

Ryan sat down by the concrete blocks. If the door was

as thick as it looked, the rabbi wouldn't be able to hear a sledgehammer.

Suddenly the door opened, and a ray of light hit Ryan full in the face. "Dr. Ben-Judah, sir," Ryan stammered.

"Come in, Ryan," Tsion said.

"I know I'm not supposed to come down here, and I'm awfully—"

"It is all right," Tsion said.

"But Mr. Williams and the others will be upset—"

"Don't worry," Tsion said. "I will tell them I needed the company."

Ryan looked around the enclosure. It was sectioned into three rooms. There was a full bath and shower, a bedroom with four double bunk beds, and a larger room with a small kitchen on one side and a living room/study on the other.

Ryan went straight to the computer. While Tsion was talking, a message came from Judd. He told the rabbi about the voices on the other side of the wall.

"Can I?" Ryan said.

"Be my guest," Tsion said.

Ryan typed, *Hey, Judd, hang in there. The troops are coming.*

Who is this? Judd typed.

Your pal, Ryan. Could you go outside and climb into a window upstairs?

The information I have is that the house is surrounded, Judd wrote. *I'm hoping to find the entrance, then sneak up there at night.*

Ryan signed off and thanked the rabbi. "I won't come down here anymore," Ryan said.

"You were no bother," Tsion said. "I will pray that you are able to make it out soon."

"I'm sure I will," Ryan said.

On Friday afternoon, Lionel was released from the building and given food. He tried not to eat too fast, but he ate and drank all that was given to him in less than a minute.

Lionel was led to a meeting hall, where all the kids sat on the floor and listened to a man talk about the Global Community.

"You came here as boys, but you'll leave as men," the man said. "Our hope is that you'll become an asset to the brotherhood of mankind."

Lionel saw Jake in the corner. They met after the meeting.

"Did you get any of what the guy was saying?" Lionel said.

Jake shook his head. "My stomach's still too empty to listen," he said. "But I do know one thing. Every one of us means more money to the guys running the place."

"What do you mean?" Lionel said.

"They've got some racket going with the Global Community," Jake said. "For every kid that comes here, they get X amount of dollars of support from the GC."

"Even if they get here the way you and I did?" Lionel said.

"The GC doesn't know that," Jake said. "And there's

something else. They're training us for something. I don't know what, but one guy said when we leave, we get to carry a gun."

"How'd you find that out?" Lionel said.

Jake pointed to someone sitting in the corner. "That kid over there," he said. "His name's Conrad."

Ryan slipped into the church office. The front doors were locked, and Loretta had gone home. Ryan dialed the number and gave his address. He went out the back of the church and stayed in the shadows. Night was falling, but he wanted to use the rest of the daylight for his trip.

When the cab pulled up in front, Ryan looked both ways, then ran. When he got in, the cabbie said, "You the only one?"

"Yes, sir," Ryan said.

"Let me see your money," the cabbie said.

Ryan held out a few wadded bills and some loose change. "I counted it," he said. "There's twelve dollars and about $1.37 in change." Ryan handed the man the address. "You think it's enough?"

When they arrived, the cabbie shut off the meter. "That's $10.50," he said.

Ryan looked at his money. "I don't know how to do tips," he said.

The cabbie rolled his eyes. "If I do a lousy job, don't tip at all. If I drive carefully and show my wonderful personality, you could give me 20 percent."

"How much is that?" Ryan said.

"I don't know," the cabbie said. "Just give me the $10.50 and we'll call it square."

Ryan handed him the whole thing. "Keep the change," Ryan said. Before he shut the door, he looked back. "I've always wanted to say that."

Late Friday night, Judd sent the final draft of his article for the *Underground*. Talking with Vicki via E-mail was fun, but it wasn't the same as being face-to-face. He admired her for the way she had kept going. That she was preparing another newspaper for the people at school showed she cared. She could have played it safe. Not Vicki.

Judd wondered whether his life would ever be "normal" again. Would he be able to go out in public? After questioning Taylor Graham and Mrs. Stahley, would the GC turn to him for answers?

He was tapping his fingers against the computer keyboard when he heard a strange thump come from the hangar. He turned off the light and moved toward the door. The hangar was pitch-black.

"Anybody there?" Judd said in a loud whisper.

Nothing.

"Oh, well," Judd said out loud. He turned, then heard it again. It was coming from the door.

Heart racing. Thinking of a way out. *If it's GC, what do I do? Surrender? No way.*

Judd heard a creak, then felt something against his

skin. Night air. The smell was wonderful. Fresh. Then
Judd realized someone had found the mechanical box
near the woods. They had probably seen the door open
by now. Judd stood back. Armed guards would descend
any moment. How could he escape?

Judd had located two motorcycles in the hangar
while jogging. One was smaller, and from the size of the
helmet, he guessed it was Darrion's. The other was a large
dirt bike. He hadn't tried to start it for fear it would alert
the GC team on the other side of the wall. Now it didn't
matter. They knew.

Judd ran to the motorcycle. He strapped on the
helmet, then looked for the ignition key. It wasn't there.
On the wall inside the study! Judd thought.

There wasn't time to retrieve the key and start the
machine, so Judd rushed to the door and hit the button
to close it. In the moonlight he saw a figure running
toward him.

Come on, door!

Judd rushed for the key, grabbed it, and turned.
Before the door closed, the figure somersaulted into the
room.

"Ryan!" Judd exclaimed. "What are you doing
here?"

Ryan smiled and cocked his head. "I came to help,"
he said. "You going somewhere?"

Judd took off his helmet and shook his head. "You
could have been shot!" he said. "You might have led
them right to me."

"I didn't," Ryan said. "But you were right about them

being around the house. There have been three out there all evening."

"How long have you been here?" Judd said.

"Long enough to know we'd better find that entrance," Ryan said.

30

JUDD and Ryan searched the room again, taking out every book and every drawer. Nothing. Early Sunday morning, Ryan suggested they have some kind of church service.

"Let's get Tsion in on it too," Judd said.

Tsion joined them by computer. Judd felt weird singing with just two other people. They sang softly so they wouldn't be detected. Tsion asked Ryan to read a passage from Luke.

Ryan read, "'As they were walking along someone said to Jesus, "I will follow you no matter where you go." But Jesus replied, "Foxes have dens to live in, and birds have nests, but I, the Son of Man, have no home of my own, not even a place to lay my head."' "

"There is a great cost to following Jesus," Tsion said. "Those who were his disciples did not realize it at the time, and I confess I am like them. And you are as well. We had no idea what would happen, and where God would take us. But here we are. God be praised."

Tsion talked further of being willing to go and do whatever God wanted. Judd and Ryan prayed for wisdom and courage for the days ahead.

As Judd prayed, he opened his eyes and looked up. He noticed a panel in one corner of the ceiling he hadn't seen before. When they had said good-bye to Tsion, he got a chair and looked at it more closely.

"What's up?" Ryan said.

"I think we may have been looking in the wrong place," Judd said. "I thought the entrance in here would be through the wall, but maybe it's up here somewhere."

Judd poked and pushed at the three-foot square, but nothing happened. When he moved the chair he saw another square on the floor the same size and in the same spot as the one above.

"I don't get it," Ryan said. "Is the entrance up there or down here?"

Judd sat back and scratched his head. "Maybe it's nothing," he said.

Ryan took a run and jumped on the square in the floor. Ryan's feet came down hard. Judd heard a noise. The panel above moved to the side to reveal a hole. At the same time, the panel Ryan was standing on raised off the floor.

"Hurry and get on," Ryan said.

Lionel tried to figure out why the men would have taken him. He received the answer from Conrad.

"They have a lot of ways to get kids," Conrad said.

"They snatch some off the street. Some they go after for a reason."

"Like you?" Lionel said.

"My older brother is in the GC," Conrad said. "My hunch is they brought me here to punish him for something."

"What about me?" Lionel said. "A guy came to my school. He had papers."

"Somebody had to have tipped them," Conrad said. "I know they have shady connections to people in prison. Does anybody in jail know you?"

"LeRoy and Cornelius!" Lionel said. "Of course."

"Who are they?"

"Two guys we helped the cops put in jail," Lionel said. "They killed my uncle. Either one of them could have given my name out of revenge."

"It doesn't matter how you got here," Conrad said. "The question is, what're you gonna do about it?"

Lionel shook his head. "These guys are gettin' in my head," he said. "They make us exercise until we drop, then only give us a little food. Then they say the same things over and over again. And most of the guys are falling for it."

"Most of the guys don't know the truth about the GC," Conrad said.

Lionel sat up. "And you do?" he said.

Vicki rode with Chaya to the service at New Hope Village Church. A week after the service for Bruce, the pews were packed. Vicki thought Bruce would be pleased. On the way home, Vicki talked with Chaya about Amanda's suggestion.

"I don't think my father would allow me inside the house," Chaya said.

"You can call him and try," Vicki said.

"Maybe I'll call the rabbi and ask him to help," Chaya said. "Perhaps the grief over my mother has softened my father's heart."

The panel lifted until Judd and Ryan were through the ceiling. A ladder was fastened to the wall and led up.

"Let's see where it goes," Ryan said.

"Not now," Judd said. "We'll wait until late tonight."

Lionel listened as Conrad talked about his brother. "He flies for the GC," Conrad said, "but he told me he doesn't trust them."

"Why does he still work for them?" Lionel said.

"He's loyal to his boss, not the whole GC," Conrad said. "When they grabbed me, I heard them tell my brother not to do anything stupid."

"What are they trying to do to us?" Lionel said.

"I can't figure it out," Conrad said. "I know they want us to be part of the Global Community in some way, but it's not clear. They're definitely using mind control on us."

"Mind control?"

"The way they make us parrot stuff back to them,"

Conrad said. "They say things over and over. In the small groups it's almost like some of the guys are in a trance."

"They're not gonna control me," Lionel said.

"How can you fight it?" Conrad said.

"I was hoping you'd ask," Lionel said.

Judd tried to sleep during the day, but he and Ryan were too excited. They heard very little movement on the other side of the walls, but they didn't want to take any chances.

Late that night, Judd and Ryan activated the entrance and climbed the ladder into the secret passageway. When they got to the top of the ladder, they stepped onto a small landing in front of a huge panel. Judd turned on his flashlight and noticed a blinking sensor on the wall. There was no slot for a key, so Judd put his hand over it.

A latch clicked. The panel moved slightly open. Judd nodded, and Ryan pushed the panel slowly. Ryan and Judd stepped through the opening. They were now inside the plush Stahley house.

On the other side of the panel was a painting of the Stahley family. "Don't close it all the way," Judd whispered. "We might not be able to open it again."

The two stood still and listened. No movement in the house. Judd saw that they were on the main floor of the house, and they would need to go up a flight to find Mr. Stahley's office.

They took a step, then realized their tennis shoes

squeaked on the tile. They took off their shoes and placed them gently by a pillar that held an antique vase.

When they reached the stairwell, Judd saw movement through the windows. He held up a hand, and Ryan stopped. A GC guard with a gun was moving back and forth on the patio.

On the second floor they tried three rooms before they found Mr. Stahley's office. If they turned on a light or even used the flashlight, Judd knew the GC might notice. Pictures and papers were strewn about the floor. Judd found the desk, then groped in the dark for the filing cabinet.

It was locked!

"Try opening the middle drawer," Ryan said. "Sometimes that releases the others."

Judd opened the middle drawer, then tried the other. It opened!

Judd patted Ryan's head.

Judd grabbed half the stack of files and moved away from the desk. Ryan followed his lead and took the other half. They slipped down the hall to the bathroom. Laying the files in the tub, Judd drew the shower curtain, placed his hand over the flashlight, and turned it on. A reddish glow provided enough light to see.

"You flip through them while I hold the light," Judd said.

The files looked like any homeowner's. There were folders for investments, bills, warranties, and taxes. Mr. Stahley was organized.

Ryan flipped through them and shrugged. "What would it be under, Secret Safe Combination?"

"What did Mrs. Stahley say about the combination?" Judd said.

"Just that it was in a file in Mr. Stahley's study," Ryan said.

Judd flipped to a file titled "Construction." Inside he found bills and contracts for the house. There was nothing listed about the underground hangar. Next he looked in the warranties. There were receipts for a home theater, several cars and motorcycles, and household appliances. In the back was a small receipt from The Stockholm Safe Company.

Judd scanned the writing but found no unusual set of numbers. "This has to be it," he said.

"Look on the back," Ryan said.

Judd turned the paper over. On the bottom corner of the page was a string of numbers. Judd stuffed the paper in his pocket and turned off the flashlight.

Judd and Ryan stopped when they heard a door open and close downstairs. Voices. Two men.

Judd's stomach tightened. His heart beat faster. If the men noticed the open picture, they were sunk. A light went on. Judd and Ryan moved into the shadows.

"What's this?" a man said. "I didn't see those here before."

"Somebody's here!" the other man said. He keyed his walkie-talkie and ordered other guards inside. "You search upstairs. I'll go downstairs."

Judd and Ryan watched as a guard ran up the stairs. The man's gun was equipped with a laser. He looked both ways at the top of the landing. Judd and Ryan were to the right. The man ran left, down the hall. It would only be a few moments before he discovered the files in the bathtub.

Judd and Ryan quickly moved down the stairs. The front door opened, so Judd waved Ryan through the kitchen. Two more guards were in the house.

"Where do you want us to search?" the man said into the microphone attached to his shoulder.

"Main floor and the kitchen," came the reply.

Judd and Ryan stole to the other entrance to the kitchen. If the guards came this way, they were dead. If they came the other way, Judd and Ryan still had a chance.

Judd saw two pinpoints of red light behind them and moved into the living room. He and Vicki had first met Mr. and Mrs. Stahley in this very room. They kept moving, quickly but quietly. They passed the stairs and heard the guard yell, "I've found something! There's stuff in the bathroom."

Now they ran full speed toward the opening in the wall. Judd wasn't about to worry about his shoes at this point. He wanted to get into the wall and latch it shut before the guards saw them.

Judd made it to the opening first and opened the picture. Ryan stumbled around the corner and fell head-long into the antique vase. It shattered on the floor with an incredible crash.

"Hurry up!" Judd said.

The men converged on the two boys. Ryan tried to stand, but he kept slipping on the waxy floor. In the darkness, he looked like Phoenix on Judd's kitchen floor when Ryan brought out a treat.

Ryan finally made it through the hole and started down the ladder. Judd closed the picture just as the red lights converged on their end of the hallway.

"Where'd he go?" a man said.

Judd trembled as he descended the ladder. He slid the last ten feet to the ground. Ryan jumped on the square, and the two were led back into their hideout.

Judd was shaking as he pulled the combination to the safe from his pocket. He fumbled for the key card but couldn't find it.

"Wait," Ryan said. "I had it last." Ryan opened the desk drawer and rummaged through it.

"Hurry up!" Judd yelled.

From the other side of the wall, Judd heard a man yell, "They're down here somewhere. I can hear them!"

Ryan found the card and shoved it in the slot. The safe rose, and Judd began punching in numbers. When he hit the last one, the door to the safe popped open with a *whoosh*.

Inside were a stash of bills, some gold coins, and a folder. Judd grabbed the folder and flipped it open.

Evidence against the Global Community and Nicolae Carpathia was written at the top of the page. What followed was a point-by-point listing of facts uncovered by Mr. Stahley after the death of his brother.

"Bring it right here," the man on the other side of the wall yelled.

"We have to go," Ryan said.

"Hang on," Judd said as he glanced at the document.

Judd heard some kind of saw grinding through the wall.

"How thick is that wall?" Ryan said.

"Not thick enough," Judd said, folding the document and stuffing it into his pocket. Ryan followed Judd into the hangar. Judd locked the door behind them. "That'll hold them for a few more minutes."

Judd showed Ryan the motorcycles. They threw the helmets away, grabbed the keys, and pumped the starters. Ryan's bike fired up immediately. Judd's sputtered and coughed but started on the third try.

"If we get separated," Judd said, "we meet at the church."

"Got it," Ryan said.

Judd punched the button to the outside door. As it slowly opened, Judd saw a rotating blade cut its way through the door behind them.

Judd took the lead down the hill. There was no headlight on the bike, which made driving dangerous. Judd looked back and saw one man talking into his microphone.

Judd was nearly to the Stahleys' driveway when a vehicle shot out of the bushes and cut him off. Judd turned and followed Ryan, the GC vehicle not far behind. Ryan pointed to the woods on the other side of the property.

While Judd and Ryan rode along the side of the hill, the GC vehicle couldn't. It went into the valley and up the other side. By that time, Judd and Ryan had neared the woods and had a lead. If they reached the trees, the GC would have to backtrack to the access road.

Judd's body rattled on the motorcycle. He turned once more to see the pursuers. Then he lost control of the bike.

Ryan looked back just as Judd's front tire hit a rock. The bike upended and sent Judd sprawling. Ryan braked hard, turned around, and raced back.

Judd was sitting up when he got there. "Go!" Judd yelled.

"I'm not leaving you," Ryan said.

"I'm hurt," Judd said. "I can't ride. They're almost here. Now go!"

Ryan felt awful leaving his friend. When he made it to the woods, he looked back long enough to see that the GC vehicle had overtaken Judd.

The documents, Ryan thought.

But it was too late. Ryan gunned the bike and sped through the trees toward Vicki's house.

VICKI could hardly believe Ryan's story when he arrived at her house early Monday morning. With the documents in the hands of the GC, she knew they had little hope of helping Mrs. Stahley, Taylor Graham, or even Judd.

Ryan nodded. Phoenix huddled close and licked his hand.

Judd was sore and dazed as he sat in the Global Community headquarters. Though he hadn't broken any bones in the fall, he had strained his neck and shoulder. The GC guards hadn't helped any with the way they had arrested him.

Judd prayed they wouldn't find the documents, but a guard at headquarters discovered them. "You were hoping we wouldn't find these," the guard said in a mocking tone.

An hour later another man was led into the room. Judd recognized him as the gunman beneath the L. "That's him," the short-haired man said. "Where's the other kid?"

"We don't know, sir," another guard answered.

"I'm talking to him," the man said.

"I'm not telling you anything," Judd said.

"Better think hard," the man said. "You've got a record." The man ticked off a list of Judd's violations and said, "You're a prime candidate for reeducation. I wouldn't be surprised to see you shipped out of here by next week."

Lionel decided his best plan of action was to obey his captors until he could find a way back home. If they thought he was one of them, he could escape. He hoped to do so with his new friend, Conrad. Lionel had told Conrad his story, but the boy seemed skeptical. Lionel backed off and prayed for him.

The group quickly tapped Lionel for leadership. By the middle of his first week in camp, he knew the GC slogans and chants by heart. He was drawn into the inner circle, where they explained their mission.

"You are part of an elite group of young people," a GC official told them. "You have been chosen to be the eyes and ears of the Global Community and our leader, Nicolae Carpathia."

Yeah, right, Lionel thought.

On Friday evening, Vicki called a meeting to pray for Judd and give an update. They had heard nothing from Judd since his arrest.

"I'm taking the *Underground* to school Monday morning," Vicki said. "I want to thank you all for your help
and ask you to pray for me."

Chaya said she wouldn't be able to drive Vicki, so
Mark offered.

"Where are you going?" Vicki asked Chaya.

"My father has allowed me one hour Monday morning
to go through some of my mother's things," she said.

The kids prayed for her, then for Lionel. Ryan asked
about Darrion. She was still with Donny Moore and his
wife. The discussion turned to Ryan's safety.

"The GC may not care about you," Vicki said. "With
Judd, Taylor, and Mrs. Stahley in custody, they might
leave you alone. But I'm not taking any chances."

"I haven't gone outside the whole week," Ryan said.

"I know," Vicki said, "but I want you to promise
me in front of everybody. You won't go outside, right?"

"I promise," Ryan said.

Monday morning Mark helped Vicki load a duffel bag full
of copies of the *Underground* into his car.

"I hear security is as tight as ever," Mark said. "How
are you going to get it inside?"

Vicki held up a key. "Shelly gave me this yesterday
morning," she said. "I had a copy made and got it back
before they knew it was missing."

"What's it for?" Mark said.

"The gymnasium," Vicki said. "I'm putting the *Underground* in the gym lockers."

Vicki thanked Mark and lugged the duffel bag to the gymnasium entrance. The key fit perfectly. She locked the door and walked across the basketball courts. Her footsteps echoed in the building. She put the bag down and looked down both halls. Empty.

She started with the boys' locker room. She placed several copies of the paper in each locker, then closed the door. Where she found a lock, she stuffed the pages through the vents in front. She hoped the first-period class would take one, then leave the rest for others.

She was nearly finished when she sensed someone watching her. She turned. No one was in the room. She saw a movement in the coach's office. She picked up the bag and headed for the door. She opened it and found Mrs. Jenness staring at her.

"Byrne," she said. "I saw someone walk through the gym on the monitors."

The cameras! Vicki thought.

Vicki backed up. Mrs. Jenness grabbed the duffel bag and pulled out a copy of the *Underground.* She looked startled. "You!" she said. "It *was* you."

Mrs. Jenness rifled through the lockers, stuffing the papers back in the bag. She marched Vicki to the office and ordered a Global Community guard to collect the papers from the rest of the lockers.

"You're staying right here," Mrs. Jenness said as she sat Vicki in her office. "This time I have evidence, and I'm not letting you out of my sight!"

For a whole week the Global Community tried to uncover more information from Judd, but he kept silent. Finally they led him to a holding cell for transport. Judd hadn't received treatment for his injuries, but he felt better. Now he was anxious to see where they were taking him. He was definitely going to a reeducation camp, but he had no idea how severe the treatment would be. The camps ranged from a minimum Level 1 camp to a maximum Level 5.

The door opened, and three other prisoners were led in. Judd gasped when he realized one of them was Taylor Graham. The man looked sick. He was bruised about the face, and he walked with a limp.

"Taylor, it's me, Judd."

The pilot's left eye was swollen shut, so he turned his head to see Judd. He smiled. "So they finally found you?"

Judd explained what had happened. When he told Graham about the secret documents, the man winced. "I wish we could have saved those," Graham said. "The GC probably destroyed them, so there's no hope for Mrs. Stahley and me."

"Where is she?" Judd said.

Taylor Graham shook his head. "They told me she was sent out of here late last week," he said.

Several armed guards led them to the transport area. "You two, get over here," one guard said to Judd and the pilot. "You're going to Level 5."

Vicki sat in the office and watched Mrs. Jenness read the *Underground.* The woman sneered as she read. When she was finished, Mrs. Jenness bundled the copies and ordered them burned.

After school was under way, Mrs. Jenness made two phone calls. "No, I do not want someone to pick her up," she said. "I'll bring her in myself."

Vicki glanced at the clock as they left the school. It was 9:00 A.M.

Chaya found her mother's clothes piled in bags for a nearby homeless shelter. She picked up a sweater and smelled her mother's perfume. In her mother's room, she found pictures and jewelry. Chaya remembered how she used to play with her mother's box of treasures.

Chaya located the family photo albums and pored through them. She wept and laughed as she remembered vacations and graduations and the way her mother was always there.

Chaya couldn't decide which memento to take— a golden brooch she had given her mother or an empty photo locket.

The door downstairs opened and closed. She looked at the clock. It was 9:18 A.M.

Judd Thompson, Prisoner #4634-227, was handcuffed and sitting by Taylor Graham in the third seat of the Security

Transport vehicle. The STV drove west of Chicago, then south along Interstate 55.

"How many Level 5 places are there?" Judd said.

"There are two in Illinois," Taylor Graham said. "One is close to the Wisconsin border near Rockford. The other is close to a little town named Streator, about two hours south."

Judd watched as the scenery changed from apartment buildings and storefronts to cornfields and farmland. They exited I-55 and headed west. Judd noticed an unusual amount of dead animals on the road. Skunks, raccoons, and deer littered the two-lane road. They passed a farmhouse and a huge grain silo. The weather vane on top swayed.

Vicki watched Mrs. Jenness drive with determination. The principal had her revenge now and was going to enjoy every minute. Mrs. Jenness's knuckles turned white as she gripped the steering wheel.

"I told you I'd get you, Byrne," Mrs. Jenness said.

"Didn't anything in the *Underground* or in the service for Pastor Barnes get to you?" Vicki said.

"If you want to believe that stuff, it's your business," Mrs. Jenness said. "But you'll never come in my school and shove it down our throats again."

Vicki looked away. The electric lines and light poles seemed to be moving, but there was no wind.

Ryan was watching television in the basement when Phoenix bounded into the room.

"Hey, boy, you glad to see me?" Ryan said.

Phoenix barked and put his paws up. Then he ran in circles around the room.

"Looks like you need to go out," Ryan said. "Sorry I can't go with you."

Phoenix raced Ryan up the stairs and jumped on the front door.

"No, you gotta go out back," Ryan said. Ryan opened the screen door and Phoenix bolted from the house, yipping and barking like Ryan had never seen before.

"That dog's goin' crazy," Ryan muttered.

Lionel was in the exercise yard of the compound when someone yelled, "Snake!"

Boys ran to the edge of the yard, then retreated to a nearby porch. Lionel watched as snakes crawled out of their holes and raced across the compound. There had to be at least a hundred of them, all slithering and hissing.

Lionel saw squirrels in a nearby tree skitter to the top, then jump to the limbs of another tree. A huge cloud of birds darkened the sky. Then they were gone.

Then Lionel felt it.

The ground.

Shaking.

He looked for a place to run. To hide. Then he remembered. There was no such place.

Chaya met her father downstairs by the piles of clothes.

"I am sorry," she said. "I got caught up with all the pictures and I forgot—"

"We agreed you would be gone by now," Mr. Stein said. "I don't want to talk with you."

"Please, Father," Chaya said.

A fine mist fell around Chaya. Then a chunk of plaster hit her on the head. She looked up and saw a crack in the ceiling and felt a rumbling beneath her.

Mr. Stein was in the doorway, ready to leave. He turned when Chaya screamed.

The van swerved to avoid hitting a Great Dane crossing the road.

"What is it with these animals?" the driver said. "They're all over the place."

Judd saw a flagpole in front of a school rocking back and forth. Road signs swayed, and suddenly the pavement cracked and opened before them.

The driver struggled to keep control of the speeding vehicle, but Judd knew it was too late. They would have to deal with *the wrath of the Lamb*.

Vicki didn't realize what was happening until Mrs. Jenness was already driving over the bridge.

"Stop!" Vicki said. "We have to go back."

"If I have anything to do with it, you're *never* coming back," Mrs. Jenness said.

"You don't understand," Vicki said. "The earthquake. It's happening. We have to get off this bridge."

The top of the bridge swayed first. Then the whole structure pitched right, then left. Mrs. Jenness screamed and let go of the wheel. Vicki grabbed it and tried to keep the car steady.

Vicki looked out her window and saw a strange sight. The bridge had tipped so far, she could almost see straight into the water. In the next instant they were tipped the other way, and the water was on Mrs. Jenness's side.

Vicki heard a crash above them. *One of the cables,* she thought. While Mrs. Jenness screamed, Vicki looked around at the windows. She wanted to make sure they were all up.

Phoenix sniffed the air and ran back to the house. So much noise. The ground was moving underneath him.

Sniff.

He had to find the boy. The boy had let him out. Why hadn't he come?

Find the boy. Find the boy. Find the boy.

32

VICKI sat in horror as the bridge wobbled and buckled. Mrs. Jenness slammed on the brakes and covered her eyes.

"Make it stop," Mrs. Jenness whimpered.

A few minutes earlier, Mrs. Jenness had been gloating over catching Vicki with a new edition of the *Underground*. Vicki knew she was headed back to the detention center, or possibly worse. Now both were hanging on for their lives.

Vicki checked to be sure the windows were up, in case the bridge collapsed and they fell into the water.

"Back up!" Vicki shouted.

"Make it stop!" Mrs. Jenness said.

Vicki heard the thundering of the great earthquake.

It roared like a thousand cannons. The normally calm river rushed by with whitecaps as the bridge rocked.

Vicki decided to jump out and run, but before she could get the door unlocked, the bridge tipped violently and the car rolled on its top. The windshield shattered. Shards of glass flew everywhere.

They came to rest on the railing, the front of the car over the edge. Several cars toppled into the water. One man had gotten out of his vehicle and raced for safety. A few steps later he was in the air, flying headlong into the choppy water.

How could the bridge last this long? If they fell with the bridge, the twisted metal and concrete would drag them down. The bridge tipped, then slammed the car against the railing again. Metal scraped against concrete. The back tires rose off the pavement. Vicki and Mrs. Jenness screamed as they plunged over the edge.

The car landed back end first but didn't sink. Water poured in through the broken windows, and the car settled. The current took them underneath the bridge, chunks of asphalt and steel plopping in the water around them.

The water reached Vicki's feet and took her breath away. Mrs. Jenness looked terrified, and she shook uncontrollably. Vicki couldn't help feeling sorry for her.

"We're gonna get out of this," Vicki said.

"I can't swim!" Mrs. Jenness screamed.

The earthquake rolled on as the car spun in the river. Water continued to rise through the floor. As the car sank, Vicki unbuckled herself and Mrs. Jenness.

"Crawl on top," Vicki shouted. "I'll help you make it to shore."

Mrs. Jenness stared past Vicki and pointed. A downed tree stuck out over the water. The car rushed toward it.

"Get down!" Vicki yelled.

The treetop rammed through the opening of the back window and stopped within inches of Mrs. Jenness's head. The car hung by the tree, a foot above the surface of the water.

"We have to get out," Vicki said. "If the tree breaks, we're dead. And if the water level rises, the tree will hold us under."

"Stay here," Mrs. Jenness said. "Wait for help."

Vicki noticed a red gash on the woman's forehead. She must have hit the steering wheel hard. Part of Vicki wanted to leave her. Mrs. Jenness had been no end of trouble for the Young Trib Force. But something inside wouldn't let her.

"We go together," Vicki said. "I'll get out and pull you through the other side."

Vicki struggled through the window. The car top was crushed. She cut her hand on a piece of glass that clung to the windshield, but she didn't let go. The river rose, and the rushing water and trembling earth were deafening.

When she got to Mrs. Jenness, Vicki looked back in horror as the bridge collapsed. Huge concrete pylons snapped like twigs. Cars were trapped in the twisting metal. Vicki braced herself as a huge wave swept over them and nearly knocked her off. When the wave passed, Vicki coughed and saw the water pouring in the windows.

"Give me your hand!" Vicki shouted above the noise.

Then it happened. Darkness. The sun went black. Vicki heard the roar of the earth and water, but she saw nothing. She felt helpless.

Vicki hung on to the roof as another violent rumble nearly shook the tree loose. A cracking, an explosion, and another deafening shake sent the water swirling around them. Vicki reached into the car and realized the water level was going down.

"You still there?" Vicki screamed.

"I think so," came the weak reply.

"Turn on your lights!" Vicki yelled.

The beams cut through the darkness. Vicki blinked and wiped her eyes. She couldn't believe it. The earth had opened from one side of the river to the other into a bottomless chasm. Water cascaded into the hole but didn't fill it. It looked like the hole just kept going to the center of the earth. The riverbed was changing, and water from both sides of the crevice rushed in. If they fell into the hole, they would never be found. If they fell into the water on either side of the chasm, the current would drag them into it as well.

The car shifted, and Vicki nearly lost her balance. She turned as a flash lit the sky and revealed a scene Vicki would never forget. The tree roots barely clung to a wall of shifting earth. Below her was black nothingness.

"Help me," Vicki muttered. "Please, God . . ."

———————————

Judd Thompson had noticed the dead animals along the road to the reeducation facility. The GC pilot he had come to trust, Taylor Graham, sat beside him in the GC transport van. Both were handcuffed. Taylor had been beaten during his time in custody, and Judd could tell he was weak. The two were on their way to a maximum Level 5 facility when the great earthquake began.

Judd noticed flagpoles and weather vanes rocking as they passed through the farmlands of central Illinois. Squirrels, rabbits, dogs, cats, and deer darted back and forth. People were used to seeing raccoons and opossums dead on the road, but now it was every kind of animal. Lifeless bodies were strewn about the road.

The driver swerved to miss another animal, and the road in front of the van buckled and heaved upward.

"Hang on!" Taylor screamed.

The van went airborne. Judd held on to the seat in front of him as they crashed to the pavement. He found himself suspended by his seat belt as the van skidded to a stop. But the earth seemed to pick up momentum.

Taylor Graham managed to unbuckle himself and kick open the emergency exit. Judd followed. He smelled gasoline.

"Good thing they didn't put us in leg irons," Taylor said.

"What about them?" Judd said, pointing to the driver and the other guard. Both men were in the front of the van. Neither moved.

"You're right," Taylor said. "We need the keys to these handcuffs."

Before Taylor could get to them, an explosion ripped through the van and set the vehicle ablaze. Judd and Taylor were thrown into a ditch.

"We'll never get them now," Taylor said. "Come on. We'll find a place that's safe."

As they ran toward a cornfield, Judd tried to balance himself. It felt like he was walking on the deck of a ship in a hurricane.

The sound was incredible. When he had been mad at his parents he would go into his room and turn his headphones up full blast. This was louder, and there was no turning down the volume.

Judd glanced back as a huge crater opened. The burning van and a section of road were swallowed whole. Black smoke rose from the wreckage. Nearby a farmhouse vanished. Horses ran in circles in their corral.

"When's this thing gonna stop?" Taylor shouted.

Judd heard crumpling metal and saw power lines. The towers fell, the deadly lines crashing with them.

"Look out!" Judd yelled.

When the sun went black, Judd couldn't see his hands in front of his face. He heard crackling nearby.

"Don't move," Taylor said.

Judd's heart beat furiously. One wrong step and they could be killed instantly.

A flash lit the sky, and Judd saw the power lines only a few feet away.

"To your left," Taylor said, and the two struggled to their feet.

Lionel Washington was in the exercise yard near the main compound building when the great earthquake began.

He had been told he had family who wanted to care for him. That was a lie. What he found in this secluded Alabama town was a Global Community training camp. Lionel and the others were being groomed as monitors. The camp leaders called them the "eyes and ears of Nicolae Carpathia."

Lionel hated the idea of helping the Global Community, but pretending to go along with them was his only chance. More than anything he wanted to get back to his friends in Mount Prospect, Illinois. If that meant memorizing a few GC chants and faking obedience, he'd do it.

The horde of snakes slithered across the compound. Moments later, Lionel felt the ground rumble. He turned to run inside a building, then stopped. A friend ran past him.

"Don't go in there, Conrad!" Lionel yelled.

Conrad kept going. Lionel followed, screaming for the boy to stop. Lionel caught him on the stairwell, grabbed his arm, and turned for the front door.

"What're you doing?" Conrad said.

"Earthquake!" Lionel said. "We have to get out!"

Conrad ran. Lionel followed. The hardwood floor vibrated. He was almost outside when the beams on the porch gave way. Lionel shoved Conrad to safety as the porch crashed down on him.

After almost being caught by the Global Community, Ryan Daley promised Vicki he would stay inside. But when Phoenix had bounded into his basement hideout, barking and running in circles, Ryan had taken the dog outside. Now he watched Phoenix scamper around the yard. The dog sniffed at the air and took off again.

At first, Ryan thought he heard a train. But there were no tracks near Vicki's house. He ran back into the kitchen as cabinets opened, spilling dishes and glasses.

What do I do? Ryan wondered. *Go to the basement? Upstairs? Outside?*

He dove under the kitchen table as a light fell from the ceiling. Through the sliding glass door he saw the ground moving. A neighbor's in-ground pool cracked and collapsed. A huge oak tree in the backyard leaned to one side, then reversed and crashed into the house, the roots tearing up the yard. Phoenix darted back and forth.

"Run, Phoenix!" Ryan shouted.

Then darkness.

Pitch-black.

Ryan rolled from under the table and snatched a flashlight from the utility drawer. He switched it on and screamed. The kitchen floor cracked. Pieces of tile snapped and hit him in the face. He tried to roll to the opposite side as the floor heaved upward, then tilted. Ryan grabbed the leg of a chair as he slipped through the opening. The flashlight fell and smacked into something hard. The chair he clung to wedged on each side of the crack. Ryan hung in the air, peering into what had been the basement. Cracked concrete and rocks filled the room.

Above him darkness. Below him the tiny beam of the flashlight.

Another shift and the chair snapped. Ryan fell into the churning debris.

Chaya Stein had gone to her father's house with mixed emotions. Her mother had died in the same blast that had killed Bruce Barnes. Chaya wanted a keepsake from her mother. Chaya's father didn't want to see her and asked that she be gone by 9:00 A.M.

Mr. Stein had spoken sharply to Chaya. She knew her father was still angry that she believed in Jesus as the Messiah.

When the chunk of plaster hit her, Chaya screamed, "It's coming!"

She grabbed the railing with both hands and held on. A chandelier in the front room fell, just missing Mr. Stein. The railing cracked and sent Chaya over the edge to the floor.

The ceiling gave way as Mr. Stein rushed toward her. A huge beam fell and landed on her legs, crunching the bones. The other end of the beam smashed into the grand piano, splintering it to pieces. Bricks from the fireplace littered the floor.

Through the dust and noise, Chaya's father yelled her name. He staggered into the room, horror on his face.

"I'll get you out!" he said.

Before he could move, the ceiling collapsed, raining boards and plaster. The room was white with dust. Chaya screamed for her father to save himself, but he didn't answer.

A beautiful morning had transformed into darkness. Chaya shivered as she struggled to move. The beam had her legs pinned. Her father lay under rubble only a few feet away. And she heard nothing but the most fierce earthquake in history.

Darrion Stahley was lonely. Her mother had been arrested a full week ago, and Darrion felt powerless to help. Darrion had been brought to Donny and Sandy Moore's house for safety. Early that Monday morning she chatted with Sandy. Donny was heading to the church. Just talking with the Moores made Darrion feel better.

Mrs. Moore had lost a baby in the disappearances. She and Donny said they looked forward to seeing their child in heaven someday.

Darrion left Sandy eating her breakfast and reading the paper. Darrion retreated into the shelter Mr. Moore had built under the house. It wasn't finished, but Darrion was able to relax there.

Darrion was angry at her mother for getting arrested. They could have gone back to their cottage in Wisconsin, and no one would have known. Now her mom was in the custody of the Global Community, falsely accused of murdering her husband.

As Darrion thought about ways to help her mother escape, she heard a rumbling. The room began to shake. She screamed for Mrs. Moore, then heard a crash above. The floor of the basement caved in. The limbs of a tree pushed through a hole in the kitchen floor.

Darrion pulled the door of the shelter closed. She knelt with the earth shaking violently around her, and she wept with fear.

33

VICKI held on. It was the only thing she could do. She was on top of Mrs. Jenness's car, her feet touching the tree that held them suspended over the chasm. The car rocked as Vicki moved slightly.

Though she couldn't see in the dark, she knew her only chance of escape was the tree. If she could make her way back along the trunk to its base, there was a chance she could climb up the bank to safety. She gingerly leaned down to the driver's window.

"Mrs. Jenness, you have to climb out," Vicki screamed. "It's the only way."

"I can't," the woman said. "I'll wait until the rescue squad comes."

"There isn't gonna be a rescue squad," Vicki said. "Can't you see? This is the worldwide quake the Bible predicted. This is what I wrote about in the *Underground*."

Mrs. Jenness held the steering wheel. Her knuckles were white. Vicki had to make a decision. If the woman didn't want help, Vicki would have to leave without her.

"Please," Vicki pleaded, "give me your hand."

"Leave me," Mrs. Jenness said.

Vicki scooted back on the roof of the car and grabbed the tree trunk. Water sprayed up from the chasm. The tree was slick.

She was only a few feet along the tree when another fierce tremor sent the ground rolling behind her. The earth swallowed the tree roots, and Vicki held on as she was moved downstream. The car submerged. Vicki was underwater before she could take a good breath of air. She held on to a small limb, surfaced for air, then pulled herself toward the car.

In the inky blackness, she felt her way down. The current was swift, and if she hadn't had the tree and the car to hold on to, she would have been swept to her death. The car lights flickered underwater. Vicki reached inside the driver's side. She found the steering wheel. Then she touched a lifeless hand. Mrs. Jenness. In the reflection of the dashboard light, she saw the tree had struck the principal in the head.

She must have been killed instantly when the car went under, Vicki thought.

For a moment, Vicki froze. She knew it would be easier to give up. But something willed her to fight.

Then Vicki realized the water current and the gaping hole weren't the worst dangers she faced. The water was.

Her hands were almost numb, and she could hardly feel her legs. With all the strength she could muster, Vicki struggled to the surface. She grabbed a limb and pulled herself up.

She slowly crawled along the length of the tree until she felt the muddy bank. She climbed the last of the roots to the top of the embankment hollowed out by the earthquake. The sky was changing now, and Vicki saw the submerged car. She looked toward the city, but there were no lights. Screams and cries echoed into the watery canyon. People staggered by in tattered clothes. A man in a suit and tie ran by in muddy shoes. He called out for his wife. Vicki cried for help but no one responded.

Vicki made her way back far enough from the bank to be safe, but another shock sent the ground at her feet crumbling into the water. The tree finally dislodged and fell into the water with a great splash. The current turned the tree around, then flipped the car onto its top. Both plunged into the chasm.

Vicki cried. She cried for Mrs. Jenness. She cried for others who were facing death. And she cried for herself.

Did you bring me through all that's happened to let me die in an earthquake? Vicki prayed.

Nothing. Just the mighty churning water and the rumbling earth that would not stop.

Judd and Taylor felt their way along in the darkness, their handcuffs clacking. Away from the electric lines, they were at least safe from electrocution. But the earth kept moving. Judd never knew when the next step might lead him into a newly opened hole.

"At least we're safe from things falling on us here," Judd said.

"Safe is a relative term," Taylor said. "You say this thing was predicted in the Bible?"

"If you'd have stuck around for the service for Bruce," Judd said, "you would have heard about this. I downloaded Tsion Ben-Judah's take on it."

"What's he say?" Taylor said.

Judd thought about the rabbi in his shelter at the church and wondered if he had survived. If it was a worldwide quake, Buck, Chloe, Amanda, and Rayford had to be caught in it as well.

"The Bible calls this the wrath of the Lamb," Judd said. "The Lamb is Jesus Christ. The Bible says the sun will be black and the moon will become like blood."

"Sure got the sun right," Taylor said. "Can't see the moon. What else?"

"I can't remember all of it," Judd said. "There's something about the mountains moving and people hiding in caves and asking God to kill them. . . ."

A section of earth gave way near Judd. He sat rigid until he felt it was safe to move. "That was a close one," Judd said.

Taylor didn't respond.

"Taylor?" Judd shouted. "Where are you?"

Something groaned beneath Judd. The wind picked up and blew dust into his eyes. When he could see again, clouds rolled back and a huge crater appeared inches from his feet.

At the bottom of the crater, Taylor Graham lay in a heap. Judd shouted to him, but the pilot didn't move. With the ground shifting, he couldn't risk going after Taylor.

Judd looked around for help. He was near the house that had disappeared. A tire swing hung from a tree a hundred yards away, but between Judd and the tree lay another huge gorge.

Judd looked at the sky and gasped. He suddenly remembered the rest of the passage.

The stars of heaven fell to the earth!

Lionel put up his hands as the porch roof crashed down. He fell backward. Support beams landed near him. If one had hit his head, he knew he would have died instantly. Wood splinters scratched his arms and tore his pants.

"Lionel," Conrad called, "can you hear me?"

"Don't come in here," Lionel yelled. "Get away from the building!"

The second floor caved in behind Lionel, and he could hear the screams of the dying. Lionel dug his way to the front door. He coughed and tried to get air, but there was so much dust he had to put his shirt over his face to breathe. There was no light. No way to see which way to go.

The earth shook with such force that Lionel thought he would be killed any minute. It was a miracle any part of the building still stood.

This was his chance. If he could get out of the house, he could make a break for it. Maybe take Conrad with him and explain the truth about the Global Community and what the Bible said was happening.

Through the shaking, Lionel found the stairwell and sat in the doorway. If there was any hope of safety, it was here.

A beam of light trembled with each rattle of the earth. Then a horn.

"Lionel, can you hear me?" Conrad yelled from a car. "Follow the headlights to find your way out!"

Lionel moved toward the light and found the biggest opening he could. He clawed at boards and rocks. The rumbling and shifting continued. Lionel heard Conrad clearing debris from the other side. As Lionel fell out of the rubble, another shock sent them both back to the ground. The headlights turned skyward as the car sank into the ground. The building collapsed behind Lionel.

A whistling, like air escaping.

"Gas leak!" Conrad said.

An explosion rocked the compound. Lionel and Conrad were thrown from the blast, along with the shattered building. Lionel landed in the dirt. Monstrous black and purple clouds formed in the sky.

Ryan braced himself to hit concrete as he fell into the basement. He imagined landing headfirst and splitting his head open. Instead, he twisted in the air and landed on his back. Something cracked, and he felt a sharp pain. Then nothing.

The earth shifted again, and Ryan was rolled over. He lost his breath as something slammed onto his back. He panicked, struggling for air and to get out from under the heavy load. When he couldn't, he settled and slowly regained his breath. There was pressure on his chest but no pain. He tried to move again.

I'll just wait a minute, he thought. *When the earth moves again, I'll get out.*

But the thing on his back didn't move. The pressure grew worse. It was hard to breathe. Then he heard dripping. The flashlight was a few feet away, but Ryan couldn't reach it. He felt around in the mud and found a splintered piece of wood. By scraping it against the flashlight, he pulled it close.

He shone the light on what was left of the basement wall. A stream of water rolled down the side and collected in a pool. The water pipes had burst. If Ryan didn't get out from under whatever was on his back, he could drown in less than two feet of water. The rumblings sounded different down here. Above ground the noise spread out. In the basement, the sound was like the beating of a drum, and the drum was the earth.

He turned the flashlight and craned his neck. A huge slab pressed into his back. He tried to move his legs. Nothing.

Ryan scratched at the mud and clay beneath. It would take him hours to dig out. The shifting ground might crush him by then. Or the water might be over his head.

He had to try. Ryan used the flashlight and dug with all his might.

Chaya struggled to free herself, but the weight of the beam was too much. Broken glass fell around her as the earthquake rolled on. She could hear the screams of people in the street. She screamed too. Furniture from the second floor toppled down. She tried to cover herself, but with each shudder of the earth, more things fell.

She called out for her father over the noise. Finally, he answered.

"I am here," Mr. Stein said. "Are you safe?"

"I can't move," Chaya said. "I think my legs are broken. And you?"

"I will try to get you out," he said. "Keep talking so I can find you."

Chaya softly sang a song from her childhood. Her mother had sung it to her at bedtime. Tears rolled down her cheeks as she choked out the melody.

"Do you remember that song?" she yelled.

"I do," Mr. Stein said. "I wish your mother was here with us now."

Chaya could hear her father moving in the rubble nearby. "She is in a much better place," Chaya said.

The movement stopped. "What are you saying?" her father said. "You do not wish your mother was here?"

A wall behind Chaya fell outward. Bedroom furniture spilled into the yard.

"I am only saying that I am glad Mother is in heaven now and doesn't have to go through this," Chaya said.

Mr. Stein resumed his search.

"I have not been able to talk with you about this," Chaya said. "You would not speak to me."

Mr. Stein was close. Chaya felt a piece of wood lift from her shoulder.

"Talk to me about what?" Mr. Stein said.

"That day at the hospital," Chaya said. "Before she died she wrote something. She was holding it in her hand. It was a prayer."

"Your mother always wrote things," Mr. Stein said. "Put out your hand. See if you can reach me."

Chaya lifted her arm and strained. She felt her father's fingertips in the darkness.

"A little farther," Mr. Stein said.

"Mother gave her life to God before she died," Chaya said. "She believed in Jesus."

Mr. Stein's hand went limp. Another surge of the earthquake brought a cascade of debris onto them. Chaya lost her father's hand. She screamed. He did not answer.

Darrion prayed for her life. She prayed for Ryan and Judd. She prayed for Vicki. For Chaya. For Taylor Graham and especially for her mother. When the electricity went out, she was in total darkness. The shelter had no windows, but through the ventilation shaft she could hear what was happening outside.

People ran from their homes screaming. The earthquake was so sudden, Darrion couldn't imagine anyone being able to react in time. Then she thought of Sandy and Donny Moore. She crawled on hands and knees to the massive shelter door. It was like trying to walk on a moving teeter-totter. She managed to get the door open a few inches, but something had fallen on the other side.

"Mrs. Moore!!" Darrion screamed.

No answer.

Donny will come for us, Darrion thought. *He'll get us out of here.*

Darrion closed the door and crawled under her bed. The quake was rearranging what little furniture there was in the shelter.

Please, God, Darrion prayed, *help me get out of here alive.*

34

VICKI trembled. The sky was changing, and for the first time she saw the wreckage clearly. Beautiful houses toppled into the river. People ran screaming into the street. Some fell into huge cracks in the earth. Others seemed to want to die. The quake roared on and on. Like a hungry beast, it devoured everything in its path.

Great mounds of asphalt shot upward. What Vicki couldn't climb over, she went around. It was slow, but she figured her chances of survival were better if she kept moving.

But where was she going? An hour ago she sat in Mrs. Jenness's office and watched her read the *Underground*. Now the woman was dead, and Vicki was fighting for her life. She wanted to find the others. Just one friend.

Traffic signs, streetlights, and telephone poles were gone. Vicki saw a row of apartment buildings. Only one

411

stood above ground. The others had collapsed or had been swallowed whole by the earth.

Vicki walked over two yellow humps barely sticking out of the ground, then realized it was all that was left of a fast-food restaurant. Across the street, cars were piled on top of each other at a car dealership. A computer store stood at a jagged angle, then slowly the walls caved in.

A bell rang behind her, and Vicki turned to see the steeple of a church crash to the ground. She wondered about her own church and who might be there. Loretta? The rabbi? Had anyone else survived? What about her school?

Then Vicki remembered Ryan. She had insisted he stay inside. Could he still be alive? A wave of guilt stopped Vicki and she knelt. *I have to get back there and find him*, she thought.

When the car had plunged into the water, Vicki could only think about getting out alive. Now she thought about the others. Where was Lionel? Was Chaya driving home from her father's house when the earthquake hit? And Judd. Where was Judd in all of this?

Though the streets had no signs, she knew she was a few miles from home. But it might as well have been a few hundred miles. Walking through the shifting rubble was next to impossible.

No emotions, Vicki thought. *I have to stay alive. Just get back to the house and find Ryan.*

The sky peeled back, and monstrous black and purple clouds hovered over the town. It looked like a horror movie.

Then it began.

Huge flaming rocks streaked to earth. The sky was falling, and it was on fire. Vicki covered her eyes. It had gone from day to night and now back to day with the glowing balls of fire.

The earth was still rolling under her feet. Vicki had to stay upright and avoid the hurtling meteors. They seemed to smash everything the earthquake hadn't swallowed.

The heat from the meteors was intense. The smell was overwhelming. When a meteor slammed into the ground, it exploded and sent molten rock flying. Vicki looked at the horizon and saw an incredible sight. Thousands of red streaks descended from the darkness above, pounding the ground with yellow bursts of light. It looked like a Fourth of July celebration reversed. Instead of sending fireworks into the air, they were coming down.

Vicki moved cautiously. The shaking of the earth was not an aftershock. The earthquake simply would not quit. Though it had been less than half an hour, Vicki felt like it had been going on for days. With each meteor, the earth shook even more.

A wild-eyed man rushed at Vicki and screamed. His head was bleeding, and his right arm hung uselessly at his side.

"Kill me!" he shouted over and over.

Vicki knew there were other survivors, but this was the first person she had seen up close.

"I'll help you," Vicki said, putting her hand on his shoulder.

The man jerked backward. His chest was heaving with

each labored breath. "They're gone," he said. "All dead. I'm the only one who got out alive!"

"But you're alive," Vicki said. "That's good."

The man ran, tearing at his hair with his good hand. Vicki put a hand to her mouth when she saw where he was going.

"No!" she screamed.

The man stopped at the edge of a crater and looked back. Smoke and flames gushed from the hole. The man gave one last scream and threw himself into the white-hot flames.

Judd peeked over the edge of the gorge. The ground was crumbling. He stepped to a small ledge to get a better look at Taylor Graham. He was on his back at the bottom.

How could anyone hear the prophecies about the wrath of the Lamb, then experience this and not believe in God? Judd thought. He recalled a comedy show shortly after Buck Williams's article had appeared in *Global Community Weekly*. The show featured a cartoon of a cute little lamb. Sappy music played in the background. Suddenly the lamb turned fierce and went on a rampage. The audience had laughed. Judd wondered if the people who had drawn that cartoon were laughing now, or if anyone would ever laugh again.

A red glow engulfed Judd. He heard a jet pass overhead. Judd looked up and realized it wasn't a plane but a fiery meteor. It slammed into the earth.

The second meteor hit near where Judd had been standing and threw molten rock high into the air. If Judd had stayed where he was, he would have melted from the heat.

But he hadn't stayed at the top of the crater. He had thrown himself down its shifting wall and reached Taylor. The man was too big for him to carry, so he tried to awaken him.

Taylor sat up.

"We gotta get you out of here," Judd said.

Taylor looked at the sky and cursed. "It doesn't matter where we go," he said. "We'll never survive this."

"We have to try," Judd said.

Judd helped Taylor climb out the shallow end of the crater. When they made it back to level ground, another shock threw them to the ground. They half crawled, half walked until they made it to what looked like a parking lot of an old elementary school. The building had been flattened.

"What's that up there?" Judd said, pointing to a hill behind the demolished school.

"Must be a lake or some kind of water plant," Taylor said. "Those concrete walls are locks that change the water level."

Judd watched in horror as one of the walls cracked. Water rushed down the slope right toward them.

"Look out!" Taylor shouted as a meteor slammed into the crumpled school building. The rubble caught fire. Judd could feel the intense heat. They ran. Judd looked back and saw the asphalt melting in a wave that was moving toward them. They were no longer running on pavement but on a gooey, melting mess. Then he heard a hissing. The hot water gushed over them and took them both with it.

Judd clung to Taylor with all his might. The water had saved them from a fiery death, but where would it take them now?

Judd went under, then recovered and gasped for air. It was difficult staying above the swells with his cuffed hands. He had lost all control. He was being led by the cascading water.

Then Judd heard a roar. The earth split not far ahead of them, and the water was rushing into the gorge. Judd watched helplessly as they neared the edge.

Before Lionel opened his eyes, he sensed the fire behind him. The heat was intense. The hair on his arms singed, and he buried his head in the dirt. He looked up. The gas explosion must have made the clouds look funny. He tried to move. His body ached, but it didn't feel like any bones were broken. Conrad sat a few feet away, shaking his head and squinting.

"You should have gotten out of there while you had the chance," Lionel said.

"I could say the same for you," Conrad said. "You risked your life for me."

Lionel looked at the car. The wheels were buried. They would never be able to move it by themselves.

A few boys staggered from the rubble. Lionel knew

many had been killed in the explosion. Two leaders barked orders and tried to gather the survivors.

"You think we should go with them?" Conrad said.

"I've got another idea," Lionel said.

Lionel and Conrad moved away from the group. When they had gone a few yards, Lionel heard a whirring. The rumbling of the earth still sounded like a freight train, but this was different.

Conrad pointed to the sky. Lionel saw the meteor and fell to the ground. The sphere slammed into the crater where they had been. The car flew in the air and landed on its top, the wheels spinning.

"Glad we didn't stay there," Conrad said.

Lionel looked up. Other meteors streaked through the black and purple clouds, some huge, some only the size of Lionel's hand. The small ones didn't do as much damage but were just as deadly.

"We gotta get under something," Conrad said.

"Not with the earthquake," Lionel said. "Anything we get under is likely to fall on us."

"Then where?" Conrad said.

Lionel scanned the area. What had been flat was now a series of hills and valleys. The main compound building was now a fiery crater. The spot where the leaders had gathered the boys was also a hole in the ground, and Lionel saw bodies a few feet away.

The meteor shower increased. One struck the over-turned car. It exploded on impact. The earth continued to roll. Lionel wondered when it would end and if he would still be alive when it was all over.

Ryan was exhausted from digging after only a few minutes. With the weight on his back it was difficult to breathe. He had moved some of the mud and rocks near him, but another rattle had sent boards and plaster falling from above. He was covered in white, chalky dust.

Through a hole in the rubble above he saw clouds. The quake had rolled the roof and upper floors so that he had a clear view of the sky.

The clouds were beautiful. He had never seen anything with such brilliant color. Then he remembered the show he had watched on television about violent storms. Every one of them had weird cloud formations. From the looks of these, Ryan was in for trouble.

He struggled against the slab, but he couldn't move or even feel his legs. He had hoped to be able to move a few inches with all the digging he had done. But he was stuck in the mud and rocks and dust.

He closed his eyes and prayed. Then he thought of his friends. Where were they? What could they be going through? Were they even alive?

He opened his eyes and saw a television remote control floating in the water. The level was rising.

A flash. A thunderous roar. He saw flames streak through the air and wondered if this was some kind of attack. It sounded like the special effects on his video games, but this wasn't a game.

Finally, he understood. This was what Bruce Barnes had written about. Rayford Steele's words came back to him.

" 'The sun became black as sackcloth of hair, and the moon became like blood,' " Rayford had read from Revelation. " 'And the stars of heaven fell to the earth, as a fig tree drops its late figs when it is shaken by a mighty wind. Then the sky receded as a scroll when it is rolled up, and every mountain and island was moved out of its place.' "

Ryan caught a glimpse of more meteors. Since it was morning, he knew he couldn't see the moon. But wherever it was shining, he knew it was as red as blood.

Chaya coughed and choked as the debris settled. She stretched as far as she could but did not find her father. She screamed for him, then prayed.

A flash. Screams in the distance. The ground shuddered.

Chaya had read much of Bruce's writings since his death. She knew other prophecies leading up to the earthquake had been fulfilled. But she was not prepared for this.

Bruce had said the earthquake would touch every place on the globe. There would possibly be volcanic activity as well. As the meteorites hurtled to earth, she recalled what Bruce believed would happen to those who were living at the time of the great earthquake.

The people of earth will believe God is responsible for all these events, Bruce had written. *And they will cry out to be killed.*

Chaya could understand that feeling. Though her belief in God made her want to keep going, others had nothing to believe in. For them, life was hopeless.

She did not see the meteors. When she heard the explosions and smelled the fire, she knew what it was.

Something moved in the rubble. Her father groaned.

"Why?" Mr. Stein cried. "Why don't you kill me now and get it over with!"

Chaya called out for her father, but he continued his ranting. "If you are so good and merciful, why are you doing this to us?" he screamed.

"Do not blame God," Chaya said.

"He has taken my wife," Mr. Stein said. "He has ruined everything I have worked for. Why shouldn't I blame him?"

"God is still calling you to himself," Chaya said. "He is merciful and gracious, even now."

"Mercy and grace are poured out with an earthquake?" Mr. Stein said. "Death and destruction are a display of love?"

"If you turn to God, he will show you mercy," Chaya said.

Chaya listened as her father struggled against the weight of his destroyed home. He was trapped. And the meteors were falling around them.

Darrion couldn't wait any longer. Though the earthquake continued to roll, she bolted out of the shelter and closed the door as tightly as she could. The basement floor was littered with computer parts, storage boxes, and broken canning jars. An oak tree stuck through the kitchen floor above.

Darrion gingerly made her way up the stairs, clinging to the rail as the quake rolled on.

"Mrs. Moore?" Darrion called.

No answer.

The drapes were open in the living room. Considering all the shaking, things looked OK. Then Darrion saw the tiny breakfast nook in the back. She closed her eyes and turned away. Mrs. Moore was still at the breakfast table, her finger curled around a cup of coffee. On top of her was the huge tree. It had flattened her and the heavy wood table.

At least you didn't suffer, Darrion thought.

Darrion couldn't stay. She didn't want to be inside with a dead body. She knew Donny was at the church. She had to tell him. She unlocked the front door and ran outside. The pavement in front was intact. Shards of glass from broken windows littered the lawn. A brick wall of the duplex had collapsed, but Darrion was hopeful. If this was the extent of the damage, others might be alive.

Then she saw the clouds. She heard the meteors before she saw their red glow. She dove under a car as the first one fell to earth.

35

VICKI could hardly believe the man had killed himself. The Bible was right; others felt the same despair. Vicki wondered what people who had a will to live would do. Who would help them?

In the distance, Vicki saw a hospital. The multistoried parking garage had fallen. Ambulances were upside down or deep in ruts. People ran frantically about looking for family members.

Vicki kept going. She scrambled over a huge stone that had fallen, then realized she was in a graveyard. Headstones lay flat. Unearthed coffins spilled bones and tattered clothes. Vicki carefully picked her way through. When she was almost on the other side, a tremendous shock sent her reeling. She fell into a soft place, then felt withered bones beside her. She was in an open casket!

Vicki climbed out. No matter how much she brushed at the dirt, she didn't feel clean again.

She made it over the stones to the other side of the cemetery. She jumped to the ground and stopped. Something was strange. The ground wasn't moving.

She looked up. No clouds. No meteors. The sun reappeared. It was a bright Monday morning.

Vicki fell to the ground on her knees. She felt relieved it was finally over. She felt sadness for Mrs. Jenness and uncertainty for her friends. And she was alone.

Judd and Taylor were swept away with the current. The water carried them back over the route they had walked a few minutes earlier. The pilot held Judd's jacket tightly and tried to stay above the surface. Judd held tightly to Taylor as well.

Judd realized where they were. The collapsed farmhouse had been here. In front of them was the tree, now perched at a weird angle. From one of the limbs, hanging just above the surface of the water, was the tire swing.

"Swim!" Judd yelled.

"What do you mean, swim?" Taylor said. "I can hardly breathe!"

"If we can move a little to the left, we can make it to the tire," Judd said.

Judd and Taylor kicked, but it didn't seem to do any good. The water had a mind of its own. At the last second, the current swirled to the left. Judd managed to reach out and catch the tire with his left hand. Taylor let go of Judd's jacket and grabbed for the swing too. He missed. He grasped at Judd's feet and caught one before he was swept away.

Judd held on, then managed to get both arms through the tire. But Taylor was floundering. He couldn't get a good grip on Judd.

"Pull yourself up!" Judd screamed.

"I can't," Taylor yelled back. "Looks like this is it!"

"Don't say that," Judd yelled. "We're gonna get out of this."

Judd tried to wrap his legs around Taylor's chest. Judd looked up and realized they were only a few yards from the chasm.

The ground stopped shaking. The sun came out. Judd heard birds. There were no meteors. Still they had to fight the water.

Judd finally got a good hold on Taylor. He reached his hand out to pull the man to the tire.

"Almost there," Judd shouted. "You can do it!"

Taylor stretched out his arms. The water was dirty brown as it swirled past him. Chunks of meteor dropped over the edge. If Judd could reach Taylor's hands, the two could stay on the swing until the lake ran dry and the water stopped.

The pilot was almost to safety when a submerged log hit them both. The log hit Judd's legs, and he nearly lost hold of the tire. The log hit Taylor Graham in the face. The man let go and was sucked under in the current.

"No!!!" Judd yelled.

Judd didn't see Taylor until he surfaced at the edge of

the chasm. Taylor looked back, blood streaming down his face. He lifted his handcuffs into the air and plunged out of sight.

Judd hung on to the tire. He closed his eyes. They had been so close to making it. Close to life. But close to death as well. The tire swung with the current. Judd put one leg through and then another. He sat there, the water rushing under him.

The sun was out. Everything seemed quiet and normal. Everything except the earth that had turned inside out.

Conrad and Lionel scooted toward the perimeter of the compound. A chain-link fence lay crumpled on the ground, the metal poles twisted or snapped in two.

Meteors slammed into the soft ground, leaving huge craters. Lionel felt like they were dodging incoming fire from an unseen enemy.

"You think we'll survive this?" Conrad said when they stopped at the base of a tree.

"The Bible says some will," Lionel said.

"What do you mean?" Conrad said.

"It's a long story," Lionel said. "Remind me to tell you when this is over."

"Where are you headed?" Conrad said.

"I have friends in Chicago I need to get back to," Lionel said.

"That's where my brother's stationed," Conrad said. "You want to go together?"

426

"Sounds like a plan," Lionel said.

The rocking of the earth stopped. The terrible noise was gone. Sunshine hit Lionel in the face. He looked at the blue sky.

"It's like it never happened," Conrad said.

"But it did," Lionel said. "Look at that."

Lionel pointed toward the compound. There was no road. All the buildings were flat. The car Lionel wanted to escape in was on fire. Remains of burning meteors dotted the landscape.

"What do we do now?" Conrad said.

"I'm getting out of here before they catch me," Lionel said.

Then Lionel heard a quick rumbling. A violent shake rattled the earth.

"Aftershock!" Lionel said.

"Look out!" Conrad yelled.

Lionel looked up as the tree they were under crashed down. Lionel dodged the trunk. He thought he was safe until a good-sized limb smacked him in the head. Lionel heard the sickening thud and felt the bark against his skull.

He slumped to the ground and passed out.

Ryan stared at the rising water. He could judge the intensity of the earthquake by the ripples. He still saw the sky through the demolished house. It had been some time since the last meteor.

Light. Glorious light. The sky turned a brilliant blue. He looked at the water. No ripples.

It's over, Ryan thought. *It's really over!*

Ryan put his hands on the muddy floor and pushed up. The water was halfway to his elbows. He couldn't budge the weight that pinned him, but he could raise up enough to see the burst water pipe. He figured it had been about twenty minutes since the pipe burst. Maybe a half hour. Another hour or two and the water would be over his head. He had to either dig out or get help.

Ryan believed the water might help lift whatever was holding him down. If he could keep digging and let the water do its work, there was a chance he could get out.

He used the flashlight until a wooden spoon floated by. Ryan grabbed it and furiously scraped at the mud under his body.

He didn't want to die. He certainly didn't want to survive the great earthquake and then drown. Focusing on the rising water made his heart beat faster, so he talked to himself to calm down.

"If I make it out of here, I'm going straight to the school and find Vicki," Ryan said. "She'll want to know that I'm OK. Then I have to find Darrion."

Ryan did another push-up, but he was still trapped.

"OK," he said, "that's the best I can hope for—get out of here and find Vicki and Darrion. Worst case, I'm stuck. Nobody finds me and I drown."

Ryan paused, then cocked his head.

"That's not without its good points, because then I'd be in heaven with Bruce. I'd get to meet his family. That'd be cool."

Ryan shook his head. "I don't think I'm ready for

that," he said. "I want to be here for the Glorious Appearing Bruce talked about. I want to see Jesus coming again."

Something moved above him. A piece of wood fell into the water.

"Hello?" Ryan yelled. "Anybody up there?"

Ryan listened carefully. Someone or something was up there.

"Can you help me?" Ryan said. "I'm stuck! Can anybody hear me?"

Then Ryan heard familiar sounds. Sniffing. Pawing. Phoenix moved around the edges of the rubble. Finally he put his head over the hole and looked down.

"Hey, boy," Ryan said.

Phoenix barked. He wagged his tail and planted his feet like he expected Ryan to chase him.

"Go get help," Ryan said. "Go get somebody!"

Phoenix just looked into the hole.

"OK, so just bark," Ryan yelled. "Come on, bark!!"

Chaya listened as the last of the shifting rubble settled. "It's over, Father," she said.

Mr. Stein furiously tried to pull himself out from under the wreckage. Then he stopped. Chaya couldn't even hear him breathe.

"Father?" she said.

Finally he answered. "You are right; it is over," Mr. Stein said. "How can I go on? How can one man lose so much and still want to live?"

"We have each other," Chaya said.

"I have lost everything!" Mr. Stein said. "I have no daughter. You betrayed me. You betrayed your family and your faith."

Chaya shook her head. She couldn't see her father, but she could imagine the look on his face. "We mustn't fight," she said. "We must pull together and try to survive this."

"What does it matter?" Mr. Stein said.

Chaya coughed and groaned.

"What is it?" Mr. Stein said. "Are you hurt?"

"Something happened to my back," Chaya said. "It is difficult to breathe."

Chaya heard her father struggle again, then lay still.

"I wish I could help, but I can't," Mr. Stein said. "Can you move at all?"

"No," Chaya said. "I am like you. Are you injured?"

"Nothing serious," Mr. Stein said.

They were silent for a moment. Then Mr. Stein said, "I suppose you believe there is some great plan in all of this."

"I don't understand it all," Chaya said, "but I do believe God is in control, if that is what you mean."

"I'm sorry I brought it up again," Mr. Stein said. "Let's not talk of those things."

"It is the one thing we should talk about," Chaya said. "It is the most important thing of all."

"You are like your mother."

"Thank you."

"That was not a compliment."

"I know. But I take it as one."

"Your mother tried to convince me to allow you back into the family," Mr. Stein said. "She wanted to forgive you and accept you."

"And you could not."

"Not after what you did," Mr. Stein said. "I suppose that's why she decided to become a foster parent."

"Vicki?"

"Yes."

Chaya wondered if Nicolae High had been damaged as badly as her house. If Vicki had been able to get the *Underground* inside, some kids had probably read it before the quake.

"What did you decide to keep from your mother's belongings?" Mr. Stein said.

Chaya moved on her side and reached in her front pocket. The jewelry was still there. "I kept the gold brooch I gave her," Chaya said. "Is that all right?"

"Why did you really come here?" Mr. Stein said, ignoring her question.

"I told you," Chaya said, "I needed something to help me remember her."

"Is that the truth?" Mr. Stein said. "Doesn't your new faith teach it is a sin to lie?"

Chaya bit her lip. "I suppose I did want to see you once more," she said. "But I swear, I lost track of time. I didn't stay on purpose."

"You wanted to see me once more, so you could break my heart."

The two were only a few feet apart, separated by wood

and debris. Neither could see the other. Chaya thought it was best this way. Her father could not get up and storm off like he wanted. He was trapped.

"How long do you think it will take until someone finds us?" Chaya said.

"If everyone is in the same shape we are in, there will be no one," Mr. Stein said. He sighed. "I suppose there will be someone who will come along within a day or two."

"A day or two!?" Chaya said.

Chaya coughed. She felt something on her lip and wiped it away. Her hand came away with specks of blood.

Darrion stayed under the car until the meteor shower ended. Soon the earth stopped shaking. Darrion climbed out and surveyed the damage.

Some houses were harder hit than others. A few, like the Moores' home, were damaged but not destroyed. Other buildings were flattened. Darrion saw a few people scurrying, rummaging through the rubble. She heard the screams of trapped victims. She heard a police siren behind her. *At least they have a working squad car*, she thought.

Not wanting to take any chances, she ducked behind a mound of dirt.

The officer spoke through an amplifier. "Stay out of your homes!" the officer said. "Do not return to your homes! If you need help, get to an open area where we can find you!"

Darrion thought of her mother. She was still in the custody of the Global Community. If their facilities were anything like the homes in the area, her mother could be dead.

However, those who might be looking for Darrion and Ryan were busy. Or they were dead themselves. That meant she was free to move about.

She wasn't sure where she was. She hadn't paid attention to street signs when they drove her to the Moores' house. But there were no street signs left anyway. She headed north. She had to find the church and tell Mr. Moore about his wife.

36

VICKI had been walking more than two hours. She thought she was going in the right direction, but it was impossible to tell by the streets. Every familiar house or business left standing stood at odd angles.

People wandered about in a daze. Some had no shoes. Others were bleeding and seemed near death. A few had survived horrible burns from the meteors and had to be carried.

Other survivors were beginning the grisly task of bringing out the dead. Bodies lay covered on mounds of dirt. Vicki felt sorry and wanted to help, but something drew her home. She had to find out about Ryan.

Geysers of water shot up from broken fire hydrants. Animals roamed about, sniffing at the rubble and whimpering. A woman clutching a bloody cloth wept in front of a demolished apartment building.

435

On a normal Monday, the street Vicki was on would have been packed with traffic. Now the only cars getting through the mess were those with four-wheel drive. A man pulled up beside the weeping woman and hopped out. One side of the vehicle was caved in, and the back window was shattered.

"I'm a doctor, ma'am," the man said. "Can I help you?"

"My baby," the woman wept. "Please help my baby."

The doctor lifted the bloody cloth and winced. "Get in my car and I'll take you to one of the emergency shelters."

The woman stood slowly.

Vicki approached. "Where could I find one of those shelters?" she asked.

"The closest is at Nicolae High," the doctor said. "Take you about twenty minutes on foot." He helped the woman in and closed the door.

"Could I have a ride?" Vicki said.

"I'm not going there," the doctor said. He lowered his voice. "I'm taking this lady's baby to the temporary morgue. It's in the other direction."

The doctor pointed Vicki toward the high school. Vicki looked at the mother as she rode away. She wanted to tell the woman something to comfort her, but she didn't know what to say.

What could anyone say at a time like this?

———————————————

Judd swayed as he clung to the tire. Water plunged over the falls. Trees, cars, huge chunks of asphalt, even parts of houses were swept into the newly formed canyon. Every few minutes Judd spotted another lifeless body going over the edge. He wondered if there was any chance Taylor Graham could have survived.

The current had slowed. Judd put one foot down to test whether he could stand. He decided to wait. One wrong step and he could fall and be swept over like the others.

Judd wanted to search for Taylor, but he knew things looked grim. He also knew he had to change clothes and get out of the handcuffs. The Global Community was resourceful. As soon as the reeducation camp was secure, someone would notice they hadn't arrived. Judd hoped they would find the burned-out van and believe he was dead.

He had to find help. Someone he could trust. He wanted to get back to his friends. That was his most diffi-cult task. On a normal day with a car, the trip would take two hours at most. But without a vehicle and with the destruction of the earthquake, he couldn't imagine it taking any less than two days.

The water was shallow now. He looked back at the collapsed locks. The earthquake had smashed the concrete walls. It looked like a monster had taken a huge bite out of it.

Judd gingerly walked to the edge of the chasm, making sure of his footing. He peered over and was horrified. A new lake had formed, much narrower and brown with dirt. Floating at the top were the mud-caked bodies of the dead. Judd looked for Taylor, but identifying him was impossi-ble.

"Can anybody hear me?" Judd shouted, giving it one last try.

Water trickled nearby. Birds flew overhead. No one answered. The only voice Judd heard was his own, echoing off the chasm walls.

He walked around the hole and went east. He knew the interstate was somewhere in that direction. He tested every new hill he climbed to make sure it would hold his weight. It was like walking through a maze. He would choose one route, then find it led to a gap too wide to cross. He doubled back and went another way.

He found the road where the van had wrecked. He picked along what was left of the highway and found crumpled bits of a mirror. Then he spotted a blackened portion of earth. The earth had swallowed the van but opened again, exposing the charred vehicle. Judd climbed down and stood near the driver's side and looked in.

Dirt filled the van completely. Judd tried to open the door but couldn't. He stuck his hands through the window and pulled at the rocks and clay. Finally he found the charred pistol of the guard. Judd fumbled for the keys on his belt, but there were none. They had melted from the heat of the inferno. Judd would have to find another way to get his handcuffs off.

Judd set off again, stepping over dead animals. He decided to stay close to the road. He would pass someone who could help. In the distance he saw a leaning farmhouse. Someone moved on the front porch. Judd decided to chance it.

"Where am I?" Lionel said when he came to.

"Trauma center," Conrad said. "Looks like a tent, but that's what they call it. That tree did a number on your head."

"Tree?" Lionel said. "Is that what hit me?"

"Yeah, you've been out almost two hours," Conrad said. "So much for you heading north. Looks like you're gonna be here for a while."

"What are you talking about?" Lionel said. "Who are you?"

Conrad looked at him strangely and held up his hand in front of Lionel's face. "How many fingers do you see?" he said.

"Two," Lionel said.

"What's your name?" Conrad said.

Lionel rubbed his head and winced. He shook his head. "I don't know," he said. "I honestly don't know my name."

"Do you remember anything about the last week or two?" Conrad said. "The ride down here, the GC camp, the earthquake?"

Lionel's face lit up. "Yeah, the meteors," he said. "I remember them . . . and the earthquake. The noise. Yeah, that's still with me."

"But you don't remember your name or where you came from?" Conrad said.

"Tell me," Lionel said.

Conrad told Lionel what he knew. Lionel was from Chicago. Lionel had told him he had friends back there, but that his parents and other family had vanished in the disappearances.

"What disappearances?" Lionel said.

Conrad patted him on the shoulder. "Sometimes I wish I could forget all that's happened," Conrad said. "You should feel lucky."

"You said something about the GC," Lionel said. "What's that?"

"Global Community," Conrad said. "Don't you remember why you're down here?"

Lionel closed his eyes. "I do remember the drills. The push-ups and sit-ups and laps if you didn't have your stuff memorized."

Lionel opened his eyes excitedly. " 'The greatest goal of the Global Community and its leader, Nicolae Carpathia, is peace. We will strive together for a world without war and bloodshed.' "

"It's coming back," Conrad said. "The problem is, I didn't think you bought into this stuff."

"What do you mean?" Lionel said.

Conrad stood to leave. "I'm going back to the dorm and see if I can salvage some of your stuff. It might jog your memory if you can see some things you brought with you."

"Wait," Lionel said. "You never told me your name."

Conrad smiled and told him. "Wait here for me," he said.

Lionel glanced around the room at the others. Covered bodies lay in one corner.

"I'm in no shape to move," Lionel said. "And I wouldn't know where to go if I could."

When Ryan rested on his elbows, the water was up to his neck. When he pushed up with his hands he could breathe easier, but his arms got tired. The water was rising, and it wouldn't be long before his strength gave out.

He had given up on digging himself out. No matter how hard he tried, he couldn't slip out from under the pile. If he was going to make it out alive, he needed help.

The water was cold. He could feel his body going numb. His fingers were already pruny, and he felt a tightness in his chest. He didn't think he was bleeding anywhere, but there was a good possibility of broken bones and internal injuries. All the more reason to get help quickly.

Phoenix was still looking down. Ryan had hoped the dog would bark his head off and alert someone. Instead, Phoenix put his head on his paws and lay down by the hole in the roof. The dog whimpered and whined, but Ryan knew that wouldn't bring people running.

Ryan recalled the old *Lassie* reruns he used to watch with his father. His dad worked long hours and didn't have much time for Ryan. On the weekends, however, they would sometimes curl up on the couch with a bowl of popcorn and watch old television programs. His dad laughed at the old style of clothes. Ryan loved the way Lassie could always figure out what to do. She saved whoever was injured or trapped. He knew no dog could do all that, but it was still exciting to watch.

"Why don't you do something heroic and lower a rope down here?" Ryan yelled. "Dig a tunnel and let the water out or something."

Phoenix panted and kept his head on his front paws.

Ryan picked up a stick floating nearby and threw it hard at the dog. It bounced harmlessly back into the water. Phoenix raised his head and whined.

"Help!" Ryan shouted. "Somebody help me!"

Chaya and her father talked on and off for about two hours. As long as Chaya stayed away from her belief in Jesus, Mr. Stein listened and answered. But when she talked about her faith, Mr. Stein was quiet.

Chaya described her studies at the University of Chicago. Finally, she couldn't resist. "I had the same reaction as you when my friend started talking about the New Testament," she said. "I told him I was a Jew. I didn't want to hear any more. But he kept after me."

"You should have told him to leave you alone," Mr. Stein said.

"I did," Chaya said. "He didn't pester me. I read some of the things he suggested—"

"You turned your back on your family and your faith for a boyfriend?" Mr. Stein said.

"He wasn't my boyfriend," Chaya said. "We never dated. We only talked."

Chaya coughed again. More blood appeared as she

wiped her cheek. As the sunlight grew brighter, she was able to see the problem. A splintered piece of wood from the piano had penetrated her back. Her left lung had probably collapsed.

"I don't know how much longer I will have," Chaya said.

"Don't worry," Mr. Stein said. "Someone will come."

"For a long time I was trying to win the argument with my friend," Chaya said. "I tried to prove he was wrong. And to prove it, I had to know what he believed. You understand that, don't you?"

"It makes sense to know your enemy's arguments." Mr. Stein sighed.

"The more I read, the more sense it made," Chaya said. "The questions I always had about my faith were answered. I didn't stop being Jewish; it was as if what Jesus said made me complete."

"I will hear no more," Mr. Stein said.

"When I finally believed in Jesus after the disappearances—"

"I said I will listen to no more!"

"—I wanted to argue with you and prove I was right. But I no longer want to win the argument."

"Stop!"

"I love you, Father," Chaya said. "The point is not about me proving you wrong. The point is God."

Chaya coughed violently and tried to catch her breath. She wondered how much longer she could hold on.

Darrion wished she were on her horse. It would have been easier to ride over the downed trees and mountains of automobiles.

She was unfamiliar with the neighborhood of the church. When she and her mother had stayed in the apartment behind Loretta's house, they hadn't ventured out. Now she felt lost.

Darrion found several survivors who were frantically searching for family members. Some had never heard of New Hope Village Church. Others didn't answer her. A few pointed her in the same direction she was going.

Darrion recognized the name of a restaurant. Vicki had ordered takeout there and said it was only a few blocks from the church. Darrion walked past bodies of people who had tried to hide from the earthquake. They had crawled under chunks of asphalt to protect themselves. Now they were crushed.

Finally, Darrion spied the steeple of the church. She climbed over fallen trees. The parking lot was a crater filled with cars and rocks and jutting concrete. The steeple was the only thing standing. The sanctuary was gone. Beautiful stained glass littered the pavement below. The Sunday school rooms and offices were a pile of bricks and glass and mortar. This was all that was left of New Hope Village Church.

Darrion walked closer and noticed some of the pews still in place. Others were pushed against each other like an accordion. She knew Ryan had been moved from his hideout, and that gave her hope. But what about Mr. Moore?

She scanned what had been the parking lot but didn't recognize his car. She sat down on a pew and put her face in her hands. When she opened her eyes, she saw a pair of tennis shoes. She knelt and found two thin legs in dark blue jeans. The small body was hidden under the pew. Darrion looked at the left hand. No wedding band! It couldn't be Donny!

She grabbed the man's feet and pulled. Darrion gasped at all the blood. One look and she was sure this was Mr. Moore. Sandy and her husband were together. Together with their child.

Darrion was not comforted by that thought. She felt so alone. Where was her mother? Would she eventually find her body too? Or would she ever see her mother again?

Darrion started crying. Uncontrollable sobs. She ran from the church, falling over debris. She knew Vicki's house was not far away, but her mind was reeling. She had to find her mother. She had to find someone she knew. But she had no idea where to go.

37

VICKI climbed over the crest of a hill and found what used to be Nicolae High. The gymnasium still stood, but the rest of the school looked like a war zone. Teachers and students ran back and forth, shouting, crying. Rescuers would pull someone from the rubble, crushed and matted with blood. Then someone else would call for help and a group would rush to the other end.

What had been a finely manicured football field was now a rolling heap of grass and dirt, mixed with cinders from the surrounding track. The goalposts had moved several yards. One was turned totally upside down. The stands were a heap of twisted metal.

Vicki rushed to see if anyone she knew had made it out alive. In the front, where the flagpole had been, Vicki spotted her friend. She was sitting on the ground, crying, holding her hand over one ear.

Then Shelly noticed Vicki and rushed to hug her. Vicki winced when she saw Shelly's wound. The girl's ear was swollen and bleeding.

"I thought Mrs. Jenness took you away," Shelly said.

"She did," Vicki said and quickly told her story.

Shelly gasped when she heard Mrs. Jenness was dead. "Most of the people in the administration wing made it out," Shelly said. "The vice-principal was in one of the classrooms. They haven't found him yet."

"Any idea how many are still in there?" Vicki said.

"There's no way to tell," Shelly said. "It all happened so fast. I barely made it out the window before the wall caved in."

"Is that how you hurt your ear?" Vicki said.

"A brick hit my head once I was outside," Shelly said. "But I stayed inside a long time."

"What happened?" Vicki said.

"I was trying to save you," Shelly said. "One of the secretaries had me working in Mrs. Jenness's office. I thought if I could find your file and destroy it, the GC might leave you alone."

Vicki put a hand on Shelly's shoulder. "How'd you find out I got caught?" Vicki said.

"Word traveled fast," Shelly said. "I had the drawer open that held your file when I noticed the watercooler shaking. I didn't know what to make of it. Then I remembered what Mr. Steele preached about."

"I wish I had thought that fast," Vicki said. "Mrs. Jenness might be here right now if I had."

"And you might be in a detention center," Shelly said, "or worse."

Vicki nodded. "I can't help feeling guilty about her," Vicki said.

"From what you said, you did everything you could," Shelly said. "And then some."

"It's not that," Vicki said. "Part of me is glad she's not around to bug us. Isn't that awful?"

"We're both sorry she had to die," Shelly said. "I'm sorry she didn't believe the truth. But you can't *make* people believe."

Vicki asked what had happened when the earthquake hit.

"I hurried back to the main office," Shelly said. "The secretary was going nuts. A basketball coach pulled the fire alarm and got on the loudspeaker. He told everybody to get out of the building. If he hadn't done that, there probably would have been a lot more killed."

"Are there doctors here?" Vicki said. "You should get your ear checked."

"There's a long line," Shelly said. "This is nothing compared to the people over by the gym."

"I need to get home and find Ryan," Vicki said.

"I'm glad he was there instead of the middle school," Shelly said. "We just heard most of the survivors were on a field trip."

"How awful," Vicki said. She invited Shelly to come with her.

"I need to check on my mom," Shelly said. "She was still asleep when I left this morning. Guess she didn't go to work. I'll try to get to your place later if I can. I hope you find Ryan."

Judd approached the farmhouse warily. He figured anyone who lived this close to the reeducation facility would recognize his uniform. If not, the handcuffs would concern them. He passed a mailbox that was still in its place with the red flag in the "up" position. There was no road next to it.

The farmhouse leaned to the left. On the porch, a woman sat in a green metal chair. Her husband stood behind her. The woman cried. On the lawn next to them a sheet covered a body.

"You can stop right there," the man said. He held up a shotgun.

"I don't mean you any harm," Judd said.

"Doesn't matter what you mean," the man said. "Get down on the ground, hands behind your head."

"I'm handcuffed," Judd said.

"I can see that," the man said, motioning with the gun. Judd thought of running, but then he heard a click.

"I just need a change of clothes," Judd said. "I'll pay for it. When I get home I'll—"

"If I were you," the woman interrupted, "I'd do as he says."

Judd dropped to the ground.

"Been expecting some escapes," the man said.

"I didn't escape," Judd said. "I was in transport and our van crashed. I got caught in the flash flood. My friend's dead." Judd looked at the sheet by the porch. "A relative?" he asked.

The man ignored his question. "You must have done something pretty bad," the man said. "This is the highest level facility around here."

"Let's just say I don't get along that well with the Global Community," Judd said.

"Meaning what?" the man said.

"Can I get my face out of the dirt to answer you?" Judd said.

"You're fine where you are."

Judd sighed. "I had some documents that exposed the GC for who they really are," he said.

"Which is what?" the man said.

Judd knew if the man and his wife were in love with Nicolae Carpathia like most of the world, he didn't stand a chance. He decided to simply tell the truth.

"The GC don't like people like me because I believe Jesus is the only person we should serve," Judd said. "That doesn't make the potentate too happy."

The man looked at the woman as Judd kept his head in the dirt. The gun clicked again. Then the man knelt and took Judd by the arm.

"Come on," the man said. "Get up."

"I don't understand," Judd said.

"We have to be careful," the man said. "You're safe with us."

Judd couldn't believe the change in the two.

"You ever heard of the Underground Railroad?" the man said.

Judd nodded.

"That's what we have here," the man said. "I'm Hank. This is my wife, Judy."

Judd shook hands with them, the handcuff chain clinking. The woman looked toward the yard. "That's our son," Judy said. "He was in the pump house when the earthquake hit. The walls caved in on him."

"I'm sorry for your loss," Judd said. "How old was he?"

"About your age," Hank said. "He was the first of us to figure out what the disappearances were all about."

Judd listened as the two explained how they discovered the truth. Jesus Christ had returned for his true followers, and they weren't among them. When they found out the GC was jailing believers, the couple felt God wanted them to help some of them escape.

"The problem is our bunker collapsed," Hank said. "We can keep you at the house as long as you'd like, but we can't guarantee you'll be safe. Your best bet is to get as far away from here as you can."

"If you're part of a railroad," Judd said, "there must be others working with you."

"I can give you some names of people and how to find them," Hank said. "We probably have a couple in your area."

The woman stood stiffly. "We won't be using our son's clothes," she said. "Judd might as well have them."

"First things first," the man said. "I'll take him to the barn and get this off."

The man found a hacksaw in the rubble and carefully

cut the bands from Judd's wrists. Judd found a pair of jeans and a shirt that fit and grabbed a jacket as well.

"Wish we could offer you a vehicle of some sort," Hank said. "Everything's ruined. Even the tractor."

"You've done more than I could ever ask," Judd said. "Especially at such a difficult time." Judd looked at the body.

"You get back to your friends," Hank said. "We'll be praying for you."

He pointed Judd in the direction of the interstate. "If anything's getting through to Chicago, you'll find it there."

Lionel felt better in the afternoon, but the knot on his head was huge. He still couldn't remember anything about his life before the Global Community camp.

One of the surviving leaders came to him. He assured Lionel his memory would return soon.

"Conrad told me what you did for him," the man said. "I'll admit we've had our eye on you for a while. You're bright. You catch on quick. You could really go far."

"I'm confused," Lionel said. "I can't even remember what I'm doing here."

"Like I said, it'll come back," the man said. "Bottom line, guys like you are going into society as morale monitors."

"What's that mean?"

"Believe it or not, there are people out there who don't like the agenda of the Global Community. Once your training is complete, you'll be in a position to keep track of them, report them to the authorities, and take action if you have to."

"What kind of action?" Lionel said.

"Approved monitors carry a side arm at all times," the man said, showing Lionel his pistol. "You have to be ready for anything."

Lionel stared at the pistol. Something seemed wrong, but he couldn't figure out what. "Like a cop?" he finally said.

"Sort of," the man said, "but no one knows you're a monitor."

"What kind of people do I look for?"

"Enemies of Nicolae Carpathia," the man said. "Especially the religious people who aren't with Enigma Babylon. They're probably the most dangerous of all."

After the man left, Conrad came in with Lionel's battered suitcase.

"Had to do some digging to find this," Conrad said, "but you've got some interesting stuff in here."

Conrad pulled out clothes and toiletries. Then came Lionel's Bible and pages of printed material.

"I hope you don't mind me reading it," Conrad said.

"I don't care," Lionel said. He picked up the Bible and leafed through it. "Are you sure this is mine?"

Ryan's arms were tired and his throat parched. He was so thirsty he tried drinking some of the dirty water in the basement. He spat it out.

He pushed up as far as he could a few inches above the waterline. He couldn't rest on his elbows without going under.

Ryan tried to yell, but his voice crackled. His throat was getting sore. Suddenly Phoenix barked.

"That's it, boy," Ryan managed to say. "Keep it up!"

Phoenix moved away but kept barking. A moment later a man stuck his head through the opening.

"Down here," Ryan said. "Get me out! The water's almost over my head!"

The man didn't say anything. He turned quickly and left.

"No!" Ryan said, trying to scream. "Come back! Help!"

Ryan smacked his fist into the mud. His other hand slipped, and he fell face first into the water. He coughed and sputtered as he pushed up. He felt like crying.

Maybe this is it, Ryan thought. *Maybe this is the end.*

A few minutes later Ryan heard Phoenix bark again. A clatter of rubbish sent pieces of tile down. The man peeked over the edge and let down a rope. Another man at the top steadied him. Then both climbed down carefully.

"Boy, am I glad you came back," Ryan said.

"Water's getting deep in here," one man said. "Let's get this off his back."

"I don't think you'll be able to move it," Ryan said. "It's had me pinned since—"

The first man easily lifted what Ryan thought was a concrete slab. Ryan couldn't believe it.

455

"It's not that heavy," the man said. "Now we have to get you out of here."

_____

Mr. Stein didn't say anything for a while. Chaya heard something outside. Mr. Stein screamed for help and struggled under the weight of the debris.

When no one came, Chaya said, "I am growing weaker. I believe I'm bleeding internally."

"Nonsense," Mr. Stein said. "We'll have you out of here soon."

"It will do no good to avoid the truth," Chaya said. "I am prepared to die."

"You are not going to die—"

"Can't you see, Father?" Chaya said. "You're treating this like you have treated my questions about faith. You don't think about it. You can't live that way any longer. You'll have to face the truth."

"You and your theology," Mr. Stein said.

"I used to think theology was something you read about," Chaya said. "It didn't really matter. Now I know that's not true. If God exists and has spoken to us, he deserves to be heard."

"He did speak," Mr. Stein said. "He gave us the law and the prophets."

"Yes, but now he has spoken to us through his Son," Chaya said.

"Jesus," Mr. Stein muttered. "You think he is the answer?"

"What do you think about him?" Chaya said.

"He was a good rabbi. He taught many things about loving your neighbor. But he—"

"How can you call a man good who says he is God?" Chaya said.

"I don't believe he said that," Mr. Stein said. "His followers wanted to believe he was God."

"If so, why did the disciples give up their lives for a lie?" Chaya said.

Mr. Stein protested, but Chaya wouldn't stop. She began in the Old Testament and described the prophecies of the Messiah. She couldn't tell whether her father was listening or not. But Chaya had the growing feeling that this was her last chance to reach him.

Darrion couldn't think straight. She had seen so much death and so many suffering people. She ran from Donny Moore's body. She wanted to be with the living, not the dead. She wanted to be with her mother or her friends.

She spotted some sort of ambulance slowly making its way through the ruins. She ran to it and caught the attention of the driver.

"Can you help me?" she yelled.

"Are you hurt?" the man said.

"Not really," Darrion said. "I'm looking for my mother."

"This vehicle is only for the injured," the man said. "Don't look for your mom by yourself, though. The houses are too dangerous to go in. Get to one of the survival posts, and they'll help you."

"Can't you use your radio?" Darrion said.

"Sorry," the man said. "Nearest place you'll find is about a half mile in that direction."

Darrion watched as the van lumbered off. She set out for the survival post and wondered if she would ever see anyone she knew again.

38

VICKI finally got her bearings and found the house on
her corner, but she realized the ground had shifted so
drastically that it was on the other side of the street.
Other houses leaned or were destroyed. The end of the
house had been blasted by a meteor. It was on fire.

A dog barked. *Phoenix,* she thought. She ran toward
him, and the dog jumped on her and nearly knocked her
over.

"Where's Ryan?" Vicki said. "Take me to Ryan."

Phoenix bounded over to the rubble that was her
house. Vicki climbed onto the roof, which was now at
ground level. Phoenix stood next to a hole. Vicki peered
down and saw the water-filled basement. She called for
Ryan, but there was no answer.

"Is he in there, boy?" Vicki said.

Phoenix barked.

459

Vicki saw the tree that was now in her kitchen. If Ryan had been there, he was dead.

He's a tough kid, Vicki thought. *He knows how to take care of himself.*

Vicki wanted to go into the basement, but she needed a rope. She raced from the house, but everyone she found was busy with their own rescue efforts. She finally found a long electrical cord she thought would hold her weight.

As she made her way back to the house she spotted a group of people in uniform. Two Global Community guards directed the homeless to shelters. Vicki walked briskly away but stopped when she saw a girl who looked familiar. Her clothes were in tatters, but Vicki recognized Darrion Stahley. Darrion was headed straight for the GC officials.

Vicki hurried to catch up, but Darrion made it first. Vicki feared the men would recognize Darrion's face.

"I have to know about my mother," Darrion said.

"Stand over there and wait," one guard said.

"You don't understand," Darrion said. "Do you know who I am?"

Vicki grabbed Darrion by the arm and turned her around. Darrion hugged Vicki.

"I'll take care of her now," Vicki said to the GC guards.

"Wait. Come back here," one guard said.

Vicki wanted to run. Then she saw their guns. They might shoot to kill if they got suspicious.

"Is there a problem?" Vicki said as the guard approached.

"There is if you plan on going back into that subdivision," the guard said.

"I was," Vicki said. "I think my friend's trapped in there."

"Which house?" the guard said.

Vicki pointed.

"There's nobody alive in there," the guard said. "If they did survive the quake, the water's gotten to them by now."

"What are we supposed to do?" Vicki said.

"We've set up temporary shelters for the less injured," the guard said. He pointed toward a tent in what used to be a park. "You and your friend go there now."

"Where did they take the serious cases?" Vicki said.

"Some went to the high school," the guard said. "They airlifted a few others."

Vicki thanked the man, and the two walked to the tent. Instead of going inside, they circled around the back and kept going toward Vicki's house.

"What were you doing?" Vicki said when they were a safe distance away.

"I have to find my mom," Darrion said. "I'm afraid she's dead."

"She might be," Vicki said, "but you won't find her by going to the GC."

"I didn't know what to do," Darrion said. "I saw all those dead people. Mrs. Moore. Donny too. I panicked."

"The Moores are dead?" Vicki said.

Darrion explained what had happened.

"OK," Vicki said, trying to calm her. "I promise we'll find out about your mom. First we need to see if we can find Ryan. I need your help."

As Vicki led Darrion back to her house, she explained what had happened to her. Darrion could only shake her head when she heard about Mrs. Jenness.

Vicki tied the orange electrical cord to the tree that had crashed into her house. A piece of rope was tied to the tree but cut off at the knot. She kept working.

Vicki dangled the cord into the hole and carefully climbed down. Darrion helped steady her. Vicki looked at what had been her home. She could make out the upstairs bedrooms, but the rest was smashed.

While Vicki explored the basement, Darrion retrieved as many clothes from the bedrooms as she could find.

A few minutes later, Vicki and Darrion sat on a downed tree limb.

"This is where the kitchen was when I left this morning," Vicki said. "Now there's a tree where the table used to be, and we're looking into what's left of the upstairs bathroom."

"Unbelievable," Darrion said.

A vehicle moved between the houses.

"Get down," Vicki said.

Someone was talking over a loudspeaker. "Stay out of your homes! By order of the Global Community, you must not return! If you need help, get to an open area. Looters will be shot!"

Darrion looked at Vicki. "If they catch us with these clothes, how do we prove they're yours?" Darrion said.

"Just stay down," Vicki said.

The vehicle passed. Vicki breathed a sigh of relief.

Something moved toward them. Before Vicki could stop her, Darrion stood.

"Hey, you!" someone shouted.

Judd couldn't remember how long the van had traveled from the interstate. They had gone at least a few miles before the earthquake hit. He tried to follow what was left of the two-lane road.

He passed collapsed buildings with farm machinery sunken into the ground. The outer walls of a post office had collapsed, leaving the inside counter standing and a mountain of mail behind it.

Judd kept moving. In the distance he saw the remnants of a collapsed bridge leading to the interstate. He was horrified to find cars underneath, smashed flat by the concrete.

Other motorists worked to rescue those trapped. They pulled bodies from an overturned bus. Judd walked around the mayhem through a nearby field. Black smoke rose from craters. He followed a drainage ditch through tall weeds until he heard a strange squeaking. He found a motorcycle, upside down. Its front wheel turned slowly.

A few yards away, Judd found the body of a man wearing a black helmet. Judd bent over the man and felt his neck for a pulse.

The man opened his eyes and screamed.

Judd jumped back. "It's OK," he said. "I'm here to help."

"I can't move," the biker said. "I've been lying here

since this morning, yelling and screaming for someone to hear me." The biker tried to sit up. "Have you seen my bike?"

"It's right over there," Judd said. He knew enough about such injuries to leave the man alone. He didn't want to move him and make things worse.

"I saw the bridge breaking up and tried to stop," the biker said. "A slab of road rose up like a ramp, and I went flying through the air like one of those daredevils."

"Stay here and I'll get someone," Judd said.

Judd found a man who said he had a stretcher they could use to strap the biker down. It would take a few minutes to free it up. Judd went back to stay with the biker.

"Help's on its way," Judd said. "What's your name?"

"Pete Davidson," the man said, putting out his hand.

Judd shook it and told him his name.

"Where are you headed?"

"Back to Chicago," Judd said. "I have friends I need to check on."

"Why don't you use my bike?"

"I couldn't do that," Judd said.

"It's not that hard to handle," he said.

"It's not that," Judd said. "It's yours. I couldn't take it."

"Look at me," Pete said. "You think I'm gonna be riding anytime soon?"

Judd smiled. "You'll be up and around in no time," he said. "Besides, we don't even know if it'll still run."

"Put it on its wheels and try," Pete said.

Judd spent a few minutes trying to get the motorcycle

right side up. He noticed a huge dent in the gas tank. It was bad, but the tank hadn't ruptured. The cap on the tank was off, and the fuel had emptied onto the ground. Judd rolled the bike close so the man could see it.

"You'll have to make sure you have gas, then plug the hole so it doesn't slosh out. I can't guarantee it'll start, but if it does, you're in business."

"Like I said—"

"Listen to me," Pete said. "You know what happened to the bridge back there. You know every bridge from here back to Chicago is probably in the same shape. Nothing's getting through except some four-wheel drives and bikes like this. You helped me. I help you. Simple as that."

"All right," Judd said, "but you have to do me two favors."

"Name 'em."

"Give me your address so I can return it," Judd said.

Pete gave Judd the information. "What's the other favor?" he said.

"I want to tell you why I helped you," Judd said.

Lionel looked through the papers Conrad had given him and saw notes in the Bible. Still, nothing clicked.

"Does this mean anything to you?" Conrad said.

Lionel read the inscription in the front of the Bible. *To Lionel, from Ryan.*

"No," Lionel said. "I don't remember any Ryan."

"You need to get to Chicago and find these people," Conrad said.

"What for?" Lionel said.

"They were your friends," Conrad said. "They know who you are. And they probably know all about this Bible stuff."

"I'm not sure I want to know," Lionel said. "I mean, if it comes back to me, fine. But I can't turn my back on what the Global Community is offering."

Conrad frowned. "You ought to at least give it a chance," he said.

"I'll think about it," Lionel said.

———————————

Ryan lay in a furniture store that had been turned into a makeshift hospital. His head was pounding. He felt cold.

He couldn't believe how easily the man had lifted the thing off his back. They had pulled him up from the hole by placing a rope under his arms. Ryan had passed out and woke up at the emergency shelter. He hadn't been able to thank his rescuers.

People around him seemed in worse shape. Some had lost arms or legs. Others wore bandages over their faces.

A woman came and took his temperature. "You're burning up," she said.

"I feel the opposite," Ryan said. "Can I have another blanket?"

The woman brought him some medicine and a drink to wash it down.

Ryan hesitated.

"What's wrong?" the woman said.

Ryan blushed. "I can't take these," he said. "I never learned how to swallow pills like this."

The woman sat on his bed. "You mean you were able to survive the biggest earthquake in the history of the world," she said, "and you're not able to swallow a couple of pills?"

She smiled, pulled the capsules apart, and dropped the contents into the glass of water.

Ryan thanked her.

"See if you can get some rest," the woman said.

"Wait," Ryan said. "How bad is it?"

The woman smiled again. "The doctor will be by as soon as he can," she said. "Rest."

Ryan pulled the covers up and shook.

Someone cleared her throat nearby. "Here," an old woman in the next bed said. She handed him one of her covers.

"You don't have to," Ryan said.

"Can't keep these old bones warm anyway," the woman said. "You look like you can use it."

The woman was too weak to throw the cover to him. She handed it as far as she could, then let it fall to the floor.

Ryan was able to pick it up but couldn't spread it over himself very well. Finally he spoke to the old woman. "Do you know what's wrong with me?" Ryan said.

"Doctor saw you earlier," she said. "Said something about a wound on your back and a possible infection. Plus some other things."

"What other things?" Ryan said.

"I think he ought to tell you," the old woman said. Ryan persisted.

The woman held up her hand. "I'm tired," she whispered. "We'll talk when I wake up."

Ryan listened to the woman's labored breathing. *What could be wrong with me?* he thought.

Though her father was silent, Chaya continued giving Scripture after Scripture that showed Jesus was the true Messiah of the Jews. He had been rejected by his own people and had been killed just as Isaiah had prophesied.

"You sound like the rabbi on television," Mr. Stein finally said after a few minutes. "He had an excellent grasp on the Scriptures, but he was misguided with his conclusion."

Chaya frowned. Vicki said she had been at Chaya's home when Dr. Tsion Ben-Judah proclaimed Jesus as Messiah on an international broadcast. Mr. Stein had been angry.

"Then you do not see anything of merit in what I say?" Chaya said.

"It has nothing to do with merit," Mr. Stein said. "I will not turn my back on my faith as you have."

"What would it take for you to believe?" Chaya said.

Mr. Stein laughed. "I suppose if God himself were to hold me down and tell me Jesus was the way, I would believe."

Chaya coughed violently, then regained her composure. "Isn't that what has happened to you today?" Chaya said. "God has put you in a position to hear the truth. You would have run if all this weren't on top of you."

"I am not afraid of the truth—"

"Then hear it and believe," Chaya said. "God is giving you one more chance to respond to his gift."

"This is a gift?" Mr. Stein yelled. "To have my wife taken from me and now my house and all my possessions destroyed?"

"God gave his only Son for you," Chaya said. "Just as the lamb was slain and its blood put on the doorposts during the Passover, so Jesus died for you and me so we would not have to die. That is the gift of God."

Chaya felt light-headed. Before her father said anything more, she passed out.

39

VICKI knew there was no use running. They were caught. When the man came over the rubble, she was surprised to see he had no uniform.

"What are you two doing here?" the man said.

"I live here," Vicki said. "At least, I used to."

"Can you prove it?" the man said.

Vicki thought a moment. She couldn't. At least not with any papers or a driver's license. She shook her head. "I don't have an ID, but this really is my house. Those are my clothes over there."

"If it's really your house," the man said, "you'll know who we found here a few hours ago."

"You found Ryan?" Vicki said.

The man smiled. "He was right down there," he said. "We pulled him out just before the water got to him."

"Is he all right?" Vicki said.

471

"He was alive," the man said, "but he didn't look good. He'd been trapped the whole day."

"Where is he now?" Vicki said.

"Don't know," the man said. "I helped put him into one of those Ambu-Vans. They took him to get help, but I don't know where."

Vicki thanked the man. She located her purse, then grabbed a few changes of clothes and stuffed them into an overnight bag she found floating by. The water was at ground level.

As Judd waited for the stretcher for Pete Davidson, he told his story of being on an airplane during the disappearances. Judd asked Pete if he could remember where he was that night.

"I'll never forget it," Pete said. "I was at a cycle convention. People come from all over the country. You see a lot of cool machines. I go because it lets me get in touch with old friends. We drink a little.

"Anyway, there's always a few groups of these Jesus bikers. Some guys don't care for 'em. They pretty much leave me alone. I was leaving a bar late that first night when a big group rode in. I knew from the crosses on their jackets that this was one of those Jesus groups.

"I got on my bike and started it up just as they were passing. Then there was this awful noise. I turned around and saw empty bikes going fifty or sixty miles an hour. There were a couple of people still in the group, but most of them had disappeared, like they'd been beamed up somewhere.

"The first bike went down, and the rest followed. There must have been thirty hogs all over the road, twisted up, some of them burning."

"Hogs?" Judd said.

"A type of motorcycle," Pete said. "The best you can buy, as far as I'm concerned. Anyway, we only found a couple of bodies. There were leather jackets spread out on the road. Boots. Rings and chains."

"What did you do after that?" Judd said.

"I went back into the bar," Pete said. "I was too shook up to drive."

"Do you have any idea what happened that night?" Judd said.

"I've heard some theories," Pete said. "Space aliens took them. They rode into another dimension. That kinda thing. Never heard anything that made sense to me."

"Did you ever actually talk with anyone from that group?" Judd said.

"Never let them get that close," Pete said.

Judd explained what had happened to his family. They had vanished too. "The interesting thing is," Judd said, "everybody I know who disappeared claimed they had a relationship with Jesus."

"Same here," Pete said. "My mother always went to church. Said she prayed for me every day. I found her clothes in a rocking chair in her living room when I went to her house."

"That's the key to understanding the vanishings," Judd said. "It wasn't just people who went to church or were religious that got taken; it was people who knew Jesus as their Savior."

"What's that mean?" Pete said.

Judd explained the gospel. "God created people to have a relationship with him, but people sinned. Since God is holy, he can't tolerate sin. When the time was right, Jesus came into the world and lived a perfect life. Then he died in our place and rose from the dead. Now, if people ask for forgiveness, Jesus comes into their life and God forgives them."

Pete put his head back and looked into the sky. "I saw this magazine article that talked about that," he said, "but I wasn't sure it was right."

"Do you admit that you've done wrong things?" Judd said.

"Yeah, plenty."

"Do you want God to forgive you?"

"If he can," Pete said.

"He can and he will," Judd said. "The Bible says if you confess your sins, God is faithful and will forgive you."

Pete stroked his beard. "My mom used to try to tell me this stuff, but I wouldn't listen."

"Now's the perfect time," Judd said.

"How would I do something like . . . what you're saying?" he said.

"Pray with me," Judd said. "God, I'm sorry I've sinned, and I ask you right now to forgive me."

Pete closed his eyes and whispered the words as Judd spoke.

"I believe Jesus died for me and that he rose from the dead," Judd continued. "Come into my heart now and save me. Amen."

Pete smiled. "If I hadn't hit that incline, or if you hadn't come this way, I'd never have prayed like that."

"God loves you, Pete," Judd said. "I'm just glad I found you."

Before the man with the stretcher returned, Judd tried to start the motorcycle again. There was enough gas in the tank to get the engine going, but as hard as Judd tried, it wouldn't start.

"You're kicking it hard enough," Pete said. "It just sounds like something's wrong with the engine. The bike took a pretty bad hit."

The man put the stretcher under Pete and secured him tightly. Pete motioned for Judd.

"If you can't get my bike going, you could go back to my place," Pete said. "I have a dirt bike, which might be better for you. Between here and Chicago you'll be able to use something that'll climb."

"Where's your house?" Judd said.

"Next exit south," Pete said. "About three miles or so."

Judd looked at the highway. No cars moved on the broken road, but he hoped someone with a four-wheel drive would come by soon heading for Chicago.

"I don't want to go the other way if I don't have to," Judd said. "Besides, we don't know if your other bike survived the quake."

Pete looked away and rubbed his eyes.

"What is it?" Judd said.

"My girlfriend," Pete said. "I was heading back to my house this morning. I was hoping you'd go back for the bike and check in on her. Maybe you could tell her what you just told me. You know, about the Jesus thing. Then you could tell her where I am."

Judd smiled. He got the directions to Pete's house and helped the man load Pete onto the back of a four-wheel-drive truck.

"You'll go then?" Pete said.

"I'm on my way," Judd said.

Pete smiled. "I guess my mom's prayers worked after all," he said.

Lionel thanked the doctor, and Conrad came into the room.

"What did he say?" Conrad said.

"Not much," Lionel said. "Other than this knot on my head and the memory loss, I'm fine."

"How long are you gonna be here?"

"As long as it takes," Lionel said. Then he lowered his voice. "But the doctor says there's no reason I can't jump right back in as long as I don't suffer any side effects."

Conrad pulled out a page from Lionel's belongings. "There's stuff in here about a Jewish rabbi who became a Christian," he said. "Interesting. I always thought Christians were people who put their brains on the shelf."

"Honestly, I can't remember anything about it," Lionel said.

"This rabbi says everything that's happened was predicted in the Bible," Conrad said. "Do you think there's any way to find these friends of yours?"

"I don't see how," Lionel said. "I don't have names, addresses, phone numbers, and even if we did, the earthquake's destroyed communication lines."

"True," Conrad said, "but we just had a briefing from one of the top guys. He says the Global Community is already rebuilding an international communications network. Before the quake, the GC bought up all of the satellite and cellular communication companies."

"But it'll take months to get that back up and running," Lionel said.

"Take a look," Conrad said. He pulled back a flap of the tent. Lionel shaded his face with a hand. A few hundred yards away, workers pushed a cellular tower in place.

"Already?" Lionel said.

"I guess being able to talk with people is more important than saving lives," Conrad said. "Don't tell anybody I said that."

"That doesn't make sense," Lionel said. "Nicolae Carpathia is a man of peace. The Global Community cares for people, right?"

"I don't want to get in trouble," Conrad said, "but from what I heard from my brother, Carpathia wants power. Control. He's bought the media. He controls the countries with the most oil reserves. Now he's in control of all the phone and communication lines. He owns and controls everything and everybody."

"But that's good, right?" Lionel said. "If somebody we can trust is in control of all that, there won't be any more wars."

Conrad frowned. "I don't know what to believe," he said. "But I want to check out what this rabbi is saying."

Lionel felt an uneasiness in his gut. Something was wrong, but he didn't know what. Since he had awakened from his injury, he felt there was more than his memory missing. It felt like a hole in his soul. He tried hard to remember. Was it something he was supposed to be doing? Was he letting someone down? He felt guilty for not remembering. He touched the knot on his head and winced. A big part of his life *was* missing, and he had a feeling he was never going to find it again.

Ryan awoke without pain. He wanted to get up and walk out of the converted furniture store and find the others, but he couldn't move. He thought they might have him strapped down.

He turned to the woman in the next bed. She was staring at him.

"I'm glad you're up," Ryan said. "I really want to know what's wrong with me. I can't wait for the doctor. Will you tell me?"

The woman didn't answer.

"Before you say no," Ryan continued, "just hear me out. I have these friends I've been living with since the disappearances. My mom and dad were killed, so I've been staying with them. Maybe you'll get to meet them. Anyway, I was thinking if I knew what was wrong, they could come get me and take care of me until I get better."

The woman just stared at him.

"Please," Ryan said, "what did you hear the doctor say?"

The woman didn't move. Didn't bat an eye. She seemed stuck in the same position.

"Ma'am?" Ryan said. Then he said it a little louder. The third time he screamed and a nurse came. She bent over the woman, then pulled the sheet over her head.

"She can't be dead," Ryan said. "She was talking to me just a little bit ago."

"Go back to sleep," the nurse said. "There's nothing you can do."

"Tell me what's wrong with me," Ryan said. "She said the doctor was checking me for an infection in my back. Is that true?"

The nurse hesitated, then sat on his bed. "I'll tell you what I know, though I'm not supposed to," she said.

Ryan nodded and said, "Thank you."

"There is a possible infection in a wound in your back," she said. "Something about a cut back there and the water being dirty. But that's not really the big problem."

"What is?" Ryan said.

"Do you know what *paralysis* means?"

"Yeah, like paralyzed, you can't move, right?"

"That's right."

"Well, that's not what I have," Ryan said. "See, I can move my arms anywhere I want."

479

"Something happened during the earthquake," the nurse said. "Either you fell on something or something fell on you. It injured the nerves in your back that make your legs work."

"Am I going to die?" Ryan said.

The nurse looked away. Ryan remembered when he was a kid getting his appendix removed. He had asked the doctor then if he was going to die. The doctor laughed and smiled at him. He wanted the nurse to do the same now, but she didn't. She looked back with tears in her eyes.

"I'm not supposed to tell you any of this," she said. "But there are so many patients, and the few doctors we have can't keep up with everybody."

"It's OK," Ryan said. "I'm not afraid to die. I just don't feel that bad."

"Can I get you anything?" she said.

"Yeah, you can get word to my friends," Ryan said. "They'll be upset if they don't know what happened to me."

"Are you sure your friends are . . ."

"They're OK," Ryan said. Then, for the first time, he seriously considered whether he was the only one who had survived the wrath of the Lamb earthquake. He pushed the thought from his mind.

"Why don't I get you a pen and some paper," the nurse said. "Writing something down to them might be the best thing in case . . ."

"In case what?" Ryan said.

"I think it would just be a quicker way to get them a message, that's all," the nurse said.

"Sure," Ryan said.

Mr. Stein was calling Chaya's name when she awoke. She tried to speak but couldn't. Finally she choked out, "I am here."

"What happened?" Mr. Stein said. "Are you all right?"

"No, I am not all right," she said. "I told you, I am hurt. I am bleeding."

Mr. Stein tried again to lift the weight from his back. The more he struggled, the more the weight shifted onto him.

"I can't get to you," Mr. Stein said.

Chaya thought of Jesus and his teachings. She knew the power of his stories. They came from daily life. The disciples could relate to the tiny mustard seed. They knew what wheat and tares were. Then Chaya thought of her own situation. She and her father were buried under a mountain of rubble. *This*, she thought, *is a perfect example*.

Chaya took a breath. "Father, you are trapped," she said. "You are helpless to save yourself. Someone from outside must come and give us assistance."

"That is why I have been yelling since this morning," Mr. Stein said.

"It is the same with your spiritual life," Chaya said. "No matter how many good things you try to do, or how much you try to follow the law, you know in your heart that there is sin."

Mr. Stein was silent.

"Only God can forgive sins, and that is what Jesus came to do," Chaya said. "He was the perfect sacrifice. When we were dead in our sins, Messiah died for us."

"You are delirious," Mr. Stein said.

"I am telling you the truth," Chaya said. "Jesus said he was the way, the truth, and the life. You can only come to God the Father through him. Please receive him now before it is too late."

Chaya felt a burning in her chest, and her breathing was getting more difficult. The dust had settled around her in a white film. Each breath sent a tiny white puff into the air.

She listened for her father's response. He was past the point of struggling against the weight. She knew he had resigned himself to wait for help. But she couldn't tell whether this last thought had gotten through to him.

40

5:52 P.M.

VICKI wanted to find Ryan, but she knew they needed shelter for the night. The sun was going down, and it was getting colder. Vicki and Darrion backtracked to the high school.

She asked about Ryan, and a man with a clipboard looked through several pages. He shook his head. "No Ryan Daley here," he said, "but we've got a bunch of victims who haven't been identified yet."

"Where are they?" Vicki said.

The man pointed to a corner of the gym where bodies lay covered.

"A doctor told me you didn't have a morgue here," Vicki said.

"We didn't a few hours ago," the man said.

"Don't you have any unidentified injured?" Vicki said.

The man looked at his clipboard again. "We do, but

there's no one who fits the description of your friend," he said. "You can look if you'd like."

Vicki and Darrion were led into the locker room. A few mattresses lay on the floor. Some people moaned and cried with severe injuries. The shower had been turned into an operating room. It was clear from a quick look that Ryan wasn't there.

Darrion looked nervously at Vicki. "You think we should look in the gym?" she said.

"He's not dead," Vicki said. "Come on, I'll prove it."

Vicki lifted sheet after sheet from the dead bodies. Ryan wasn't there. As they were leaving, Shelly returned. Vicki could tell she had been crying.

"I made it back to our trailer," Shelly said, "but the whole place was destroyed. Trailers on top of each other, twisted, broken in two."

"What about your mom?" Vicki said.

Shelly shook her head. "I found our neighbor next door who got out," she said. "The ground opened up and swallowed my house whole. I assume my mom was still inside, but there's no way to tell."

Vicki hugged Shelly. "Come on, you're with us now," Vicki said.

The next shelter was a mile away. Vicki was told there were injured being treated there and beds for those who needed a place to sleep.

"I can't believe the house is gone," Vicki said. "I wonder if Judd's place is still standing."

"I saw Mark before I got to the high school," Shelly

said. "He and his aunt made it, but they can't stay in the house. He did have some good news, though."

"What's that?" Vicki said.

"He said he saw Buck Williams driving his Range Rover near the church," Shelly said. "At least Buck made it."

"But what about Chloe and Loretta?" Vicki said. "And Tsion Ben-Judah?"

Shelly shook her head. "Mark only saw Buck."

Judd rode with Pete a few minutes on the back of the truck, then walked to the exit Pete had described. The exit sign was facedown.

Judd had to climb down a culvert and cross some twisted railroad tracks. He climbed up the other side and followed Pete's directions. A few minutes later he came to a creek. He crossed it and found the road Pete had described. He found several leveled houses.

Pete's house was a small, white ranch. It had a separate garage in the back. Judd went to the house and managed to crawl into the kitchen through a window. The ceiling had collapsed but was still a few feet off the floor. Judd had forgotten to ask the girl's name, so he called out, "Hello?"

Judd's voice echoed in the rubble. No one answered. Judd crawled through the kitchen. He saw no sign of the girl. A ray of light came from a utility area.

He saw the woman's hands first. She had been doing laundry when the quake occurred. Or perhaps she had

485

run in there for safety. Judd felt for a pulse, but he knew there was no use. Her skin was chalky white and cold. He could barely make out her face in the midst of the wood and plaster.

Judd couldn't find a way out, so he retraced his steps to the kitchen. The refrigerator had toppled but was still closed. If he was going to drive to Chicago, he would need some food. He grabbed a loaf of bread and a package of ham that was still cool in the fridge. He found a jug of bottled water and stuffed a few other things into a garbage bag he found under the sink.

The garage was crumpled. He finally got the door open but saw there was nothing inside that could be saved. The quake had tossed old lawn mowers and tillers onto motorcycles. The dirt bike wasn't there. In the grass behind the garage, Judd found it. He figured someone had used it, then propped it against the garage before the quake had hit.

He jumped on and tried to start it. The bike sputtered a few times. Then the engine took off with a deafening sound. He opened the gas cap and rocked the bike. Half full.

As Judd tied his provisions onto the seat, he saw someone in the distance waving and running toward him. Would they believe him if he said Pete had given him permission? Judd decided not to chance it. He roared away and followed the creek until he came to the main road.

Judd wanted to tell Pete about his girlfriend, but the light was fading and he had a long way to go. He decided to wait until he returned the bike to tell Pete.

He clattered around the bridge, still littered with
survivors and the dead. Where other vehicles couldn't go,
Judd plowed through. In some areas, Judd had to get off
and walk. As the sun faded, Judd looked for the headlight
and was surprised the bike had none.

Guess I won't be driving all the way home tonight, Judd
thought.

Judd came to a stop at the edge of the Des Plaines
River. The top of the bridge stuck out of the rushing
water. Judd stood on the bank and looked across. Unless
he could find a raft or some other way across, he was
stuck.

Judd rode east into a wooded area. He dodged
uprooted trees and stumps until he came to a cliff overlooking the river. Judd stopped the motorcycle and
leaned it against a tree. It was peaceful here. Squirrels
played in the fallen trees. Birds sang. It was a perfect day,
except for the fact that the earth had shaken itself so
violently that morning.

Farther east the river narrowed. A dam still stood. If
Judd could get to it, there was a chance he could drive a
few more miles before dark.

He turned to retrieve the motorcycle but stopped dead
in his tracks. Three men stood around the bike silently
watching Judd.

Lionel ate a small dinner and looked through his belongings. He closed his eyes and tried to remember. The ID
card in his wallet showed his name and his picture and

said he was a freshman at Nicolae Carpathia High School in Mount Prospect, Illinois. Lionel turned the card over and over.

He picked up a spiral notebook and leafed through it. It was a journal of sorts. Random thoughts and verses written out. Notes on sermons he had heard. Lionel found names. Judd. Ryan. Vicki. Bruce. Something had happened to Bruce. Lionel had taken it hard.

I don't know what we're going to do without him, Lionel read. *He was more than just a teacher; he was our friend.*

Lionel also found references to something called the "Trib Force." He closed the book and lay back. The words made no sense. He couldn't deny the journal was his.

Lionel's superior walked in. He pulled a chair close to the bed and sat.

"How are you feeling?" the man said.

"As good as I can be," Lionel said. "Ready to go, I guess."

"Good," the man said. "We've been meeting this afternoon. The top brass feels this is the perfect time to put our monitors in place. The earthquake has changed everything. If you'll agree, we'll put things in motion and get you transferred to a monitor station as soon as transportation is open."

"Monitor station?" Lionel said.

"The program is just getting started," the man said. "Each location will have two monitors. You'll report to a regional commander in your district. They'll report to us, and we report directly to Global Community Command."

"So I'll go with somebody else?" Lionel said.

"You can suggest someone if you want," the man said. "I would expect to have you out of here within the week if you agree."

Lionel felt the bump on his head. "A lot's happened since I got here," he said. "I've been reading things I wrote and trying to figure out who I am."

"It'll come back to you—just give it time."

"Would it be OK if I slept on it and told you in the morning?" Lionel said.

"Sure," the man said. "You think about it."

The nurse brought Ryan a pen and paper and left him alone. Ryan stared at the blank page. He felt hot. Beads of sweat popped out on his forehead. He wiped them away and tried to prop himself up, but again, he couldn't move. Someone came to take the dead woman away. Ryan bunched up the covers enough to put the pad of paper in the right position.

He wrote down Vicki's address and gave the location of New Hope Village Church. Someone would get the message to Vicki.

I'm writing this to you, Vicki, but I'm hoping you'll be in touch with Judd and Lionel as well.

First, I shouldn't have been surprised at what happened because this was everything Bruce said. The wrath of the Lamb and all. We can be glad God keeps his promises, I guess. The nurse said I should write to you. I never was a letter writer, but she thought it was a good idea.

Ryan lay back and rested. His arm was already tired from trying to hold the pad in the right position. He had to shake the pen so the ink would come out. He continued.

You've been like a big sister to me. I never had one. Judd was a big brother, and Lionel was a good friend. I hope I wasn't too much of a pain to have around.

I guess there's a chance I could get up and walk out of here, but it doesn't look good. So I want to tell you all to hang in there. God didn't let us survive this long without there being a reason. No matter where you go or what happens, I want you to remember how much you mean to me. I can't thank you enough.

Maybe somebody else will come and take my place at your house or in the Young Trib Force. I hope they do. If you care for them half as much as you cared for me, they'll be really happy.

Ryan's strength was running out. The light in the room was fading.

Promise me you'll take care of Phoenix. Tell Chaya and Shelly and Mark and John that I was thinking of them. I hope you all made it through the earthquake. I'll never forget you.

Love,
Ryan

Ryan put the pen down and wept. The nurse returned and removed the pad. She took his temperature and gave him more medicine.

"When do you think somebody could take this letter?" Ryan asked.

"I'm not sure," the nurse said. "But we'll get it to someone you know."

"Promise?" Ryan said.

The nurse looked at him and smiled. "I'll take it myself if I have to," she said.

The nurse turned to leave.

"Wait," Ryan said. "I want to ask you something."

"You need a drink, something to eat?" the nurse said.

"No," Ryan said. "It's about God."

"I don't think we have a chaplain here," the nurse said.

"It's not that," Ryan said. "I want to know if you believe in him. Do you know God?"

Chaya tasted blood again. She had read stories of people on the brink of death and what it was like, but she hadn't pictured it this way. She wanted her father to believe in Christ, pray, and be rescued. But after her description of Jesus as Messiah, Mr. Stein didn't speak. He either went to sleep or ignored her.

The sunlight faded. Soon it would get colder, and she knew she could not survive. Chaya wheezed and coughed.

God, please help my father come to the truth before it is too late, she prayed.

In her brief time as a Christian, Chaya had memorized many sections of Scripture. Bruce Barnes suggested she commit key portions of the book of Revelation to memory. As she lay in the dust of her prison, she recalled the apostle John's words. He described a silence in heaven, followed by an angel who stood at the golden altar before the throne of God.

"The smoke of the incense, mixed with the prayers of the saints, ascended up to God from the altar where the angel had poured them out. Then the angel filled the incense burner with fire from the altar and threw it down upon the earth; and thunder crashed, lightning flashed, and there was a terrible earthquake.

"Then the seven angels with the seven trumpets prepared to blow their mighty blasts."

The words brought a strange comfort. She felt the earthquake was her final earthly glimpse of fulfilled Scripture. She knew the judgments of God would get progressively worse, and she was relieved she wouldn't have to experience what was coming next.

Still, to die without seeing her father accept Christ overwhelmed Chaya. She began to weep for him.

"Why are you crying?" Mr. Stein said after a few moments.

"I weep for you, Father," Chaya said. "I have prayed for you since the day I made my decision."

"And I have prayed that you would come back," Mr. Stein said.

"Your heart is so hard," Chaya said. "You are like the pharaoh in Egypt. Though you have sign after sign, you still will not believe."

"You compare me to an Egyptian pharaoh," Mr. Stein said, "and I say you have forsaken the God of Israel and gone after other gods."

Chaya wanted to argue more, but she knew it would do no good. Her father had made his decision.

"If you make it through this," Chaya said, "would you please find my friends and tell them what happened?"

"You are going to be fine," Mr. Stein said. "Just rest. Don't try to talk."

"Promise me," Chaya said weakly.

"I will find them," Mr. Stein said.

"Thank you," Chaya said.

She closed her eyes. The pain made her shiver. She thought of her mother and clutched the brooch tightly.

"Father?" Chaya whispered.

"Shh," Mr. Stein said. "Don't talk. I think I hear someone outside."

"I love you," Chaya said.

41

VICKI was exhausted when the girls made it to the shelter. The camp was a series of tents salvaged from a nearby sporting goods store. Volunteers handed out sleeping bags and blankets to those straggling in. Families huddled over small fires.

While Shelly and Darrion scoped out a place to sleep, Vicki went to the large tent in the center. The injured lay on air mattresses or on the ground. As she entered, a young woman let out a piercing scream.

"No!" she yelled as she gripped the hand of a pale woman.

Vicki found a nurse and asked about Ryan. The nurse showed her a list of the dead.

"That's the best I can do for you," the woman said.

Vicki thanked her and scanned the names. There was

no Ryan Daley. She walked through the tent but couldn't find him.

She rejoined Darrion and Shelly in a small, two-person tent. They held steaming cups of soup and bread. Shelly had a bandage for her ear.

"No spoons," Darrion said, "but it's pretty good."

They handed Vicki a cup, and she dipped the bread in the broth. The meal was simple but satisfying.

"You think we can all fit in here?" Vicki said.

"We'll have to," Shelly said. "It's supposed to get chilly, and they could only spare two blankets."

"The soup was good," Darrion said when she had finished, "but I'd go for some shrimp cocktail right now."

Shelly cackled. "You've spent too much time at the country club," she said. "I'd go for a cheeseburger. Extra cheese."

"Stop," Vicki said. "I was happy with the soup. Now you guys are making me hungry for dessert."

"Cheesecake," Darrion said.

"Apple pie and ice cream," Shelly said. "My mom, when she was sober, used to bake it from scratch. Then the ice cream would melt on top."

"Did your mother ever . . . I mean, was she . . . ," Darrion stammered.

"Was she a Christian?" Shelly said.

"If you don't want to talk about it, I understand," Darrion said.

"It's OK," Shelly said. "Vicki knows I tried to talk to her. Sometimes she'd listen, but most of the time she'd get mad."

Vicki shook her head and shivered.

"What is it?" Darrion said.

"The graveyard," Vicki said. "I can't stop thinking about it."

"I'd still be screaming if it had happened to me," Darrion said.

"Plus, Mrs. Jenness," Vicki said. "It helps to talk."

"Then go ahead," Shelly said.

"When we were on the bridge, it was like she was a little kid," Vicki said. "She froze. Couldn't move. Then we were in the water and I got out. But I felt guilty leaving her."

"You can't force people to do what they need to do," Shelly said.

"The look on her face will haunt me forever," Vicki said.

"You know what I think?" Darrion said. "I think we ought to be thankful for the miracle that you're alive. You could have gone down with her."

"I was so scared," Vicki said. "I could tell God was helping me because I just seemed to go on autopilot. I didn't even think about what could happen; I just did it."

Shelly and Darrion recounted their experiences. Finally Shelly said, "I wonder how everybody else is. We know Mark's OK, but what about Lionel and Ryan?"

"And Judd," Darrion said.

Judd.

The mention of his name made Vicki tremble. "If I know Judd," Vicki said, "he's out there somewhere in a lot of trouble, but he's alive."

The girls stopped talking and listened to the crackling fires and the moans and cries that came from the main tent. Vicki thought of Judd. She imagined what it would be like to tell him how she really felt about him. She felt he was alive. Whether he was in the custody of the Global Community or not, he had to be alive. She wished he were here. He would know how to find Ryan.

"I think we ought to pray," Vicki said.

And they did until all three fell asleep.

Judd nearly lost his breath when he saw the men staring at him. His first instinct was to run. He was in danger.

"Are you GC?" one man said.

"No," Judd said.

"What are you doing up here then?" another man said.

"I'm trying to get home," Judd said. "I thought I could cross over the dam up ahead."

The first man motioned to the others to move away. They walked toward Judd and down the side of the hill.

"Middle of the dam fell in," the man said. "Can't get across that unless you jump it."

"I can try," Judd said. "Looks like my only choice."

"Probably is for now," the man said. "But we could use a machine like this. It'd help us and our families."

"Families?" Judd said.

"When the quake hit, a few of us ran up here for safety. Caves all over this area. A couple of them collapsed. Those who survived are in that one, but we don't have many supplies."

Judd untied the bag on the back of the bike and handed it to the man. "It's not much," Judd said, "but it's all I have. I need the bike. You keep the food."

"It's dark now," the man said. "Why don't you stay with us for the night? We have a fire. You'll be warm."

"That's kind of you," Judd said, "but I have to keep going."

"How?" the man said. "You'll kill yourself if you can't see anything."

"I want to take a look at what I'm up against," Judd said.

Judd started the motorcycle and looked back at the man. Members of his family peered out of the darkness of the cave. Judd gunned the engine and headed for the top of the ridge.

He knew the man was right. He had to stop at some point and rest, but he didn't want to stay here. Something about the people unnerved him.

The dam was ten feet wide and nearly a hundred yards across. The moon shone a ghostly glow on the water below. Judd stopped the bike and walked to the center of the dam. A gap of about fifteen feet had opened.

I could put a tree across here and crawl over, Judd thought. *But I'd never cross on the bike.*

The man was right about jumping the gap. Judd had done that type of thing as a kid on a regular bicycle, but he'd had a ramp. He would have to jump this without one.

The rest of the bridge seemed to be in good shape. There were cracks and a few pieces of loose concrete, but there didn't seem to be a danger of collapse. Judd noticed the earthquake had pushed the other side of the dam slightly lower and forward. That would help, but it also meant he would have to jump at an angle.

Judd retreated and looked at his target from a distance. *If I miss, I'm dead,* he thought. I *could camp here and jump in the morning, but those guys might decide they want more than just my food.*

Judd decided to take the risk. He started the motor-cycle and rode to the edge. He could clear the gap at forty miles an hour. But he wouldn't know if he could make that speed until he tried.

He drove up the bank and revved the engine.

"Do or die," Judd said.

Lionel asked to see the GC leader. The man returned a few minutes later and sat by Lionel's bed. He was carrying a leather case.

"What's up?" the man said.

"I've thought about it enough," Lionel said. "I don't need to wait until tomorrow. I'm in. I want to be a part of what you're doing, and I'll go wherever you send me."

"That's good news," the man said. He pulled some papers out of the case. "I have you paired with Conrad Graham."

"He's a friend," Lionel said.

"Good. We're sending you both to Chicago. Maybe

you'll piece things together personally once you're back near your home."

The man had Lionel sign some documents. Then he unzipped a smaller pouch and took out a tiny phone.

"You'll keep in touch with this," the man said. "Solar powered. Once the lines are in place, you'll be able to talk with anybody you need to in the world."

"When do I leave?" Lionel said.

"You'll need to go through a bit more training," the man said. He pulled something else out of the case. "And you'll need to get familiar with this."

The man pulled out a gun. Lionel knew accepting it meant he would be part of the Global Community. He hesitated a moment.

"It won't bite you," the man said.

Lionel took the gun. He felt its weight. He knew his life had changed forever.

Ryan was glad the nurse had listened to his story, but he was frustrated. His thoughts were jumbled, and he couldn't remember some of the verses he'd memorized.

The nurse felt his head and wiped it with a towel. She took his temperature and strapped something around his arm.

"Your blood pressure's falling," the nurse said. "I'll need to get the doctor."

Ryan rolled his head back and forth on the pillow. *What is that verse?* he thought. *Something about God and the world.*

When the nurse returned with the doctor, Ryan was excited. "I remember now," Ryan said. "Not word for word, but—"

"Just lie still," the doctor said.

"He's been going on like this," the nurse said.

"God loved the world," Ryan said, "and he loved it so much he gave his Son."

"His pulse is erratic," the doctor said.

"That's Jesus," Ryan said. "And anybody who believes in him won't die. They'll have eternal life."

"Should I get someone?" the nurse said.

"There's no one who can help him now," the doctor said.

"You have to trust him," Ryan said. "Do you believe in Jesus?"

The room spun. Ryan closed his eyes. He wished Judd were here. Or Vicki. He thought of Phoenix and the long bike rides they used to take. The dog was beside him all the way.

Ryan opened his eyes. "Am I going to die?" he said.

"We're doing everything we can," the doctor said.

"Doesn't answer my question," Ryan said. The doctor was changing the medication in Ryan's IV. Ryan grabbed the man's coat and held on.

"I asked if you think I'm gonna die," Ryan said.

The doctor looked at him gravely. "I choose to believe all my patients will make it," the doctor said, "but I'll admit I have my doubts."

Ryan let go. "It's not so bad," he said. "I have some friends waiting for me up there."

"Lie still and try not to talk," the doctor said.

Ryan closed his eyes again. He was so hot. So tired. He just wanted to sleep. He wanted to go home.

Mr. Stein screamed for help. Finally someone came. Flashlight beams lit the room. Layer after layer of debris had to be cleared. Finally the rescuers reached Mr. Stein. He was cold, and he knew he had lost a lot of blood.

"Don't worry about me; find my daughter," Mr. Stein said. He pointed.

It had been some time since Chaya had spoken. She had passed out, then revived, only to pester him again to consider Jesus. It seemed the only thing on her mind.

The men lifted the beam on top of Mr. Stein enough to pull him from the rubble. He grabbed one of the flashlights.

"Uh, sir, you might not want to look over there," one of the men said.

"I have to find my daughter," Mr. Stein said.

The light flashed on something. Mr. Stein gasped. The brooch. A few inches away he saw his daughter's delicate hand.

"Help me here!" Mr. Stein yelled, but he was in no shape to move, let alone pull his daughter from the rubble.

Mr. Stein picked up the brooch as the men tried to remove Chaya. A wall shifted, and plaster fell on them.

"It's not safe in here," a man said. "We have to get out."

"Not without her," Mr. Stein said.

"You can stay if you want," the man said.

Mr. Stein knelt and cradled Chaya's head in his lap. He felt for a pulse, but there was none. He brushed the hair from her face and cleaned a streak of blood from her mouth.

"You look just like your mother," Mr. Stein said as he wept. "So beautiful."

He looked at the night sky through the shambles of his home. Stars and the bright moon.

"Why?" he said softly. "Why did you take the only one left to me?"

Louder and louder he wailed. "Why? Why?"

JUDD raced down the bank to the dam. He was up to thirty miles an hour when his front tire hit a stick. Judd swerved and slammed on the brakes. He stopped a few feet short of the edge. *Maybe this is God's way of telling me to stop*, he thought.

Judd turned around and cleared the path, making sure there were no hidden obstacles. He took the bike farther back and revved the engine again.

"If you don't want me to do this, God," Judd said out loud, "then stop me."

Judd plunged down the hill and picked up speed. He was going thirty-five before he made it to the pavement. He knew he had enough speed, but something felt wrong.

He was still bouncing when he hit the concrete, like he was on uneven ground. The speedometer said 40 mph. Judd slammed on the brakes. He heard thunder and felt the dam rocking.

Aftershock, Judd thought.

He was nearing the edge, sliding, burning rubber, when he realized he was not going to stop. He put the bike down and slid with it to the edge. The motorcycle, still running, plunged over the side. Judd put out his hands and grabbed the railing. His momentum nearly took him over, but he managed to hold on, his feet dangling over the edge.

He looked below and saw the green motorcycle splash into the murky water. It floated a moment, then sank.

Judd held on. The water seemed to rush by faster. He couldn't survive the fall, and the current would take him if he did. He tried to get a foothold on the side of the dam, but the concrete crumbled with each try.

OK, Judd thought, *I guess I wasn't supposed to do that. Now what?*

He was alone, hanging on for his life, the earth shaking again, and there was no one to help him.

ABOUT THE AUTHORS

Jerry B. Jenkins (www.jerryjenkins.com) is the writer of the Left Behind series. He owns the Jerry B. Jenkins Christian Writers Guild, an organization dedicated to mentoring aspiring authors. Former vice president for publishing for the Moody Bible Institute of Chicago, he also served many years as editor of *Moody* magazine and is now Moody's writer-at-large.

His writing has appeared in publications as varied as *Reader's Digest, Parade, Guideposts*, in-flight magazines, and dozens of other periodicals. Jenkins's biographies include books with Billy Graham, Hank Aaron, Bill Gaither, Luis Palau, Walter Payton, Orel Hershiser, and Nolan Ryan, among many others. His books appear regularly on the *New York Times, USA Today, Wall Street Journal,* and *Publishers Weekly* best-seller lists.

Jerry is also the writer of the nationally syndicated sports story comic strip *Gil Thorp*, distributed to newspapers across the United States by Tribune Media Services.

Jerry and his wife, Dianna, live in Colorado and have three grown sons.

Dr. Tim LaHaye (www.timlahaye.com), who conceived the idea of fictionalizing an account of the Rapture and the Tribulation, is a noted author, minister, and nationally recognized speaker on Bible prophecy. He is the founder of both Tim LaHaye Ministries and The PreTrib Research Center. He also recently cofounded the Tim LaHaye School of Prophecy at Liberty University. Presently Dr. LaHaye speaks at many of the major Bible prophecy conferences in the U.S. and Canada, where his current prophecy books are very popular.

Dr. LaHaye holds a doctor of ministry degree from Western Theological Seminary and a doctor of literature degree from Liberty University. For twenty-five years he pastored one of the nation's outstanding churches in San Diego, which grew to three locations. It was during that time that he founded two accredited Christian high schools, a Christian school system of ten schools, and Christian Heritage College.

Dr. LaHaye has written over forty books that have been published in more than thirty languages. He has written books on a wide variety of subjects, such as family life, temperaments, and Bible prophecy. His current fiction works, the Left Behind series, written with Jerry B. Jenkins, continue to appear on the best-seller lists of the Christian Booksellers Association, *Publishers Weekly, Wall Street Journal, USA Today*, and the *New York Times*.

He is the father of four grown children and grandfather of nine. Snow skiing, waterskiing, motorcycling, golfing, vacationing with family, and jogging are among his leisure activities.

COMING SOON!

Look for the next two books in the Young Trib Force Series!

www.areUthirsty.com

well . . . are you?